To Love a Dark Lord

ANNE STUART

MILLS & BOON

Published in Great Britain 2013
Mills & Boon, an imprint of Harlequin (UK) Limited,
Eton House, 18-24 Paradise Road, Richmond, Surrey TW9 1SR

© Anne Kristine Stuart Ohlrogge 1994

ISBN: 978 0 263 90248 8

013-0413

TO LOVE A DARK LORD

What can I say about this book? It tends to be the most memorable of all my historicals and yet it had a very troubled beginning. At that point in my career I didn't necessarily write heroes who were that dark. Oh, they were alpha, and cynical, and brooding, occasionally, but they weren't dark, dark, dark. Killoran was my first hero who was really over the top.

I really wanted to write him. I had a clear vision of him early on and I wanted to go for broke. Just throw everything in, no matter how dark, and see what happened. By that point in my life I'd lost a number of my family, all too young and without warning, and I was angry and grieving. I wanted to put all that emotion into the book and I wrote the required three chapters and an outline, convinced of my brilliance, and sent them off.

My editor wasn't so sure. She sent it back to me, wanting me to pull back on just about everything. Now I've always been fairly arrogant, but I also try to listen to opposing opinions, so I dutifully went in, toned everything down and sent it back to her.

It came right back, with fourteen pages of notes, saying pull back more. Frustrated, I did, cutting everything and softening everything I could while still keeping my vision of what the book should be.

It came back. Remember I said I was arrogant, right? At that point I said no. I said I would write the book, send in the rough draft and if it didn't work, then I'd pull it. But I couldn't keep tweaking and tweaking and losing my passion.

So I did. I tried very hard to shut out the worried voice of my editor and write the book that was in my heart and in the end she accepted the book the way I'd written it. Later, when my extremely dark first contemporary came out (for another publisher and editor), she read it and asked me if that was what I'd had in mind for *To Love a Dark Lord*. I said yes. And she, bless her heart, said she'd been wrong to try to tame me.

So Anne Stuart, Queen of Darkness, was born, not without a long, hard labor, a contrary midwife and birthing pains.

In the end, I'm very proud of it. But I'm still wondering what the original would have been like, if I hadn't had to sweeten it.

CHAPTER ONE

Just Outside London, 1775

Emma Mary Catherine Langolet stood in the middle of the small, private bedroom at the Pear and Partridge. She was silent with shock. There was blood on her hands, she noticed absently. It was little wonder. The man who lay at her feet seemed composed almost entirely of blood, and most of it now formed a pool beneath him, staining the inn's shabby carpet, staining her slippers and the hem of her dress.

She stared down at her uncle. He'd been an unpleasant, unattractive man in life, and death hadn't improved him any. Cousin Miriam was going to be most displeased with her, she thought.

She hadn't meant to kill him. Indeed, when she'd picked up the smallsword to ward him off, she hadn't thought the ornamental weapon would actually do such extensive damage. Nor had she truly believed her uncle by marriage was intent on hurting her, despite his peculiar behavior.

Until she'd looked into his small, piggy eyes and seen her death reflected there. And she'd known, incomprehensible as the notion was, that Uncle Horace intended to kill her.

But she wasn't the one lying dead on the floor. The smallsword that Horace DeWinter had set on the table had proved to be fatally efficient. She could still feel it slicing through flesh and bone, and the expression of astonishment on her uncle's murderous, lustful face would haunt her dreams.

He still looked faintly startled. Emma considered sinking to her knees in a proper attitude of repentance. She ought to feel sorry for such a mortal crime.

But she couldn't.

He had been an evil, miserable man. Everyone, with the notable exception of her formidable cousin, Miriam, had felt his fists. There had been tales of his lasciviousness with the female servants, tales of his brutality toward all and sundry. He was wicked and evil and cruel, and he deserved to die.

It was simply a great misfortune that Emma had to be the one to kill him.

They hanged women, she knew that, though not often. They would surely hang her. After all, her uncle and his spinster daughter had taken her into their home when her father died, providing her with an austere, godly existence. She had no one to turn to for help—her father had been an extremely wealthy man, but tainted by trade. Her shy, aristocratic mother had been cast off by her family for marrying a foundry owner, and his substantial earnings from the armament trade hadn't softened their attitude. Emma's mother had died in childbirth, her doting father some twelve years later. And during the last seven years Emma had lived with the DeWinters in their large house near Crouch End, obedient to Miriam's strict demands that bordered on religious fanaticism, dodging her uncle's increasingly determined efforts to put his soft, pudgy hands on her body.

It had been a game of wits, to keep from being alone with him, but she'd never realized how very serious it was. How determined and vicious Horace DeWinter could truly be. Her face was numb from the blow he'd struck her. She ought to pull herself together, she knew it. The maid who'd had the bad timing to appear had taken one look at the body on the floor and run off screaming. It would be only a matter of minutes before the noise she was making summoned the inhabitants of the old inn.

Emma wondered idly whether they'd drag her out into the stormy evening and hang her there and then. It might be preferable to facing Cousin Miriam.

Someone was watching her. She wanted to summon the energy to look, but for the moment she was distracted by all the blood on her hands. She had never thought he'd lunge for her like that. That he'd doubt her determination.

She could still feel the blade sinking into his flesh.

Killoran's mood was not particularly sunny that winter afternoon. For one thing, he had a terrific headache, and the bottle of cognac he'd brought with him to cheer him during the journey didn't seem to make any difference except to make his head pound even more fiercely. He'd regretted his acceptance of Cousin Nathaniel's visit within one day of agreeing to it, but he'd been oddly loath to cancel it, and he'd let the invitation stand. If Matthew Hepburn, a country squire in the tiny Northumberland village of St. Just, had been a more worldly soul, he would have known better than to send his only son, Nathaniel, to the care of his distant cousin James Michael Patrick, the Earl of Killoran, for a bit of town bronze. The connection was so remote it was almost nonexistent—Hepburn's wife's sister was cousin to Killoran's aunt's husband—and indeed, Killoran could have ignored the request, since all the principals in the matter were long dead. He didn't need Hepburn's money, or gratitude, and he was never one to let himself be bothered by responsibility or guilt.

But he accepted the imminent arrival of one Nathaniel Hepburn with a kind of cool grace, for one simple reason.

He was bored.

The cards always fell his way; the women did the same. He had conquered society, with the small and unlamentable exception of the proper young females, and he no longer had any interest in removing himself from his comfortable house on Curzon Street in London and returning to the charred ruins of Killoran House, the run-down horse farm that made up the bulk of his inheritance. If it were up to him, he'd never set foot in Ireland again. He had no family left, no land worth anything, no ties. He would die an Englishman. And if his current boredom didn't abate, that happy day would come damned soon.

Nathaniel Hepburn, age twenty-three, sounded, according to his father's spiky, flowing script, like an absolute prince of young English manhood. Sober, earnest, hardworking, intelligent. Determined to learn a bit of the ways of the world, he would then retire back to Northumberland and take up the reins of his father's comfortable estate.

If he hadn't been drunk at the time, Killoran would have simply ignored the letter. Unfortunately, he'd taken to drinking deeply of late—it didn't fill the emptiness inside him or relieve his monumental ennui, but it made him less aware of the deficiencies in his elegant, comfortable life.

Instead Killoran decided to welcome his splendid young cousin into the ways of London society. He would open the eyes of this stalwart paragon, teach him something of the seaminess that lay beneath the pretty surface of the ton. When the task grew tiresome, as everything always did, far too quickly, he would send Nathaniel back to the bosom of his trusting family, older and wiser. If he needed to see a bit of the world, Killoran could be prevailed upon to show him. Including a tour of some places most country squires never even imagined could exist in the wicked environs of London.

He was drunk, definitely, gracefully drunk, when he had come up with the notion and written the letter to Hepburn's father, signifying his agreement. He was sober, definitely, irritably sober, when it had come time to fetch the young man at a posting house on the outskirts of London. Killoran considered getting drunk once more and ignoring the assignation. Instead he decided to take his bottle with him.

He'd considered heading for the Continent—he missed Paris, missed the gaiety of Versailles, where the perspicacious inhabitants were some of the few who rightly preferred the Irish, and indeed any nationality, to the English. He wanted to spend a week in the arms of a plump French mistress who understood his needs and how to please him. He was mortally tired of people and their endless blathering. He wanted sex and silence, and he had no objections to paying for them. There was a certain honesty about such arrangements, devoid of the tiresome and false declarations of affection or even interest outside the bedroom.

He flicked his cuff, noting the heavy fall of Mechlin lace against the inky-black satin of his coat. It was a particular conceit of his to dress only in black and white, ornamented with silver. His acquaintances would deride him for it—"You look like a demmed parson," his acquaintance Sanderson would tell him, dealing with a skill untouched by the number of bottles he'd imbibed. But it was an effective conceit. He moved through society, watched by all. It provided a certain amusement.

He put his long fingers to his temples, massaging them. He seldom bothered with wigs, and he kept his own luxuriant black locks unpowdered and tied back in a queue. He had a pounding headache, and was entirely ready to take his temper out on the so-perfect Nathaniel Hepburn.

Of course, there was always the possibility that Nathaniel had managed to fool a doting parent and was a precocious sinner, old in the ways of wickedness. But he doubted it. Nathaniel Hepburn would be as sober and stalwart as his father assured him, a dead bore unless Killoran managed to bring him down to his own level. He certainly had every intention of trying.

The Pear and Partridge was a small inn on the edge of the heath, and by the time Killoran's chaise pulled up, it was growing dark, with a strong wind picking up. He dismounted with the languid grace that had become second nature to him, then strolled into the taproom and surveyed the inhabitants with a weary sigh.

Nathaniel Hepburn was easy enough to pick out. He looked younger than his twenty-three years, with chestnut-brown hair tied back in a simple queue, a handsome face, and distrustful, disapproving blue eyes. Killoran noted with interest that the disapproval was directed at him.

"Lord Killoran," he said, surging to his feet with enough energy to make Killoran's head pound even more. "I was afraid something might have happened to you."

"Please," he said faintly, holding out a slim white hand. "Call me Killoran. Everyone does. Dear me, am I late?"

Nathaniel stared at him uncertainly. "It's past four in the afternoon, sir. I arrived early this morning."

"'Sir' is almost as bad as 'Lord Killoran,'" he murmured. "I gather I've been remiss. Order me a bottle of French brandy, and once we've toasted your arrival and the horses are properly rested, we'll start back to the city."

"But, sir..."

"Not at all, my boy," Killoran said with an airy wave of his hand. "Not another word. I know you're grateful..."

"Actually, I'm not."

Killoran halted. He refused to let his amusement show. Instead he reached for his quizzing glass, held it to his eye, and looked the young man up and down with a leisurely air. Insolent pup. "How fascinating," he said faintly, his tone conveying his complete disinterest.

"I'll tell you now, sir, that I didn't wish to come," Nathaniel announced stiffly. "I have no need for town bronze, no need to expose myself to the fleshpots of a wicked city such as London. My father insisted, and I am, above all things, a dutiful son. But I don't wish to be here, and I most particularly don't wish to partake of your hospitality. My father may not have heard of your reputation, but when I was at Cambridge, there were tales enough of your excesses. The Irish earl is notorious, as I'm sure you have little doubt. Young men were warned not to gamble with you if they met you in society. If I had any choice in the matter, I wouldn't be here, I promise you. I'd be back in Northumberland, I'd be married, I'd be—"

"Ah," said Killoran, still bored, "there's a young lady involved. Tell me, child, is she unsuitable? The daughter of a dairymaid, perhaps?"

"Miss Pottle is from one of the finest Northumberland families!" Nathaniel said furiously. "How dare you!"

"You will discover, after a few weeks in my company, that I dare just about anything," Killoran murmured. "And you will be spending several weeks in my company, won't you?"

"Unless you send me back early."

Killoran's smile was far from reassuring. "I see. I was wondering whether your monumental ill manners were the result of ignorance or design. Obviously you were hoping I'd be so appalled by your rudeness that I'd send you packing. You forget, I'm an Irishman living in England. I'm quite used to rudeness and insults."

Nathaniel was temporarily at a loss for words. Killoran accepted that fact with gratitude.

"In the meantime," he continued before Nathaniel could gather together his prodigious powers of speech, "I'm going to lie down. Heroic emotions before dinner give me the headache. I intend to bespeak me a bedchamber for a few hours, and you can sit here and nurse your grudges. I believe there's a mail coach heading north within the next few hours. If I come back downstairs and find you gone, I will assume your duty to your father proved unbearable." He tilted his head to one side, surveying the young man silently. "If you stay," he added gently, "you may discover that you lose all interest in the divine Miss Pottle."

"It doesn't matter," Nathaniel said in a sulky voice. "She's lost all interest in me."

"Has she, now? Women are ever fickle. In that case, you might as well remain in London and drown your sorrows. There are any number of pleasing women in town, most of them with much pleasanter names."

"How dare you!" Nathaniel exclaimed.

"You already said that," Killoran pointed out in a deceptively mild voice. "Don't be tiresome, my boy. Leave or stay, it's up to you. I'll be ready to drive back to town as soon as the horses are rested."

"Damn you," Nathaniel snarled, but it was in a low voice. There was a limit to the young man's bravado, after all.

Killoran smiled sweetly. "Indeed."

The bedchamber mine host provided for him was damp, the linen unaired; the fire smoked, and the noise was appalling. Killoran was beyond objecting. He had tossed himself down on the lumpy bed with a complete disregard for his elegant clothes, unfastened his torment-ing queued hair, and closed his eyes. The rain was com-ing down in earnest now, and the bedchamber was far from warm. The windows rattled in their casements, de-termined breezes swept through the room, and Killoran's mood did not improve. One hour of sleep, that was all he asked. Just enough to take the edge off the miserable pounding in his skull.

The voices in the next room were muffled, angry. He heard a thump, and a cry that was cut off abruptly.

Another man might have evinced some level of curi-osity. Not Killoran. He had seen enough in his life to be particularly disinterested in the violent doings of others. It sounded as if someone had just met his demise, vio-lently. He could only hope things would now quiet down.

He was just drifting off into a pleasant, wine-benumbed slumber when a shrill scream sent him leaping off the bed. Whatever semblance of a good mood he'd possessed, and there'd been precious little, had vanished. He strode to the door, slammed it open, and advanced down the hall, in the direction of the witless screaming.

All was silent now. The door stood open to a private bedroom, and there were only two inhabitants. One was a bedraggled, bloodstained, and astonishingly lovely young female.

The other, at her feet, was quite dead. And so it was

that he found himself at the Pear and Partridge, on the outskirts of London, embroiled in a cold-blooded murder.

Things, he thought faintly, were definitely looking up.

"Are you going to swoon?"

The voice was cool, ironic, with the faintest trace of a lilt. It was enough to gain Emma's attention. She looked toward the door, to the man lounging there, surveying her with a bored air.

He was a startling figure, dressed in deep black satin, with ruffles of lace trailing down his cuffs. His waistcoat was embroidered with silver, his breeches were black satin as well; his clocked hose were shot with silver. He had no need of the diamond-encrusted high heels on his shoes to add to his already intimidating height, nor to show off the graceful curve of his leg. His hair was midnight black, falling loose on his shoulders, and his eyes were green, cold, amused.

"I don't think so," she said, finding her voice from somewhere. She wanted to wipe the blood off her hands, but the only possible spot she could find was her full skirts, and that would only make things worse. She wasn't used to men. Cousin Miriam kept the house almost cloistered, a fact which Emma had accepted without argument. She didn't see many men, and she'd certainly never seen one like this.

"Because if you are," the elegant man continued, moving into the room and closing the door very quietly behind him, "I suggest you take a step or two back so that you don't fall on the corpse."

Emma swallowed. "I'm not going to swoon," she

said with a fair degree of certainty. "I might throw up, though."

He didn't appear alarmed at the notion. "Surely not," he murmured. "If you've survived this much, you won't succumb to such paltry behavior. I presume you killed him. Why?"

"I... I..."

"Not that it's any of my business," he added casually, skirting Horace's body. The smallsword lay on the floor beside him, and the man picked it up. "But I do confess to a bit of curiosity. Logic impels me to assume you're a doxy, set on robbing one of your customers. Frankly," he said, glancing at her as he hefted the weapon, "you don't have the look of a doxy. The clothes are wrong. And there's something about your eyes as well. I could be mistaken, though. Are you?"

"No."

"Pity," he murmured, letting his green eyes slide down her disheveled body. "You could make a fortune."

She already had a fortune, inherited from her father's manufactories. Not that it would do her a speck of good. "He was trying to rape me."

Again that long, assessing, intimate look. "I can sympathize with the temptation," he said, half to himself. "Still, he's paid for his crime. Do you know the fellow?"

"He was my uncle. And guardian."

"How delicious," the man said with a faint, heartless laugh. "Do you have an aunt as well?"

"A cousin. His daughter. She doesn't like me very much."

"I don't expect her affection is about to increase."

"It's not likely to matter. They'll hang me."

He tilted his head to one side, watching her. The mane of black curls was disconcerting—the few men allowed in the house in Crouch End wore their hair tied back in queues, or powdered and bewigged. The loose curtain of hair was somehow disturbing, intimate.

The haphazard elegance of his clothes was equally unsettling. Emma was used to men who dressed conservatively and properly. Men of sober habits and dour demeanor, who kept their vices behind closed doors.

This man was slightly drunk. He was surveying the scene of a murder with a combination of faint curiosity and amusement, and her sense of unreality grew.

"That would be a great shame," he said. "Such a pretty little neck." He sighed. "I suppose I'll have to do something about it."

Emma could hear the thunder of footsteps approaching, the babble of voices. The maid's high-pitched squeal rose above the rest, her voice carrying through the closed door. "She was standing there covered with blood, as cool as you please!" the woman shrieked. "I saw her. She killed the poor old gentleman, stabbed him through the heart, I swear..."

Emma barely saw the man move. He strode past her, graceful, swift, and pushed open the door. A crowd of people gathered there, wide-eyed, bloodthirsty.

"I'm afraid you're mistaken," he announced in a cool, arrogant voice. He still held the smallsword in one hand, and he swung it with a negligent air. Blood still clung to it, and Emma had to control her stomach with sheer force of effort. "I'm afraid I killed him."

"Lord Killoran!" the innkeeper exclaimed, horrified. "Were it a duel?"

"I'd hardly stab the man in cold blood, now, would I, Bavers?" he said. "The man was deranged. He attacked this young lady, and when I came to her rescue, he tried to kill me. I had no choice."

Bavers stared at him, clearly astonished. "You rescued her?"

"From the brutish hands of her father," he said.

"Uncle," Emma corrected him unhelpfully.

"Ah, yes. We didn't have time for proper introductions."

"Lord Killoran, you can't just walk into one of my rooms and spit a guest," Bavers said in a reproachful voice.

"He didn't seem inclined to meet me outside. The floor will come clean, if you don't leave his moldering corpse for too long."

A necessary, Emma thought longingly. A few short moments of privacy to cast up her accounts, and she'd face her fate with all the grace she could muster.

Except that fate seemed to have been spared her, due to the lazy ministrations of this glittering stranger.

"There'll need to be an inquest," Bavers warned.

The man referred to as Lord Killoran leaned forward, and the heavy coin that passed between his pale, elegant fingers and the landlord's rougher ones took care of matters quite nicely. "I'm sure I can count on you to see to things." He glanced up, toward the doorway. "I think we'd best be on our way, Nathaniel. This inn is far from peaceful."

And without another glance at either her or the corpse of her uncle, he walked out of the room.

The other witnesses followed, no longer interested in something as mundane as a dead man, and the landlord was alone with Emma.

He bit into the gold coin, then grunted with a fair amount of satisfaction. He looked up at Emma. "You there," he said, his earlier deference vanishing. "We don't need your sort here. I heard what his lordship said, and I don't believe a word of it. Lord Killoran wouldn't lift a finger to save his own mother. Be off with you, doxy."

He was the second person in a matter of minutes to assume she was a whore, though Lord Killoran had at least been polite enough to ask. "If you'll have the horses put to..." she said faintly, watching as the landlord knelt in the blood, going through her uncle's pockets with a singular lack of squeamishness. He came up empty.

"I'm keeping the horses," he said. "Something's owed me for dealing with all this. They aren't yours, anyway— they're this poor, dead gentleman's—and I'd be remiss in my duty if I let you take them without so much as a by-your-leave."

Frustration made her curl her hands into fists. She had no money—her cousin, Miriam, had always seen to that. She was alone, penniless, with no one to turn to for help, least of all her family. She considered this for a moment, feeling an unlikely surge of hope.

Destitution was one side of the coin. Freedom was the other. No one to touch her, pinch her, hurt her. No one to watch her, questioning her every move. To force her to spend hours on her knees, recounting nonexistent sins.

In Miriam DeWinter's stern household, Emma had had little opportunity for sinning and no temptation to do so whatsoever.

Suddenly she was free. She could simply walk out the door and not a soul would stop her. The thought was absolutely terrifying.

Before the greedy innkeeper could change his mind, she ran into the hallway, racing down the narrow stairs, not daring to slow her pace for fear that reaction and reality would set in. She would escape, disappear into the city, and no one would ever find her. She would be safe from Cousin Miriam; she would be happy. And then she looked down at the blood staining her hands and shivered.

Killoran stood alone in the private room, staring into the fire, a glass of brandy in his hand. Nathaniel had been sent to make certain the horses were put to with all possible dispatch. Apparently he'd decided to keep Killoran company a bit longer. Killoran viewed that prospect with a jaundiced air but he was too weary at the moment to bestir himself and send the young hothead home.

The young woman upstairs was far more interesting, and he was requiring a surprising amount of self-denial to keep from taking her with them. Not that he had a great deal of experience in self-denial, but something told him the young woman would be more trouble than she was worth.

For one thing, she was quite astonishingly beautiful. Not at all in the common style, she was possessed of a thick mane of impossibly flame-colored hair, a tall, lush body of dangerous voluptuousness, and the warm, honey-colored eyes of a complete innocent. That red hair called to him, a siren lure, but he assumed it was only nostalgia and misplaced sentiment. Not that he'd ever been known to possess those two qualities.

She reminded him of another redhead, long dead, albeit a more subdued one. The creature upstairs, despite her shocked eyes, was far from demure. The blood on her hands only added to her allure.

Ah, but innocent females could be very dangerous indeed, and it wasn't anything as mundane as his worthless hide Killoran was concerned about. He'd had virgins before, and knew just how uncomfortable that could be. They tended to imagine themselves in love, and when they discovered their seducer was a man who simply didn't believe in love—didn't believe in much of anything at all, for that matter—they grew furious, subjecting one to tears, rage, bitter protests, and the like. All for the sake of clumsy, untried sex.

No, he would leave this fascinating, murderous virgin alone. He wouldn't even offer her a ride back to London in his carriage—there was a limit, after all, to his self-control, and she was quite the most tempting female he'd seen in years. With luck, he'd never set eyes on her again.

He still couldn't quite fathom what had inspired his quixotic act in the upstairs bedroom. The words had been out of his mouth before he'd realized it, claiming responsibility for the man's death. Indeed, it had been no sacrifice on his part. He'd killed before, in duels, and he was known to hold human life in very low esteem.

Besides, as he'd observed, she had such a lovely neck. It would be a shame to bruise it with a thick hemp rope.

He'd done his good deed—it should shave a year or two off his stay in purgatory. Assuming he didn't go straight to hell, a far more likely eternity for a man like him. And he was a man who believed in hell.

There were times, he thought, staring into the fire, when he wearied of it all. Years ago he had decided, quite simply, that goodness and decency had been denied to him by the vagaries of fate. The innocent rashness of youth had led him to disaster, and made victims of those he loved. He had chosen, then, to be a villain. Never again would a moral imperative cause others harm. He had no morals. Nor any other qualities he could think of, apart from his skill with horses, with women, and with gaming. All of which bored him heartily.

It was far more comfortable to live without soul or conscience. He knew it, since those discarded commodities occasionally attempted to return to haunt him. But he was finding it easier and easier to banish them once more. Soon they wouldn't trouble him in the slightest.

For example, the fate of the young woman upstairs was nagging at his brain, when he should have been far more interested in concentrating on the landlord's fine brandy instead of thinking about her and his odd gesture. It had been a whim, brought on by the large amounts of brandy he'd already imbibed, or perhaps by a momentary madness brought about by that flame-red hair, and if he didn't get away soon, there was no telling what kind of noble behavior might take hold of him. The thought was chilling.

He had no intention of succumbing to a lamentable resurgence of conscience. He drained his glass and started for the hallway, suddenly quite desperate to escape the Pear and Partridge and the titian-haired innocent in the upstairs chamber.

Before he betrayed his determined lack of principles again.

CHAPTER TWO

He was alone in the darkened hallway, her savior, when Emma reached the bottom of the narrow stairs. He halted at the sight of her, and she could see the startled wariness in his silhouette. She started toward him, ready to fling herself at his feet in gratitude.

His hands reached out to catch her, stop her. Hard hands, pale in the gloom, hauling her to her feet. "Not that I couldn't find any number of interesting things you could do in such a position," he drawled, "but this is a public place."

She had no idea what he meant, but she flushed, anyway. "I owe you my life," she said. "How can I repay you for your kindness and nobility—"

"Don't deceive yourself," he interrupted her, his voice cool and ironic. "I have not a trace of kindness or nobility in my entire body."

"But you saved me. You risked your own life, your reputation, all out of the goodness of your heart."

"I have no heart," he snapped, that mocking drawl sharpening. "Nor a reputation to be damaged, child. And

I ran no risk. He wouldn't have been the first man I've killed, and he won't be the last. One more corpse on my head is of little account."

"But still…"

"But nothing, my love. I didn't take the blame for your bloodthirsty dispatching of your father out of goodness, kindness, or even for the sake of your magnificent, tear-filled brown eyes."

"My uncle," she said numbly. "My cousin's father."

"Details," he replied airily. "I did it because it amused me."

"Amused you?" she echoed, disbelieving.

"I was bored. Heartily bored. It entertained me to take the blame for your uncle's death. But now you're boring me once more. Do go away."

She stared at him in shock. He was surveying her with all the interest one might bestow upon a tankard of flat ale. Perhaps even less.

"Go away?" She heard the helplessness in her voice and hated it.

He raised a dark eyebrow. "Were you thinking you might come with me? I assure you, I have no need for a mistress, and you're a little too well-bred for a scullery maid. Of course, you could always work as my paid assassin, but in general, I like to do my own killing."

His mockery was like a blow, one she almost reeled under. She backed away from him, staring at his black-and-white elegance with a kind of numb contempt. "Forgive me," she said in a husky voice. "I didn't mean…"

His smile was wintry sweet. "You're very pretty, child," he said, reaching out with one of his slender, strong hands and brushing it against her cheek. She jerked, but he merely smiled at her reaction, and ran his fingertips over her soft lips. "If you just sit in the taproom with your magnificent eyes filled with tears, I'm certain you'll find someone to take care of you." He glanced down at her. "You might, however, endeavor to wash some of the blood off your hands. It might put a man's appetite off a bit."

She tried to pull back from him, but he was surprisingly fast and surprisingly strong for such an indolent-looking creature, and she found her wrist caught tightly in one of his deceptively pale hands. "Then again," he murmured, leaning closer, "it does seem to whet mine." He was dangerously, hypnotically close, and she wondered dazedly what would happen if he moved closer still.

"Killoran!" A young man stood in the doorway, his body radiating outrage and horror.

The dark man's smile was sudden, rueful, and oddly charming as he released her, released her hand, released her from his dark, entrapping gaze. "My conscience calls, sweeting," he murmured. And he walked away from her, clearly dismissing her from his mind.

Emma watched him go. She found she was trembling. She could still feel the heat and strength of his hand on her wrist, still feel the caress against her face. She had the sudden, unmistakable conviction that the threat from the dark man was even more devastating than the bloody death her uncle had planned for her.

And that she'd had a very narrow escape.

* * *

"You can't be meaning to just leave her there," Nathaniel said, running to keep up with Killoran as he strode toward his carriage.

He stopped, glancing at his new charge with deliberate boredom. "What do you suggest, dear boy? That we bring her back to the city with us? You were looking at me with such an outraged expression on your face that I assumed you disapproved of any lustful designs on my part."

"She's an innocent."

"So she is. As much as any woman ever could be. And that's one reason we're not taking her with us. She's far too pretty. Let me give you a bit of warning—it doesn't do to tamper with the middle classes. They're alarmingly rigid. You can't despoil their daughters and hope to get away with it. The lower orders are one thing—they're grateful for the attention and benefits. The upper classes as well—they're beyond rules. Ah, but the middle class is tied up in the most tedious knots of proper behavior, and even the young lady, as compromising a situation as she was in, would have very strict notions of propriety. You'd find yourself leg-shackled in no time, and I expect your father wants better for you. If Miss Pottle wouldn't do, then I think it even less likely that he'd approve of the young lady upstairs."

"Damn it, man, you killed her father!"

"Uncle," Killoran corrected him dryly, having finally gotten it right.

"We can't just leave her here."

Killoran paused by the carriage, utterly weary. "If

you're so desperate to tumble her, I suppose I can content myself with the landlord's brandy, even though I'm used to far better. I can wait for an hour or so."

"I should mill you down for that," Nathaniel said angrily.

"On whose account? That of the damsel in distress?"

"My own honor."

"You'll lose it soon enough," Killoran said. He sighed. "What do you propose I do for the girl?"

"It was by your act she's alone and destitute—"

"Oh, I wouldn't say that," Killoran drawled. "After all, she came here in the first place."

"She's not the one who ran her...uncle through with a smallsword."

Killoran's smile was gentle. "I would say I'd already done her a great service." He reached into his pocket and drew out a gold coin. The landlord was hovering close by, ready for just such an eventuality, and he caught the coin with a deft hand. "Make certain the girl receives it," Killoran said in a deceptively pleasant voice.

"He won't," Nathaniel muttered sulkily.

"You have a soft heart, child," Killoran murmured. "I do hope you won't be bringing home stray kittens and chimney sweeps during your sojourn with me." He fixed the landlord with his suddenly steely gaze. "You'll oblige me in this matter, Bavers, or it might grow very unpleasant for you. Give the girl the gold, and tell her to apply herself to Mrs. Withersedge, on Mount Street. She'll find something for her to do."

"Mrs. Withersedge, on Mount Street," Bavers repeated dutifully, casting the gold coin in his hand a sorrowful look.

Nathaniel climbed into the carriage behind his lordship, bristling with anger and contempt. "You are, in truth, the very devil," he said in a sullen voice.

"I'm delighted that I live up to your expectations," Killoran said, leaning back against the tufted velvet squabs. "Exactly how have I managed to convince you of that fact?"

The carriage started smoothly. "Within moments of making your acquaintance, I find that you murder a man."

"Believe me, it had nothing to do with your so-charming manner," Killoran said sweetly. "If it had, I would have murdered *you*."

"And then you send a poor, innocent girl off to a...a brothel."

"What makes you think Mrs. Withersedge runs a brothel?" he asked lazily.

"Why else would you know such a woman?"

Killoran closed his eyes with sudden weariness. "You will learn soon enough, dear boy, that men in our position do not need to visit brothels unless we care to. And we certainly do not need to help recruit for them. I doubt the young lady would be a great success as a doxy. Despite her glorious figure and that mane of red hair, she hasn't the look of one."

"How so? I would think her looks would aid her if she wished to—I mean—" He broke off, flustered by the conversation.

"Did you fancy her?" Killoran murmured, just the faintest thread of steel beneath the lazy drawl. "Dear boy, you should have said so. We could have brought her back with us—"

"I will never love again!"

"So you say. We'll see how long that lasts. And I don't believe we were talking about love, but something almost as short-lived and a great less complicated." He stretched out his long legs in front of him. "However, if you didn't lust after the young lady, then I fail to see why she occupies your mind to such an alarming extent. She's not at all in the common style—it would take a connoisseur to appreciate one such as she, and you're far too young to be a connoisseur. Don't worry about her, Nathaniel. She'll do well if she keeps her wits about her, and I expect she'll be more than able to do just that. A remarkably coolheaded young lady," he added with a faint, reminiscent smile.

"You're a devil," Nathaniel muttered again, throwing himself back against the seat with a surly expression marring his handsome young face.

"I never denied it, dear boy. Cheer up, my child. You can always visit Mrs. Withersedge yourself if you wish to make certain you've forsworn the pleasures of the flesh as well as the travails of the heart."

"You said she wasn't a procuress!"

"You do rise to my bait so nicely," Killoran said. "How else would you expect a young girl to make her living on the cruel streets of London?"

"Bastard," Nathaniel muttered underneath his breath.

"Quite daring of you, my boy," Killoran murmured lazily, closing his eyes. "And if I hadn't already killed my quota for the day, I would skewer you for just such a remark. Your first lesson in polite behavior is never to call into question a man's parentage. You won't survive a week in London if you do, and I would hate to have to answer to your father."

"She'd be sorry," he said, more to himself.

"Doubtless the divine Miss Pottle would. She might even name her firstborn after you. But that would be the extent of it. You wouldn't be around to enjoy her grief. Your second lesson, Nathaniel. Women are ever fickle, jades every one of them. They have their delights, but they'll be the ruin of you if you let them."

"Was it a woman who ruined you?" Nathaniel asked, bold as ever.

"I shall thrash you, quite soundly," Killoran said calmly. "The only woman who ruined me was my sainted mother who made the mistake of bearing me in the first place."

"Lord Killoran…"

"Enough," Killoran snapped. "If you don't possess yourself in silence for the remainder of this trip, I'll send you to Mrs. Withersedge myself. There's a definite call for handsome young men in establishments such as hers."

For doubtless the twentieth time in the past hour, Killoran had managed to shock him. "You mean women patronize these places?"

Killoran found his first real amusement of the day, "Seldom, dear boy. You'd be reserved for the gentlemen with refined tastes."

Nathaniel finally subsided into blessed silence, and Killoran closed his eyes once more, dismissing both his new companion and the far more distracting vision of a voluptuous, bloodstained, red-haired female from his thoughts. Dreaming, instead, of Ireland.

There had been a time, some twelve or so years ago, when he had been as young as Nathaniel. Perhaps never quite so stalwart and innocent, but he had once believed life held possibilities. That certain things were worth fighting for, and that right always triumphed over might.

It had taken a bloodbath to disabuse him of the notion, and he hadn't been the one to suffer. It had been his parents who died in his place. And his punishment had been to live with that knowledge through the rest of his endless, empty days.

Nathaniel sank back into the lushly cushioned seats of Killoran's carriage. Although his father was wealthy enough, he wasn't used to such luxury. There was a sybaritic elegance about the thick velvet squabs that seemed almost decadent.

The man who'd agreed to take on his social education was an enigma. He sat across from Nathaniel, eyes closed, having dismissed both his young guest and that poor girl without a trace of regret, not to mention the corpse he'd left behind. But then, it was all of a piece with what Nathaniel knew of the man. Even as far north as Northumberland, he was notorious. Any number of people had been willing to tell Nathaniel all about him, and everything he'd seen so far had lived up to that reputation.

James Michael Patrick, the fourth Earl of Killoran, was a notable figure in London society. Not that he was accepted everywhere—for one thing, he was Irish. Which, according to Nathaniel's informants, automatically made him a wastrel, a scoundrel, a gamester, and a sot. Killoran had never been known to do anything to disabuse society of that opinion.

Being Irish, he was also possessed of a certain lethal charm, a ruined estate somewhere back in Ireland, and eyes the color of Lady Winnimere's world-famous emeralds. Add to that an almost sinful beauty of face framed by black curls, a tall, graceful body and quite the most elegant hands in all of London, and Killoran, who disdained to use his title, was indeed a dangerously attractive member of society.

Dangerous because the man was reckless, decadent, and far too handsome for his own good. A wicked tongue and a care-for-nothing attitude made him a force to be reckoned with. He had come from nowhere (or Ireland, which some accounted to be the same place), and in the years he'd been in London he'd amassed a prodigious fortune, all through his astonishing success at the gaming tables. His current worth was so impressive, it was rumored that he either cheated or had made a pact with the devil. Of the two possibilities, the latter seemed far more likely.

Though if he wasn't a Satanist, there was always the dread possibility that he might be far worse—a Catholic.

Most gossips considered that such slander might be going too far. To be sure, Killoran had been educated abroad at one of the Irish colleges in France, but few of the Protestants of Ireland were even allowed an education in that boggy country. He seemed to have no interest in papist notions; he held lands and a title, both a bit shabby, to be sure, but Catholics weren't allowed those possessions. In other matters he was as English as one could possibly wish. He could drink large quantities of port and claret and never show the cost, he could stay up all night gaming and walk away, winner or—on the rarest of occasions—loser, with a singular lack of regard. He could ride, hunt, shoot, and box, and he'd been known to kill his man in a duel on more than one occasion. What would be considered a liability in a lesser man, his very Irishness added to his allure. He was a great favorite with some of the more adventurous ladies—those who were considered mature enough to withstand his dangerous, drawling charm—and with the gentlemen as well. Those who didn't mind his mordant streak of humor or his withering contempt.

There was no doubt among the cognoscenti that Killoran had arrived in London with the sole purpose of making his fortune and bringing prosperity back to his name and estates. The most logical way to go about such a commendable course was to marry well, but Killoran, being Irish, hadn't been given that option. He'd had a number of close calls, including rumors of a clandestine elopement, stopped at the last minute by an angry brother, and the near alliance with a certain unpleasant widow whose jointure was almost as impressive as her bulk. That had come to nought, and Killoran appeared to have settled into a life of indolent, cynical ease. After the first year, he never even spoke of Ireland, and the faint traces of a brogue vanished from his deep, drawling speech.

It was also rumored that he'd once been in love.

Foolishly, impetuously in love with Maude Darnley, the reigning toast of London when he'd first arrived, a red-haired, blue-eyed innocent who made a perfect foil for his dark beauty. No one knew for sure whether he'd actually made an offer. Some held that he knew it would never have been accepted and he'd simply been amusing himself, another one of his infamous little games. Others hinted darker possibilities, that despite his already wild reputation, he'd made an effort to mend his ways and earn the hand of his love, and had gone so far as to declare himself.

Impossible, of course. Maude was a beauty and an heiress, of impeccable lineage and family. She would never be allowed to throw herself away on a penniless Irish peer. She was dead now anyway, and it was all past history.

Some counted the Darnley affair as the start of Killoran's descent into truly determined decadence. Others insisted he had already been well on his way. In either case, it mattered not the slightest. As long as Killoran could play cards, hold his liquor, and behave like the titled gentleman he was, no one minded how swiftly he went to hell.

His acquaintances were many; his friends, almost non-existent. "Fine fellow, Killoran," they would harrumph. "Wouldn't do to get too close to the man, though. Irish, y'know. Not quite like us. Knows his way around a bit of horseflesh though. And a demmed fine card player."

And Killoran was known to have overheard these loud, drunken encomiums and simply smile his cool, cynical smile.

He should have stood up to his father, Nathaniel thought bitterly, and not put himself in Killoran's graceful, decadent hands. But indeed, his father was a kind, blustery soul who seldom asked for much from his son and heir. And with Elspeth Pottle's defection, there was no real reason to resist. He could just imagine her reaction when he returned, jaded and cynical, a man of the world. She'd regret her hasty actions, she would, but it would be too late.

Nathaniel shot a surreptitious glance at his host. It would be foolish to underestimate the man and he had no intention of doing so. He was condemned to London and Killoran's corrupting influence until springtime. He would make the most of it.

The trip back to London was short and silent. If Killoran hadn't known better, he would have thought his reluctant guest was asleep, but from the occasional grunt of displeasure emanating from the young man's shadowy form, he surmised that Nathaniel was sulking. The day, which had started out so miserably, had brightened for a short while during Killoran's run-in with the murderous female, but life had once again subsided into bleak boredom. He'd been counting on Nathaniel to entertain him. Instead the young man merely made Killoran long to toss him into the Thames.

Perhaps he'd been foolish to dismiss the temptation the redhead had offered. It would have been much more entertaining to have left his unwilling guest back at the Pear and Partridge and take up the bloodstained female in his place. It had been years, perhaps a decade, since

Killoran had had any interest in virgins, but the innocent young female with the bloody hands was unlike any virgin he'd yet to encounter. There might have been a certain spice to deflowering her in the carriage during the drive back to London.

Ah, but then there would have been the problem of what to do with her once he'd finished with her. He had little interest in rape, even less interest in true love. If he brought her pleasure, she'd follow him like a ghost. If he didn't, his own physical pleasure would diminish, and there would have been no need to bother in the first place.

He cast a curious glance toward his companion beneath half-closed lids. Nathaniel was staring out into the darkness, his full lower lip thrust out. Perhaps he should have brought the young female as well as Nathaniel, and simply sat back and watched his guest do the honors.

Doubtless the starched-up Nathaniel would be unwilling to provide even that much entertainment. Killoran sighed. There was no help for it; he would drop the tedious creature off at the house at Curzon Street and then repair to his club. There he would drink a very great deal, enough to provide a warm glow to his bleak heart, and then he'd endeavor to lose a great deal of money at Faro. Chances were, things would go from bad to worse and he'd end up winning. He had the devil's own luck.

"What will happen to her?"

Killoran wasn't expecting the sudden gruff voice from his companion. He glanced across the carriage toward young Hepburn, trying to gauge his reaction by the muffled timbre of his voice. "Who knows?" he said casually. "I suppose she might go back to wherever she came from.

I didn't bother to ask how she happened to be in a private bedroom with her uncle, but I imagine there could be a perfectly innocent explanation. Perhaps she was eloping, and her uncle had come to put a stop to it. In which case her intended should show up at any moment, and they'll be off to Gretna Green."

"I don't think so."

"Don't you? For some reason, I don't think so either." Killoran leaned back. "She might very well take that money and present herself to Mrs. Withersedge. Or she might simply head out into the streets and earn her crust of bread that way. I do hope not."

"Why not?"

"Because it would be such a waste. She's worth more than a ha'penny a tumble."

"We shouldn't have left her," Nathaniel said.

Killoran yawned. "You will discover, young Nathaniel, that there are a great many strays and lost souls in this life. You can't waste your time worrying about them. Granted, few of them are quite as luscious as Miss Incognita of the Pear and Partridge, but few of them are as dangerous."

"Dangerous? Why would she be dangerous?"

Killoran contemplated telling the truth, and only one good reason stopped him. If he informed Nathaniel Hepburn that he'd taken the blame for the old man's death, the young fool might mistakenly think he'd done something noble. Killoran certainly had no interest in no-bility, no interest in anything other than his own amuse-ment. And he had no desire for anyone's good opinion, least of all that of his sullen companion. The very thought alarmed him. "Dear boy," he said faintly, "all beautiful women are dangerous. Haven't you learned that at your advanced age?"

"I don't—"

"We're here," Killoran said abruptly, interrupting him as the carriage drew to a halt outside his town house. He glanced at the huge gray-and-white structure and sighed. "And I doubt we're alone."

"You have guests?" Nathaniel was horrified.

"Presumably just one. I should have expected her."

"Her?" His voice rose in shock.

It was almost going to be too easy, debauching this stalwart innocent, Killoran thought fondly. Perhaps he'd start tonight, with the aid of the woman who was waiting for him.

The house was warm and well lit, the rich, almost decadent elegance of the place soothing to his soul. Nathaniel followed behind him, staring around with unconcealed wonder. Doubtless Killoran's house on Curzon Street was like nothing he'd ever seen in Northumberland, full of ornate, Oriental colors and furnishings, more like a sultan's palace than an English town house. It amused Killoran to keep it that way, a reaction to the simple country farmhouse in Ireland where he'd lived with his parents. Until that wretched day his father had inherited the title from his drunken older brother, the second Earl of Killoran, who had a tendency to ride too fast and too carelessly when he'd had too much to drink. And Killoran's life had never been the same.

Jeffries, his majordomo, was waiting, an expression of vague concern marring his usually imperturbable face.

"Don't look so distressed, Jeffries," he drawled as his servant and guest trailed him into the salon. "I gather Lady Barbara is here."

The concern vanished. "She is, your lordship."

"And where, may I ask, is she?"

"In your bed, your lordship."

"Lady Barbara grows very tedious," he murmured. "Send Mrs. Rumson up to inform her that I'm here with a guest, and if she doesn't get her delectable little arse out of my covers, then I'll have her tossed into the street in what she's wearing. Which I imagine isn't much."

"Would his lordship object if it were phrased as a polite request?"

"His lordship would object," Killoran said, throwing himself into a chair by the fire. "And bring me some brandy. Three glasses, assuming Lady Barbara will dress and join us."

"I don't drink brandy," Nathaniel said, sounding shocked.

"Yes, you do," Killoran corrected him lazily.

"I shouldn't be here. Your...friend would be embarrassed to meet a stranger under such circumstances."

"You mean my mistress, do you not? Friends do not usually arrive at a house uninvited and avail themselves of the master's bed. Though Lady Barbara is not, as yet, my mistress. She's merely campaigning for the post."

"Sir!"

"Nathaniel!" he mocked in return. "It's time for your education to begin. Meeting Lady Barbara should be a most felicitous start."

"I couldn't—"

"Killoran!" Her voice, powerful, melodic, demanding, sounded from the stairwell. A moment later the door was slammed open, and a vision stood there, all rage and beauty and quivering emotion.

Lady Barbara Fitzhugh was surprisingly young for a female of her reputation and habits. A mere two and twenty, she'd been reputed to have had more than a dozen lovers, though Killoran knew he was counted as her current paramour, and he'd yet to lay a hand on the delicate white skin that was quite deliciously exposed by the half-fastened gown. Her blond hair tumbled down her back, her blue eyes flashed, and her color was high as she marched into the room.

"Lady Barbara," he murmured, deliberately not bothering to rise.

"How dare you!" she shrieked, unaware of the silent young man standing in the shadows, staring at her. "Threatening me! You coldhearted bastard, I could have any number of men call you out for the insult."

"I doubt it," he drawled, feeling wicked enough to goad her. "I'm quite deadly in a duel, and most of your paramours know it. You're not worth dying for, my dear, as neither of us is certain you have any honor to save."

Her face was pale, and she reached out to slap him. The unfastened dress began to tumble, and she wisely hauled it up again. If she'd slapped him, he would have been obliged to slap her back, and then Nathaniel would have called him out, and the fun would be over even before it began.

"I hate you," she said in a tight little voice, turning to leave. And then she halted, as her magnificent eyes fell on Nathaniel's tall, silent figure.

She blushed. Killoran watched in amused astonishment as a faint wash of color spread over Lady Barbara's porcelain skin. Nathaniel was just as bad. While his mouth was pursed in unhappy lines, his eyes were staring at her with complete, smitten adoration.

"Lady Barbara," Killoran murmured, rising at last. "Let me make you known to my guest. Nathaniel Hepburn is the son of a distant connection of mine, come to London to see a bit of the world." His tone of voice left no doubt as to what part of the world Nathaniel was currently viewing as Lady Barbara was struggling with her dress.

Ah, but Barbara was up to the challenge. She tilted her chin defiantly, sailed forward, gown still clasped to her fabled chest, and held out a slim white hand bedecked in diamonds. Diamonds that Killoran had, in fact, paid for when she'd been bold enough to request them. "Mr. Hepburn," she greeted Nathaniel regally. "Welcome to London."

He took her hand. Indeed, he had no choice, but Killoran expected he wanted the excuse to touch her. He looked like a child at Christmas, surrounded by fantastical treats, the most delectable of which was the spun-sugar fairy holding out her hand.

"I am honored, Lady Barbara," he said, and the poor fool meant it, bringing her delicate hand to his lips with perfect courtesy.

Killoran considered giving vent to a snort of derision. Oddly enough, he couldn't quite bring himself to do it. "This is Lady Barbara Fitzhugh, Nathaniel. A dear friend of mine."

She stared at the young man, an odd expression on her

face, and Killoran found he was beginning to enjoy himself. He fancied himself a great black spider spinning a web, and Lady Barbara and Nathaniel were two succulent flies, caught for his amusement. It was a wondrously entertaining prospect, he assured himself.

"I'll see you to your carriage, Lady Barbara," Killoran murmured, coming up behind her and breaking Nathaniel's surprisingly firm grasp of her. "I'm certain you're anxious to be on your way."

She glared at him, hiking her dress up further, before turning to glance at Nathaniel. "Watch out for him, Mr. Hepburn," she said frostily. "He'll steal your soul if you don't have a care."

Killoran followed her out into the hallway. He caught her shoulders and held her for a moment. "You'll catch your death, Barbara," he said softly, fastening the tiny hooks that traversed down her narrow back.

She pouted. "You wouldn't care."

"On the contrary. You provide me with a fair amount of entertainment."

She glanced up at him, her coquettishness so blatant an act that he wondered that it managed to fool most of London. "I could provide you with a great deal more than that," she said in a husky drawl.

"I doubt my young guest would approve."

The sultry expression vanished from her face abruptly. "Why is he here?"

"I thought I explained. An act of kindness. I promised his father I'd give him a bit of town bronze."

"You've never done an act of kindness in your life," Barbara hissed. "Leave the poor boy alone."

"He's hardly a boy. He's older than you are."

Barbara's laugh was mirthless. "No one is as old as I am," she said bitterly. "Send him back home before you destroy him, Killoran. Leave some innocence in the world."

"I seldom waste my time with innocence," he replied, reaching out and stroking her perfect skin. "Not when debauchery is so much more interesting."

She preened under his casual caress, a practiced gesture, and no warmth reached her bleak eyes. "Send him away Killoran," she murmured, "and let me stay."

He smiled at her, gently, and gave her a gentle nudge toward the open door. "You forget, I know you too well. Good night, Babs."

Killoran had little doubt that Lady Barbara Fitzhugh's blasphemous response, echoing all the way to the library, made Nathaniel Hepburn's love-struck countenance darken in embarrassment once more.

CHAPTER THREE

Emma had always considered herself to be possessed of a few fortunate qualities, offset by the same number of drawbacks. She was brave, but when someone raised a threatening hand to her, that calm, faintly contemptuous expression on her face usually made the punishment far worse. She was strong, which made her able to withstand greater pain, both physical and emotional, whereas a weaker soul might dissolve into tears that would stop the torment. She considered herself to be passably pretty, though not quite in the common style, since she was built on large lines, but her height and her quiet life kept over-eager swains at bay. Her face was lovely enough, yet her pale skin was marred by an unfortunate arrangement of freckles, and her brown eyes, pretty though they were, were alarmingly nearsighted. And there was the problem of her most unfortunate shade of hair. She would have given anything to have hair a plain, mousy brown, rather than the flame red she'd been born with. Miriam called her hair devil's silk.

On top of everything, Emma was far too intelligent for

a woman. That intelligence, however, had served her in good stead. Were she not possessed of more than a mere competency of brain, she would never have guessed what her uncle had in mind when he entered her room at the Pear and Partridge.

Apart from all her other mixed blessings, she came equipped with a fortune. Not a sufficiency, not a comfortable independence. A fortune. Little good it did her. Cousin Miriam had ruled the household in Crouch End and Uncle Horace with an iron hand, and she had made certain Emma had no claim on even a penny of the money her father had left her. The income went to God's works, Miriam had righteously informed her, though Emma had yet to see evidence of that. Doubtless if she were a pauper, they never would have bothered with her in the first place, much less planned to kill her.

The notion still astounded her. She had never liked Uncle Horace, with his soft hands, his rounded belly that always seemed to brush up against her, his sour breath overlaid by peppermints. She had never liked the glistening look in his pale eyes when he thought no one was looking, or the cruel pinches, but she'd been naive enough to ascribe them to a misplaced lust. Not that she had much acquaintance with lust in her nineteen years. Cousin Miriam was twice her age, a woman of unassailable virtue and morals, and she'd kept Emma so well protected that she was practically immured behind the walls of the ugly house in Crouch End. The few men who'd been admitted to her cloistered presence were either very old or suitably terrorized by Miriam DeWinter.

But Gertie, Cousin Miriam's overworked maid, had explained it all to her in terms that, while shockingly frank, were also quite fascinating. The details of procreation sounded disgusting, particularly when coupled with the image of Uncle Horace DeWinter, and Gertie left her with little doubt that that was exactly what Uncle Horace had in mind with his seemingly endless soft touches and the gleam in his eyes when he thought no one was looking.

She'd learned to enlist Cousin Miriam's aid, subtly, of course. If that thin, overdressed martinet suspected her father of harboring any indecent tendencies toward Emma, she would have made life a holy hell for both of them. Not that she didn't already.

But Miriam loved her father, inasmuch as she was able to love, of that Emma was certain. And Miriam cared not one whit for her orphaned cousin with the vast inheritance that would all, one day, go to Emma's husband, and not a penny to herself. She wouldn't take the news of Uncle Horace's death well.

Emma had no idea when Uncle Horace's rapacious designs on her had turned deadly—the idea was so outlandish that even now she couldn't quite believe it. Any more than she could believe he was actually dead, killed by her own bloodstained hand.

But he was. She had stood over his body, numb with horror, the small part of her mind that functioned telling her to run before they dragged her outside and strung her up on the nearest tree.

And then He had appeared. That strange, drawling creature who'd mocked her, shocked her, taken in the desperate situation, and then quite calmly accepted the blame.

His professed motive shouldn't have astonished her. She had looked into the glittering depths of his eyes and seen only cold emptiness. That he'd saved her life out of boredom should have come as no surprise. She only wondered why she didn't want to believe it.

She could hardly object, since he had saved her life. And indeed, if his professed motive was true, she no longer owed him anything. It was a fair enough trade for a winter's evening—her life for his entertainment. They were quits.

She still wasn't sure why the landlord had appeared with a gold coin and the name of a mysterious woman in London, any more than she could fathom why that previously distrustful fellow had been willing to arrange a ride back to the city. She imagined it had something to do with her mysterious rescuer, but she had no intention of questioning her erratic luck.

The first welling of panic had filled her, and she squashed it down, ruthlessly. She was young, she was strong, she was—as her cousin had often informed her—lamentably intelligent. Surely she could find a way to survive.

She didn't want to become a whore, which was doubtless the profession that mysterious Mrs. Withersedge would offer her. There was little enough for a female to do on the streets of London, and the gold coin wouldn't last long. Indeed, it was a judgment upon her, one she should be willing to pay. She'd taken a life. If Mrs. Withersedge offered her a suitable penance, she would accept it.

Surely it would be preferable to life on the streets, and

two days later, she presented herself at Mount Street, ready to begin life as a high-priced doxy.

She still wasn't quite sure what that life would require of her. Her information on the act that gentlemen seemed to set such a store by was sketchy at best, and she preferred it that way. She had little doubt she could manage to lie in a bed in the darkness and allow someone to fumble beneath her nightdress and take liberties with her. After all, she would have to do the same thing if she ever married. It was a woman's duty, a woman's curse, and she might as well be paid for it.

The house on Mount Street didn't look the slightest bit like a brothel, but then, Emma had no idea what a brothel would look like. The doorman who ushered her inside didn't appear to be steeped in the ways of sin, and there were no dissipated females lounging around. Mrs. Withersedge was even more of a surprise. Her simple gray wig seemed better suited to a widow than a procuress, and her striped gown was high-cut with a wide white fichu. The only adornments to her face were thick white powder and a very discreet beauty mark near her fearsome nose.

Emma stood in the middle of the room, not having been invited to sit, when Mrs. Withersedge entered. Emma had bathed, arranged her unruly tangle of red hair as best she could, and dressed as boldly as her demure wardrobe allowed. Cousin Miriam had always made certain Emma's clothing was dull, drab, and discreet, better suited to a parish orphan than an heiress, and the few pieces Emma had brought away with her, while slightly more colorful, seemed rather unfit for a whore.

Mrs. Withersedge said not a word, walking around Emma's tall, upright figure, her eyes narrowed. "You have definite possibilities," she said abruptly, her voice rich and plummy as gentility overlaid her working-class upbringing. "What did you have in mind, child?"

Emma blinked. "I'm not quite sure."

Mrs. Withersedge moved away from her to sit behind an elegant, spotlessly neat desk. "I'm very particular about who I work with, my girl," she said. "I don't take on just anyone. I like references."

"References?" Emma echoed faintly. *For a whore?* she thought with wonder. "I'm afraid I can't provide you with any."

Mrs. Withersedge tapped a pale finger against the mahogany desk. "Fallen on hard times, have you?" she asked. "You're a better breed of female than I usually work with, but I'll consider it nonetheless. What are your qualifications?"

Emma blushed. She hadn't the faintest idea what the proper qualifications for a doxy were, apart from the obvious physical accoutrements, and she assumed most women came equipped with the basics. "I'm a virgin," she said abruptly.

Mrs. Withersedge simply stared at her for a moment. And then she laughed, a deep, rolling belly laugh. "Good for you, child," she said, wiping the tears from her eyes. "That's not something you see too much of nowadays, though I doubt it'll have much bearing in my finding a position for you. Sit down, child. You're too tall as it is, and it hurts my old neck to stare up at you."

Emma sat, also abruptly. "Position?" she said, afraid she was sounding like a lackwit.

"Isn't that why you're here?"

"Er...of course." *Position,* she thought, racking her brain. Gertie had mentioned something about different positions, with the man behind, or perhaps beneath, the female, but she hadn't paid much attention...

"Any other qualifications aside from your pure state?" Mrs. Withersedge demanded. "Can you read and write? Sew a fine seam? Paint with watercolors?"

"Of course," Emma said, surprised. Her education had included that much, even if her watercolors were confined to religious subjects and her reading material consisted of improving tracts that bordered on the fanatic.

"Of course," Mrs. Withersedge muttered underneath her breath. "Doesn't everyone?"

"Is there much call for that?"

"In governesses, yes."

"Governesses?"

"Do you have trouble hearing, young lady?" Mrs. Withersedge was losing a bit of her temper. "I run an employment agency. I specialize in finding upper servants for the wealthy. Isn't that why you're here? Don't you want a job?"

"Of course I do," she said, the stiffness in her shoulders relaxing fractionally. "And I should love to be a governess."

"Not if you had much experience at it," the older woman said wryly. "I know who sent you here. It could be no one but Killoran, curse his hide."

"Killoran?"

"The Earl of Killoran. If you've met him, you're not likely to forget him easily. A most unnerving gentleman, dressed in black and white and silver, with no heart and soul but the most malicious wit—"

"It was his lordship," Emma said hastily, remembering those deep green eyes so devoid of life and feeling.

"And exactly what did you think he was sending you to when he gave you my direction?" Mrs. Withersedge asked sternly.

Emma had never been one for discretion. "A brothel," she replied.

Mrs. Withersedge shook her head for a moment. "You're not likely to be paid as well, and you'll work a great deal harder," she said. "If you've a desire to be a whore, I could always make some arrangements…"

"No, thank you," Emma said swiftly. "I think I would make a very good governess. I'm very fond of children."

Mrs. Withersedge surveyed her doubtfully. "Fondness for children and an ability to paint with watercolors won't take you very far in this life, my girl. What's your name?"

"Emma," she said, without thinking. Belatedly the need for subterfuge stopped her. "Emma Brown," she added.

"Brown, is it? The most common name in England. I don't have many possibilities, Miss Brown. I try to avoid sending young women such as you into households where there are impressionable young men, but I'm afraid in this case I have no choice. Mrs. Varienne isn't the most genteel of employers, and she has not one but two older sons, just of the age to get into mischief with an attractive young female beneath their roof. You'd best keep an eye out for them if Mrs. Varienne is willing to take you on."

Unexpected hope had began to fill Emma, stiffening her shoulders and brightening her eye. "I'll devote myself to my charges," she said. "Besides, I don't suppose I am the sort to appeal to man's baser instincts."

Mrs. Withersedge looked her up and down and then emitted a genteel snort. "And I thought you were acquainted with Killoran," she said obscurely.

The house was cold and dark, the shades and curtains pulled tight. The smell of old cabbage drifted from the spotless kitchens, and in the front salon came the sound of footsteps, pacing, pacing.

Miriam DeWinter moved slowly, deliberately, back and forth across the room. Mourning made no change in her apparel—she always dressed in black. She had put off colors when she was a plain, thin twenty-three-year-old, mourning her mother's death, and when the year was over, she decided black suited her very well indeed. It gave her a maturity, a sense of power she craved, and by the time she was thirty she had the bearing of a matriarch.

She hadn't wanted to bring that little brat into her household, but she hoped she knew her Christian duty. Besides, Uncle Roderick had turned a small foundry into an obscenely profitable armament business, and Miriam had a passionate devotion to money that almost rivaled her passionate devotion to the jealous and vengeful God she worshipped. As long as Emma grew up in the confines of Miriam's household, there would be no distractions, no temptations, no young men to marry her and lure her fortune away. Miriam would teach her everything she knew, to love and fear her God, to live chastely and humbly. To leave the tawdry business of finances in her cousin's capable hands.

If only Horace had managed to control his ungovernable lust. If only Emma hadn't looked like a whore, with her disgustingly feminine body and her sinful hair. Miriam had prayed, but God hadn't been disposed to obey. And now she had to live with the consequences.

He was supposed to have killed her. The plan had been simple, but her father, much as she'd adored him, had never been one to listen to her teachings. The lure of fornication and strong drink had weakened his mind, that and the presence of Emma in their household.

She needed to die, Miriam's father had had no quarrel with that. They were running out of time; sooner or later Emma would run off, or some young man would steal her away, and all that lovely money would be out of reach. It would be a simple enough matter, a fall down the wide, bare, highly polished stairs, or a runaway carriage mowing her down and no one ever discovering the hapless culprit of such an unfortunate occurrence.

But Horace hadn't listened. He didn't want accomplices, he'd said. Other people involved, people they'd have to pay, people who could take it into their heads to demand more and more. He was a man; he could do it himself.

But Miriam hadn't been fooled. She'd seen the damp bog of lust in his eyes, and she'd known. There was nothing she could say, however. She was a righteous daughter, and obedient. She'd remained silent when he'd taken Emma off for the day, knowing it would soon be over. Knowing it would be none of her concern, what Horace did with Emma before he cut her throat.

But Horace was the one who had died. By his own sword, at the hand of some decadent Irish lord. And Emma had disappeared, beyond Miriam's reach.

If only she could find Emma. The slut would pay for her sins, her crimes. She had to be responsible for Horace's shameful death. She must have encouraged that Irishman to kill him, and then run away.

They'd brought her father's body back to her. She'd mourned, loud and long. And then she'd stiffened her poker-straight back, and turned to revenge with a prayerful intensity.

Emma would pay for her crimes. Spectacularly. And there would be no one left to inherit her considerable fortune. Except her dear, devout cousin, Miriam.

If only she could find her.

"I have the most amusing story to tell you, Killoran."

He looked up from the book he was perusing. It wasn't something he was particularly interested in—a treatise on agriculture he'd purchased more than a decade ago, when he still thought he might return to Ireland. He used it more as a tool with which to bother his companion, and as such it was very effective.

"Do you?" he murmured lazily.

Lady Barbara's delicate mouth thinned for a moment, and then she smiled. It was a good thing Nathaniel was nowhere to be seen. He was already absurdly smitten with

Lady Barbara, and there was no denying that she had a truly enchanting smile. If one cared to be enchanted.

"You recall my neighbors? That dreadfully common Varienne family?"

"Not particularly." He set the book down, surveying Lady Barbara with a bored expression. In truth, she didn't bore him. Her determined pursuit, combined with a complete lack of sincere interest in his innumerable attractions, fascinated him, almost as much as Nathaniel's instant, passionate devotion to her. The menage they had formed continued to enliven his days, what with Lady Barbara as usual throwing decorum to the wind and arriving on his doorstep morning, noon, and night, thereby convincing the polite world, erroneously, that she was his latest mistress. He gave her very little encouragement, which only seemed to fire her determination all the more. She wouldn't rest until she had managed to entice him into bed, and he couldn't imagine why. He knew women very well indeed, and there was no real sensuality in her practiced gaze, no lush longing in her full lips. She had as much honest interest in the delights of the flesh as she had in the agriculture tomes which he used to ignore her, and he was almost tempted to take up the challenge. The men she had bedded were legion, including most of his acquaintances and those who were misguided enough to call themselves his friend. None of them seemed to have noticed she was playing a game. A game he wasn't particularly interested in learning.

Ah, but young Nathaniel made it so much more interesting. When he looked at Lady Barbara with all the fierce passion that Killoran doubted he'd ever felt in his entire, jaded life, Nathaniel even managed to startle such a practiced flirt. She tried to keep away from him, albeit subtly, which amused Killoran greatly. Young Hepburn, studiously correct in all of his dealings, made the manipulative Lady Barbara extremely nervous. It was enough to cause Killoran to tolerate both of them.

"They're a family of cits," Lady Barbara said, rising and drifting toward him. It was half past four of a Friday afternoon. Lady Barbara had arrived for lunch, and despite Killoran's complete lack of hospitality, she had refused to leave. "One of their spotty young sons kept sending me flowers." She shuddered extravagantly.

"Not that you aren't deserving of all floral tributes," Killoran said idly, "but why?"

"You've never sent me flowers," she said in a surprisingly soft voice.

"You aren't interested in flowers from me, my sweet," he replied.

Her smile was bright, bold, never reaching her china-blue eyes. "True enough. And the young man was most appreciative of my charms. He would watch me from his bedroom window. It looked directly into mine."

"Fascinating," he remarked. "And did you do anything to merit his adoration?"

"The poor lad was so furtive about it. Always snuffing the light and lurking just out of sight, but I could see him from behind the awful lace curtains with which his mother festoons everything. Night after night he would watch, hoping to catch a glimpse of something. I thought such devotion deserved some reward."

"I'm certain you did."

"In a way, I'm afraid it might have provoked the current contretemps."

"I'm expecting you to amuse me with the eventual conclusion of this convoluted tale," Killoran murmured. "Or I shall return to my agriculture text."

She crossed the room to the settee beside him, perching close to him on her knees. Her dress was far too low-cut for day wear, exposing her small, undeniably lovely breasts, and she smelled like violets. He'd never cared for violets. "For a week, Killoran, I had my maid undress me in front of that window. I always left the candles brightly burning, and I made certain Clothilde stood behind me so as not to obstruct the boy's view." She sighed. "Wicked of me, wasn't it?"

"Indeed," he said. "Though not unexpected."

"You never find wickedness unexpected, Killoran. That's why I find you so interesting. I did it for a week. And then I stopped, abruptly. The poor boy would never leave his room. He was distraught, waiting for one more chance to view me. I have quite a lovely body, you know, Killoran. Many men have told me so."

"I've seen it," he said blandly.

"But you haven't taken it."

He smiled into the lost depths of her eyes. "Finish your tale, Scheherazade."

"I decided to watch him. I was much more adept than he was, and he had no idea I would come up in the darkness and sit behind my curtains. He had a very strong body. A spotty face, but that wasn't visible across the mews."

"You are a lustful wench," he said dryly, knowing it to be a lie. "I trust you enjoyed yourself."

She smiled, running her tongue over her full lips in a gesture as practiced as it was meaningless. "This morning I saw something far more interesting than a naked male body."

"I pray you, don't tell me you watched him tumble the upstairs maid. I would think a woman of your experience would have long ago tired of voyeurism. There are, after all, only a limited number of variations, and I imagine you've tried most of them. Certainly more than a spotty adolescent could think of."

"Oh, it was far more interesting than fucking, Killoran," she said, using the word deliberately, as if to prove she could say it without flinching. It sounded sad and absurd on her lips. "I got the chance to watch murder being done."

He closed the book. "Indeed," he murmured. "And who was murdered? The spotty little voyeur?"

"Presumably. She bashed him over the head with a fire poker, and even from my vantage point I could see the blood."

"She? The upstairs maid, I presume. This loses interest, darling. It's far too predictable."

"I was hoping it was his sister," Lady Barbara said, "but I gather that young lady is still in leading strings. I'm guessing it was the governess, though I've yet to find out."

"Why should the governess kill him?"

"He was trying to rape her. Ripping at her clothes, tearing at her. I'm afraid it's my fault. I must have driven him to a frenzy."

Killoran managed a faint snort. "A flattering notion, beloved," he said. "So what happened?"

"She hit him with the fire poker, he went down in a bloody heap, and she stood there staring at him, frozen, for what must have been minutes. I kept waiting for someone to burst into the room, but nothing happened. Eventually she set the poker down and went about tidying herself. Even from that distance I could see her hands were shaking."

"Not everyone has your sangfroid, my dear."

"And then she leaned down, and was out of sight for a while. I don't know whether she was finishing him off or trying to help him. After a bit she rose, repinned her hair, and left the room."

"And?"

"And I waited for an hour, to see whether there'd be a hue and cry, but no one seemed to have realized what happened. No one entered the young man's bedroom, and I assume his body wasn't discovered. So I came here for lunch. You don't mind, do you, darling? After all that excitement, I needed some companionship."

"You've probably missed all the fun. By the time you return, your murdering governess will have been hauled off to jail, the young man's corpse removed, and the shutters to his room closed. Your entertainment is at an end. If I were you, I'd hurry back home in case it hasn't quite concluded."

"Are you trying to get rid of me, Killoran?"

"Yes."

"You prefer a treatise on the growing of corn to the

delights I could offer you?" She dropped her voice to a husky note, and her slim hand rested on his thigh.

"The delights you are so eager to offer are nothing that I haven't already experienced in abundance. I doubt you could provide me with anything novel."

"Why are you so cruel to me, Killoran? Don't you want me? I assure you, I would dedicate myself to pleasing you. I'm very…inventive."

"I'm certain you are, Babs. But the fact remains that your inventiveness is mental, not sensual. You have no desire for the men you bed, and no real desire for me. Therefore I have no intention of boring myself by tumbling a cold, lying, aristocratic slut. If you're going to be a well-bred whore, Babs, you might at least be more convincing."

She snatched her hand back. "You are a blackhearted bastard," she said bitterly. "If I were that strapping, red-haired governess, I'd be tempted to kill you myself."

He was about to abandon her, but he stilled for a moment. "Strapping, red-haired governess?" he echoed. "Now, that I find a great deal more interesting than spotty adolescent males. You forgot to mention that part."

"You have a streak of the voyeur in you as well, Killoran?" she mocked him. "Young Varienne didn't manage to rip all her clothes off. I imagine she was taller than he, and strappingly built. Quite an armful—it was no wonder the young lad was overcome with lust. He was able to rip the front of her dress and yank down her hair. It was a fiery red color—very Irish. That was probably why she killed him. They say that fiery color eats into the brain and makes one mad."

"Had the governess been there a long time?"

"How would I know?" Lady Barbara said crossly. "The domestic staff of an upstart family such as the Variennes is hardly of interest to me."

"Only their sex lives."

She made a face at him. "As a matter of fact, I don't believe she'd been there long. No more than a fortnight. They tend to go through servants rather quickly. The older boys are lustful and the mother's a tyrant."

"A fortnight," he echoed lazily.

"Almost as long as your guest has been here. How much longer is he staying, Killoran?"

"Don't you care for Nathaniel, my dear? He's a most devoted admirer of yours."

"I don't care for devoted admirers," she said flatly.

"So I've noticed." He rose abruptly, moving away from her clinging, scented presence. "I'll escort you home, Babs."

He'd managed to surprise her. "You're coming to my house?" she said, wariness and triumph warring in her eyes. With absolutely no anticipation.

"Yes."

"You've refused all my invitations, Killoran. Why have you suddenly changed your mind?"

He held out his hand, and she placed her smaller one in his pale, hard grip. "I have a pronounced weakness for red-haired murderesses."

Emma sat in the stillness of her attic room, waiting. It was very cold up there, and she hadn't gotten used to the chill during her two-week tenure at the house of the

Variennes, any more than she'd grown accustomed to the pawings of Master Frederick.

Mrs. Varienne's eagle eye and pinch-penny behavior were nothing new; compared with Cousin Miriam, she was almost the soul of amiability. And indeed, Master Frederick had seemed no more than a minor irritation, like an errant flea, to be brushed away with a polite laugh and careful avoidance.

But now he lay in a welter of blood on his bedroom floor, dead, and Emma knew herself for the murdering wretch that she was. One man's death at her hands was a simple matter. It had been her life or Uncle Horace, and she hadn't thought twice about it. But killing a second man within a month went beyond the level of what was acceptable in polite society. She was a monster, deserving of whatever harsh justice was meted out.

So she sat in her room, and waited.

It was growing dark, and the night air was chilly in the room. Mrs. Varienne didn't hold with fires for the servants, and on the best of nights the most Emma could hope for was a call to join the family for dinner. That happened more often than not when the family was entertaining, and it hadn't taken Emma long to understand the reason behind the intermittent affability.

The Variennes were wealthy and indisputably vulgar— they made her uncle Horace seem positively genteel. Whenever guests arrived, Miss Brown was brought downstairs and treated with the most astonishing toadying, and Emma realized she must resemble her aristocratic mother more than she had ever realized. There could be no other reason behind the Variennes' desire to show her off to their various guests.

There was a price to pay for those warm, well-fed evenings. For each flattering occasion, Mrs. Varienne followed it up with an even greater degree of condescending hostility. And then there was Frederick.

Mrs. Withersedge had warned her. Indeed, Frederick's younger brother, Theodore, had been far too busy bedding the scullery maid even to notice Emma's presence in the house. But Frederick, who had a habit of spending far too much time immured in his room, had taken one look at Emma and begun to pursue her, much to his mama's displeasure.

He had kissed her once, a great, wet, slobbery attempt that had convinced her she was not cut out to be either a doxy or a wife. He had pinched her buttocks and pawed at her breasts one evening when he knew she wouldn't dare cry out, and she had done her best to keep herself away from him, locked in the nursery with little Amalia and young Master Edward, a budding roué of eleven who looked to surpass his elder brothers in lechery once he attained a few more years.

But Mrs. Varienne had called Emma into her bedroom for a morning diatribe. And on her way back up the stairs, the door to Master Frederick's room had opened and he'd dragged her inside, his soft, cruel hand clamped over her mouth before she could scream.

He was stronger than she would have thought, stronger than Uncle Horace. She'd fought wildly, silently, only longing to get away. She'd grabbed the first thing her flailing hand could reach, and it wasn't until she'd heard the sickening thud, and watched him collapse on the floor, that she realized what she'd done. Again.

She'd stared down at him in mounting horror. So very much blood from the wound on his spotty forehead, and he'd lain lifeless on the carpet, his eyes closed. Her body still felt bruised, mauled, by his hands.

Instinct had taken over. She'd caught those hands and dragged him out of the way, hiding his motionless body behind the bed. And then, she'd run up the flight of stairs to her small, cramped room on the third floor, locking the door and waiting.

But no one had come for her. The children had left on an outing to their grandmother's home in the country. This was, perforce, to have been her day off. If she had any sense at all, she would make a run for it.

But two dead men in less than a month were her limit. She would sit, and wait, and take her punishment. There would be no decadent, elegant rescuer like the Earl of Killoran this time. This time she would die. And her cousin, Miriam, would likely be there, to read religious tracts of vengeance and then do a stately gavotte on her grave. Except that Miriam never danced.

In the distance she could hear the noise. The Variennes had no plans for entertaining that evening, so there could be only one reason for the sudden influx of people. They had come to arrest her. Frederick's body had been discovered, and it was now simply a matter of time.

She rose, squaring her shoulders. She would sit here cowering no more, waiting for vengeance to come and drag her down, screaming and fighting.

The hallway was dark and warm, the heat rising

through the four floors. She descended slowly, her mind
in a fog, her hands clasped tightly beneath the heavy
linsey-woolsey apron Mrs. Varienne insisted she wear
when there were no guests to impress. She could hear
the sound of a woman's laughter, light, lilting, drifting
upward, a voice she'd never heard before. It made no
sense to her, but then, she was beyond the point of un-
derstanding.

She moved in a fog toward the main salon. Mrs.
Varienne's deep voice boomed outward, coy and arch,
flirtatious. Another voice replied, too low for Emma to
hear the words, but there was a strange, disorienting fa-
miliarity to the sound. It was a voice she'd heard in her
dreams, in her nightmares, drawling, masculine, with a
faint lilt.

She pushed open the door without knocking. Mrs.
Varienne, seated on a brocade sofa like a fat black spider, looked up at her and glared. Beside her stood quite
the most beautiful woman Emma had ever seen, a fairy-
tale creature dressed in some diaphanous, gauzy creation.

She turned, and to her horror she looked into the face
of Frederick Varienne, not dead at all. He appeared most
aggrieved, and the thick white bandage on his forehead,
set at a deliberately rakish angle, covered some of his
worst spots.

The sight of the man she thought she'd killed should
have been horror enough. But he was a mere bagatelle
compared with the dark figure that moved out of the
shadows into the bright candlelight.

Dressed in stark black and white trimmed with silver
stood her rescuer from the Pear and Partridge. His thin

mouth curved in a mocking smile, his green eyes glinting with amusement, he looked at her, and then his gaze slid knowingly to the bandage on Frederick's forehead.

Emma opened her mouth to say something, anything. She had wits, strength, self-possession. She could carry off this impossible situation; she could say something cool and polite and then absent herself. She could move into the room as if nothing had happened, as if she hadn't tried to kill the young heir to the household, as if she hadn't been caught bloody-handed by the malicious rake who had suddenly reentered her life.

She could do all this with ease. She made a tiny, choking sound. And then slid to the floor in a dead faint.

CHAPTER FOUR

The room was dark, and much too warm. An unusual circumstance—ever since Emma had left the dubious safety of the DeWinters' household, she'd been abominably cold.

She didn't move. She could hear the faint hiss and pop of the fire at the far end of the room, the flames dancing up the darkened walls. She was in the back parlor, Mrs. Varienne's private retreating room. And she wasn't alone.

She'd fainted, she remembered that much, which was odd in itself. She'd never given in to a crise de nerfs. But Mrs. Varienne wasn't a great one for either feeding her servants or keeping them warm, and the stresses of the day had taken their toll.

Emma sat up, a little too swiftly, and a fresh wave of dizziness washed over her. She hadn't killed him. She hadn't even damaged him badly. Frederick Varienne's pale eyes had looked at her with acute dislike, but he hadn't denounced her, hadn't had her hauled away from the house on a charge of attempted murder. Perhaps he was simply going to overlook it.

She didn't think so. Frederick *was* a bully, a young man prone to grudges as well as to spots. And she didn't care to consider the price he might exact for keeping his mouth shut.

She would have to leave. Though exactly where she could go was another problem—she doubted the estimable Mrs. Withersedge would approve of the botch she'd made of her first position.

She lay back down again, closing her eyes. She didn't want to go anywhere. She was tired, she was hungry, and she was humiliatingly close to tears, she who seldom cried. If only she could remember what had happened just before she'd toppled into her ignominious fate. And who in the less-than-friendly Varienne household would have seen to her comfort and brought her to this warm, quiet place to recover herself, who would have loosened her clothing and—

She sat up again, horror filling her as the memory came flooding back. "Oh, no," she said out loud, quite distinctly.

And out of the darkness his voice, the low, cool drawl with the faint trace of a lilt, said, "Oh, yes."

Emma slid her legs around, putting her feet on the thick French carpet. Her dress was tumbling down around her shoulders, and she knew whom to thank for that service. "You," she said, not bothering to disguise the horror in her voice.

"Me," he agreed. "Come to your rescue once more, my sweet. You do seem to have a talent for running into trouble."

She digested this seemingly innocent statement carefully, trying not to let panic swamp her. "I wasn't aware that I was in trouble," she said.

"Then why did you faint when you saw young Master Frederick?"

There was no way he could know. But then, the devil knew everything. She couldn't see where he was in the room—his dark clothes hid him in the shadows—but she knew he was watching her.

Emma had spent the past seven years of her life with Cousin Miriam. She wasn't about to let the likes of Killoran shake her concentration. "I fainted at the sight of you, my lord," she said coolly. "That night at the Pear and Partridge has haunted me."

"Haunted you, has it? Not enough to stop you from taking a fire poker and coshing young Frederick over the head, obviously. Such a very violent young lady, it quite astonishes me," he said lazily. "Are you certain it wasn't the sight of your second victim, risen from the dead, that sent you into that dramatic faint?"

"He told you," she said in a horrified voice.

"Actually, he didn't. I rather fancy he's too embarrassed. That mother of his is a tartar as well—I suspect she wouldn't be any too pleased with him."

"Then how did you know?"

"I have a spy." He moved then, materializing out of the shadows like a ghost taking shape, and she could see the whiteness of his lace and linen, the somber black of his coat and smallclothes. His hair was unpowdered, midnight black, and his pale face was unreadable. He was as dark, as handsome, as mesmerizing as she had remembered and tried so hard to forget. "He is, however, not about to let you get away with rebuffing his advances. He's been talking about a diamond-and-gold stickpin that appears to have turned up missing from his room. And he told his mother he saw you leaving his room this morning looking guilty."

"I didn't touch his stickpin!" she said furiously. "Though it's true enough I did leave his room, and I felt very guilty indeed. However, he wasn't in any shape to see me."

"I imagine his mother is about to call in the Bow Street runners, if she hasn't already. Either that, or young Master Frederick will find a way to exact penance. It doesn't appear that your sojourn at the house of Varienne will continue as comfortably as it has."

"I wish I *had* killed him." She made no effort to keep the bitterness from her voice.

"I had noticed that you have a bloodthirsty streak," Killoran remarked appreciatively. "There's a small matter that interests me. If you thought he was dead, why didn't you make a run for it? Do you have a sudden desire to end your own existence?"

"To kill one man is a great deal unfortunate," Emma replied flatly. "To kill a second is criminal."

"Some might argue that fact with you. The law would say the first death was just as criminal. Personally, I think anyone who would rid this world of that spotty, tedious young creature should be accorded all honors. So, my dear young lady, what is your desire?"

She peered at him through the darkness. She wished she could see his expression, but then, upon remembering, decided she was better off in the dark. He was far too handsome, far too cool and malicious-looking. There would be no light of concern or kindness in his dark green eyes, no gentle smile on his thin, mobile mouth.

"My desire, sir?"

"Will you stay here and await your punishment? Or will you escape? You have only to say the word."

"I don't trust you," she told him. "I've heard of your reputation, and it's beyond unsavory."

"So it is. A fitting companion to a murderess, don't you think?" he said gently.

"I'm not..." she protested, and then the words failed her as she remembered that indeed, yes, she was a murderess. Uncle Horace lay dead, and Cousin Miriam would doubtless be in deep, furious mourning. Plotting revenge.

Killoran was a dangerously patient man—it was one of the many things about him that made her uneasy. He waited while she considered all the ramifications and possibilities, none of them pleasant.

She finally spoke. "I think, given the alternatives, that I would rather escape," she said quietly.

He nodded politely, passing no judgment on her decision. "My carriage awaits."

She just looked at him. Doubtfully. "You'll help me?"

"I told you, I have once more come to your rescue. Like a deus ex machina, I appear where I'm most needed."

"You don't seem the slightest bit godlike to me," she observed. "Quite the opposite, as a matter of fact."

She'd finally managed to startle him. He laughed, a sudden, surprised sound. "I'm no envoy of Satan," he said softly. "It only seems that way."

She looked up at him, for a moment totally lost and

completely gullible. He held out his hand to her. It was an elegant hand, pale-skinned, with long, deft fingers and a narrow, graceful palm. He wore a quantity of gold rings, and the foaming white lace brushed his knuckles. They were beautiful hands, deceptively strong. And Emma was afraid to touch him.

She rose carefully, making certain she was able to maintain her balance. The loosened dress hung around her, and she clutched it against her, holding her tangled hair away from her face. She didn't dare ask who had carried her into this room, who had loosened her clothing. She knew she wouldn't care for the answer.

"Won't they try to stop us?" she asked, staring up at him. She was a tall woman, used to looking most men directly in the eye. This man's height only added to her unease.

"I imagine they will. Lady Barbara will keep them occupied while we leave through the garden." He had dropped his hand, no longer commanding her, but she knew her reprieve wouldn't last. Sooner or later she would have to touch him, and she had the oddest notion he would make her pay for her cowardice.

"There's no gate in the garden wall," she pointed out.

"Then we'll have to climb over it, won't we?"

She looked askance at his silks and satins, his dripping laces. And then she looked at his calm, enigmatic face, and didn't say a word.

The night was cold, and there was the promise of snow on the air. Emma shivered, wishing she'd brought a shawl. She'd already made one escape with little more than what she could carry in a capacious carpetbag. This time she'd leave with even less.

She glanced up at the man beside her, moving through the frost-deadened moonlit garden like a ghost, and for a moment she considered whether she might not be better off with a Bow Street Runner. Or the hangman.

But she'd never been one to turn coward. She'd stood up to adversity time and time again, and now wasn't the moment to cave in like a whimpering ninny. She'd gone from a safe, cosseted childhood as her indulgent father's only child to the stern and unbending asylum of Miriam DeWinter's house in Crouch End. She had adapted, grown strong, and never surrendered her spirit, her hope. She wouldn't start now. Squaring her shoulders against the bitter night, she started after him, keeping well out of sight of the windows and Mrs. Varienne's distressing eagle eye.

Either he had preternatural knowledge, or he'd already canvassed Mrs. Varienne's back garden for the low point in the wall. He moved toward it unerringly, turning to wait for her.

Her courage almost failed her. He stood watching her, silent, still, as she came to him, and through the scudding clouds the moonlight shone down all around him. He was a man of moonlight, she thought fancifully. Cold and silvered, a creature of the night and shadows. And she was putting herself at his mercy, though she sincerely doubted he was possessed of that particular commodity.

He held out his hand, and this time she knew she would have no choice but to accept it. "Someone's waiting on the other side of the wall," he said. "Go with him, and he'll take you to my house on Curzon Street."

"You aren't coming?"

His smile was as cold and dormant as the winter garden. "I'll be along soon enough. Possess yourself in patience, my child."

She looked at him, wondering whether the hangman's noose might not be preferable. And then she put her hand in his.

His flesh was cold to the touch. The lace that dripped from his sleeve covered their entwined hands, hiding them from sight, and for a moment she stood motionless, unnerved.

He moved forward smoothly and lifted her up, up, over the wall, his body strong and hard beneath the silk and satin and lace, his arms like bands of steel, entrapping her.

And then he released her, and she slid down in a heap on the other side, landing in another pair of strong arms.

"Got her, Killoran," her second rescuer announced from the darkness.

"Go with Nathaniel, my love." His voice floated over the wall. "And I pray you, don't try to murder him. He's the champion of the poor and misguided. And he's your only protection against me."

Emma gazed at the handsome, uncomfortable-looking young man staring at her. She pulled away from him, yanking her dress down around her hips. She didn't remember him, but he seemed to know her.

Nathaniel moved swiftly, stripping off his sober wool jacket and wrapping it around her. "She'll be perfectly safe with me, Killoran," he declared firmly, putting a protective arm around her shoulders, which were almost even with his.

A distant laugh, faint and mocking, echoed from the other side of the stone wall. "I know."

"Come with me, miss," Nathaniel said, pulling her away from the wall.

She let herself be moved along to the carriage, allowing herself to be cossetted for the first time in what seemed like her entire life.

He helped her up, followed her inside, and by the time she was safely settled, wrapped in a fur robe that covered her up to her neck, the carriage had started forward along the dark London streets.

She looked across the carriage to the man opposite her. "Do I know you?" she asked in a low voice.

She half suspected the boy of blushing. Not that he was truly a boy—he was perhaps three or four years older than she was—but compared with his unlikely companion, he seemed boyish indeed.

He cleared his throat. "I was at the Pear and Partridge," he said hesitantly. "You were too overset to notice me, of course, but I was most distressed for you. Killoran is a monster."

In the name of fairness, Emma felt called upon to disagree. "He saved my life."

"I suppose so. Doubtless out of no noble motive. You've been through a great deal, but I promise you, as long as you're under Killoran's roof, no harm will come to you. I'll see to it."

"What about Killoran?" She managed a faint trace of wryness.

"He won't touch you." Nathaniel was very stern for such a young man.

He couldn't see her doubtful smile in the darkness, and for that Emma was glad. She didn't want to hurt this innocent champion, but she knew that if a man like Killoran took it into his head to have her, then no fierce, noble young hero was likely to be able to stop him.

However, she doubted that Killoran would be bothered. She wasn't the sort to appeal to men of his lordship's jaded interests; she was the stuff of spotty adolescent urges and old men's dreams. For the time being, she'd be safe. Long enough to catch her breath and decide what to do next.

"I'm certain Killoran's motives toward you are of the purest," Nathaniel added.

"I doubt there's anything pure at all about my lord Killoran," she said. "And I have no illusions about his reason for coming to my aid this time, any more than I mistook his actions last month. He's bored. And he finds me entertaining."

She waited for Nathaniel to refute her theory. He said not a word for a long moment, and it wasn't until the carriage had come to a stop that he spoke. "Perhaps you're right," he said slowly. "But it wouldn't do to underestimate Killoran. There's more to him than meets the eye."

"Of that," said Emma, "I have no doubt."

She barely noticed her surroundings as Nathaniel ushered her into the house, the fur lap robe still wrapped tightly around her. She had the vague sensation of candlelight and elegance, impassive servants and warmth. The oversize and surprisingly soft settee next to the blazing fire in what must have been a library was much more comfortable than she would have expected, and she had the errant, distracting notion that Killoran might have stretched his elegant body out on its length and slept there. The idea made her extremely uncomfortable, but not uncomfortable enough to leap up.

"You'll be wanting something to eat, no doubt, and perhaps a cup of tea," Nathaniel said solicitously. "Rest for a moment, and I'll see what I can do…"

The words faded into the thick velvet of her mind. The warmth had finally reached down into her bones, turning them to jelly, and she closed her eyes, drifting into a deep, helpless sleep before Nathaniel could even finish speaking.

"What are you going to do with her?"

Killoran turned to look down at Lady Barbara, wondering lazily why the miraculous perfection of her face left him so unmoved. He could see her well enough in the dim light of the carriage, and while he admired her beauty, it ignited no spark of desire. "I doubt that's any of your concern, my love."

"Don't call me your love, Killoran," she snapped, momentarily distracted as he'd meant her to be. "Not if you don't mean it."

"I never mean it, my love," he said deliberately. "You should know that."

"I don't make the mistake of assuming you're going to take the wench to bed," Lady Barbara continued.

"And why not?"

"Because you've refused to take what I've offered," she shot back. "I doubt whether you're a real man at all. Perhaps you prefer the attentions of others of your sex."

He laughed softly. "Perhaps I merely seek a challenge, dear Babs. You've made it more than clear I can have you anytime I evince the slightest interest. Perhaps I like the hunt."

"Perhaps you like other men."

"Perhaps," he murmured, unruffled by her attempt to be provoking. "Doubtless you'd like me to throw you down on the carriage seat and prove how wrong your supposition is."

"Doubtless," she purred, suddenly all preening sensuality with no real emotion beneath it. He wasn't fooled by her, and never had been. Barbara's wiles were for the likes of gullible young men such as Nathaniel.

"Sorry to disoblige you, darling," he said, "but right now I'm more interested in seeing how our little Miss Brown is faring."

"I'd scarcely call her little," Barbara said waspishly.

"No, indeed." Killoran allowed a certain amount of detached appreciation to enter his voice, just enough to enrage Barbara further. "She's quite a luscious handful, is she not?"

"You know her, don't you?" she said shrewdly. "The moment I described her, you knew who I was talking about. Who is she? And don't expect me to believe her name is really Brown. Mrs. Varienne might call her that, but I've never had any opinion of *her* intelligence."

"I doubt that it is. I have no idea what her real name is; for all I know, it could be Pottle."

"Pottle? What a revolting name." Barbara shuddered.

"Indeed. Just don't let Nathaniel hear you say so. He was devoted to Miss Pottle."

"I'm getting confused, Killoran. Is Nathaniel in love with the girl we just rescued?"

"Of course not, darling. He's in love with you, poor sod, and well you know it. Before that he was in love with a Northumberland lady with the unfortunate name of Pottle, and next he'll probably fall in love with Miss Brown."

"Which would be a great relief to me," she said, possibly not even aware that she lied. "You still haven't told me where you've seen her before."

"No," he said gently, "I haven't."

Barbara's carriage had barely come to a halt outside Curzon Street when Killoran opened the door and leaped out. It had begun to snow lightly, the thick white flakes drifting downward to blanket the street. "I know you'll refuse to come in, so I won't even bother asking you," he said smoothly, looking up at Barbara as she leaned out the carriage door.

Soulless she was, but that experienced body could still provide him with a night of sweet oblivion. For one brief moment he wondered if he could let himself be tempted.

"But, Killoran," she said, and the possibility vanished as swiftly as it had come.

"Good night, Babs," he said, closing the door firmly in her pouting, pretty face.

He didn't care much for servants hovering around him,

and the front hall was blessedly empty when he let himself in. He tossed his thin kid gloves on the gilt-and-ormolu table, then wandered through the public rooms, glancing at them with new eyes, wondering what his new guest would think of such bizarre magnificence. He couldn't quite place her background. On the one hand, it seemed more than likely that she came from yeoman stock, decent, middle-class blood, perhaps tainted with trade. A cit, solid and unimaginative.

But for all that he didn't care much about people, he was very observant, and Miss Emma Brown was no cit. There was breeding in her fine, strong bones, in the cool bravery of her eyes, in the elegance of her hands and that indefinable air of grace. She was an enigma, was Miss Brown, a fierce, murderous enigma. One that was blessedly entertaining.

He had a use for her. The notion had been playing around the back of his mind these past few weeks, merely a fancy that he'd been considering. At that time he'd had no idea whether he could find her again, nor was he certain he wished to. Mrs. Withersedge might provide him with her direction, but there was no guarantee that the girl had taken advantage of his offer, no guarantee that she was even still alive.

But fate had taken a hand, and Killoran was Irish enough to believe in fate. A beautiful red-haired waif had, for the second time, been brought to his attention. He'd have to be a fool not to make use of her.

Nathaniel was nowhere to be seen. The fire in the library beckoned Killoran, and that night he gave in to creature comfort, moving toward the one room in the house in which he allowed himself to drop the armor that protected him so well.

He stripped off his coat, tossing it on a chair, then placed his lacy cravat and a handful of diamond-and-emerald studs on the desk. He had moved closer to the fire and was turning his laced sleeves back when he saw her.

Her red hair was a blaze across the white ermine lap throw in which she was wrapped. She was sound asleep, lying on the settee, and he could see the pinched white misery of her face, the paleness of her lips, the faint spattering of freckles against her skin. He wondered if he could redden those lips.

Would she pay the logical price for rescue? She was in his house, in his power, and if she were even the slightest bit knowledgeable about the way the world worked, she'd know what was expected of her. She was probably lying naked beneath that soft white fur, expecting him.

A sudden rush of desire washed over him, and he examined it, surprised. It had been a very long time since the thought of a soft, sweet body had aroused his interest, not to mention another, more demanding part of him. But Emma Brown, with her murderous ways, her soft, shy mouth, and her astonishing bravery, had done just that.

He moved to stand over her. He considered unfastening his breeches and taking her there on the sofa. After all, she must be a doxy, despite that innocence. No one could look as she did, find herself in the situations she did, and remain untouched.

He reached out a hand, tugging the fur down, hoping to see exposed skin. Instead he saw that miserable gray serge that he'd wanted to rip off her when he'd unfastened it earlier. She wasn't made for gray serge. She was made for silks and satins and furs. And the pristine whiteness of bed linen and smooth skin.

"What are you doing?"

His damnable guest, Nathaniel, appeared in the doorway, his brown hair ruffled from sleep, a glowering expression on his face.

"Admiring Miss Brown," Killoran said lazily, turning his gaze back to the sleeping woman. The sound of voices didn't rouse her, and he imagined she would continue to sleep quite soundly.

"Where's Lady Barbara?"

"I sent her home."

"Killoran…" Nathaniel's voice was strong with disapproval.

Killoran glanced at him. "Yes?" His voice was chilly enough to daunt even hardier souls, but Nathaniel was a hero, intent on defending the flower of womanhood from a dedicated villain. It should have been amusing, but Killoran's malicious sense of humor was abandoning him when he most needed its protection.

"Leave her alone, Killoran. I promised her you meant her no ill."

"And did she believe you?"

"Not for a moment."

Killoran looked back at her. "Wise girl," he murmured. "But for now, she's safe. I promise to keep my marauding hands off her fair young body. For the time being."

"Damn it, Killoran, she's an innocent!" Nathaniel protested hotly.

"My dear Nathaniel," Killoran said, utterly weary as he turned away from the sleeping girl, "no one is innocent." And without another word he left the room. Before he could change his mind.

CHAPTER FIVE

Emma lay still beneath the thick covering, alone in the darkness of Killoran's library, and although that ought to bother a decent, God-fearing young woman, she found she couldn't rouse much indignation. She was wonderfully warm, and even though her stomach was still quite hollow, she had no desire to go in search of food.

Cousin Miriam would be horrified if she saw her, but then Cousin Miriam was easily horrified. Having spent the majority of her almost forty years addicted to good works, and to increasing the general misery of any poor soul unfortunate enough to cross her path, Cousin Miriam had very little tolerance for moral laxity. And Emma was definitely feeling lax.

She rolled onto her back and opened her eyes, staring into the firelit darkness. Why had the notoriously decadent Earl of Killoran rescued her once more? Would he want payment this time? It was unlikely in the extreme that he should find her over-tall, overripe body desirable, but then, she'd never been one to fathom the way gentlemen's minds worked. If Killoran wanted her, she would have to pay her debt. It could hardly be worse than Frederick Varienne.

She sat up in the darkness, secure in the knowledge that she was, at least for the moment, alone. Her body felt the same beneath the thick fur throw—if anyone had despoiled her, she didn't seem the worse for it. Besides, she sincerely doubted she'd sleep through *that*.

She had a headache. Her stomach growled ominously. And the heat from the fire penetrated only a few feet into the elegant room.

She didn't want to run away again. She didn't want to end up on the icy streets of London with no cloak, no money, no prospects.

But she had no desire to lie naked in the Earl of Killoran's bed and wait for him to take her. Given that she found the earl unnervingly attractive, the experience probably wouldn't be unpleasant. Given the turmoil of the past few weeks of her life, it seemed unlikely she would end her days a virgin or find a decent husband. Failing those two preferable fates, the dark and dangerous Killoran should begin to take on a certain appeal.

She was being soundly impractical. If she ran off, she would doubtless end up selling her body. She'd been resigned to the notion once before, when she'd presented herself to Mrs. Withersedge. The Earl of Killoran was a beautiful man, far better than anyone who'd be willing to buy her favors on the streets.

Why didn't she count her blessings and let herself be debauched?

She sat up and began to fasten her clothes slowly, deliberately, as she considered the notion. It was perhaps his very beauty that unnerved her. The cool amusement in his handsome face, the banked emotion in his dark green eyes. The grace in his tall, strong body. She didn't want that body touching hers. She didn't want those long, beautiful hands caressing her. The very idea terrified her.

Her hair was a loose tangle down her back, and she quickly bundled it behind her neck, securing it with a strip of silk. Moving to the window, she pushed the heavy velvet aside to stare out into the city street.

It would be getting light soon. Snow was falling, a lovely blanket of white covering the cobbled street. Emma looked down at her thin shoes and shivered.

Killoran was a man who appreciated elegant trifles. A small pile of diamond-and-emerald studs gleamed from the center of the walnut desk, catching even Emma's myopic eyes. She moved toward them, picking them up and weighing them in her hand.

His coat lay there as well. She stared at it, uncertain for a moment. It was black satin, embroidered with silver, and she'd look ridiculous in it. She would also be protected from the snow.

It lay on a chair near the fire. When she picked it up, it was warm, as if it had just come off his back. She slid her arms into the long sleeves, and the froth of lace covered her hands entirely. The coat encased her shabby dress in silken elegance, and it smelled wonderful—of leather, and spice, and whiskey, and fire-warmed satin. It smelled like Killoran.

She found she was stroking the sleeve absently. She almost stripped the garment off there and then, disgusted with herself. It was a good thing she was possessed of a certain amount of determination. It would be dangerously easy for her to stay in the mesmerizing presence of her wicked rescuer.

She'd rather take her chances on the streets of London. She dropped the jeweled studs into a silk-lined pocket, pulled the capacious folds of the coat around her, and started for the door.

At the last moment, caution halted her. She hadn't seen or heard any sign of a servant in this night-shrouded place since just after she arrived, but that didn't mean they weren't lurking. Most servants rose at the break of dawn, and if she dared wander the hallways, she might run into someone.

Indeed, she thought she could hear the sound of approaching footsteps. There were no other doors in the room, only windows overlooking the snowy dawn. She didn't hesitate. By the time the door to the library opened, she had already slipped out the casement, pulling the window closed behind her.

She landed in the snow. It was very wet, the temperature not yet being extreme, and it soaked immediately through her skirts, drenching her thin leather slippers as well. She struggled upright, tugging Killoran's coat around her. It no longer felt quite so cozy.

She started forward, and an icy blast hit her full in the face, rocking her backward. For a moment she thought longingly of the warm fire and the fur throw. And then she thought of Killoran's cool, malicious eyes, and she kept going, head down, into the early morning storm.

* * *

Leaning negligently against the window frame, Killoran watched her vanish into the swirling snow, his new coat wrapped around her tall figure.

He glanced at his desk. The jeweled studs were gone as well, and if he instituted a search, he'd probably find other artifacts missing. He smiled faintly. Another man might swell with outrage. Another man might call in the runners, or at least send his servants after her to retrieve the stolen property. Killoran did no such thing.

He found he was properly in awe of her, as well as amused. She seemed to have an essential grasp of how to survive, even if she was uncommonly interested in preserving her virtue to the point of murder. She hadn't succumbed to the vapors when she'd skewered her uncle, and though she had fainted when she discovered her latest victim bloody but unbowed, he sensed it was his presence that had delivered the coup de grace, not the resurrection of Frederick Varienne.

She had stolen his jewels and his coat and climbed out his window to disappear into a snowstorm. If only all women could be so resourceful.

He considered letting her go. She was undoubtedly a great deal of trouble; if he hauled her back, she might grow agitated, and try to skewer him.

The notion had a certain oblique charm. No one had tried to kill him for a number of years, ever since he had dispatched his third man in a duel. He was considered possessed of the devil's own luck, both in dueling and in cards, and most people avoided both those pursuits with him.

So circumspect were the majority of his acquaintance, in fact, that he found them deadly boring, as well as vicious, petty-minded snobs. On the other hand, Nathaniel's ill-concealed dislike managed to provide him with some much-needed distraction. And despite being vastly irritating, young Nathaniel, with his stern disapproval and heroic ways, was twice the man any of Killoran's London acquaintances were.

Of course, he wasn't nearly so distracting as the strapping, flame-haired murderess who had so conveniently dropped into his lap. He was convinced she'd been brought into his life for a purpose, not by mere chance, and he found the thought curiously soothing. In the past five years only one human being had managed to rouse him from his ennui, and that was Jasper Darnley.

The score he had to settle was an old one. He'd worked away at it, bit by bit, until the sport was almost gone. But still, Darnley managed to surprise him and come back. Emma could provide the means for the long-awaited coup de grace.

However, she was a double-edged sword. Killoran knew Darnley would take one look at her and be consumed with lust. That was exactly what he counted on.

The only danger was that he might fall prey to the same weakness he offered his enemy.

She was almost at the edge of the garden now, and her tall figure was obscured by the blowing snow. Her thin shoes would be worthless in the deep slush. Her clothing was rough, cheap, unimaginative, and too flimsy. And his satin coat would provide little protection from the elements.

Would she freeze to death within sight of his house? He considered the notion absently. It would certainly make things interesting. He could well imagine the rumors that would abound. People would assume she was a serving girl, seduced and abandoned. Or some indigent relative, turned away without a crust of bread. People believed the worst of him, and rightfully so. He was a heartless bastard, worse even than they imagined.

She might get as far as the stews of London. She wouldn't last long on a night like this. If the cold and the storm didn't stop her, one of the denizens of the night would. He couldn't imagine how she'd survived before, but he had seen her pale face and shadowed eyes and known she was at the limit of her endurance.

If he didn't go after her, she'd be dead before the sun rose. It was just that simple.

A villain wouldn't care. The heartless, soulless creature he prided himself on being would accept her fate as her just deserts. He'd rescued her twice now, and the night was cold and wet. Only a sentimental fool would go after her.

He turned away from the window and poured himself a leisurely glass of brandy.

Her feet were numb. Surely she'd been this cold before, but at the moment, Emma couldn't remember the occasion. Odd, that her feet would hurt so much when all feeling was gone. Every step was torment, yet still she moved onward through the blinding snow.

The wind had whipped her hair free from the knot at the back of her neck, and it blew in her face. Several strands were caked with ice, and she could feel frozen tears against her eyelashes. The sun must be rising, but she couldn't see a thing in the swirling storm.

Freezing to death wasn't supposed to be an unpleasant way to die. She wasn't sure where she'd garnered that piece of information, but it lay in the back of her mind, embedded there like all useless bits of knowledge yet she needed that knowledge now. Because freezing to death looked to be very unpleasant indeed.

She didn't know whether she'd reached the limits of Killoran's property, and she didn't care. She ran into something, hard, iron, slamming against it in her blind dash for shelter, and she sank down, huddling against it. It had to be a fence of some sort, and it provided no comfort at all, but she was beyond the point of hoping for comfort in this lifetime. All she desired was a swift, merciful end.

She wasn't going to cry. She couldn't stand the thought of any more ice on her face. She was shaking so hard she could hear her teeth rattle, and she kept waiting for that blissful, disorienting blanket of approaching death to wash over her. Where was it, damn it? She'd had enough of this vale of tears.

He loomed up, out of the blinding storm, before she had a chance to run. One moment she was alone, an ice princess. In the next she was being hauled roughly upward by a caped figure.

She tried to struggle, but her movements were hampered by the numbing cold, and the creature simply scooped her up with almost uncanny strength. She managed a feeble shove, and he responded with a resounding curse. It was Killoran, of course.

"If you don't hold still," he said through the thick snow, "then I'll drop you and let you freeze to death."

It was hardly reassuring. She made one more vain attempt to free herself, and his response was swift, leaving her to subside with a pained whimper. He moved swiftly through the storm, taking less than a quarter of the time to cross the area it had taken her so long to traverse.

This time there were servants when Killoran kicked savagely at the door. Heat and light surrounded her, the chatter of voices, and then he dumped her, unceremoniously, so that she stood for a moment, ice-caked, weaving, in the front hallway.

"Poor lady," an elderly woman's voice clucked. "Where did you find her, my lord?"

She wanted to faint. She wanted to sink to the floor in a graceful escape, but she was made of sterner stuff than that. She squared her shoulders and looked up into Killoran's face through ice-caked eyelashes. He was staring at her with a cool, unreadable expression.

"I fished her out of the snow, Mrs. Rumson," he replied. "Take her and thaw her out, would you?"

"Where would you have me take her, sir?"

His smile would have struck terror in the heart of a Bow Street Runner. "I haven't the faintest idea," he said lazily. "She's a bedraggled creature, is she not? Perhaps she might be presentable, but right now she doesn't do much to excite my interest. See that she's well taken care of, Mrs. Rumson. Doubtless I'll find some way to make use of her."

Emma was beginning to warm up. She didn't like the sensation. "I'm not your possession," she said, the effect somewhat ruined by the chattering of her teeth.

Killoran's smile was sweet indeed. "Certainly you are, my dear Miss Brown. But we shan't call you Miss Brown—that's much too humdrum a name for a mad creature like you. I shall put my mind to it while you're thawing out."

She opened her mouth to say something, then shut it abruptly. It would be a waste of time. She needed to conserve her energy for another escape.

"Don't even think it," he said gently.

"Think what?" she blurted out.

"You aren't leaving here until I'm ready to let you go. It's extremely simple, and you strike me as a bright enough creature."

"You can't keep me here."

"Of course I can. And the more you try to escape, the more you interest me. Your wisest course of action, my dear Miss Brown, is to become very conciliatory. Labor to do my bidding, please me in all matters, and I shall soon grow beastly tired of you and send you on your way."

"No."

"No?" he echoed, much amused. "Then consider your options. Here you have a warm bed, decent food, and I'll replace those hideous clothes with something a great deal more suitable. Your alternative is selling your body on the streets."

"At least I'd have a choice."

"Don't deceive yourself, Miss Brown. You'll have no

choice at all. You'd be dead before long, from a knife to the belly or the pox, it wouldn't make much difference. One takes a bit longer, but you're dead either way."

"I'm not afraid of death."

"Obviously not, since you're not loath to deal it out on occasion. Come, child, you're being foolish. Would it appease you to know that I have absolutely no interest in your enchantingly voluptuous body?"

She looked at him warily. "You don't?"

"Not a bit," he said calmly. "I can have quite any female who interests me. Ones, I regret to say, who are a great deal lovelier than you are, pretty though you may be. I've lost interest in affairs of passion, my child. I'm more intrigued by affairs of cunning."

"Then where do I come in?"

"I have need of you, Miss Brown. I'm counting on you to help me with a small problem concerning an acquaintance. Once that's taken care of, I'll see you're suitably rewarded and sent on your way. Your options are not extraordinary, my dove. You can assist me and be generously recompensed. Or you can find a swift end on the streets of London. Trust me, child. I have no intention of touching you. You believe me, don't you?"

She looked up at him. Her body was racked with shivers, her feet were blocks of ice, and her skin fairly screamed with pain. She ought to run, but she knew she'd finally reached the end of her endurance. He was looking down at her, faintly bored, slightly amused, and she believed him. She knew as well as anyone what she looked like, and in her current half-frozen, half-melted state she could hardly flatter herself by thinking he desired her.

Besides, she'd seen his current mistress, Lady Barbara. The man would be mad to want her instead.

"I believe you," she said, her voice not much more than a rusty whisper.

For a moment she imagined she saw a flare of triumph in his cool green eyes. If she had, it was gone in an instant. "I knew you were an intelligent child."

"I'm not a child."

"Compared to me you are. Mrs. Rumson should have your bath ready by now."

She hesitated. "My lord..." she began.

"Call me Killoran. Only servants pay attention to the Irish peerage," he said coolly.

"Are you certain...?"

"Don't be tedious, Miss Brown. God, what a wretched name. Almost as bad as Pottle."

"Pottle?" She was confused.

"What's your name, child?"

She didn't like being called child, but she had no intention of telling him her name. Cousin Miriam would like nothing better than to have her cousin returned to the bosom of her family. "Brown," she said firmly. "Emma Brown."

"Emma," he said. "How very disappointing. You should be named Boudicca. You're far more like some mythic warrior maiden than plain Emma Brown. Up to the bath with you, Emma. You look as if you're going to melt into a puddle in the middle of my Aubusson carpet, and that wouldn't please me, you know."

She looked down at her feet. She was standing in a very wet spot, and shivers were still racking her body.

The flight of stairs looked very long indeed, and she wondered how in the world she would make it up them without assistance.

One step at a time, she reminded herself. She turned from him slowly and began to mount the stairs, secure in the belief that the cool green eyes that followed her progress held no interest whatsoever.

She was a ridiculous creature, Killoran thought idly. And so very gullible, to believe his arrant lies. He would use her to destroy Jasper Darnley. He would use her for his own pleasure, if and when he chose to. And then he would dismiss her without another thought, and if she ended up on the streets after all, it wouldn't be his responsibility.

He didn't give a damn who spent his or her foreshortened life on the streets. He still wasn't certain why he'd decided she'd help him, why he'd drained his bowl of brandy with unappreciative speed and gone out into the storm after her. It was surely senseless to keep rescuing her, just on the chance she'd help him effect his final revenge.

Ah, but perhaps that was part of the sport. Her very unwillingness to be rescued from the consequences of her rashness amused him. Her lack of reaction to him, when he'd grown weary of impressionable young women willing to fall at his feet and into his bed, stirred his pique. And her luscious, pale-skinned beauty aroused him in ways he hadn't even begun to consider.

She'd believed his promise, poor child. Believed he had no more interest in her than she had in him. She wouldn't know what he was about until she was lying on her back in his bed, her legs wrapped tight around his hips, her strong hands digging into his shoulders, her voice crying out in pleasure and release.

Ah, yes, she had an education in store for her, one she couldn't begin to fathom. He would seduce her, slowly, delicately, and so thoroughly that there wouldn't be a waking hour in her life when she didn't think of him.

And he would haunt her dreams as well.

Ah, he was a bad man. A very, very bad man. With a faint smile on his face, he headed back to the library, to devote the proper appreciation to his French cognac.

CHAPTER SIX

"What are you planning on doing with her?"

Killoran looked up lazily from his breakfast of warm ale and sirloin. It was close to dusk, and he found he'd awakened with less of a headache and more of an appetite than he'd had in years. He hadn't forgotten why. The luscious Miss Emma Brown was somewhere in the vastness of his London house, and that bleak, cold spot within him seemed temporarily alive. He had no doubt she was still there. His servants were rightly terrified of him. They wouldn't be likely to let her escape, and if by any chance she outsmarted them, every single servant would have disappeared rather than face his wrath.

Unfortunately, he didn't seem to have the ability to quell Nathaniel's righteous indignation. Really, the young man was most irritating. If he weren't so infatuated with Lady Barbara, Killoran would have sent him back to his father posthaste.

But Nathaniel's heated, respectful passion for a notorious light-skirt was almost as entertaining as Emma Brown. Besides, his disapproval was doubtless good for

Killoran's benighted soul. Assuming he still had one, which Killoran strongly doubted.

"I'm not planning to do a thing with her, dear boy," he drawled, leaning back in his chair. "Your suspicions wound me. She's a waif, in need of protection from the harsh winter winds. Though, in truth, I don't consider her particularly waiflike," he added.

"I can't countenance—"

"You don't need to countenance a thing, Nathaniel. I would hardly have any interest in seducing the poor girl. After all, I could have Lady Barbara anytime I signify, could I not?"

The shot hit home, and Killoran wondered why he felt no pleasure at Nathaniel's miserable flush. "It's not my place to say."

"You've never let that stop you before," Killoran said lazily. "You feel no qualms about passing judgment on my designs for Miss Incognita. Why shouldn't you give me your opinion of my relationship with Lady Barbara?"

"Miss Incognita," Nathaniel said, deliberately ignoring the provocation. "I thought her name was Miss Brown."

"That creature is no more Miss Brown than she is Miss Pottle." Killoran decided to allow him to avoid the more emotional issue of his would-be mistress. "As a matter of fact, our little stray is a relation of mine." He considered the notion, then smiled. "My half sister."

"What?"

"Of course, we don't acknowledge it openly. We'll simply call her a connection by marriage, though unfortunately, marriage had nothing to do with the situation.

Who would have thought my proper father would have proved so licentious?"

"She's not your sister!" Nathaniel snapped.

"No? Well, I doubt you can prove it. Particularly since I have no intention of claiming the relationship openly. Merely a word or two, a hint, and the information will pass through society quite swiftly."

"I'll deny it."

"Of course you will. So shall I. It will do no good. The ton will believe as it wishes. But they'll accept her, knowing her pedigree is decent. Let's see, who shall her mother be? Some titled English lady, perhaps? The daughter of a duke, who fell for the wiles of a dashing Irishman and succumbed to a moment of passion?"

"You're a bastard."

"In point of fact, I'm not," Killoran said. "Would you rather I set her out on the streets? Your notion of Christian charity is at odds with reality, Nathaniel."

"I don't…"

"Consider this, my boy. If I'm amusing myself with my newfound relative, I'm less likely to spend time with Lady Barbara—giving you a chance to enjoy her bounteous favors."

"Lady Barbara isn't a plaything to be passed back and forth!" Nathaniel said furiously. "She's not a whore!"

Killoran leaned forward and rang the crystal bell at his left hand, summoning Jeffries. "Why don't you ask her yourself?" he suggested. "You may not like the answer."

If Jeffries hadn't appeared so promptly, Killoran would have laid odds that Nathaniel would have flung himself on him, doing his best to pummel him. Killoran counted his narrow escape unfortunate. Sooner or later he and Nathaniel would come to blows, and he was looking forward to it immensely. Particularly since he wasn't at all certain of emerging the victor. Nathaniel was some ten years younger and possessed of the fire of youth and principles. All Killoran could offer was the wisdom of age and treachery. In a fair fight Nathaniel would win. But then, Killoran had no intention of fighting fairly.

"Jeffries," he said, his voice dismissing the furious Nathaniel, "find my sister and bring her to me."

"Your sister, sir?" Jeffries said, aghast. "And where would you suggest I look for her, my lord?"

"In the green room."

"I beg your pardon, your lordship. Is the young lady your sister?"

Killoran smiled sweetly, never a reassuring sight. "We don't acknowledge the relationship, of course. Perhaps we should call her my cousin. I know I can count on your discretion, Jeffries. I wouldn't want the other servants to hear of this."

"Absolutely, my lord," Jeffries said. "I'll find the young lady and bring her here."

Killoran turned to Nathaniel once the door had closed behind the servant. "You see? It's that simple. I shan't have to say another word. By tomorrow morning every acquaintance will hear that I've taken my bastard sister under my wing, and society will be agog, waiting to take a look at her. It should be most amusing."

"Is that why you brought her here? For amusement?"

"Among other reasons, none of them particularly licentious. Ah, Nathaniel, you're beginning to understand me. If I lusted after the creature, I would scarcely decide to pawn her off on society, would I? She'll make a lovely sister."

"Until when?"

Killoran blinked. "I hadn't thought that far ahead. Until she ceases to serve a useful purpose. I suppose, once she becomes tiresome, I'll send her away. That's what I usually do. So behave yourself, Nathaniel. I could dispense with your company just as well if you continue to be so tedious."

"That would please me no end."

"Of course it would. Which is exactly why I have no intention of sending you away. Hostility entertains me."

"You're adept at inspiring it."

Killoran blinked again. "Why, thank you, dear boy. I believe that's the first compliment you've given me."

Emma didn't want to see him again. She wasn't being missish or unreasonable in that desire; when she'd emerged from the bath, her clothes had disappeared, and the silk dressing gown of deepest black satin and bright silver buttons could only belong to one person.

It carried the same elusive scent his coat had held. Leather, and whiskey, and spice, and if she were a braver soul, she would have disdained the use of the robe.

But the alternative, walking around in nothing at all, was immodest and made her chilly, so she wrapped herself in his dressing gown and tried to pretend it belonged to the stalwart young man who had brought her to this strange house in the first place.

She slept fitfully on the wide, soft bed. She ate everything Mrs. Rumson brought her, then curled up in the window seat, the dressing gown tucked around her long legs, and stared out into the gathering snow. With the warmth of the fire it should have seemed pleasant. But all Emma could think of was life on the streets of London, wading through drifts, and she pulled the satin dressing gown closer around her body and shivered. Why in heaven's name did this late winter have to be so harsh?

She didn't hear the door open, but she knew he was there. He was a very silent man, something that would have unnerved her if she hadn't developed a sixth sense about his presence. She was used to noise. Uncle Horace had been loud, blustering, and Cousin Miriam's voice had quite often been raised in strictures or prayers. Even behind the closed curtains of the DeWinter house, there had been no stillness, no peace.

Stillness surrounded Killoran like an uneasy cloud. Emma was already burrowed deep within the dressing gown; she controlled the urge to pull it closer around her as she turned to look at him in the gathering twilight.

"You remind me of a magpie," she said unexpectedly.

He stood in the doorway watching her, a rare look of interest in his eyes. "I make you think of a noisy, chattering bird?" he said. "How very lowering."

She swung around, careful to keep her long legs covered. Her red hair was a tangled curtain around her, impossibly curly, but there was no way she could restrain it with what they'd left her, so she decided to ignore it. "There's more to magpies than noise," she said severely.

"I stand corrected. I never was a bird fancier. Are you about to educate me?"

"They are very handsome birds, you know. All black and white, with elegant plumage."

He bowed. "You reassure me."

"They also have a weakness for glitter. If they see something shiny, they simply steal it, carrying it off with them to their nest."

If she weren't so near-sighted, she would have known for sure whether there was a glint of amusement in his green, merciless eyes. "I rather thought you were the one who stood accused of thievery." His voice was as cool as silver. "There was the small matter of that young man's diamond stickpin."

"But you know that's not true."

"I don't know anything at all about you, child, apart from your unusual thirst for violence." He moved closer, but his expression, as always, was guarded. She had no idea what he was thinking as his eyes traveled over her oddly dressed figure. "And then there's the undeniable fact that you helped yourself to my coat and my diamond studs. I suspect there's a strong streak of larceny in your soul as well."

"I presume you got them back," she said, squashing her immediate guilt.

"I did. But that doesn't necessarily absolve you, or answer my questions. I don't suppose you care to enlighten me as to who you are?"

"Do you really care?"

He smiled then. "No."

"I thought not. Miss Brown will do."

"On the contrary—'Miss Brown' will not do at all. I refuse to have someone living under my protection with such a tedious name. 'Emma' will suffice. You seem rather like an Emma, despite your exotic appearance. There's something definitely well ordered about the name Emma. Calm and reasonable, warmhearted and generous."

"You think I'm calm and reasonable?" She was astounded. While that sounded a bit more flattering than she tended to view herself, he'd painted a fairly accurate picture of the real Emma. Well ordered, sensible, kind, and serene, despite the storms that surrounded her. But how could he possibly know that?

He sat down beside her on the window seat, carefully arranging the black-and-silver brocade of his coat so as not to crush it. He was too close to her, and she tried to scoot away, surreptitiously. She had little doubt he was aware of her every move, little doubt that she could edge away only because he allowed her to.

"I know a bit about human nature," he replied.

"And you don't care much for it."

"What reasonable human being could? But I'm not a monster. Unlike the magpie you accuse me of being, I'm not about to carry you off to my nest and keep you there like a shiny new toy. If you wish to leave, you need only say the word and you're free to go. Wherever."

It was hardly the most appealing offer. The silk was soft against her bare skin, the fire warm. "And if I prefer to stay?"

There was no flare of triumph in his eyes. "Then you will abide by my decisions. You will wear what I choose, eat what I choose, go where I choose. You will be my creature, living the life I decide for you."

"I would be your whore?"

He laughed then, hardly a reassuring sound. "You needn't sound so dismayed about it. Most women would feel honored. You keep harping on that, child. I thought I made it clear that I'm not about to expire with passion for your undeniably lovely body. I have far more interesting plans for you."

"What kind of plans?"

"Such a suspicious mind," he murmured. "Nothing you need to worry about at present. We shall have to see how things unfold. In the meantime, I plan to present you to society as my ward. Ah...we're not likely to run into any real member of your family, are we?"

"No."

"Good. You look charming in that dressing gown of mine. Black suits you. I think I shall arrange for a suitable wardrobe. Your manners are genteel enough, perhaps better than mine, so there's no need of working on them. After all, what can one expect from the Irish? We'll dress you appropriately and take you to the opera. To start with."

"I love the opera," she said, a faint note of hope creeping into her voice.

"You aren't going to listen," he said. "You're going to observe and be observed."

"Why?"

"Why do I do anything? Because it amuses me. But you must make one thing very clear to all and sundry. Make certain you tell them you are not my sister."

"Your sister? Why should anyone believe such an absurdity?" she said hotly shaken by the very notion.

He touched her then. His elegant, pale hand reached out and touched her chin, tilting her face up to his. He looked at her carefully, his dark green eyes revealing only cursory interest. "I cannot imagine," he said after a moment. "But people do come up with the oddest notions. As long as you deny it every chance you get, things should be fine." His hand left her, and he rose, tall, elegant, distant.

Her face felt warm and cold where he'd touched her. She had never wanted a man's touch before in her life. She certainly didn't want the touch of this beautiful, cold-eyed, coldhearted lord, did she?

She was unwilling to give in so easily. "Are you certain this is quite wise on your part?" she called after him as he started from the room.

He halted, turning to look at her. "Perhaps I'm dull-witted this afternoon," he said. "Not that I've ever been particularly concerned with wise actions, but why don't you explain your concerns?"

"You're taking into your house a woman who's already killed one man and almost killed another. Aren't you worried I might take a sudden dislike to you?" she inquired in her most dulcet voice.

He wasn't the slightest bit discomfited, blast him. "A sudden dislike?" he echoed. "Does that mean that for the time being you cherish a fondness for my worthless self? How very encouraging. Trust me, my dear Emma. I shall keep sharp objects and dueling pistols out of reach. If you find your murderous tendencies have suddenly become overwhelming, apply them to Nathaniel instead of me. I'm afraid I'm a very difficult man to kill."

"Has anyone tried?"

"A number," he said very gently. "And they're no longer among the living. Keep that in mind, my pet." He closed the door very quietly behind him.

"He's a devil," Nathaniel said bitterly.

Lady Barbara raised her eyes, careful to keep her expression guarded. The painted chicken-skin fan was perfect for that; she could spin and tap it, distracting the eye from any stray emotion that might flicker across her face. She couldn't match Killoran's ability to hide his feelings. Doubtless he no longer had them. If only she could reach that same, blissful state.

"Don't be tiresome, Nathaniel," she said. "He's a man, like all men. Quite human, underneath his airs and graces."

Nathaniel flushed. She shouldn't have said it, she thought. She shouldn't have made him more miserable, reminding him of her relationship to the fourth Earl of Killoran. As far as he knew, she was Killoran's mistress.

But he needed reminding. When he looked at her out of those adoring blue eyes, he started her thinking of what life could have been like, and she had no choice but to give him a setdown. For her own sake as well as his.

Not that she was, in fact, mistress to Killoran. And she could well agree with Nathaniel's calling him a devil. It made no sense that he resisted her. Despite her gibes, she knew perfectly well that he had no interest in bedding those of his own sex, and his amorous exploits were well-known. He hadn't had a mistress in keeping for more than a year now, but it was put to the account of boredom rather than to alternative interests.

She'd toyed with the idea that he might be ill, might have suffered some grave wound during his last duel. But he hadn't fought a duel in over four years, and the entire ton knew about the time he'd been caught in flagrante delicto with Lord Marlborough's wife, sister-in-law, and the governess, all at the same time. Those who hadn't shunned him had remained in awe of his prowess, and Barbara had every intention of sampling that prowess. After all, who was more deserving of the most dedicated rake in London than one of its most dissolute whores?

She glanced at her reflection in the mirror above Nathaniel's head. She always preferred to sit in a place where she could see herself. That way she wouldn't run the risk of forgetting exactly who and what she was.

She should use a little more paint. In the past few weeks she'd been oddly tempted to dress less outrageously, to paint less starkly, and she was horribly afraid the distracting presence of Killoran's young cousin was responsible. She'd seen adoration in young men's eyes often enough to recognize it. She'd never allowed herself to be moved by it before. But for some reason, Nathaniel moved her.

It was all Killoran's fault. If he'd simply take her, use her, as so many other men had, then she would be distracted from the impossible temptation of pure young love staring at her.

And that pure young love was flawless. Nathaniel Hepburn was absurdly handsome, with broad shoulders, long legs, a flat stomach, and strong, tanned hands. He wore simple perukes when he wasn't tying his chestnut hair back in a queue, and his clothes, while nowhere near Killoran's elegance, were quiet and well tailored, fitting his strong young body almost too well.

He was intelligent, he was kind, he was honest and fierce and noble. An absolute paragon, with only one besetting sin.

He was fool enough to love her.

He must know about her. Gossip in London was rampant, and she'd never made the slightest effort to be discreet. In fact, she'd sought out notoriety, for her own reasons, and been well rewarded in her quest. By the age of nineteen, she'd already discarded five lovers, one of them a royal duke three times her age. She moved through society with a seemingly bright, cheerful amorality, taking her pleasure where she found it, with no interest in the consequences, and certainly no interest in besotted young men from the country who wanted to take her away from all this and breed babies.

She had no doubt that was exactly what Nathaniel wanted to do. If she gave him the slightest hint of encouragement, he'd be down on one knee, offering his heart, his hand, his fortune, and a future in the wilds of Northumberland, far from shops and theaters and civilization.

She gave him no encouragement whatsoever, apart from the occasional cool smile. She hadn't yet been cruel to him, though that time would doubtless come. Sooner or later she would need to drive him away, before she was tempted by something she could never have.

Maybe she would have to seduce him. The boy might

be a virgin, though she doubted it. Perhaps if she took
him to bed, showed him things that some of her more
jaded partners had taught her, it would be enough to convince him of the truth.

The truth was that Lady Barbara Fitzhugh was a
whore. Deserving of no better or worse than a blackhearted rake like Killoran, who would use her and then
discard her like the worthless creature she was.

Except that Killoran seemed to have no use for her.
Anxious, Barbara looked up once again to the mirror. Her
beauty was still there—her golden curls, her translucent
skin, her huge eyes and soft mouth. She hadn't yet begun
to fade—there was no reason for Killoran to resist her.

"He means ill by her, I know it," Nathaniel was saying
in a bitter voice. "I don't trust him for a moment. He's
never had a kindly impulse in his life, and he certainly
hasn't taken the girl in out of the goodness of his heart."

"Are you talking about Killoran's sister?" Barbara
asked idly, stifling her irrational jealousy.

"She's no more his sister than you are, despite what
he wants the ton to believe, and you know it as well as
I do. For the life of me, I can't figure out what he wants
with her."

"Does it matter?"

"I can't stand by and let him debauch an innocent."

"Why not?"

Nathaniel stared at her, momentarily speechless. "You
don't know what you're saying, Lady Barbara."

"Of course I do. Why is it your concern whether he se-
duces the girl or not? She's pretty enough, I admit, though

not quite in the common style. Why should it bother you if he takes her to bed? Do you have a *tendre* for her?"

It was almost too easy to watch the color stain his face, the look of misery enter his wonderful blue eyes. "No," he said.

And, of course, that was all he said. His code of honor prevented him from declaring himself to his host's mistress. His code of honor should probably have prevented him from feeling those feelings in the first place, but Barbara was not misled. She knew that yearning look in his eyes. She knew it because, unaccountably, she felt the same fierce, fragile longing. She was experienced enough to know better, but still it persisted, irrationally, dangerously.

"In that case, I suggest you keep your concern and your opinions to yourself. I've known Killoran for several years now, and his nature is legendary. He will do exactly what he wishes to do, and no stalwart young hero will be able to distract him."

Nathaniel flushed, as she'd meant him to. She rose, crossing the room to him, letting her body sway slightly, just a tiny bit, so that she could enjoy the dubious pain/pleasure of watching his eyes glaze in longing. She ought to bed him, she thought again. To remind herself that he was just like every other man who'd possessed her body and believed her moans of pleasure.

He looked up at her and she lifted a hand to touch him, then let it drop again, wise for once in her life. "If I were you, Nathaniel, I would go find myself a plump young mistress to entertain you. Then you wouldn't waste your time worrying about Killoran's affairs."

He didn't miss her gently worded message. "I have no interest in plump young mistresses, my lady," he said. And he caught the hand that she'd let drop.

He was strong. His hands were hard, unlike the soft, pampered flesh of the men who'd touched her. She looked at him, and she almost had hope.

But there was no hope for the likes of her. She'd gone beyond it, years past. She pulled her hand away. "La, sir," she said, laughing lightly, "you're developing quite a gift for flirtation. Don't let Killoran catch you at it— he's scarce a jealous lover, but he holds what he has."

"Does he have you, lady?" Nathaniel's voice was low, intense, and its timbre thrummed through Barbara's body.

"Me, sir? No one has me. And no one ever will." And without another word she left him, almost at a run.

CHAPTER SEVEN

It was three days before Emma saw Killoran again. She should have found that a relief. Her plain governess's garb never made a reappearance, though fine lawn underclothing supplemented the doubtful modesty of Killoran's dressing gown. She was well fed—not only did Killoran possess a gifted chef, but the other servants were discreet and alert. Emma had only to feel a faint chill and the fire was replenished without her saying a word. Tea arrived a moment before she knew she wanted it, including cakes and scones with lashings of butter. Indeed, Emma, who always had a weakness for food, decided after the first day of piggery that she'd best find ways to distract herself from the bounty offered her. At Cousin Miriam's house, the meals had been remarkably Spartan, even during holidays.

During the three-day sojourn she wasn't entirely alone. Nathaniel, all respectful concern and unaffected charm, taught her to play cards. It had been a knowledge she'd lacked, since Miriam considered cards to be instruments of the devil, and she showed a decided talent for it, beating Nathaniel soundly by the second day.

"I like this," she announced ingenuously. "I think I have a real flair for it."

Nathaniel glowered. "Just don't do it for money, Cousin Emma. It's hard enough on a man to lose to a female of greater skill. If any sum of money were involved, the consequences would be disastrous."

She looked up from the cards with curiosity. "Why do you persist in calling me Cousin Emma?" she asked. "We're no kin."

"Indeed. But Killoran occasionally proves adamant, and he insists you're his by-blow sister. We both know otherwise, but I can scarce call you Miss Brown, since that's just as unlikely, and you don't seem eager to share your real name with me. And simply calling you Emma is too forward."

"Don't you think sitting around playing cards with me while I'm wearing your host's dressing gown should loosen the proprieties a bit?"

"Do you want them loosened?" he asked, suddenly intent.

She looked across the table at him. In truth, he was a very handsome young man, something she hadn't taken the time to notice. She'd never been one to be distracted by handsome faces—granted, there'd been few enough in her cloistered existence at Cousin Miriam's, but even so, she simply hadn't been interested. She'd spent most of her time reading, preferring the fictional characters to those gentlemen with far too many frailties.

Nathaniel Hepburn was, without a doubt, the handsomest young man she'd ever seen. With his clear blue eyes, ruddy complexion, thick brown hair, and firm jaw, he should have been enough to melt her untouched heart.

But he wasn't. And even as he gazed at her, she knew she didn't want him to be.

"No," she admitted. "I just want us to be comfortable with each other."

"We are, Cousin Emma," he said, and there was only the faintest irony in his firm voice. "We're bound together by our dependence on Killoran's hospitality."

"And my ability to best you at cards," she added cheerfully. "I may decide to earn my living at it. Isn't that how certain gentlemen support themselves?"

"It's how Killoran acquired his current fortune," Nathaniel said frankly.

"Does he cheat?"

"God, don't let him hear you say such a thing!" Nathaniel said, aghast. "Don't even think it, much less utter the possibility out loud. I doubt your femininity would protect you from his wrath."

She doubted it herself. For all his cool, distanced charm, she suspected Killoran could be very dangerous if riled. "Perhaps you'd best warn me," she said, shuffling the cards with recently acquired dexterity. "What else am I not allowed to think?"

"It would probably be best if you didn't allow yourself to think at all," Nathaniel told her. "Society frowns on women with minds."

"I hardly think I'm going to spend much time in society, despite what Killoran said." She glanced down at the embroidered dressing gown. "Though I would have liked to go to the opera."

"You're fond of opera? I can't abide it myself. A lot of fat women running around screeching." Nathaniel shuddered. "Though, come to think of it, Killoran seems to like it. I can't imagine why."

"I've never heard it," Emma said. "We weren't allowed much music in the house. If Father had stipulated that my lessons were to be continued—"

"What kind of house was that?" Killoran's voice was smooth, cool, and completely unexpected.

He couldn't have thought she'd answer him. Instead she jumped a mile, pulling the dressing gown more tightly around her throat as she turned to look at him. Nathaniel had risen, and there was a faint, guilty color on his cheeks. She wasn't sure why. She only knew she had a touch of the same guilt herself.

"My father's house," she said after a moment, then felt herself blush. She always blushed when she lied.

"And what was your father's name?"

"Mr. Brown."

There was a trace of amusement in his eyes at her pert answer. And then he dropped the subject, though Emma had no doubt that it would resurface sooner or later. Probably when she was least able to deal with him.

"I was teaching Cousin Emma to play cards," Nathaniel said in a slightly defensive tone.

"Were you indeed? Does she show any aptitude?"

"Too much," Nathaniel muttered, aggrieved. "She's decided to become a professional gamester."

Killoran sank down in Nathaniel's vacated seat. "I

imagine you would do very well, my love," he said. "Men would be so busy admiring your loveliness that they'd pay no attention to their cards."

"Don't be ridiculous," Emma said, uneasy.

"I've seldom been accused of being so," he murmured. "To what do you object?"

"First of all, I know perfectly well that I'm not lovely. Not like Lady Barbara. I may have lived a…a quiet life, but I know what is the current style, and I am not it."

"Pray tell, what is the current style?" he asked politely.

"Petite brunettes," Emma replied frankly. "And fragile blondes. I am too tall and too…robust for fashion, and my coloring is lamentable."

"Fishing for compliments, my dear?"

She snorted, enjoying the unladylike sound. "Hardly, my lord. I believe in honesty and plain speaking."

"I hadn't realized that. Why don't you tell Nathaniel and me about your childhood, then? Indulge us in a little honesty and plain speaking."

She looked past him, to the deserted doorway. "Nathaniel has left us."

Killoran didn't bother to turn and check the veracity of her words. In truth, he'd probably been aware of Nathaniel's desertion before she was.

"So he has," Killoran said smoothly. He leaned back, stretching his long legs out in front of him. His stockings were clocked with tiny diamonds, hard and cold as his heart. "Go along to your room, child. Mrs. Rumson awaits you."

"Why?"

"Your clothes have arrived. Your introduction to society is at hand."

She had the sudden, horrid vision of her plain, fustian wardrobe that scarce took up a quarter of the space in her cupboards at Cousin Miriam's house. "What clothes?" she asked hoarsely.

"Why, something to set off your...what did you call your dazzling attributes? Over-tall, over-robust, with lamentable coloring?"

She couldn't very well object. She glared at him, more openly this time. "If you won't return the clothes I came in, something simple would suffice."

"I thought pink and apricot," he said in a mild voice. "You should see your face, dear Emma. Do I look like the sort of man who would dress you in pink and apricot? Does my house look like the abode of a man with execrable taste? Go find Mrs. Rumson. I'll be along in a matter of moments. We've the opera tonight. *Orfeo and Eurydice.* I only hope it will be bloody enough to please your violent soul."

Emma rose, torn between the desire to tell him she had no interest in new clothes or the opera, and her very natural desire to indulge in such rare treats. She stiffened her back, the ornate dressing gown gathered around her. She wanted to tell him her soul wasn't the slightest bit violent, but recent history disproved that. Besides, she was currently possessed of the rather violent urge to throw something at her host. "As you wish," she said stiffly, sweeping from the room.

She half expected to hear his mocking laughter follow her. But as she closed the door behind her, she heard nary a sound.

Killoran's house was less than a mile from the DeWinter house in Crouch End, but it might as well have been a continent away. Miriam DeWinter favored drab colors, stiff furniture, function, and formality. Compared with that austere atmosphere, Killoran's house was like a seraglio, all bright, jeweled colors, silks, and cushions. Emma's third-floor bedroom was a sybarite's dream, with thick Persian carpets beneath her feet, a bed so soft she felt as if she slept on clouds, and silken hangings at the tall windows that overlooked the snowy London streets.

Her room at Cousin Miriam's had been a nun's cell, with a narrow, hard bed, bare floors, and scratchy wool blankets. It was little wonder Emma had a difficult time reminding herself that this household was no better for her than the DeWinter manse.

She should leave. She would, she promised herself, as soon as she found some decent clothing. Unfortunately, the shimmering black silk gauze Mrs. Rumson was holding reverently didn't seem to qualify as decent.

"His lordship said you were to wear this one tonight, miss," the elderly woman said, as Emma stripped off the dressing gown and stood there in only the lacy white linen undergarments.

"How can you tell?" she countered, glancing at the heap of new garments on the bed. "All the clothes look the same—there doesn't seem to be much choice."

"His lordship's orders. He has a very strong sense of beauty, he has. You're to dress entirely in black and white and silver."

"Why?"

"Ask him yourself, miss. He'll be here in a minute."

"He certainly won't!" Emma cried, leaping for the black dress and pulling it over her head, slapping away Mrs. Rumson's clumsy attempts to assist her. The gown was barely around her shoulders when the door opened, without so much as a knock. Beneath the yards of filmy material, Emma allowed herself a quiet snarl.

"Arguing with Mrs. Rumson again, my angel?"

Emma yanked the gown down, half hoping it would rip. It didn't, and the clinging black silk gauze settled around her curves perfectly. "I'm not used to dressing in front of an audience," she said sternly.

Killoran had already availed himself of the most comfortable chair and seemed prepared to enjoy himself. "Accustom yourself, Emma," he said. "It is quite the fashion. Great beauties have their cicisbei to guide their choices of jewelry and maquillage. Think of me as merely a servant to your exquisite loveliness."

She scowled. "I am not a great beauty," she said, advancing on him as Mrs. Rumson struggled behind her, trying to fasten the myriad of tiny black buttons. "I don't wear maquillage, and I have no jewelry."

She halted, her anger carrying her so far and no farther. She was already dangerously close to him, and he simply looked up at her, that cool, assessing expression on his face. He said nothing for a long moment, merely let his eyelids droop as he surveyed the length of her.

"Perhaps you're right," he said finally. "You are no common beauty. You are, however, quite…magnificent." There was an undercurrent of heat in his words that terrified her, but a moment later it had vanished, and he was leaning back, watching her with detached interest. "You don't need maquillage yet, just a beauty mark or two. As for jewelry, I intend to remedy that lack."

She backed away, completely unnerved, both by his heat and by his coolness. "I can't accept jewelry from you," she said.

"Why not? You've accepted clothing, food, a bed, and my humble assistance in certain—ah—other matters. There's no reason why you shouldn't accept jewelry as well. Believe me, child, the expense is no worry. I have more money than I can rid myself of, no matter how hard I try."

"I won't."

He rose, and she backed farther away. Mrs. Rumson had vanished, leaving Emma alone with Killoran, closing the door behind her, the swine. Killoran advanced, stalking Emma, and she told herself there was nothing to be frightened of. Still, she kept retreating.

The wall came up behind her back, far too soon. Killoran kept coming closer, and closer still, so that his clothes brushed against hers, and she felt the heat of his body penetrate hers. Odd, when she wouldn't have thought there was an ounce of warmth in the man.

"You will wear what I choose, do what I choose," he said in a silken voice. "You know that, don't you?"

She wanted to agree. She wanted to do anything to get him to move away from her, release her from his impaling gaze. She felt like a hunted rabbit caught in a snare, facing the inexorable death in her hunter's eyes.

But she couldn't. She couldn't cower and waffle and let

him know how very much he terrorized her. "And if I re-fuse?" Her voice quavered slightly, but at least she fought.

The dress was very low-cut, exposing a great deal of her chest. Her tangled red hair lay around her shoulders, and he picked up a strand, running it between his long, bejeweled fingers like a merchant testing silk. And then he brushed it slowly across the exposed swell of her breast.

She couldn't control her start of shock at the subtle caress. It shouldn't have affected her, it was only her own lamentably red hair, yet the touch against her soft skin was shocking, arousing, and she made a frightened little noise.

"You won't refuse, Emma," he said softly, repeating the caress. "You're a very clever child, far too wise for your own good. You know when you can win a battle, and you know when the price of putting up a fight is too high. You'll wear what I want you to wear. Won't you?" For a third time the lock of hair danced across her breast, dipping below the décolletage to slip inside the bodice of the dress. Emma wanted to scream.

Instead she bit her lip. "For now," she said, amazed that her voice didn't shake. She kept her expression stonily unmoved, but he was too observant to miss the rapid rise and fall of her chest, the heightened color of her cheeks. Doubtless he would make of it what he wanted.

For a moment he didn't move. And then he released the strand of hair. Emma had barely taken a deep breath of relief when instead his fingers touched her skin, dancing across the top of her bodice, a light, devastating caress.

"Diamonds," he said in a musing voice. "Set in white gold. And your hair loose and unpowdered."

She gasped. "I'll look like a whore!"

"You'll look like an original. No one would dare to call my sister a whore."

"I'm not your sister."

He was still touching her breasts. The dark smile that lit his face was far from reassuring. He leaned closer, so close she could sense the warmth of his breath against her parted lips, and she felt herself weaken. If the wall weren't at her back, she would have been unable to stand. As it was, she held herself very still, not daring to breathe, aware only of his dark green eyes staring into hers, his breath on her mouth, his hands on her breasts.

"Remember that," he whispered, so close, so desperately close. And then he moved away, abruptly, releasing her from his touch, his gaze, his intensity, and it was all she could do not to collapse on the floor.

But her spine was made of sterner stuff. She didn't move, merely waited until he was at the door. "Why are you dressing me like this?" she asked in a deceptively calm voice, determined not to let him know how he affected her.

"A particular conceit of mine."

"You wish people to think I'm your property."

He smiled. "Such a brutally frank way to put it, my love. Let us say merely that I want to extend my protection to you. With you dressed in black and silver, no one will assume you are fair game."

"I hate black."

"A shame. It looks splendid on you. Besides, you happen to be in mourning. Or had you conveniently forgotten your uncle's unfortunate demise?"

She stared at him, momentarily shaken. "You are a very bad man," she said.

His smile was beatific. "Bless you, child. I wasn't certain you'd noticed."

CHAPTER EIGHT

There were times, Killoran thought, when he almost missed his humanity. He sat directly behind Emma in the box, silent, watching, for once not bored. The public amused him—the covert glances toward Emma, sitting there almost unaware, enraptured by the spectacle onstage and not the slightest bit interested in the spectacle offstage.

The diamonds around her throat glittered in the lamplight, and he had no doubt that half the matrons there knew the price of those jewels. Not to mention the gentlemen with mistresses in keeping. He'd made a statement, with diamonds of that size and clarity. And the shock waves were still resounding.

Word of her supposed relationship to him had spread throughout the ton, Nathaniel had informed him bitterly, even before her first appearance. Killoran had greeted that information with a bland smile. If things continued at their present pace, he could look forward to a most satisfying spring, replete with revenge and a delightfully distracting passion.

He glanced at his protégé, who sat in front of him, totally unaware of his presence, her entire being concentrated on the rather mediocre performances of Orfeo and Euridyce on the stage.

She fairly vibrated with pleasure. He sat at an angle so he could watch her, and he saw the delight in her eyes, the flush in her cheeks, her dreamy, dazed expression as the music flowed around her. Beneath the diamonds her creamy chest rose and fell, and her red hair streamed over her shoulders like a shawl. Her mass of unbound hair was a lure and an affront to proper society. Exactly as he wished.

Her lips were parted in wonder, and he felt his own sense of wonder: what those lips would taste like.

Absurd, of course. He didn't like kissing, didn't like to be kissed. Sex was one thing, a scratching of an itch, a mutual pleasure to be explored between two experienced and willing partners. A kiss was another matter entirely. It was intimate, and there was no room in his life for intimacy.

And yet he wanted to kiss her.

It was probably the tears that did it. She'd looked at him with rage and fury, with despair, yet her warm brown eyes had never filled with tears. She'd been brave and defiant, no matter what she faced.

She cried tonight, when Orfeo sang about his lost Euridyce. The tenor was mediocre, his pitch uncertain, his habit of pausing for deep, painful breaths unnerving. Emma didn't notice. She sat there listening to the music, and she cried.

He didn't want to remember a time when he was that

innocent. That easily moved. It brought back a pain and a guilt so powerful, they threatened to crush him. He was willing to do anything, *anything,* to drive those feelings away.

It was Emma's fault. She was making him remember. Painful memories, like the smell of the green earth, the warm untidiness of the horse farm where he'd been raised with his impractical, caring parents. There was a time, so long ago it seemed like a dream, when he'd been happy, and loved.

But then everything had changed. And he had no one to blame but himself.

His only defense had been to close everything off. All feeling, all decency. He'd buried his parents and left Ireland, never to return. For the past ten years he'd barely even thought of it.

But Emma was bringing it back. The memory, and the pain. He missed it. Missed the fire of passion, the noble cause, the idealism that was in reality a cruel trap for the unwary. He could see Emma glow with it, and he wanted to take her slim white shoulders and shake some sense into her. He wanted to take her mouth and see if he could drink some of that innocence. One last taste.

He didn't move. He'd positioned himself so that although he remained in the shadows, no one could have any doubt that he was there, watching.

He waited until the most tedious part of the opera, for a time when most eyes would be directed at the upper box and not at the stage. Deliberately he leaned forward, resting his hand on her bare shoulder, splaying his fingers across her cool skin, and putting his mouth next to her cheek.

She jumped, but he held her still, with a gesture that would appear to be a caress. "We'll leave now," he murmured against her temple.

She kept her face forward, but he could feel the shiver that ran through her body. "It's not over yet."

"We have another engagement."

"But…"

"Come." He tightened his fingers marginally, not enough to hurt her, just enough to compel her compliance. She rose, obediently enough, following him into the dark recesses of the box before flinging off his hand. By that time, he was ready to let her go.

"Where's Nathaniel?" she whispered, a ridiculous concession when the rest of the audience was talking loudly enough to drown out most of the music from the stage.

"He doesn't care for opera." Killoran draped the black velvet cloak around her shoulders, covering her hair as well. Now that they were in private, there was no need for him to touch her. He resisted the impulse to push her hair back from her face. "He'll meet us at the Darnleys. We've only just begun to introduce you to society."

"Isn't it a little late for a party?" she asked.

He held out his arm, and she took it, though he could tell that she didn't want to touch him. "The evening, my love, is very young. We'll go to the Darnleys' ball and spend perhaps half an hour, depending on how things go. You're not to dance," he added.

"I don't know how."

He paused at the door to the box, astonished by her mournful tone of voice. "Everyone dances."

"Not me."

"Where did you grow up, dear Emma? A convent?"

She glanced at him. The tears were gone, replaced by a sparkling hostility. "The workhouse," she replied flatly.

"Of course," he said pleasantly. "Come along, dear one. It's time to see who else we can horrify."

Emma wasn't sure what made her feel the most conspicuous, her unbound hair or the vast expanse of her chest that had never before been displayed to the world. The shackle of heavy diamonds around her neck, or the chain of Killoran's imprisoning hand on her slender wrist.

Whatever caused it, the eyes followed her as Killoran led her through the maze of people, pausing occasionally to exchange a few murmured barbs, never once introducing her.

If she'd been able to shrink into the background, it would have suited Emma perfectly well. But he kept her close, his hands possessive, and there was no way the vast crush of people could have ignored her presence.

For a short while she was distracted, by the light and the color and the music. Covertly, she watched the dancers; she watched Killoran. Mostly she kept her eyes lowered and her mouth closed, as Killoran settled her with deceptive concern on a settee near the dance floor. He sat beside her, and though he released her hand at last, his long, muscular thigh was too close to her full skirts.

There were layers and layers of clothing between them, hooped skirts and petticoats, underskirts and boning.

Yet she could feel him next to her, as if it were skin to skin, and she bit her lip in discomfort, casting a surreptitious glance at his cool, amused profile. For all her miserable awareness, he seemed to have forgotten her presence. Except that she already knew Killoran never forgot a thing.

"This should prove entertaining," he murmured suddenly, his dark green eyes focusing on an extraordinary figure heading in their direction.

No woman had spoken to him since his arrival. Indeed, the ladies kept their distance, if not their attention, from him, practically pulling their skirts out of his pathway as he moved by. The gentlemen, particularly the more raffish-looking, were the only ones who conversed with him, but they were nothing compared with the puce-clothed dandy who minced drunkenly toward them.

His clothes, satin and jewel-bedecked, were magnificent to the point of absurdity. Even with her limited experience, Emma could see that much, and she felt a momentary amusement. Until he drew close enough so that she could observe the real malice in those drunken blue eyes. He was no figure of fun, after all. There was something strange about him, unnerving.

"Who's the girl, Killoran?" Clearly the puce dandy had far more temerity than the majority of the guests, or else a great deal more to drink. Killoran glanced up at him lazily, and once more his hand captured Emma's. Since her hands were resting in her lap, it meant that he'd placed his hand on her thigh. When she tried to pull away surreptitiously, his fingers tightened, and she knew it was useless.

"Darnley," Killoran greeted him with just the edge of malice. "I'm glad to see you've recovered."

"No thanks to you," Darnley replied, and there was more than an edge to his voice. "They say she's your mistress, but I can't believe even a blackguard like you would dare bring your whore to my mother's party."

"You underestimate me. There's very little I wouldn't dare," Killoran said lazily. "And if you call my sister a whore again, you'll find out just how far I'm willing to go."

"You'll defend her honor?" Darnley demanded with mock astonishment. "I didn't know you recognized the concept. And she's not your sister."

Killoran released her hand, and Emma breathed a sigh of relief. One that strangled in her throat as he deliberately slid his hand down her silk-covered thigh. "You can scarcely be aware of all the vagaries of my family, Darnley," he said. "Emma, may I present to you my very dear friend and boon companion, Jasper Darnley? And, Darnley, this is my...distant cousin, Miss Emma Brown."

If Darnley was a very dear friend and boon companion, Emma hated to think what Killoran's enemies were like. The animosity was so intense, and yet so banked, that waves of it washed over her like a stoked fire, making her light-headed. Though, of course, that might have been caused by the long, beringed hand slowly caressing her thigh.

She glanced up and saw the myriad pairs of eyes, almost everyone in the huge ballroom, watching them through the candlelight, taking in each shocking detail: the veiled hatred between the two men; the affront of her unbound hair; the slow, deliberate caress of his hand on her thigh.

She rose abruptly, so suddenly that Killoran couldn't stop her. "I feel unwell," she announced, desperate.

The look in Killoran's green eyes didn't bode well for her. "Coward," he murmured, rising with his usual grace. "I'll take you home, my dear. We've accomplished what we need to. Good night, Darnley. I have little doubt we'll be seeing you quite soon."

"Have no doubt of that at all, Killoran," the puce dandy said in an icy, drunken voice.

Once more the women moved out of their path as they made their way toward the front of the house. Once more the gentlemen ogled, the women gossiped. "What did you need to accomplish?" Emma asked, glancing up at him, unwilling to meet anyone else's gaze.

"To let Darnley get a good look at you."

"Why?"

"Because Darnley likes redheads. Craves them, as a matter of fact."

"But you don't like Darnley."

"Very perspicacious of you, my pet. Most people don't seem to realize that. They assume I feel the same, generalized contempt for him that I feel for everyone. They've forgotten old gossip, and they assume I have as well. But they're wrong. I reserve a very special level of dislike for my lord Darnley." He glanced at her. "It brightens my drab days."

By that time they were out in the anteroom, alone. "I still don't understand why you brought me here," she said stubbornly.

"Oh, any number of reasons," he replied airily. "To see what the ton thinks of me flaunting my bastard sister under their noses. They have a difficult enough time dealing with a decadent Irish peer. Having a bastard thrust upon society only makes it worse. Particularly when I evince a little too much fondness for my own sister." He paused. "And then, of course, there's Darnley. I enjoy seeing him squirm."

"Why should he squirm?"

"Because he wants you, my dear. You didn't see him when you came in, but I did. He couldn't tear his eyes away from you, and all the claret in the world couldn't distract him. He lusts after you, and he can't bear the thought that you share my bed and not his."

"I don't share your bed," she said, barely controlling her fury.

"But Darnley doesn't know that. And wouldn't believe it if you swore it to be true. All of which simply adds to my enjoyment of the situation," he concluded suavely.

"What about your reputation? Won't it harm you, people thinking you cherish unholy feelings for your own sister?"

"You don't understand the magnitude of the reputation I already possess. A rumor such as that will only enhance it."

She stared at him silently for a moment. "Are you completely without a soul?" she asked.

For a moment the mockery left his face, and he stood there, cold, bleak, empty. "Yes," he said.

"Killoran!" A harassed-looking gentleman scuttled out of the ballroom and grasped Killoran's black satin sleeve. "You've got to help me out, old friend. I'm in desperate need."

"What is it now, Sanderson?" Killoran asked wearily, carefully detaching his arm from the man's clinging fingers.

Sanderson cast an embarrassed glance over at Emma's waiting figure. "Could I have a moment's privacy, old chap?"

Killoran sighed. "Wait for me here, Emma," he ordered, turning his back on her and following the other man.

Emma watched him go, wondering quite frankly if she hated him. On the one hand, he was cynical, sarcastic, and manipulative, using her for his own mysterious ends. On the other, he'd saved her twice—no, three times, if she counted her abortive attempt to run off into the snowstorm. And he'd made no attempt to bed her. Surely she should be grateful.

And she *would* be grateful, if he ever managed to convey even a hint of gentleness. If he didn't make her feel like a prisoner, even though she knew she could leave, anytime she wanted to. If only she had a place to go.

And if he weren't so wickedly, dangerously handsome.

She wasn't used to handsome men. If she had any sense at all, she'd be infatuated with Nathaniel, with his broad shoulders, his heroic manner, his charm, and his sincerity.

But apparently she didn't have any sense. She was fascinated by Killoran. Obsessed with him, with the very danger of him. She, who prided herself on her calm levelheadedness, was being drawn to that which could do her the most harm. And no amount of mental harangues seemed able to deter her sudden willfulness.

She tossed her head, unused to the heavy curtain of hair that fell around her shoulders. She felt cold, exposed, standing alone in the hallway. Several people glanced out at her, then quickly looked away, as if she were contaminated. It shouldn't have bothered her, but it did.

She moved away from the doorway, toward a tall, leaded window that overlooked the street. The Darnleys' ballroom was on the second floor of their town house, and it commanded a decent view of Kensington Park. Snow still lingered there, though it had long ago turned to black slush in the filthy streets. If she ran away now, would she find any place to hide? She had a fortune's worth of diamonds around her neck—surely they would be enough to secure her a safe life, far away from London.

The problem was, she didn't want to run away. Not now, not yet. Not until she found out what Killoran really wanted from her. Not until she understood him. He was like a puzzle, one that fascinated her, both drew and repelled her. If she ran now, he'd haunt her for the rest of her life.

She felt eyes on the back of her naked shoulders and shivered, without turning. Presumably it was Killoran, and she had nothing new to fear. But a strange tightening in the pit of her stomach warned her, and she slowly turned her head.

It was the drunken dandy in puce, watching her. She wondered for a moment why she had ever thought him comical. The extravagance of his clothes was pure foppery, but there was nothing foppish about his small, blue eyes or the twist to his thick lips. "I assume this is a trap," he muttered, coming toward her.

"I beg your pardon?"

"He wouldn't just leave you alone like this, not when he's brought you here on purpose to waft under my nose like the scent of a bitch in heat. He knows me well enough, damn him."

"What?"

"Then again, he's not the man to hurry things. Where is your brother?"

"He's not my brother," she said instantly.

Darnley shrugged, moving closer. "I doubted that he was, but it matters not to me. If he were, it would only add spice to the game."

"What game?"

Darnley had come up to her. He smelled of wine and a rich, heavy perfume. "An innocent, are you?" he muttered under his breath. "He brought you here for me, you know."

Emma stared at him, willing her face to be perfectly expressionless. For all she knew, Darnley could be telling the truth. Killoran's motives were mysterious in the extreme, and he had already admitted interest in Darnley's reaction to her.

"Excuse me," she said, trying to move past him.

He was very fast for a drunk, and vicious. He caught her, pushing her, and a moment later he'd tumbled her into darkness. She heard the slam of the door as he shoved her up against a wall. His mouth was wet against her neck, his hands pawing at her breasts, and she felt a sharp pain as he yanked at the diamond collar. She fought him instinctively, but this was no callow boy, no lust-crazed old man. She fought him, scratching, clawing, kicking at him, but he was too strong.

The diamond necklace broke, tearing against her skin, and in the back of her mind she heard the rattle as it fell to the floor. But Darnley had no interest in diamonds. He was pulling at her hair, moaning, and his body was pushing at her, pushing at her, and there was nothing she could do to stop him.

A sudden light pierced the darkness, blinding her. A moment later the weight was plucked off her, and she was back against the wall, feeling like a cornered animal, panting, panicked.

Darnley lay in a crumpled heap on the floor, dazed, staring up at his nemesis. Killoran shook out the lace from his sleeves with a careless, elegant gesture and glanced down at the man. "You're lucky I arrived, Darnley," he said in a smooth voice. "Emma has an uncertain temper, and she doesn't care to be mauled. I may very well have saved your life."

Darnley tried to sit up and failed. "It was a trap," he said through his bloody mouth. "I knew it."

"Then why, dear fellow, did you fall for it?" Killoran asked gently. "With you so lately risen from your sickbed?" He stepped over the man's fallen body, moving to Emma's side. She glared up at him, still trying to catch her breath in the shadowy room. "Well done, my dear."

If she had a weapon she would have killed him without hesitation. As it was, she could just stare at him with hatred in her eyes knowing he couldn't see her expression in the darkness.

She knelt and scooped up the fallen diamond collar. She had no idea whether any of the stones were missing, but she wasn't about to institute a search. She wanted to get away from the man lying there on the floor, staring at her with equal parts hatred and lust, and from the man beside her, who doubtless felt a cool satisfaction that she'd danced to his tune.

She tried to slip past him, but he took her arm, and her efforts to yank herself free were a waste. He paused at the doorway, looking back at Darnley.

"You can't have her, Darnley," he said in the gentlest of voices. "And if you touch her again, I'll kill you."

She waited until they were out in the carriage, her cloak pulled around her, the diamond necklace held tightly in her hand. Killoran leaned back, seemingly prepared to ignore her, and Emma's rage, already simmering, burst forth.

"That's what you want, isn't it?" she cried. "To kill him?"

He glanced at her. In the murky shadow of the carriage lamp he looked cool and distant, but then, he looked the same in the full light of day. "Indeed," he drawled.

"They why don't you just do it? Why drag me into it?"

"Because a simple death would be boring. Darnley is, after all, an English peer. He deserves a more spectacular demise. I want to prolong it, make it something exquisite. I want him to die knowing it was his own lust and uncontrollable desire that killed him."

"Is that where I come in?"

"As I said, he has a weakness for women with red hair."

"What about you?"

"Oh, I have no weakness at all where women are concerned."

"Why do you want to kill him?"

"Any number of reasons," he said gently, and in the darkness his eyes narrowed, watching her. "Our enmity is of long standing. I believe it started with a disagreement over my courting of his sister. He didn't approve of a penniless Irish peer aspiring to Maude Darnley's hand. He made that more than clear. In turn, I expressed my disinterest in his approval. Things went from bad to worse."

"How long ago was this?"

"Oh, nearly ten years ago. I've been biding my time. We've had our little set-tos in the succeeding years, including one just a few short months ago that left Darnley bedridden for a deliciously lengthy period of time. I probably would have let him worry for another year or so, but you so fortuitously dropped into my lap. The perfect tool."

"How gratifying," she said.

He laughed. "I'd be half tempted to lock the two of you in a room and see who emerged the victor. I'm afraid that Darnley is too much for even such a vixen as you. But you'll do very well. He won't be able to keep away from you. The fact that he believes you're my sister only makes it more intriguing."

"And what happened to his sister?"

"Oh, she died," he said, his voice devoid of feeling. "It was rumored that she died in childbed, but since she hadn't yet married the wealthy British peer she'd become engaged to, no one admitted the truth of it. It could be that she took her own life."

"Did you love her?"

Killoran's expression was pitying. "Trust me, child, I've never wasted a moment of my time on such a maudlin emotion. I desired Maude Darnley. I desired her for her perfect English breeding and her perfect white body. I desired her for her passionate nature and her flame-colored hair. But I didn't love her."

"Was it your child she was carrying when she died?" Emma couldn't really believe she had the temerity to ask him that question. The night had been long and filled with shocks, her neck felt raw where Darnley had ripped the necklace from her, and she was cold, angry, and oddly near tears. She wanted someone to put his arms around her and comfort her. And yet, strangely enough, she wanted to put her arms around Killoran and press his head against her breast.

"You do have the most astonishing audacity," he said. "That's one of the many things I find irresistible about you."

"You don't find me irresistible," she said in a low voice. "Thank God."

He reached out and took her hand in his. It was the fist holding the broken necklace, and he opened her fingers with no effort, staring at the jewels. "You didn't care for the diamonds?" he asked, and there was no way she could fathom the expression in his voice.

"It broke." She dumped the necklace into his hands, backing away from him in the cozy interior of the carriage.

"Unlikely, my dear. I do not buy my women shoddy jewelry."

"I'm not your woman…"

"It doesn't matter," he said, leaning back, allowing her to escape. "We'll simply replace it. It wouldn't do to have Darnley think I wasn't properly appreciating you."

"I won't be a party to this."

"You have little choice, Emma." There was sudden steel in his voice. "You can live a life of comfort and ease, with nothing asked of you but your cooperation, or you can be out on the streets and dead within a matter of weeks, perhaps even hours."

"What if I choose the streets?"

"I doubt I'd let you go."

"You said I had a choice."

"I lied."

She stared at him, mute, furious. The carriage had come to a stop, and already the coachman had opened the door. It had begun to snow again, and the air was very cold.

"Why do you have to kill him?"

"I don't need to explain myself to you, child."

"Why do you want to kill him?" she persisted, ignoring the coachman's white-gloved hand, staring at Killoran in the darkness.

Killoran sighed with exaggerated weariness. "Because it wasn't my child Maude was carrying when she died," he said sweetly.

"Then whose was it?"

"Her brother's," said Killoran. And he moved past her, out of the carriage, leaving her sick with shock.

* * *

When Killoran strolled into the library that night, he almost strolled right out again. Nathaniel was waiting for him, a judgmental expression on his handsome face. "You can't do this, Killoran" he announced.

"Don't be absurd, Nathaniel. I can do anything I please. What are you racketing on about this time?"

"You can't foist Emma off on society as your sister. You can't take her to a place like the Darnleys' and fondle her like some incestuous…"

"My, my," Killoran murmured. "Word does travel fast. And you weren't even in attendance. How very gratifying. And since you've obviously lain in wait to give me a piece of your mind, you must enlighten me."

"You can't continue with this disgusting charade."

"Why not?"

The simple question stalled Nathaniel for a moment, and Killoran went back to contemplating his snifter of cognac. He drank too much. His mother had warned him about the evils of too much drink, but she was gone, along with his father, and there was little that made life endurable. Large amounts of brandy were one of the few things that hadn't palled. And even that was losing its effect.

"Because it's…it's not done."

"You're presuming to lecture me about the ways of society, dear boy?" Killoran drawled. "You've learned such a great deal in the past weeks?"

"Damn it, you can't just introduce a mysterious young lady as your sister. You have no idea who she really is, where she comes from."

"Nathaniel," his host said wearily, "I can do anything I please. I thought you were fond of my young guest."

"Too fond of her to see her become a victim to your games."

"You are all victims to my games," Killoran replied. "As for society, it's like a huge, voracious monster, feeding on gossip. The appearance of Emma has simply provided more fodder for its insatiable appetite."

"Let her go, Killoran."

Killoran favored him with a deceptively pleasant smile. The one calculated to strike terror into innocent hearts. As usual, it worked. Nathaniel whitened.

"I have no intention of letting her go anywhere. May I remind you, Nathaniel, that you are here as my guest. I've had no difficulty with your keeping Emma company, but there it will end. You may throw yourself at Lady Barbara's feet all you want, but you will keep your hands and your noble motives away from Emma. Is that understood?"

"I don't understand…"

"Then let me make it a bit clearer. Lady Barbara is fair game. You're obviously besotted with her, and for some reason, she's been extremely patient with you. If you need to rescue a fallen damsel, concentrate on Babs. She should provide a suitable challenge for you."

"I ought to black your eye."

"You wouldn't get very far in the attempt," Killoran murmured. "Take your pick, Nathaniel. Who do you want to rescue? Who would you rather have be the object of my dangerous attentions? The unknown Miss Brown? Or Lady Barbara? It's your sacrifice."

Ah, he was a very bad man indeed. Nathaniel looked ready to explode in rage and frustration. He could consign neither woman to Killoran's careless regard, so he simply stood there, fuming.

Killoran drained his cognac, refilled the snifter, and poured one for Nathaniel. "Don't waste your emotions, my boy," he said, putting the glass in Nathaniel's unwilling hand. "In six months neither of them will matter in the slightest."

Nathaniel looked at him, his big hand closing around the crystal. "I don't know who I pity more," he said slowly.

"Pity neither of them. Babs is doing her best to go to hell, and she's making a competent job of it. Miss Brown, on the other hand, will depart this house with sufficient money to keep her quite happily until she finds some young fool to marry her. Neither of them deserves your pity."

"No," said Nathaniel. "It's you whom I pity."

Killoran was momentarily startled. "Dear me," he said faintly. "Maybe I will have to kill you, after all."

CHAPTER NINE

Dawn was breaking over the city of London. Snow lay melting on the ground, and spring was approaching, but there was no sense of joy or anticipation in the air. Not that Killoran would be likely to notice merriment. He sat by the fire, legs stretched out in front of him, a snifter of brandy cradled in his hand. Irish crystal. For some odd, sentimental reason, he preferred it.

He could see the gray light through the window, and it suited the bleakness of his mood. Somewhere above him, Emma lay sleeping, her curtain of red hair spread around her. He told himself he was unmoved by the thought, but he knew he lied.

He never needed much sleep and, in truth, didn't care for it. Dreams come when he slept, memories, events he'd banished from his life. He hated letting them sneak up on him while he dozed.

Things had gone extremely well tonight, he thought, wondering why he wasn't feeling more triumphant. Jasper Darnley had reacted even more strongly than he'd hoped. In truth, Emma's appearance was nothing less than a gift from fate, and Killoran would have been foolhardy in the extreme to ignore it. The instrument of his revenge, dropped so conveniently into his life, lay upstairs in bed, her red hair spread out around her. He had every intention of using her.

He thought with fleeting fondness of the feel of Darnley's drunken body beneath his strong fingers. He could have broken the man's neck with little difficulty, and it had taken a portion of his legendary self-control to keep from giving in to the impulse. Particularly when the cold, killing rage that had sustained him for ten long years had suddenly burned white-hot at the sight of his enemy mauling Emma.

Perhaps that was what was troubling him. He'd ruthlessly stripped himself of all weakness, all emotion, anticipating little from this life except a passably entertaining evening and the bloody death of Jasper Darnley. And yet, suddenly, desires were churning inside him, stronger than he'd felt in years. He didn't like it.

Emma didn't like it either, he thought absently. He had felt her animosity, hot, intense, almost sexual, radiating out at him during the ride home. It had been very…arousing. That, and the memory of her face at the opera, eyes shining with delight. He'd wanted to reach for her, put his hands on her, and pull her against him, to touch her and wipe out the touch of Darnley's fat-fingered hands. She'd have fought him, of course, and he had yet to find the struggles of an unwilling woman to be the slightest bit entertaining.

But the interest lay in how long it would take him to make her cease struggling. What kind of sounds would

she make when he pulled the black silk down to her
waist and freed her breasts from the soft chemise he'd
bought her? What kind of sounds would she make when
he pushed her down on the bed upstairs and drove into
her? Would she be easy to pleasure? Or would she be shy,
wary, making him seduce her oh, so carefully?

He had no doubt whatsoever that he could do so. She
was fascinated by him. She didn't like him much, which
was to be expected, but like most women, she made the
mistake of thinking there was still a spark of decency in
him. If she allowed herself to fantasize, she'd probably
deceive herself into thinking she could save him.

He was past saving. When he'd finished with Darnley
and was ready to let Emma go, he would show her just
how far gone he was. He would take her then, and no
sooner, and he would teach her a profound lesson about
just how black a soul could be. He would show her the
delights of the flesh, both the common and the more so-
phisticated pleasures. He would turn her into a creature
who lived only for him, and for his touch. And then he
would release her. Knowing she would never be able to
find a man who could make her come alive as he could.

He tipped his head back and closed his eyes for a moment. It was far from a worthy motive, but worthiness
had little to do with his powerful needs, most of which
centered dangerously on the young woman upstairs. He'd
tossed his coat across a chair, discarded his diamond
studs and his peruke. His hair hung loose around his
shoulders, and the heat from the fire added to the heat
of the brandy, warming him. He listened to the faint hiss
and pop of the dry wood, and then another, quiet sound

intruded. The soft sound of bare feet on the stairs. His eyes opened again.

Was she attempting to run off once more? He was getting mortally tired of chasing after her. To be sure, she was important to his convoluted plans. But if she proved more trouble than she was worth, he might simply give in and skewer Darnley and to hell with Machiavellian justice. And then there would be no need to deny himself any longer, and he could finish with Emma as well.

He was in the library, the door open to the hallway. When she reached the bottom of the stairs, she could head straight out the front, without passing his door. And then he'd have to bestir himself, when he didn't want to.

She paused at the bottom. For some odd reason, he held his breath, waiting to see what she would do. And then the footsteps moved closer, toward him, away from the front door.

She stood silhouetted in the entrance, her hair a cloud around her pale face. She was dressed in a thick white nightgown that revealed absolutely nothing of her luscious curves, and he cursed himself for not having paid proper attention to that particular detail when he'd ordered her clothes. Not that he planned to touch her. But it wouldn't have done him any harm to observe.

She paused there, a startled expression on her face. And then she squinted, staring at him. "You're still awake?"

"Obviously." He wondered idly whether she'd come to seduce him. It seemed unlikely, given his estimation of her character, but there was always the remote possibility that he was wrong about her. "Why are you here?"

"I have something for you."

His instantaneous response would have amused him under other circumstances. He wasn't a randy boy, and he'd certainly bedded enough women to know there was nothing new under the sun, and certainly not from an awkward virgin. He only knew that this barefoot, night-railed girl who approached him now, offering God knows what, was the most arousing sight he had seen in years.

It was her resemblance to Maude, he told himself with a trace of totally uncharacteristic panic. It brought him back to a time when he had been marginally more vulnerable.

And yet he knew it wasn't true. Emma Brown was nothing at all like Maude. Maude had been a victim, sweet, helpless, with a touch of treachery that had proved her downfall. He had been oddly fond of her, though he'd never made the mistake of thinking he loved her. He'd met her soon after he came to England, with the death of his parents still burning a black hole in his mind. Maude was pretty, silly, and innocent, a perfect distraction. And far too easy to dismiss when she'd come to him in desperation.

Emma was no victim. Had Maude possessed one-tenth of Emma's strength, she'd be alive today.

To be sure, they had the same cloud of hair. But Emma's was more fiery, her body more voluptuous, her eyes more innocent. Despite a superficial resemblance, there was no connection between Emma Brown and Maude Darnley. Except for Killoran's plans. And Jasper Darnley's perverted lust.

She came right up to him, bravely enough, he thought,

and as her eyes focused on him in the murky glow of dawn and firelight, a faint color rose to her cheeks. So it wasn't seduction she had in mind. He accepted that fact with only a trace of disappointment.

He was beginning to realize she was quite short-sighted. One of the few weaknesses this flame-haired virago seemed to have. He glanced up at her, lazily, making no effort to rise.

She held out her hand and dropped something into his lap. It glittered as it fell through the air, and when he caught it, he realized it was a section of the diamond collar. He'd thrust the other piece in his pocket, not bothering to examine it closely.

"I was going to keep it," she said in a stiff voice that signaled confession. "I was going to use it to run away from here, and I've been lying upstairs, trying to decide how I could manage it. But I can't. You've been too good to me, too kind, and I can't betray your generosity by stealing from you."

He wanted to hit her. He doubted he'd ever hit a woman in his life—he received little pleasure in physical cruelty, particularly on those smaller and weaker, but he found he wanted to hurt her.

"I have no kindness, no goodness, and no generosity," he said through gritted teeth. "Are you slow-witted? How many times must I tell you?"

Oh, God, she was sinking to her knees beside him, capturing one of his hands between hers. "I don't know why you're so determined to convince me that you're a villain," she said. "The world may believe that of you, but I know there's a decent man beneath the…the…"

"Magpie?" he suggested. He turned his hand within hers, capturing one, holding it, his fingers caressing her deliberately. "You're a child, Emma. A child and a fool. There's no decency in me whatsoever. I saved you at the Pear and Partridge because it amused me. I saved you from Mrs. Varienne because I remembered an old score I had yet to settle. Had you had mousy brown hair, I would have left you to your just deserts."

"I don't believe you."

"Come now, child, you can't believe I spend my time doing good deeds, rescuing damsels in distress?" he drawled, observing the whiteness of her face, the hurt and denial in her eyes, and not giving a damn. "You can enable me to take care of some unfinished business. That is your worth to me, and that alone." He put the diamonds back in her hand, curling her fingers around them. "Keep them. In the end, you'll find you have more than earned them."

Oh, sweet Jesus, she looked like a hurt puppy. "What is it you want me to do for you? Whore for you? Sleep with that puce-colored creature? Kill him for you? I thought you said you didn't need a paid assassin."

"You have a good memory, child," he murmured.

"Don't call me child!"

"Then don't behave like one. The puce creature, as you so aptly term him, already knows what you're here for. You're a trap. One he's helpless to resist. You will draw him to his doom, and I will administer the coup de grace. And then, my dear, we will be blessedly free of each other."

She looked at him. Somehow she'd managed to banish

that hurt expression, but the quiet, assessing gaze was almost more unnerving. "I wonder," she said softly, and started to rise.

The dawn sent a shaft of early morning light through the window, illuminating her as she pulled away from him, illuminating the high neck of her night rail. He swore suddenly, savagely, and rose, catching her before she could back away, clasping her arm tightly as he reached for the neckline with his other hand.

"Don't," she said, but she wasted her breath. He ripped open the chaste white gown, scattering buttons on the floor, ripped it without considering the body beneath, only the bruised neck.

She tried to run, but he caught her, holding her immobile by the simple expedient of wrapping one arm around her body and capturing her against his, while his other hand tipped her head back so that he could survey the damage.

"Darnley did this," he said, his voice flat.

She didn't make the mistake of underestimating his reaction. "He wasn't trying to hurt me, Killoran. It was the necklace."

"It doesn't matter, my pet," he murmured. "I'm going to kill him anyway. I'll simply make it hurt more." He ran his fingertip lightly across the abraded skin.

She shivered in his arms, though her voice was deceptively prosaic. "It looks far worse than it feels. As a matter of fact, I thought it looked as if I'd been hanged. Fitting, don't you think, for a murderess?"

If she'd hoped to goad him, she failed. "Very fitting," he agreed. Her skin was warm beneath his hand, and he could feel the ripe curves beneath the lawn nightdress. The material might be opaque, but it did little to disguise the feel of her.

He was not a man who resisted temptation. Nor was he a man who prided himself on honor, decency, or fair play. He thought of her eyes as she had listened to the opera, and he tilted his head and pressed his mouth against the base of her throat, beneath the ring of bruises.

The pulse leapt beneath his mouth, hammering wildly. In panic or in longing? Or perhaps both? He didn't care. He turned her in his arms, so that her front pressed up against his. She was a tall woman, taller than those he was used to, and he found she fit him quite nicely, her hips cradling his, her breasts against his chest, her neck within easy reach of his mouth as he traced his way along the abraded flesh. She shivered again, and he liked it. Releasing her face, he slid his hand down between their bodies, into the ripped-open front of her nightdress, and encountered soft female flesh, gently rounded, tantalizing, enchanting, mesmerizing. She was trembling in his arms, with fear, with longing, and the shiver that ran over her warm, scented flesh was irresistible.

He wanted her. Wanted to lose himself in her sweet body, wanted to kiss her mouth, her breasts. He wanted oblivion, hot and dark, but oblivion with her, and the hell with his plans, with waiting. He was going to swing her up in his arms and carry her over to the sofa, he was going to drag her upstairs to his bed and strip off her clothes, slowly, and then make love to her, making it last, over and over again, until they were both wet and shaking, and he wouldn't let her escape for days. He would do her with agonizing slowness, he would do her hard and fast, he would take her and take her and never let her go...

The realization rang in his head like a death knell. He released her, suddenly, keeping a hand on her arm so she wouldn't fall as she stumbled away from him. If she'd seemed shocked and vulnerable before, it was nothing compared to the expression on her face now. Her breasts were rising and falling rapidly beneath the ripped V of her gown, and her mouth was pale and trembling. He hadn't kissed her mouth, he thought, almost in surprise. Thank God.

She was too shattered to notice that his hands were shaking. "Very nice," he managed in a cool drawl, carefully schooling his own idiotic reaction to her. "You should have Darnley eating out of your hand in no time. With luck, you might not even have to bed him."

He said it on purpose, to goad her. He wanted her rage, he wanted her fury. He wanted her to storm from the house with his diamonds, and this time he wouldn't make the mistake of going after her. She was too damned potent for his peace of mind.

But she said absolutely nothing. She simply looked at him, with infinite sorrow in her honey-colored eyes. And then she turned and walked away.

He stood still, listening. Back up the stairs she went, her barefoot tread whispering along the walnut floors and the thick French carpets.

And then the closing of a door and all was silent.

Killoran turned to his bottle of brandy, plastering a cynical smirk on his face. And it took half the bottle to still the tremor in his hand. To wipe the memory of her warmth, her scent, from his restless mind. To put him into a fitful, nightmarish sleep.

Miriam DeWinter's God was well trained. Indeed, she wouldn't tolerate a deity who didn't behave Just As He Ought. In the usual course of things she seldom read the daily paper, and she certainly didn't waste her time with anything other than the financial and political news. Financial, because she loved money above all things. Political, because politics usually meant war, and war meant more money for the Langolet Ironworks.

But that Wednesday morning differed from her usual routine. Differed because she had dreamed of Emma, and that nightmare had roused in her such a fury that she was unable to do more than pace, back and forth, back and forth, in the small, dark salon where she conducted her business affairs. She had already taken out her fury on any hapless soul who had been unfortunate enough to stray within her orbit, boxing the upstairs maid's ears, blistering the cook's, excoriating the pale and stolid Pringle, her discreet and obedient secretary. She seldom gave in to the heat of temper, preferring to dispense justice with chilly control, but once alone in the dark, stuffy room that suited her perfectly, Miriam DeWinter picked up a supremely ugly china dog that Horace had always doted on and smashed it against the fireplace.

She then tossed her thin, well-corseted frame down on the horsehair sofa, which immediately groaned in protest, and snatched up the newspaper, intending to scour the shipping news and look for trouble.

And that was when her own particular Almighty directed her attention to the society section of the paper. And the news of a mysterious, flame-haired newcomer.

"Pringle!" she screeched, her voice thundering through the gloomy halls of the old house.

Pringle, a funereal-looking man of indeterminate age, appeared promptly in the doorway of the salon. "Yes, Miss DeWinter?" he said in his sepulchral voice.

Miriam stabbed a thin finger at the newspaper. "I want you to find out who they're talking about, Pringle," she ordered sharply. "They simply say Lady X and Lord Z and Miss dot-dot-dot. I want to know the names. I want to know the directions of these people. And I want them today."

Pringle moved warily into the room, as one might enter the cage of a man-eating tiger, and peered at the newspaper. "They don't give proper names in the society section," he observed cautiously.

"Why not?"

"I rather think the newspapers feel that everyone knows who everyone else is, at that level of society, and if you don't, then you have no right to."

Miriam picked up the newspaper and flung it at him. "There are seventeen people mentioned, Pringle. Seventeen people who attended the opera. Lady X's ball, and Lord and Lady Q's soiree. I want those names, Pringle. I want them now."

Pringle deftly caught the paper. His mistress seldom threw things, but the disappearance of her cousin and the death of her father had tried her icy self-control most harshly. "I will endeavor to do my best, Miss DeWinter."

"You will succeed, Pringle," she said with a dangerous stillness.

Pringle swallowed. "Yes, Miss DeWinter."

Jasper Darnley was on his knees, puking his guts out. He'd grown used to starting the day in such a manner— in the past year or so, his body rebelled after a certain amount of alcohol, but he had no intention of lessening his intake. He simply drank more, to drive the pain away, to make the nausea no more than a trifling inconvenience.

Killoran had known about the pain in his stomach, though Darnley couldn't imagine how. Last fall, when he'd happened to come across him on a deserted stretch of road between London and Barnstaple, he'd assumed their altercation would be a duel. Instead the fight had been bare-fisted and bloody.

Darnley was still surprised at the outcome. He was much burlier than Killoran, with a capacity for taking punishment like a bear. But Killoran was faster, wilier, and taller, and he'd landed those killing punches solidly to Darnley's gut, so that he'd reeled from the blows. And when he'd fallen in the road, unable to rise, Killoran had used his boot and kicked him, not in the head, where it might have killed him, but solidly in the gut.

He'd puked blood for a month.

Still, he'd been glad to see that Killoran had as few scruples as he did. In another lifetime they might have been friends. Well, perhaps not friends. Neither of them counted friendship as worth much. But they could have whored together. Though, in fact, they *had* ended up sharing the same woman.

It was all Killoran's fault. If he hadn't dared to aspire to a woman like Maude, Darnley might never have noticed. He hadn't touched her in years, not since she was still in the schoolroom, and he might have forgotten if it hadn't been for the upstart Irishman daring to court her. It had brought back all of Darnley's possessiveness. He would have had no objections to marrying her off to a decent English aristocrat, but there was no chance on this earth that he'd let a filthy Irishman put his hands on her.

Darnley stared down at the contents of the chamber pot, then slowly sat back on the floor, leaning his pounding head against the wall and breathing heavily. The dreams had come again. That seductive whore had lured him once more, and while he'd tried to beat the devil out of her, he'd been unable to resist. But this time, as he'd wrapped his thick fingers around her neck, it hadn't been Maude's blue eyes staring up at him. It had been her. Killoran's half sister.

He knew she couldn't be his sister. It was too coincidental, too irresistible, but he wanted to believe it. He'd looked across his mother's ballroom at the two of them, seen Killoran's long, possessive hands on her body, seen the indecent veil of red hair, and thought he'd gone mad. Word of the Earl of Killoran's long-lost sister had already reached Darnley—there wasn't much in gossip, particularly gossip that touched his nemesis, that he wasn't apprised of early on. But no one had mentioned that Killoran's sister looked like Maude.

Maude was shorter. Maude was weaker. Maude was thinner. And Maude hadn't fought him, at least not so wildly. He was a mass of aches and pains, there were scratch marks on his cheek, and damned if she hadn't aimed a well-placed knee dangerously close to his privates. He would make her pay for that. He would enjoy it. And he would make Killoran watch.

He had no notion how he was going to accomplish that. In the past few months his brain had grown increasingly muddleheaded. A certain amount of brandy would clear it, combined with just the right dose of laudanum. But he had a tendency to overdo, and the moments when his mind was sharp were not as frequent.

His head ached abominably. His stomach was in an uproar, but there was nothing left to spew. Clutching his gut, he leaned forward, moaning. He would have to moderate his indulgences. Just for a short while. Just long enough to take Killoran's remarkable sister, and to finish up with that Irish bastard. There was a reckoning due between them, long overdue, as a matter of fact. The sooner Darnley finished with him, the sooner he could get on with enjoying life.

A few weeks' relative abstemiousness wasn't too high a price to pay, surely? His stomach and head would thank him for it. And the rewards, in the shape of Killoran's ample, redheaded sister, would be remarkable.

She could feel his mouth at her throat. Emma lay in bed, the curtains drawn, the gloomy winter weather shut out, and touched the side of her neck lightly. Remembering his caress, the heat of his long, hard fingers against her flesh. The dreamy, lost expression on his face as he brought his mouth to her neck. And the sudden, chilling withdrawal that left her cold and shaken.

Why? Why had he done that? That, and no more? She was surely too stupid to deny him, and he must know that full well. But then, why should he want someone like her when he had Lady Barbara Fitzhugh for a mistress?

Odd, though, he never took her to bed in the house on Curzon Street. And he never seemed to spend enough time away to partake of her notorious pleasures.

Perhaps it was out of kindness for the clearly besotted Nathaniel, but Emma doubted it. Without question Killoran was a better man than he fancied himself, but that wasn't saying much. And he was not the type to restrain his animal urges for the sake of an impressionable young man who had the poor sense to have fallen in love with his host's mistress.

It must be part of the elaborate game Killoran was playing. He probably thought he needed to buy her participation, with diamonds, with caresses that went so far and no further. If so, then he wasn't nearly as good a judge of human nature as he cynically professed himself to be. She would do exactly what he wanted.

Her reasons were myriad, and they had nothing to do with diamonds or caresses. Well, at least not much to do with caresses, she amended with brutal honesty.

She would do what he wanted because she had the sense that no one ever had in a long, long time. No one had simply done for him, with no thought of gain. If he wanted her to pose as his sister, to move through society, to entice his enemy, then she would do that. She suspected she would even bed his enemy if Killoran asked her to.

Lord, she was mad, there was little doubt. And she

knew what caused it. She, who had spent the majority of her life cloistered away, never seeing or speaking to any personable young man, had fallen completely, desperately in love with the very first man she had met.

And the fact that that man was neither young nor personable but was, in fact, the darkest, blackest, most cynical of gentlemen, titled and moneyed and decadent, didn't seem to have any effect on her good sense. He was dissolute beyond her wildest imaginings, and her imaginings were wild indeed.

She'd always considered herself a reasonable young woman, and as she lay in the darkness, she considered the predicament in which she found herself. It wasn't so odd for her to develop an irrational passion for Killoran. After all, he'd appeared out of nowhere, like a knight in slightly tarnished armor, and saved her from certain death. That his motives were far from pure didn't particularly matter. He'd saved her, and he was wickedly handsome. It was small wonder she was both enchanted and repelled.

She might have forgotten him eventually if he hadn't reappeared just when she needed him most. And in truth, she was still a little scared, a little uncertain, still reeling from those days spent in the worst part of London, and from the memory of Uncle Horace lying dead at her feet.

If she didn't fight these feelings, they would doubtless pass soon enough. Killoran was far from admirable, and while he was quite the most mesmerizing creature she'd ever set eyes on, given a few weeks in London society as he'd planned, she'd probably find even handsomer gentlemen, men who weren't loath to admit they were possessed of honor and decency and kindness.

She might even marry one. A far-fetched idea, of course, but she had a very great deal of money, and the gentlemen of the upper classes were notorious for needing heiresses. Assuming there was any way she could pry her inheritance away from Cousin Miriam's grasping hands, there might very well be a happy ending for her.

Except for the small, stubborn part of her that couldn't quite imagine a happy ending that didn't include Killoran.

CHAPTER TEN

"There are flowers," Nathaniel said abruptly.

Emma lifted her head from her somnolent perusal of her plate. She'd barely managed more than a few hours of sleep, and by late afternoon she was fairly dragging. Even tea served in Killoran's exotic sitting room couldn't wake her up, particularly since she was doing her best to ration her intake of cream biscuits. At least her host was nowhere to be seen. What little sleep she had managed had been haunted by the most disturbing visions of her enigmatic savior. Though perhaps "vision" wasn't the right word. The dreams had been filled with much more tactile sensations.

"There are always flowers," Emma replied. "I don't know how he manages to secure them at the very end of winter, but woe betide anyone who fails to do his high-and-mighty lordship's bidding."

Nathaniel laughed. "Not much in charity with him this afternoon, are you, Emma? Not that I blame you. What happened at the Darnleys' ball? Did you enjoy yourself?"

"Not particularly. Everyone stared at me, no one spoke

to me, and I don't know how to dance. Not that Killoran would have let me."

"Then why did he take you?"

"To be seen, I gather. I didn't like it much."

"And what did you think of Jasper Darnley?" Nathaniel inquired in the most innocent of voices.

All of Emma's drowsiness vanished, and she put a hand up to her high-necked gown. "How did you know I met him?" she countered.

"The flowers," he reminded her. "They aren't Killoran's usual. They're for you, and they come from Lord Darnley." He jerked his head in the direction of the window.

"I hadn't noticed," she said, rising and moving over to examine the floral tribute through her nearsighted eyes. She recoiled in horror. The blooms were ugly— overblown almost to the point of rot, with deep reds and purples that looked like blood. The smell was thick and cloying as well. She took a step backward, unaccountably shaken.

"They're ghastly," she said in a flat voice. "What makes you think they're for me?"

"They arrived while I was breakfasting with Killoran. He looked quite pleased when he read the note, which surprised me. There's bad blood between the two of them, something that goes way back. I wouldn't have thought he'd be happy to have his old enemy sending flowers to his sister."

"I'm not his sister," she said through gritted teeth, resisting the impulse to knock the flowers onto the floor. Now that she'd noticed it, a noxious odor seemed to permeate the room, and she couldn't rid herself of the absurd notion that those overblown flowers seemed somehow evil.

"It's a losing battle," Nathaniel remarked. "So what did you think of him?"

"What did I think of whom?"

"Don't be deliberately dense, Emma. I know only too well what you think of Killoran."

"I'm glad you do, because I am not in the slightest bit certain."

"You're in love with him, just as all the ladies are." Nathaniel couldn't control the bitterness in his voice. "Women are fickle creatures, valuing danger and the lure of a rake above decency and honorable intentions."

"I don't think Lady Barbara is in love with him, Nathaniel," Emma said gently.

"And who's talking about Lady Barbara?" he shot back, affronted.

"You are."

Silence reigned for a few moments, while Emma contemplated the impossible hand fate had dealt her, and presumably Nathaniel did the same. "You said you can't dance?" he said suddenly. "How can that be?"

"Killoran seemed just as surprised. Not everyone has the elegant upbringing you two had."

"I doubt Killoran's was terribly elegant, given the state of Ireland and his own inheritance," Nathaniel observed wryly. "His father inherited the title late in life, and his mother was a Catholic. As it was, they didn't have long to enjoy themselves. Bad trouble there, or so my father told me."

"But—"

"Killoran wouldn't like me gossiping, and I'm not in the mood to let him run me through," Nathaniel said, abruptly changing the subject. "Put your tea down, Emma, and come with me. I'll teach you to dance."

"I don't want to—" She wasn't even able to finish her sentence before Nathaniel had whisked the cup out of her hand, caught her wrist, and dragged her from the room. She followed, not out of docility but curiosity.

She'd never noticed the ballroom on the third floor. Nathaniel pushed open the doors, and she stepped inside, momentarily astonished.

Obviously the rest of the exotic, elegant house had once looked like this. The walls were water-stained and shabby, the parquet floor worn and scarred. The room was dark—the skylight overhead let in the murky light of a late winter afternoon, and the sconces on the walls held only the occasional candle stub.

In one far corner stood an old clavichord, its painted sides faded with age and stained with damp. Chairs lay haphazardly here and there, as if tossed about by a giant in a rage, and the huge fireplaces at either end of the vast room were cold and dead.

"Why hasn't this room been redecorated?" Emma asked, moving across the floor toward the clavichord, drawn by emotions she couldn't begin to fathom.

"Killoran won the place from a young sprig of the aristocracy," Nathaniel said, following her, his feet scuffing the dust-bedecked floor. "The boy had just come into his very sizable inheritance and was in the midst of fixing this house up when he had the bad luck to meet Killoran.

It was only a matter of time before young Whitten had no house, no fortune, and indeed, no future."

"No future?" She paused at the clavichord, glancing at him. She'd tied her hair back with a simple ribbon; despite the variety and luxury of the black-and-white wardrobe with which Killoran had provided her, it came unequipped with anything to fasten her hair. She'd had to snip a piece of trim off one of her new dresses.

"He killed himself, poor boy. Couldn't face the disgrace, I suppose. Needless to say, society blamed Killoran, and made it clear he'd have no need to refurbish a ballroom."

"Oh, the poor man," she said in a hushed voice.

"Some might say it was his own fault, for gaming with Killoran in the first place," Nathaniel said idly.

"I don't mean Whitten. I mean poor Killoran," Emma corrected him. "It is scarcely his fault that he has the devil's own luck with cards."

"In this case, I rather believe it was dicing," Nathaniel said. "Give me your hand."

Emma regarded him suspiciously. "Why?"

"So I can show you how to dance. We'll start with a simple quadrille, I think. You're naturally quite graceful, so I imagine you'll pick it up rather quickly."

"I'm not sure…"

"Come on, Emma," he said, sounding rather like a bossy older brother. "I'm not going to bite you." And he took her hand, drew her out toward the center of the room, and began to hum under his breath.

Unfortunately, he was completely tone-deaf. The sounds emanating from him had nothing to do with music whatsoever, though at least the rhythm was fairly decent. Emma moved as he did, mirroring each graceful step to the best of her ability, and wondered what it would be like to dance with Killoran.

"What in God's name are you doing?" Lady Barbara's voice carried from the doorway, arch with amusement. Nathaniel dropped Emma's hand with unflattering haste, and even in the dim light Emma could see the faint stain of color on his cheekbones.

"Emma doesn't know how to dance," he said with a trace of defensiveness in his voice. "I was endeavoring to teach her."

Lady Barbara sailed into the ballroom. She was dressed in bright teal, her skirts so wide they filled the doorway, her powdered hair carefully dressed. She had a beauty mark placed enticingly at one corner of her full mouth, and another just above her décolletage. Emma thought she could hear Nathaniel's heart grind to a halt, but Lady Barbara was intent on other things. She was shorter than Emma, more delicately made, and when she came right up to her, she had to tilt her head back, a smile tinged with malice on her lovely face.

"You look none the worse for wear, my dear," she said frankly, letting her blue eyes trail down Emma's statuesque form. "We haven't met formally, but I'm so fond of Killoran that I feel any sister of his is a sister of mine as well."

"I'm not his sister," Emma replied helplessly.

"Yes, he told me you'd say that," Lady Barbara said. "And since I'm the one who brought you to his attention, I'm perfectly willing to believe that. But the rest of polite society won't. The more you deny it, the more certain they'll be that it's true. If I were you, my dear, I'd cease protesting. Simply smile mysteriously, and that will start their doubts." She turned to Nathaniel, and Emma could feel his temperature rise several degrees.

"You're a lamentable teacher, Nathaniel," she said sternly. "But a very graceful dancer. Perhaps Emma will play for us and we can give her a demonstration. You do play, don't you? Or has that part of your education been lacking as well?"

"I play," Emma replied, not certain what she thought of Lady Barbara. On the one hand, the elegant creature was going out of her way to be irritating. On the other, Emma could detect no real ill will from the woman who was at least nominally Killoran's mistress.

The clavichord was dreadfully out of tune.

The ivory keyboard was yellowed and covered with dust, and the bench with the ripped damask seat cover felt dangerously rickety when Emma lowered herself down on it. None of that mattered. The moment the music started to flow, Emma was transported, beyond discomfort and questionable tone, beyond doubts and worries and even ridiculous infatuation.

It had been the one thing Miriam couldn't take away from her. By the time of her father's death she was already proficient, and as long as she confined her playing to religious works, her cousin had allowed her to continue, even though she shunned the sound. Emma was never quite certain why, unless it was to keep her docile. Without even her music, she might have run away by the time she was thirteen.

She played, reveling in the half-forgotten feel of the keys beneath her fingers; and, half in a trance, she watched Nathaniel and Lady Barbara move around the ballroom in perfect synchronicity.

The shadows darkened. Lady Barbara's swirling skirts stirred up the dust of ages, but the three of them were caught in a dream, lost in the music. Emma played, her eyes half closed as she watched them dance, and she could feel the hopeless longing that flowed between them. Not just on Nathaniel's part. She had only to glance at Lady Barbara's upturned face, the cynicism temporarily washed away. She looked innocent, sweet, and ten years younger, a child discovering life.

The slow, mocking sound of applause brought them all to a stop. Killoran lounged against the open door, a shadow at the edge of shadows, watching them. A servant stood behind him, holding a candelabrum, and the glow was eerie, magical.

Emma's hands landed on the keyboard with a crash. Nathaniel stumbled, and even Lady Barbara looked guilty. More proof, Emma thought, that she was indeed Killoran's mistress.

"I grieve to interrupt this touching scene," Killoran murmured, "but I arrived home to find we have visitors. Not just the esteemed Lady Barbara, but a lady downstairs asking for my dear sister."

Sheer panic sliced through Emma. Miriam must have found her, though the notion seemed incredible. "Who is it?" she demanded in a hoarse voice.

Killoran crossed the room, ignoring the motionless dancers, secure in the knowledge that his servant would follow with the candles. He stopped when he reached her, staring down at her hands as they rested on the keyboard. "At least you come equipped with some social graces," he remarked. "You play quite well, you know."

She wouldn't be distracted. "Who is asking for me?"

"You look pale," he observed. "Could it be that you're afraid of some mysterious woman? Perhaps your first victim's wife? Or the so-dear Mrs. Varienne?"

Lady Barbara's stillness vanished. "Her first victim?"

Killoran didn't even bother to glance in Barbara's direction. "My dear sister has a habit of trying to kill any gentleman who attempts to take liberties with her. She succeeded once, though she only managed to maim your young neighbor. It's fortunate indeed that you don't share her bloodthirsty proclivities, Babs. Half the men in London would be lying dead."

"Killoran!" Nathaniel's voice shook with outrage.

"Go away, you two," Killoran said, still looking down at Emma. "Go entertain my guest, and tell her my sister is indisposed." He took the candelabrum from the servant, placed it on the clavichord, and then shooed him away.

"And who is this guest, Killoran?" Barbara demanded.

"Lady Aurelia Darnley. Jasper's stepmother. Not my favorite person in the world, quite frankly. We'll deny her the pleasure of my sweet sister's company."

Emma couldn't even begin to hide the relief that swamped her. Her shoulders slumped, and she noticed that her hands were trembling as they lay on the keyboard. She quickly tucked them in her lap, out of sight, though she had no illusions that Killoran might have missed her panic. "I'm not your sister," she said once more.

He turned away from her, leaning against the narrow box of the clavichord and surveying the room. It had emptied quickly. Lady Barbara and Nathaniel hadn't hesitated in making their escape, and the discreet servant had closed the door when he left. She was alone in the darkness and shadows with Killoran, alone in the dust and stillness.

"Perhaps I should redecorate this room," he said idly. "Throw a ball to introduce my sister to society."

"Nathaniel said they wouldn't come."

He looked back at her, his smile completely lacking in humor. "He told you about my scarlet past, did he? I'm the destroyer of youth and innocence, with no soul and no conscience. But then, what's to be expected of an Irishman in London? Everything that's been laid to my door is doubtless true, plus a dozen other, more discreet crimes as well. I'm generally believed to have made a pact with the devil, you know. I cannot lose—at cards, at dicing, at any form of gaming. It gets quite tedious."

"I'm sure it does," she said, watching him. His black clothing was austere, unornamented today, a perfect match for her own dark clothing. And yet no one would ever make the mistake of confusing him with a soberly dressed churchman.

"Will you play for me some more?" he asked. "Or shall I teach you to dance?"

"That was Nathaniel's intention."

"He is to keep his hands off you," Killoran said pleasantly, "or I'll break them."

It was a sign of jealousy, unexpected and, in truth, un-believable. "Why?" she asked.

"Because I have plans for you, my dear. I didn't im-port you into my household for your spectacular looks, as pleasing as I may find them, and I didn't bring you to warm Nathaniel's bed or my own. You have a purpose, definite and brief. You are here to be a lure, a trap for Jasper Darnley. Which seems to be working splendidly so far, considering he managed to send his stepmother in search of you. He must be desperate."

Emma glanced up at him. "And that was the only rea-son you brought me here?"

"What else, pray tell, could I have had in mind?" He seemed genuinely mystified, but Emma pressed on.

"Christian charity?" she suggested.

His laugh was rich and full-bodied. "An Irish Catholic isn't considered a Christian by British standards, dear Emma. And I believe I'm singularly devoid of charita-ble instincts." He reached over and with one deft gesture stripped the black ribbon from her hair, freeing it around her shoulders. "Will you dance or will you play?"

She rose abruptly, angry, though she wasn't quite sure why. He was so determined to prove himself a villain—she could hardly have expected him to admit to honor-able impulses. Still, she'd half hoped for a gentle word. Silly, of course.

"Neither, my lord," she said, pushing away from the clavichord and starting past him, carefully out of reach.

She should have known better. He barely seemed to move, but her hand was caught in his. "Dancing it is," he murmured.

She had learned long ago that there was no escape
from a man like Killoran. The hand holding hers was
neither tight nor painful, but it was a prison as he led her
through the same, intricate moves that Nathaniel had.

There was no music, no off-tune humming, no sound at
all but the rhythmic swish of her black skirts against the
floor. The gathering darkness, broken only by the candlelight, threw eerie shadows that danced with them, ghosts
of a darker time, hovering, watching them, mimicking
their footsteps, embracing them with the chill of night.

Emma sank into a deep curtsy as Killoran bowed, all
mocking flourish. She stayed down. Her heart was racing, her pulse pounding, her face flushed. Without music
the silent dance had been strangely, frighteningly intimate. It made her think of the stories Gertie had told her,
of entwined limbs and sweat.

His cool fingers were under her chin, tilting her face
up to his. "You dance very well," he said, but instead of
the usual mockery, there was a faintly husky note in his
voice, and his eyes were intent on her. "You have the
gift of grace."

She stared up at him, caught in his gaze. And then, almost without volition, she turned her face, pressing her
cheek against his hand.

His fingers cupped her, long, cool fingers, and his
thumb feathered her lips, lightly. She opened them beneath the faint pressure, and she knew she was trembling, captured in a moment of magic and wonder, with
his hand on her mouth, their eyes caught, and she waited,
breathless, knowing that the world was about to change.

He bent down, blotting out the light, and she closed her eyes the moment before his mouth touched hers, his lips warm, damp, open against hers, and the shock of it sent her senses reeling, and she was falling into a hot velvet mass of glorious confusion.

She was falling toward the hard parquet floor. His mouth left hers, almost before the brief kiss had begun, and his hand wrapped around her wrist, hauling her to her feet before she could collapse entirely.

"A word to the wise, dear Emma," he said in a voice as cool and unmoved as the frozen ground outside. "When you engage in a dalliance on the dance floor, remember to keep your balance. It's better not to let your partner kiss you while you're still in a curtsy."

"I wasn't expecting to be kissed," she said stiffly, hating him.

"Weren't you? Another lesson, my dear. Always expect to be kissed. You have the mouth for it."

She watched him go. He left the light behind, disappearing into the cavernous shadows of the room with his usual fluid grace. It had to be her imagination that made her think he was running away from her.

She was no threat to him. She was just a pawn in his elaborate game, unwillingly doing his bidding.

She touched her lips wonderingly. They were still warm and damp from his mouth, and she felt a strange tightness in her chest that had nothing to do with the boning in her undergarments. She was no threat to him whatsoever.

And he would likely be her downfall.

* * *

There were no servants in sight when Killoran left the dusty ballroom. A fortunate fact for them, he thought wryly. If anyone had had the misfortune to cross his path at that moment, he very likely would have taken the person's head off.

When he reached the solitude of his rooms, he found he was shaking. Absurd. His lust for revenge, combined with his lust for that ridiculously innocent girl, was making him mad.

Why in God's name had he kissed her? He couldn't remember when he'd last put his mouth against another. He avoided it at all costs. Yet she'd looked up at him, so delicious, so trusting, so needing to be kissed that his body had betrayed his brain and all his well-defined defenses.

And the feel of her lips against his, the shock of it, the warmth of her breath, had been his undoing.

He'd almost had her down on that stained, dusty floor, her black skirts over her head, holding her down and taking her like a rutting boar.

He shook his head in remembered shock.

Not only had he kissed her, but the act had actually increased his desire for her. Almost to a fever pitch. And for the first time he wondered whether things might not be a great deal simpler if he simply skewered Jasper Darnley.

Ah, but he'd never been a man for simplicity. And if he let Jasper die too easily, Maude would still haunt him. To banish her ghost forever, he had to pay the price, and if the seductive danger of a pair of honey-brown eyes, a fiery mane of red hair, and the most voluptuous body he'd ever seen on an innocent was all part of the bill, then he'd accept it.

He pushed away from the door, catching a glimpse of his reflection in the mirror. He looked like the devil, he thought with a trace of wry amusement. And dear, sweet, murderous Emma was a Botticelli angel, ripe for debauching. If only he could resist temptation for a little while longer.

He poured himself a glass of brandy from the bottle he insisted be kept in his bedroom. He drank it down fast, without the proper appreciation it deserved, then splashed more in the tumbler. He needed to blot everything out, the sight of her, the sound of her, the touch of her. She kept reminding him of all he had lost, all he had turned his back on. She was luring him with her innocence, and he hated her for it.

Jasper would know if he bedded her. Part of Emma's allure for his enemy was her indefinable purity. If he took it from her, he would lose a major weapon in his arsenal.

No, he wasn't a lust-crazed youth, unable to keep his breeches fastened. He could always take Barbara. The fact that Babs wouldn't enjoy it shouldn't trouble him. He had no doubt whatsoever that Babs didn't enjoy any of the countless men upon whom she'd bestowed her favors.

Nathaniel, however, might take exception to such a course. And being such a hothead, he'd doubtless challenge Killoran to a duel. For some reason, he didn't want to kill the boy. More foolish sentiment on his part, he reasoned, but there it was. He didn't want to kill Nathaniel, bed Lady Barbara, or jeopardize his plans for Jasper Darnley.

That left him alone on a late winter evening with the doubtful comfort of brandy. He poured himself another glass, then stopped.

The house was still and quiet. And somewhere, faintly overhead, he heard the sound of music. Emma was playing again, something soft and lilting and unexpectedly sad. A moment passed before he recognized it. It was an old Irish lullaby, one he'd heard from his nurse thirty years ago.

And James Michael Patrick, the fourth Earl of Killoran, the man without weakness, honor, or decency, closed his eyes in quiet desperation.

Lady Barbara descended the broad stairs of Killoran's town house in an uncharacteristic rush, her wide skirts sweeping the steps as she ran. Nathaniel was close behind her, but she had no intention of allowing him to catch up with her. She felt breathless, uneasy, after that dance in Killoran's ruined ballroom. Dancing was a social art, as meaningless as flirtation or afternoon tea. As meaningless as making love.

And yet, when she'd put her hand in Nathaniel's, felt the strength and warmth of his skin against hers, strange sensations had raced through her body.

She'd fought them. While part of her wanted to pull away from him with a light, airy laugh, another part wanted to drift closer, ever closer.

She'd been relieved and infuriated when Killoran had interrupted them. But sanity had taken hold once more, and she was running, from temptation, from despair.

Nathaniel caught her near the bottom of the final

flight, his hand closing on her arm, whirling her around to face him. His color was high, and his blue eyes were blazing with an emotion she didn't dare try to identify.

"Why are you running away from me?"

"Running?" she echoed with a breathless laugh. "From you? La, sir, you flatter yourself. Your dancing wasn't *that* inexpert."

She expected him to flush, but he didn't; he continued to stare at her, mercilessly, his hand strong on her arm. "I won't hurt you," he said in a gruff, still voice.

The words reverberated through her body painfully, and she yanked herself free. "I should think not," she retorted coolly, arching her neck to stare up at him. "I would have to care about you in order for you to hurt me and I don't care about you in the slightest. You amuse me," she said, her voice high-pitched and undeniably nervous as she began to back away from him. "You're like an importunate puppy, leaping up, trying to lick my hand." He was following her, almost stalking her, and yet the threat was no real threat at all. "Such devotion is entertaining for a bit, dear Nathaniel, but after a while it grows wearing. I think I shall—"

He silenced her by pulling her into his arms and kissing her.

He didn't touch her breasts or paw at her. He didn't force her or hurt her. He simply pulled her startled, pliant body against his and kissed her, with far more expertise than she would have expected from a country bumpkin.

She put up her hands to ward him off, to push him away. But instead she clutched his shoulders, and allowed him to kiss her. What harm could it do?

She knew the answer to that question almost immediately. She was beginning to like it. To like the feel, the scent, the strength, and the taste of him. A dangerous liking, which would lead only to disaster.

Far above them, the sound of the piano drifted down, and Nathaniel marginally relaxed his hold on her as his mouth moved across her cheekbone.

It was enough to effect her escape. She pulled away from him, staring up with startled, frightened eyes. And this time when she ran, he let her go.

"What do you mean, you didn't see her?" Darnley demanded harshly.

His father's second wife, a plump, pale-faced biddy who was frankly terrified of him, cowered. "I said I didn't see her. I called, but she wasn't receiving guests."

"How dare he?" he fumed. "To withhold that slut from a member of my family, instead of being properly grateful! I should like to thrash him."

"Jasper, don't!" Aurelia pleaded. "The Earl of Killoran is a very dangerous man, and you've been ill..."

Darnley thought he might explode in rage. "My dear stepmama," he said with biting cruelty, "I am a very dangerous man as well. Killoran knows he can get away with slights, since I've been indisposed. But that time will pass."

"But I thought you wanted to heal the breach," Aurelia said, confused as always. "You told me you wanted me to befriend the girl, as a step toward uniting our families."

He looked at her with withering contempt. "You really are a fool, aren't you?" He noticed the family retainer,

Bombley, hovering at the door. "What do you want, man?" he snarled.

"A person has called to see you, sir. A female person."

Bombley's contempt for the shocking occurrence of a female visitor was obvious, but Darnley was suddenly eager. "Is she young and beautiful with red hair?"

"No, sir."

"Then send her away."

"Very well, sir."

"Jasper," Aurelia had the temerity to say in a troubled voice, "why would Killoran's sister come here?"

"She wouldn't," he said, starting in on his second bottle.

A moment later Bombley was back. "The person says you would wish to see her."

"Be damned to her impudence," Darnley said drunkenly. "Thrash her from the house."

"She says it concerns a young lady."

"That's what they all say. I haven't debauched anyone in months—been too sick to get it up," he said with deliberate coarseness. "Tell her she'll have to bleed someone else."

"She said it has something to do with the Earl of Killoran's sister."

For a moment Darnley didn't move. "Get out of here, Aurelia," he said thickly.

"But, Jasper, dearest…"

"Leave me alone. It appears that where you have failed, fate has decided to lend a hand. Bring the female person up here, Bombley. Is she pretty?"

"No, sir."

"Well, it makes little difference. And bring me more brandy. Someone's watered this dung."

He threw himself down to wait. The fire was too damned hot. Ever since his lingering illness he'd always been too hot or too cold, and nothing seemed to alleviate either condition. Despite Bombley's words, the plain, badly dressed woman he showed into the drawing room was a sore disappointment.

She must have been at least forty, with gray-streaked brown hair pulled back from a horsey face completely devoid of attraction or human warmth.

Darnley raised his quizzing glass, staring at her with all the haughtiness at his disposal, only slightly marred by his inadequate state of inebriation.

"Yes?"

She wasn't the slightest bit discomfited, which irritated him even more. She stood there, thin and bony and uncompromising, staring down at him. with complete disapproval. "Lord Darnley?"

"Obviously."

"I believe we have interests in common."

"My dear woman, I find that impossible to comprehend."

The drab creature smiled. It was not a pretty sight. "I have my sources, sir. I'm interested in finding my young cousin."

"I didn't lay a hand on her," he said instantly. "I've been sick."

"You know my cousin?"

"I doubt it. I don't make it a habit to socialize with the bourgeoisie," he said. "You told my servant you had information concerning the Earl of Killoran's sister. What makes you think I'd be interested?"

"Because that was when you agreed to see me, sir," she said. "And she's not Killoran's sister. She's my cousin, Emma Langolet, and she's a whore and a murderer." There was a note of malicious triumph in her voice. "I intend to see her and her paramour in hell. With your assistance."

Her pale eyes were glowing with hatred and intensity. Darnley looked at her for a moment. And then he smiled.

"Have a seat, dear lady," he murmured. "Let me ring for tea."

CHAPTER ELEVEN

Killoran hadn't planned on taking her out again so soon. He'd given society enough to gossip about the night before, and Darnley's response had been gratifyingly immediate. It had seemed the wisest course to absent himself from his usual haunts for the next few days and let the malicious gossip build to a crescendo.

But he couldn't do that. As much as he wanted the world to think he was immured in his own den of iniquity, debauching his half sister, he simply couldn't sit back and wait. He told himself he was too restless, too easily bored, yet he knew the truth. James Michael Patrick, fourth Earl of Killoran, rake and dissolute gamester, care-for-nothing scoundrel with nerves of steel and a heart of ice, wasn't sure he could keep his hands off his unwilling pawn.

She said nothing when she arrived downstairs, suitably dressed. He looked at her critically, observing the bruising around her pale neck. "They'll think I tried to strangle you," he observed pleasantly.

"Given your reputation, that should come as no surprise," Emma replied. "It's only unlikely that you didn't succeed."

"Oh, I'm not noted for cold-blooded murder," he said. "Dissolution, debauchery, and torture, perhaps. But the wholesale slaughter of virtuous young ladies has yet to be laid to my door."

"Am I considered a virtuous young lady?"

He surveyed her thoughtfully. The stark black of her dress molded to her lush form, and the neckline, though demure by Lady Barbara's standards, was scandalously low for a proper young lady. Her gorgeous hair hung down her back, and her mouth was soft, damp, abominably kissable.

There were also her eyes. Honey-brown, staring up at him with an unassailable innocence that only a complete fool would miss.

But then, how many people would waste their time looking in her eyes when there were so many other delectable attributes to gaze upon? "Not likely," he said. "Anyone who spends time in my presence is tainted." He advanced on her slowly, giving her time to run.

She didn't, but she wanted to. He could see the faint startled reflex in her eyes, the momentary flash of panic. But she held firm, tilting her chin up with just a trace of defiance. Poor child. Little did she know that her defiance enchanted him as much as her panic.

He fastened the pearls around her neck, their rich luster luminous against her skin. He resisted the temptation to stroke her bruised flesh, the need to touch his mouth to that abrasion. He resisted the impulse to turn away from her, lock himself in his study, and immerse himself in brandy.

He stepped back, a deceptive half smile on his face. "Lovely," he said. "We're going to a small dinner party and musical soiree tonight. Only a hundred or so of the most select people in London."

"Really?" she said coolly, her courage clearly mounting in proportion to his distance from her.

"Are you wondering, then, why I am invited?"

"No." She looked genuinely perplexed.

"I'm a peer, my pet. An Irish one, to be sure, but a peer nonetheless. Besides, our hostess, Lady Seldane, has a weakness for me, and she has the fortune and the lineage to get away with anything she pleases. Hence my invitation to the sort of affair where I'm usually not welcome. And, of course, my dear sister is invited as well."

He waited for her to deny the relationship. He was almost disappointed when she said nothing, merely accepted her black velvet cloak with deceptive grace.

She wasn't quite so ready to accept his arm. She didn't like to touch him. He found that fascinating, and very hopeful indeed.

Emma was not enjoying herself. Once again she was the object of everyone's interest, both covertly and openly. Few people spoke to her, and Killoran kept his hand on her arm, a possession that was both nerve-racking and oddly stimulating. She was too nervous even to taste the food placed before her, and her dinner partners addressed only the bare minimum of polite conversation in her direction, consisting mainly of comments on the weather.

After dinner, things grew worse. The musical soiree was ghastly, with an off-key tenor, a gasping soprano, and a young lady playing harpsichord with all the delicacy of a brawler. Emma sat in her gilt-backed chair, Killoran beside her, all the rest of the seats within her radius vacant, and suffered. It would do her little good to beg him to take her home. Killoran had doubtless come for a reason. At least tonight there was no sign of Lord Darnley, a fact for which Emma could only be profoundly grateful. The veiled animosity and open curiosity of the well-bred ton was hard enough to bear without the added onus of Darnley's covetous gaze.

Emma winced at a particularly crashing discord. The sound from Killoran might have been a laugh, except he didn't laugh. "Young Miss Seldane doesn't play nearly so well as you do, my dear," he murmured, his mouth dangerously close to her ear. "Shall I offer your musical services? You would put them all to shame."

"Don't you dare," she whispered furiously.

"It would be a waste of time. For one thing, your talents would be vastly unappreciated. For another, unless Lady Seldane happens to be nearby, the guests would most likely decline the honor of hearing you." He moved his mouth closer, so that it glanced along her chin. Somewhere in the distance she heard a shocked gasp.

He was doing it for show, for the perverse pleasure he received in horrifying people. He reached out his hand and moved her heavy mane of hair away from her neck, stroking her, and he shifted his chair closer, so that his leg pressed against hers through the heavy layers of black silk. His fingers slid lower, brushing against the neckline of her dress, drifting against the swell of breasts.

"Stop it," she hissed, trying to keep all expression from her face. "What will people think?"

"Exactly what I want them to think, my pet," he said.

She tried to scoot her chair away from him, but beneath the flow of her skirts, he'd managed to hook one foot around her chair leg, effectively trapping her against him. In the distance the soprano screeched, the accompanist pounded, and Emma felt uncharacteristically close to tears.

"You said you were doing it for Darnley," she shot back. "He isn't even here."

"But he'll be well informed." He slid his hand up her neck and caught her chin. The strength in those long, pale fingers was palpable, but he wasn't hurting her. Shaming her, arousing her, tormenting her. But there was no brute force in his touch.

In a way, that almost made it worse, Emma thought. Cruelty, brutality, pain could be dealt with, shut out, endured. They were straightforward, something you could fight. But the velvet caress, the banked glance, the knowledge that it was all an elaborate game and she was nothing more than a convenient pawn, a toy to be moved back and forth on the chessboard, made the situation unbearable.

She couldn't help it. A stifled murmur of misery escaped her before she could stop it, and Killoran suddenly stilled. His fingers still cupped her chin, but they were no longer stroking her. He simply stared at her, and for once there was no mockery, no wickedness, in his dark green eyes. He stared at her as if seeing her for the first time, and if she didn't know better, she would have thought it was his conscience making a belated appearance.

And then the moment passed, so swiftly it might never have existed. He leaned forward and put his mouth against the swell of her breast. His hand caught hers, holding her there, and her eyes fluttered closed as she felt the shocking caress. He used his tongue.

"Killoran, you devil!" The old woman's voice broke through Emma's mortification, and she opened her eyes, to stare at an immensely huge, immensely decorated woman of advanced age. "Leave go of the girl at once."

Killoran drew back, and the malice returned to his gaze, the humor to his thin mouth. "And why should I?" he murmured, glancing up at the old lady.

"Because I'm the only one you ever listen to," the woman said sternly. "Introduce me to the gel, Killoran, and then absent yourself. Methinks you're a bit over-whelming for the child."

"Lady Seldane, may I have the honor to present to you my...ah...relative, Miss Emma Brown?" he said smoothly, rising and pulling Emma up with him. She almost tripped over their entwined chairs. "Emma, this is our hostess, Lady Seldane."

"She knows that. The gel's not a fool," Lady Seldane said. "Why have you dressed her in black? Granted, it suits her. You make a striking pair, the two of you. But isn't it a bit theatrical?"

"I'm very fond of theatrics," Killoran said gently. "It's in my tainted blood. And my...dear Emma has suffered a recent loss."

Lady Seldane looked unimpressed. "Who died?"

"Her beloved uncle," he said, smooth as ever. "Murdered in a posting house just a few short weeks ago. It's been very difficult for the poor child."

Emma wanted to kill him. His words were mocking and deliberate, a warning. He'd saved her once, no, more than once. But he could remove his protection anytime he chose.

"Very sad, I'm sure," Lady Seldane said with a sniff. "Though I hardly think a mere uncle is cause for casting off one's colors. Nevertheless, I'm certain it suits your plans very well, Killoran." She waved her delicately painted fan. "You come with me, child, and tell me about yourself. This monstrous creature will find us some champagne and leave us to talk about him."

"The thought unmans me," Killoran said faintly.

Lady Seldane slapped him with her fan, hard. "Nothing could unman you, Killoran. That's what I like about you." She gazed at Emma. She had small, dark eyes sunk into a broad white pudding of a face. Her towering wig was bedecked with birds' nests and bits of lace, and her red silk gown would have been better suited to someone a quarter of her advanced age and half her weight. When she moved, she creaked. "Come along, child. We'll find us a place to be private."

Emma had no choice but to follow her. Lady Seldane was almost a foot shorter than she was, and much, much broader, and her exaggerated skirts only made the comparison more extreme. But Emma's alternatives were untenable. To stay with Killoran, to allow him to touch her again, was more than she could bear. And the salacious, horrified curiosity of the other guests was almost as unsettling. Lady Seldane provided escape, even if it was only temporary. Even if it came with a price.

She hadn't realized she'd been holding her breath until they reached the unexpected quiet of a small withdrawing room. The walls were pale rose, the furniture cozy and surprisingly shabby. Lady Seldane shut the door behind them and waddled over to the unfashionably comfortable-looking sofa.

"This room surprises you, doesn't it?" she said shrewdly, sinking down with a great amount of creaking. "I don't wonder. Not at all in the style of the rest of the house, is it? I married well. Twice. But I grew up in a vicarage, shabby and poor and well loved, and I brought this furniture with me. When I need to feel truly myself, I come to this room and close the door. I never invite guests in here."

Emma looked at her, startled. "Then why did you invite me?"

"Because you interest me, child. And because I have a great fondness for Killoran, difficult as he makes that. I want to know where he found you. Don't look at me like that. I know perfectly well you're no sister of his. It's all part of his games. I want to know what he intends to do with you. I don't want him hurting an innocent child."

"Why?"

"For God's sake, sit," the old woman said, exasperated. "You're too bloody tall as it is, and I'm likely to get a crick in my neck from staring up at you. Never liked being such a tiny dab of a thing. Not that you could call me such nowadays," she added, wheezing once more.

Emma sat, gingerly at first, but the chairs were just as shabby and just as sturdy as they appeared. She settled back with a grateful sigh. "Why should you care what happens to me?" she persisted.

"You're a wise child. There's no reason why I should. Despite the fact that you seem a good sort, not like the hoity-toity ladies who sail through my salon nowadays, it's Killoran I care about. If he hurts an innocent, it would go hard on him."

"Who would punish him? Killoran seems quite invulnerable to me."

"La, child, I may have to revise my opinion of your intelligence. Killoran would punish himself, of course. Don't tell me you're fool enough to believe that prince-of-darkness mask he shows society? He's done his best to wipe out any trace of humanity or decency he has left, but it crops up at the most inconvenient times. I'm fond of the lad. I don't want to see him hurt."

"I don't see that anyone could stop Killoran from doing just as he pleases," Emma said.

"True enough. But when I saw you, I wondered…"

The pause was maddening. "Wondered what?"

"What do you know of Killoran?" the old woman asked abruptly. "Of his past, his family, his childhood?"

"Very little," Emma said. "Nathaniel told me his mother was Catholic and that his father came into the title just before he died."

"And do you have any idea what it means to be a Catholic in that land? You can't hold office, can't own land, can't even receive an education. His father was a Protestant, the brother of an earl, which offered the family some protection during the early years. They were happy enough—they lived simply, with Killoran's father raising horses and keeping clear of politics."

"Has he told you all this?"

"Heavens, no. Killoran doesn't air his linen in public. I was his mother's godmother. Maeve was a sweet, gentle thing, never harmed a living soul, and her husband was a good, decent man as well."

"I take it Killoran doesn't favor either of them," Emma said wryly.

Lady Seldane's response was a wheezing laugh. "True enough. He was always a wild child, full of devilry. If only Killoran's uncle hadn't broken his fool neck. James inherited the title and they had to leave the horse farm and take up residence at the grand manor house. And things went from bad to worse."

"I wouldn't think inheriting a title and a mansion would be considered unfortunate," Emma observed.

"Ah, but you're forgetting his Catholic blood. The slights, the taunts, the restraints were unbearable for a wild boy just turning into a man. He decided to fight back." Lady Seldane leaned against the shabby sofa, waiting for Emma to ask for more.

"What did he do?"

"Did you ever hear of the White Boys? Probably not. You would have been too young at the time, and why should a young English girl be conversant with Irish politics? The White Boys were a group of reckless young Catholic boys. They wore white shirts and rode through the Irish countryside like avenging knights, causing trouble, tearing down fences, assaulting tax collectors and unfair landlords. It was only a matter of time before the Protestant bullyboys retaliated. But their retaliation was extreme. They hanged the leaders they could find. They went after Killoran, knowing the heir to a title would be particularly dángerous to the cause. They burned the manor house to the ground. Killoran was away that night. His parents were home."

"Oh, God," Emma whispered.

"He blamed himself, of course. That he wasn't there to save them. That it was his youthful idealism that brought it on them in the first place. He's never discussed it with me, but I have little doubt that it was then that he chose never to care about anything or anybody again."

"What happened to the men who burned the manor house?"

Lady Seldane shook her head, and the towering wig trembled. "There were rumors, of course, but no one knows for sure. Killoran didn't leave Ireland for a year after his parents were killed, and I imagine he was busy during that time. The strange thing about revenge, though, is that it can destroy the avenger as well as the criminal."

"Did it destroy Killoran?"

"I don't know," she admitted. "For a while I thought the lad was beyond hope. Until I heard about you. And I began to wonder whether he might have salvation in him, after all."

Emma didn't want to hear this. Suddenly she wanted to run away, but she stayed rooted to the chair, and the words came out unbidden. "What have I got to do with it?"

But Lady Seldane had had enough. She leaned back on

the sofa, amid various creaks, and fanned her face vigorously. "I imagine you'll discover that soon enough," she said wearily.

"I don't want to." Emma spoke in barely more than a whisper, but the old lady heard her.

"Cowardice, child? You don't strike me as that sort. You have the heart of a lioness. I can see it in your eyes." The old woman nodded. "He'll need a lioness. To save him from his demons. You could do it, child. If you were brave enough and strong enough. Willing to risk it all. Risk heartbreak and death and even your soul for him. With little assurance of reward."

"Why should I want to?"

Lady Seldane laughed, the fat chuckles rolling from her body. "Because you love him, child. Any fool can see that. And it dooms you. Even if you wanted to escape, it's too late. You'll save him. Or destroy yourself in the attempt."

She lapsed into silence, her crepey eyes staring down at the plump, beringed hands that rested in her capacious lap.

A thousand denials sprang to Emma's lips. None of them were uttered. She waited, for some final word of wisdom from her enigmatic hostess, some warning, some absolution. What she got, instead, was a snore. The old lady had fallen asleep.

She loved Killoran. Any fool could see that. And Killoran was far from a fool. Emma wanted to run, to hide from the truth that was plain to others. But there was nowhere to run.

She closed the door very quietly behind her, leaving

Lady Seldane fast asleep. At first glance the hallway appeared deserted, the noise from the party far in the distance, and she wondered how she would ever face Killoran again. And then the shadows moved, a dark figured separated itself from the blackness, and she knew he had found her.

"Did you unburden your girlish heart?" Killoran asked pleasantly.

"No."

"Did Lady Seldane unburden hers? 'Struth, she could make even Babs blush if she set her mind to it. She's lived an adventurous life, and she tends to believe in plain speaking."

You love him. She could hear Lady Seldane's wheezing laughter in her head. *Any fool can see it.* "She does that," Emma agreed faintly.

She should have known Killoran wouldn't miss a nuance. "What did she want from you? The scarlet details of your past? Did she try to find out whether you were really any kin of mine?"

"She knew perfectly well I wasn't your sister." Emma managed to sound severe. "As a matter of fact, she simply wanted to warn me."

"Warn you? How surprising. Did she think I was going to seduce and abandon you?" He seemed no more than mildly interested in the notion.

"I don't know. She was more concerned for your well-being than mine."

"Ah. Perhaps she thought you were going to seduce and abandon *me*. Fortunate that she doesn't know about your violent tendencies, or she'd be even more worried."

He took her arm in a formal, polite gesture, and she managed not to quiver. "I'm sending you home."

"Why?"

"Why? Because I intend to remain longer, and I don't wish to be responsible for you. There are several enlivening games of chance going on in the green room, and Lady Seldane's stepson is a wealthy, small-minded idiot. I wouldn't mind lightening his pockets."

"You don't need his money."

"No, in fact, I don't. But I need the distraction of teaching him a lesson."

"What do you need to be distracted from?"

He was silent for a moment, dangerously so, and his green eyes swept over her, slowly, languorously, with such heat that it was more potent than a touch. And then he did touch her, his hand sliding along the side of her neck, beneath her loose hair. "Perhaps it's you," he whispered, bending his head close to her, and she wondered whether he would kiss her again, as he had that afternoon in the dust-shadowed ballroom.

She wanted him to kiss her. She wanted him to pull her into his arms and take her. Any fool could see it, the words whispered in her ear. And this time she did quiver.

He released her then, with a mocking smile on his thin mouth. "More likely I simply need distraction from ennui, my pet. I am bored, dismally bored, and it will take winning a fortune or bedding a whore to entertain me."

She was glad the dim light hid the flushed unhappiness on her face. "Won't Lady Seldane take exception if you deprive her stepson of his money?"

"No. Nor will she take it amiss if I deprive her step-daughter of a good night's sleep, as long as I leave her virginal granddaughter alone. She's a liberal old dame, and passes no judgment on her offspring or on me."

They were already at the door. A servant draped Emma's cloak around her shoulders, and Killoran handed her up into the carriage. "I trust you'll enjoy yourself," she said.

"I can but try," Killoran said. "Forgive me if I don't escort you home. John Coachman will see to your well-being." He stepped away from the carriage, dismissing her, forgetting about her, she thought miserably.

"I shall be perfectly splendid," she said in her brightest tone of voice. "Perhaps Nathaniel will be at home to keep me company."

He paused, his back to her as he mounted the stairs, and for a moment she wondered whether she'd gone too far. He turned to glance at her, his expression oblique. "Nathaniel is wiser than you think," he said. "He won't endanger his life unnecessarily." And he left her.

The night was cold. She wrapped the fur robe around her, shivering, as the coach started forward with a jerk. They moved through the night-dark streets of London, only the sound of the horses' hooves on the cobbled street breaking through her abstraction.

She must have drifted off to sleep, wrapped in the furry comfort of the robe, when the sudden jarring of the carriage brought her rudely awake once more. The door was hauled open, and hands reached in, rough, dark hands, grabbing at her, hauling her from the safety of the carriage.

She fought, clinging to the door and kicking out at

them. She heard her dress tear, and then she was out in the cold night air.

She couldn't tell how many of them there were, and she didn't care. Someone bundled something dark and evil-smelling over her head, and tried to hoist her over a burly shoulder, but she was too much of an armful, and her thrashing brought them both down on the pavement. She'd been too busy struggling to scream, but she chose that moment to tilt her head back and shriek at the top of her lungs. And then one of the brigands was upon her once more, flattening her to the pavement, knocking the breath and fight from her.

She found herself floating, in the distance, wondering whether they were going to kill her, or rape her, or simply carry her off for God knew what dastardly reason. She felt the pearls rip from her neck and scatter on the frozen street beneath her, and she had the absurd notion that Killoran was going to tire of providing her with jewels if she treated them so poorly.

She couldn't breathe. Darkness and scratchy, foul-smelling wool was all around her, and the body that pressed down upon her was heavy and smothering. She was going to die, it was that simple, and she could feel very little regret. Her only sorrow was somehow wrapped up in Killoran, with his merciless eyes and oddly gentle hands.

The explosion was thunderous. The body covering hers jerked and went still, and she could feel a wash of hot fluid that she realized was blood pouring over her. She shoved, hard, and the creature above her fell away,

There was another sound, and this time she recognized

it as a gunshot. She struggled out of the entrapping material in time to see one of her attackers disappear into
the night. The man beside her lay dead, his blood staining her clothes, and another lay bleeding in the gutter.

She looked up. It was Killoran, of course, holding a
set of matching pistols and looking not the slightest bit
surprised. He was on a huge black horse, one she'd never
seen before, and he seemed entirely at ease.

He pocketed the pistol and held out his hand to her.
"You'd best climb up here with me. John Coachman isn't
in any shape to drive you home."

The street was hard and cold beneath her, and wet with
blood. She heard the groan of the other man and saw
Killoran turn, suddenly intent, the other pistol pointed
straight at the wounded man.

"Don't kill him!" she cried in horror, clambering to
her feet.

"Why not? He would have killed you. Doubtless other
people will try now that these singularly inept villains
have failed. If I kill them both, it might serve to deter
others."

"Why would anyone want to kill me?"

In the empty, icy street, she could see the vapor from
Killoran's breath as he smiled a wintry smile. "I expect
you could answer that better than I. Though perhaps they
only wanted to kidnap you. Take you as a hostage for
Darnley to play with." He nudged the horse closer. "Are
you coming with me?"

She glanced at the carriage. The horses were standing
obediently still, but John Coachman's figure was huddled

on the box. On the ground beside her, the living villain moaned.

She took Killoran's hand. He was wearing thin black leather gloves, but the heat of his flesh burned through them. The strength was shocking, palpable, as he hauled her up, up through the air, settling her in front of him. She'd known he was strong. But this sudden reminder, in the midst of blood and death, was beyond disturbing. It threatened the very core of her being.

"How did you happen to get here so quickly?" she asked in a quiet voice as he nudged the horse forward. His arms were on either side of her, holding the reins, his body devastatingly close.

"I was following the carriage."

"You knew something was going to happen." She wanted him to deny it. Wanted him to tell her that he hadn't sent her out as a trap.

But Killoran wouldn't give her comfortable answers. "I expected as much."

"And you used me."

"That's why you're here, my pet," he said calmly. "A tool, to be used, and to be well rewarded once your usefulness is at an end. It works out well for both of us. You're in need of gainful occupation, and I'm in need of a young woman with your undeniable...attributes. It's a perfect match."

"Scarce made in heaven," she said bitterly.

"No," he agreed. "A match made in hell. But count your blessings, dear Emma."

"And what are those?"

"At least you'll get to escape."

CHAPTER TWELVE

Killoran stood in the front hallway, watching Emma as she dashed up the long, curving stairs, practically falling in her effort to get away. He felt an odd, momentary unease. Had he hurt her when he'd killed that creature? Had she sat stiffly in his arms in pain, bleeding, saying not a word?

He shook his head, discounting the image. Emma was not the sort to suffer in silence. If he'd managed to hurt her, she would have informed him of that fact most bitterly. He found he could smile at the notion. For some reason, Emma made him uncharacteristically lighthearted. If such a thing could be said of a man who possessed no light, and no heart at all. And therein lay the very real danger she posed for him. She started making him feel things he had no right to feel.

"What happened to the poor lady?" Mrs. Rumson demanded with her usual temerity, wiping her hands on her apron. "Did you hurt her, my lord? For if you did, you may have my word on it that—"

"She was attacked by ruffians, Mrs. Rumson," he said

wearily. "In fact, I presume I saved her life." He forbore
to mention that he was the one who'd put her in danger
in the first place. He had no conscience, and the uncomfortable twinges that were assailing him must have more
to do with an inferior lobster sauce than with guilt.

"The poor dear. I'll see to her." Mrs. Rumson started
for the stairs, and Killoran almost stopped her. He controlled the urge, once more wondering that he felt it at all.

"Do that," he said lightly. "And where is young Nathaniel?"

"Lady Barbara came by, sniffing after you," she informed him in stern tones. "I can only presume she decided to make do with young Mr. Hepburn."

"You sound disapproving."

"It's not my place to pass judgment on my betters."

"Remember that," he said pleasantly.

Mrs. Rumson sniffed.

There were candles burning in the library, and a crackling fire lent a specious warmth to the room. He stood in
front of the grate, staring into the flames, and wondered
whether Nathaniel was enjoying himself. It was a fairly
certain thing that Barbara, despite her noisy groans of
pleasure, would not be. He could have warned Nathaniel.
Warned him that her sultry glances, her touches, her provocative smiles and indecent clothing were nothing but an
act. That no matter how many times she gave her body,
at heart she was as cold as he was.

But Nathaniel was young enough that he might not
even notice. He could take quick pleasure in Barbara's
flesh and not realize he'd been duped. Few of Barbara's
lovers were so perspicacious. It was unlikely that a

twenty-three-year-old country bumpkin would prove more discerning.

Killoran closed his eyes, leaning against the marble mantel. He'd had no qualms about sending Emma out alone. John Coachman had been warned, though his attempts to protect her had been worthless. And he himself had been right behind, fully armed. She'd come to no harm, and a little blood and gore wouldn't send her into a state of shock. Emma was made of sterner stuff than that.

Still, it had been a close call. They'd attacked the carriage sooner than he would have expected, and by the time he'd arrived on the scene, Emma was lying beneath that burly villain, cursing and kicking and struggling. To no avail.

He didn't like remembering how he had felt. The surge of white-hot rage, the guilt that was so foreign to his nature that he almost didn't recognize it. And the murder in his soul.

He'd blown the back of the man's head off, without hesitation, and it had taken all his remarkable self-control not to leap from his horse and beat the corpse into the cobbled street.

Even now he could see Emma, her dress torn, her face pale in the moonlight, her eyes wide and dark with shock. He'd stared at her, and thanked fate for the darkness of the night that covered his own, unfathomable reaction.

He opened his eyes and stared down into the fire. He would drink. He would drink a very great deal, and by morning his temporary aberration would have vanished. By morning he would warn her, calmly, determinedly, that Darnley meant to have her. And that Darnley would do anything to get her.

There was just one thing about tonight's adventures that didn't ring true. The man struggling with Emma hadn't been trying to kidnap her. For some reason, he'd been more than ready to kill her.

"She won't let me in her room," Mrs. Rumson announced abruptly, appearing in the doorway. "She's locked it, and she told me to go away. She doesn't want to see anyone. Are you certain she's not been hurt?"

"Certain," Killoran said, lifting his hand. And then he noticed the dark stain of blood.

"But—"

"I'll see to her," he said quickly, shrugging out of his jacket, wiping his bloody hand on one thigh. "You may go to bed now."

"I'd prefer to make certain she's all right. Women need other women around at times like these."

"You will go to bed," he said in his most menacing voice. "She has no need of anyone but me." The moment the words were out, unbidden, he felt a strain of shock. Not that he'd said such a thing, but how right it felt.

Mrs. Rumson was wise enough not to argue. Few people ever dared argue with him when he used that tone of voice, and even fewer were still alive today. She vanished, and he mounted the stairs slowly, leisurely, as if the blood on his palm weren't burning into his flesh.

Emma's rooms were far removed from his. He'd put her in the green suite on purpose. In this huge house most rooms remained empty, and she stayed at the end of one hallway. The master suite was in the middle—no one would have any excuse to pass his door unless on the way to see Emma. And no one would make the mistake of going after Emma and survive.

Someone, presumably Mrs. Rumson, had left a lamp burning on the table at the far end of the hall, and the shadows it cast were decidedly eerie. Killoran strolled into the darkness, paused before her locked door, and casually considered his alternatives. He could knock. He could leave her alone. The sanest course would be to dismiss her from his mind, leave her alone for the night. But he'd never prided himself on his sanity. It was a vastly overrated commodity.

And then he kicked the door open, splintering the wood with the force of his blow.

He filled the doorway to her bedroom. The *broken* doorway, Emma amended, staring at him. She kept forgetting how very tall he was. How intimidating. Despite his not being the slightest bit bulky, there was a lean and deadly power to his body, one that disturbed her far more than brute mass.

And then, belatedly, she realized how little she was wearing. She'd torn off the ruined black dress and now stood in only her petticoats. The bowl of water on the dresser in front of her was dark with the blood she'd been washing from her skin. The water had soaked through the fine lawn underclothing, molding it to her flesh, and she felt half naked.

But he wasn't looking at her breasts. He was looking at the bloody water, and the expression on his face was terrifying. Except that there was no expression on his face. None at all. It was that very stillness that was so disturbing.

"You've been hurt," he said, his voice flat. He moved into the room so quickly, with such lethal grace, that she hadn't time to move, to cover herself, to do more than stare at him, mouth agape, as he pulled her into his arms, against the snowy whiteness of his linen shirt. "You're bleeding."

He was warm. He was strong, and large, and his heart was beating against her breasts. For a moment all she wanted to do was close her eyes, sink her head against his shoulder, and give over.

But that was the greatest danger of all. Instead she pushed at him, her hand still holding the damp, blood-soaked rag. "I'm not," she said in a reasonably cross tone. "That man bled all over me. Apart from being black-and-blue and angry, I'm fine."

He released her with unflattering haste. She'd dampened his shirt as well, and she hoped he caught a cold. "You're always angry, my pet," he said. "What enraged you this time? The fact that you were attacked? Or that you didn't get the chance to kill him yourself?"

"Must you always make a joke out of things like life and death?" she shot back furiously.

"Yes."

He turned away from her, ignoring her dishabille, ignoring the broken door, wandering over to the far window to look out into the night. "Why would anyone want to kill you, Emma?" he asked in a meditative tone.

He almost lulled her into telling him the truth. "No one wants to kill me," she said. "I thought you decided it was Darnley, looking for a bit of sport. I wouldn't provide much sport if I were dead." Her white lawn powdering robe lay across the high bed, and she grabbed for it, pulling it around her body. "Besides, what makes you think you weren't their intended victim? I can easily imagine any number of people who'd like to see you dead."

"You included, my precious?" he murmured. "Feeling a bit waspish tonight, aren't you? They knew I wasn't in the carriage. If they thought I was, they would have shot first and asked questions later; my reputation guarantees that. Who wants you dead, Emma?"

"No one."

"Then why did you kill your so-called uncle?"

"He *was* my uncle!" she snapped. "And I didn't mean to. He was trying to kill me..." Her voice trailed off.

"You told me it was a case of attempted rape. That, of course, would be unremarkable." He paused for a moment. "Why would he want to kill you?"

"I don't know," she said.

"And since you were competent enough to dispose of him, who would be trying to finish what he started? Perhaps a jealous wife?"

"Aunt Tilda died before my father did."

"Aunt Tilda," Killoran echoed, turning from the window to look at her. "And Uncle Horace. We're beginning to make some progress, my pet. The last name."

It wasn't a request. It was an order, not to be refused. "I won't tell you."

Killoran sighed wearily. "Of course you will, my angel," he said in a deceptively pleasant voice. "I have any number of ways of discovering that which I desire to know. I can do it nicely." He'd come closer, too close, and his hand caught hers, his long fingers stroking her palm, slowly, insistently, cleverly. "I can touch you in ways that you can't even imagine." His voice was low, heated, and she felt a disturbing, answering shimmer deep inside. "I can take your darkest secrets, I can take anything I want from you, and you'd be willing, eager, to give to me. Everything."

For a moment she was unable to speak. Her pulse leapt in her throat, and she knew he could feel it, pounding beneath her pale skin. "You underestimate me," she said in a hushed voice, struggling against the hypnotic effect he had on her.

His smile was small, cynical, and heartbreaking. "No, my love. I know you very well indeed. Better, perhaps, than you know yourself. You want me to let go of your hand, don't you?"

"Yes," she said hoarsely.

"You want me to go away and leave you alone?"

"Yes."

His other arm slid around her waist as he bent over her. "You want me to kiss you, don't you?"

"Yes," she whispered, helpless, angry. Angry at herself for making no effort to escape. Angry at him for making her want him.

"You're safe from me, you know," he said, still in that low, enticing voice. "I won't bed you. If I did, you'd lose half your appeal for Darnley, and I can't have that. So you're entirely protected from my random lusts."

"Random lusts?"

"I usually have more control in these matters. You

do seem to have a habit of affecting me strangely." His cool tone was entirely deceptive. His body was hot and hard against hers, and she could feel the tension running through him. Odd, to realize that it was somehow she who had made him tense.

"I'm sorry," she said, staring up at him.

"Oh, don't be." He moved his head toward hers, and she had the strange notion that he was going to kiss her. "At least it breaks my boredom."

She jerked away, furious, and he let her go. He'd done it on purpose, but that knowledge didn't assuage her anger. "I'm delighted to hear you're able to resist my abundant charms," she said in an icy voice. "I wouldn't want to spoil your plans. I assume you'll be wanting me to sleep with Lord Darnley?"

"You would be unwise to assume anything."

"Unfortunately, my education in such matters is sadly lacking. Perhaps I should go back and see Mrs. Withersedge, and she could instruct me in the duties of a whore."

"Lady Barbara could doubtless tell you more," he said, moving away from her. "She's an exceptional actress."

"Did you love her very much?"

He turned his head to stare at her in unvarnished amazement. In the dim light of the bedroom he looked dark and saturnine, almost satanic. "Lady Barbara? Don't be ridiculous, child."

"No. Darnley's sister. The woman you're so intent on avenging."

She'd hoped to goad him into anger. Into some show of emotion. Instead he merely smiled at her. "I thought I'd already explained it to you, my love. I have no heart.

Darnley took something I wanted and broke it. My pride demands suitable punishment. Maude is long dead—it could hardly matter to her what I do with her despicable brother."

"Does she haunt you?"

This time it worked. And she was very sorry that it had. His face whitened, his green eyes blazed, and he was very angry indeed. She wondered, quite suddenly, whether he could hurt her.

A moment later he had himself under control once more. "You're right," he said casually. "I did underestimate you." He started toward her. "But I imagine it will be a simple matter to teach you a salient lesson. It would be wise not to provoke a sleeping lion, my pet. You will always come off the worse for it."

She backed away from him, against the table, and the water in the basin sloshed noisily. She wasn't afraid of pain, she told herself. She'd been hit and hurt before. She closed her eyes and steeled herself.

It was far, far worse than she had imagined. He pulled her up against him, his hands not the slightest bit gentle, and his body was hard and strong against her softness. "Let me give you a little demonstration of what I'm sparing you," he whispered against her mouth.

She'd been kissed before.

She'd fought Frederick Varienne's assaults, and her uncle's too fond salutes, and she had always thought she didn't like kissing.

She was wrong.

He put one hand behind her neck, his long fingers holding her head still, while his other arm encircled her waist.

He lowered his mouth to hers, leisurely, brushing his lips against hers, back and forth, slowly, oh, so slowly. She wanted to push him away, she wanted to draw him closer, so instead she simply let her hands rest at her sides. As long as she didn't respond, didn't participate, there could surely be no harm in it. Besides, she didn't have much choice in the matter. If Killoran decided to kiss her, for whatever dark reasons, then kiss her he would.

His thumb was stroking the side of her face. He was pressing his hand against the small of her back, so that her hips were thrust up against his, and she let her eyelids flutter closed as he just touched the surface of her lips, his brandy-flavored breath warming her.

The sensation was disturbing and enchanting, and she wanted more of it. He started to withdraw, a mere fraction of an inch, and her mouth followed, clinging to his.

The faint sound of his laughter made her eyelids fly open in sudden dismay. "You're too easy, child," he murmured. "I need more of a challenge. You're supposed to despise me, remember?"

She couldn't trample on his foot; she wasn't wearing shoes. She couldn't slap him; her hands were trapped by her sides. She considered using her knee, a tactic that had served her well in the past, but some latent sense of self-preservation stopped her.

She could only use her mouth. "I *do* despise you," she said furiously. "You're a bully and a coward, a mean, nasty man who's not grateful for the advantages he's been given, but instead—"

"Advantages?" he interrupted calmly, untouched by her rage. "What advantages do I have? I wasn't one of your

English lordlings, born with a silver spoon in my mouth. I'm Irish, child. That ranks slightly higher than a Gypsy, but not much. It didn't give me a particularly sanguine view of the world. Anything I have today I earned."

"You've the devil's own luck at the gaming tables," she countered. "Nathaniel told me so."

"Nathaniel's been busy," he observed. "What about Lady Seldane? Did she bore you with similar tales of my misspent youth?"

Emma wasn't about to tell him, or to let herself be distracted. She glared at him. "You're sinfully handsome, women everywhere fall at your feet, you have a beautiful house, friends, companions, anything you might desire. Surely you could be happy…?"

For a moment there was real humor in his dark green eyes. "Sinfully handsome, Emma? Women fall at my feet? Then why, pray tell, aren't you there?"

"I'm not interested in being one of your conquests."

"I don't conquer women, Emma," he said in a low, sinuous voice. "I seduce them. Charm them into doing exactly what I want them to do. Does that surprise you, that I would hold that much charm?"

She looked up at him. Indeed, she had no choice— he was still holding her close against his body, and she could either look at him or close her eyes. She wasn't sure which was more dangerous.

"No," she said. "It doesn't surprise me."

"Then why haven't you succumbed yet?"

"I'm stronger than most women."

"So you are," he agreed. "But you're no match for me." She hadn't realized he'd been moving her slowly, carefully, backward, until her body came up against the side of the high bed. She halted in sudden panic, but it was too late. He carried her down onto it, his body covering hers, his weight warm and solid.

She fought him, but it was useless. Within moments she was on her back, staring up at him, breathless with fury and frustration. His hips trapped hers, pressing her body into the soft feather bed, and his hands held her wrists firmly against the white damask sheets.

"And now, dear Emma, I'll show you just what you have to be wary of," he said, and his head moved down, blotting out the light.

This was no slow, sensuous caress of mouth and lip. This was no chaste salute, nor was it the wet awkwardness of an untried boy or a randy old man. He opened his mouth over hers and kissed her, using his tongue, his teeth, and all the clever weapons he had in his arsenal.

She told herself she was being kissed by a practiced rake. She told herself it meant nothing, it was a trick, an act, a small skill that anyone could acquire. She told herself that as her body trembled and melted beneath him, as her mouth opened to his skillful insistence.

She told herself it meant absolutely nothing as his tongue pushed into her mouth, and the moan that came from deep inside her had to be one of displeasure, didn't it?

It wasn't one kiss, it wasn't twenty, it was a long series of unending kisses, leading one into another, so that she barely had time to begin to regain her sanity when he stripped it away once more. He kissed her eyelids, the side of her mouth, the beating pulse at the base of her neck. He kissed her nose and her chin, he bit her earlobe, and then he covered her mouth once more, kissing her with a devastating thoroughness that had her damp and trembling in his arms.

His hands were on her petticoats, slowly drawing them up her long legs, and her hips cradled him. He was hard against her, she belatedly recognized that fact, and the knowledge panicked her. He wanted her, his body wanted to claim hers, and there was no way she could stop him. No way, God help her, that she wanted to stop him.

He broke the kiss, rising up over her as she lay on the bed, staring down at her with a hooded expression in his eyes. His mouth was wet from hers, and his breathing was slightly labored. It would have been the only sign of his arousal, had it not been for the heat pressing against her hips.

"Do you want me, Emma?" he murmured, his voice low and insistent. "You don't have to say a word. Just put your mouth against mine.

Oh, God she did want him, as terrifying as that notion was. She wanted to touch him, to feel his skin against hers, and she felt a dark burning deep inside her that she knew only he could assuage. She wanted his mouth, she wanted his heart, she wanted his soul.

But he had no heart or soul to give her. And he would take hers without a second thought,

"No," she said. Calmly, firmly, with a sureness she was far from feeling.

There was no hint of regret on his dark, dangerous face. No argument, or attempts at persuasion or force. "A wise choice, child," he said.

And he rose from the bed, leaving her there in a tangle of clothing.

He was almost out the door when she called after him, "Did I really have a choice?"

He paused, considering. And then he smiled, a bleak, bitter smile. "You'll never know, will you?"

"You buggered this up nicely."

Miriam DeWinter stared at the elegant wastrel who sat sprawled in one of her straight-backed chairs. Her thin fingers curled into claws in her lap, but she didn't move.

"You don't like my language, do you, my gel?" he continued, slurring slightly. "That's too damned bad, it is. You'll have to get used to it, and a lot more. Like paying attention to who's calling the shots around here. Those men were supposed to bring me the girl. Instead one lies dead, another won't survive much longer, and the third's long gone."

"It's hardly my fault if you hire inferior employees," Miriam said in her icy voice.

"This kind of work doesn't attract the finer elements of society, woman," Darnley sneered. "And they would have done just fine if they'd obeyed orders."

"What makes you think they didn't?"

"Hendries had twice the amount of money I'd paid him tucked in his pocket when he managed to crawl back to my house. Had a devil of a time explaining him to my man."

"Maybe he stole his partners' share."

"Maybe. Or maybe someone paid him double, to make

certain things came out her way instead of mine. You want the girl dead, and well I know it."

Miriam maintained her icy demeanor. "I really don't care what happens to the girl as long as she ends up dead, and spectacularly so. She's a whore, and you may use her as such if you wish. Just as long as you don't let her go."

"Kind of you," Darnley muttered. "Killoran will be on his guard now. It'll be twice as hard to get her away from him."

"He was already on his guard," Miriam said. "Why do you think your henchmen failed?"

"Damn it!" Darnley said bitterly. "They won't fail again."

She looked at her cohort with withering disdain. He was her superior in rank, in wealth, in breeding, in gender. He filled her with contempt. "See that they don't," she said calmly. "Or I shall have to see to it myself."

And she knew Darnley had no doubt she could do just that.

CHAPTER THIRTEEN

"I love you."

Lady Barbara looked up in surprise, the cards dropping from her hands. She'd been waiting for hours for the inevitable declaration, but now that the moment had come, she found herself uneasy.

She would bed him, she had decided that afternoon after she'd run from Killoran's house. The hell with Killoran, and with Nathaniel. She would take Nathaniel into her bed and let him hunch and groan and sweat on her, and she would put her arms around him and make the requisite sounds, all guaranteed to convince him of her sublime pleasure. And then she would dismiss him. She'd gone back and enticed Nathaniel away with her, planning to end this farce quickly and efficiently. But for the past two hours they'd simply played piquet in her small, exquisitely decorated withdrawing room, while Nathaniel had watched her.

She picked up her hand and smiled at him, resorting to the cards. "You're very young, aren't you?" she murmured.

"I'm twenty-three. Older than you are."

"I doubt it. I was older than you when I was twelve," she said idly, laying a card on the green baize table. "Pique."

He tossed his own cards down. "I don't want to game with you, Lady Barbara."

She smiled at him, not fooled for a moment. "I'm certain you don't," she murmured. "You want to bed me."

"I don't—"

"You don't want to bed me?" she interrupted his protest, sourly amused. "How very unflattering, Nathaniel. Are you telling me you don't find me desirable?"

"Of course I do. You are the most beautiful, desirable woman I've ever seen in my life."

"But then, you've spent most of your life in the wilds of Northumberland, have you not?" she said.

"Don't toy with me, Lady Barbara," he said, frustration and anger beginning to creep into his voice. "Don't mock my devotion."

"Devotion, is it? I thought it was lust, pure and simple." She leaned back in her chair, stretching slightly, arching her back like a cat. It showed her well-formed, partially exposed bosom to advantage, and she knew his eyes would glaze over and his noble protestations would vanish.

Except that he wasn't playing the game properly. He kept his expression glued to her face, as if the look in her eyes were somehow more important than her perfect curves.

"Barbara," he said, his voice gentle, irritatingly so.

She wasn't used to men being gentle with her. She didn't like it.

"If you want me, you have only to say so, Nathaniel," she murmured, pushing back from the green baize table. "I've been waiting for you to evince some interest. Don't you listen to gossip? Don't you know that I make myself available to any man who appeals to me? I've been thinking about you ever since you kissed me. You're a very handsome young man. I imagine you'll be an energetic lover, and I've grown tired of jaded, older men. A little enthusiasm wouldn't come amiss." She reached behind her and unfastened the diamond necklace, setting it on the table in front of her. "Will you help me with my dress, or shall I call Clothilde?"

"Barbara…" he said, rising, and there was anger and denial in his beautiful blue eyes.

She came up to him. He was a great deal taller than she was, and strong. He smelled clean and fresh, like soap and wool and candlelight. She put her small hands up to his shoulders and smiled at him. "Don't be afraid, Nathaniel," she mocked him gently. "Surely you've bedded women before. You know the pleasure I can offer you." She began to remove the plain gold studs that fastened his white linen shirt.

He brought his hands up and covered hers. "No, Barbara," he said, very gently.

"No?" she echoed, deliberately misunderstanding him. "Then it will be my pleasure to be your first. I can teach you a great deal, Nathaniel. I have endless experience."

She tugged at her hands, but he wouldn't release them.

"No, Barbara," he said again. "I don't want to bed you. Not now. Not this way."

She heard the words, and for a moment refused to believe them. Stunned, she yanked herself away from him. "Then why are you here, Nathaniel?"

"Because I love you."

"Don't be absurd. Men don't love me. They lust after me. And I assuage their lust. It's what I do, boy. If you want me, I'll lift my skirts for you. If you don't, go away."

"I love you," he said simply.

"Stop saying that!" Fury swept over her. "You're a child, with a child's emotions. How many women have you fancied yourself in love with? There's Miss Pottle—Killoran told me about her. And you've shown a strong protective streak toward Emma—perhaps you're in love with her as well. And now me, your cousin's mistress. Whom else do you fancy yourself in love with?"

"You're not his mistress," Nathaniel said. "No matter how hard you try to convince me of it."

"Not for want of trying," she shot back. "And if he won't bed me, I'm more than willing to settle for second best. Namely you. But if you don't get on with it, I'll withdraw the offer. I don't like to be kept waiting."

Reaching up, she yanked at the far-from-demure neckline of her dress. The delicate material ripped, and she pulled it down her arms, exposing her breasts in their lacy chemise.

He didn't move. Didn't look at her breasts, a fact which terrified her. Was she losing her beauty? Would men cease to want her? Cease to spend their futile desires in her well-trained body? What, then, would she do with herself?

The silence grew between them, long and harsh, and she was suddenly ashamed. She pulled the torn material back up around her, covering herself. "Get out," she said, enraged.

If only he weren't quite so handsome. If only he didn't look at her with that damnable compassion, the kind of look that made her want to scratch his eyes out. He started past her, slowly, and she wanted to fight, to goad him.

"What were you planning to do with me, Nathaniel?" she called after him in her most shrill voice. "Rescue me from my evil ways? Immure me in a convent? Pray for my soul? It's too late—my soul's long gone. Which is why Killoran and I deal so well together."

He turned to look at her. "I want to save you," he said.

She closed her eyes for a brief moment. And then she smiled brightly. "Don't you know people can't be saved? They each go to hell by their own choosing, and neither you nor anyone else can stop them. You can't save me, you can't save Killoran, and I doubt you can save Miss Emma Brown, either. The best you can do is to save yourself. And the way you do that is very simple. Keep away from me. Keep away from all of us. Go back to Northumberland, find yourself another Miss Pottle, marry her, and have fat, healthy babies."

"I want to marry you," he said. "I want you to be the one who gives me fat, healthy babies."

Something inside her snapped. She didn't know how she moved so swiftly, but she was beside him, slapping him again and again, pounding at him, furious, fighting, fighting Nathaniel, fighting the insidious seduction of what was impossible for a woman like her.

He let her hit him. He stood absolutely motionless as she pounded at him, beat at him, at his chest and his face, until finally his arms came up around her, pressing her close against him, entrapping her with a terrifying tenderness.

"Barbara," he said, his voice suddenly weary and old before his time.

She heard the sound, but she couldn't recognize it at first. The great, tearing sobs had to come from somewhere, but she couldn't pinpoint their source. Nathaniel wasn't weeping, he was holding her tightly. It must be a maid somewhere, suffering from the toothache. But Lord, that hideous weeping noise seemed to fill the quiet room!

He stroked her hair, pushing it away from her face, and his hand felt damp. She had no idea why. She was cold, so very cold, and her body was trembling. But he was warm, he was strong, he was all that was decent and good. He was not for her.

She pushed him away, suddenly, abruptly, using all her strength, and he released her. "I want you to go," she said in a raw, cold voice, shaky with some confused emotion. Her face was wet, and she backhanded the moisture from her cheeks. "I want you to leave me alone. Clearly you're not interested in what I have to offer, and I'm not interested in what you would give me in return. Go back to Killoran; go back to Northumberland. Go." Her voice was rising, and she was powerless to stop it. Rage and despair had taken hold of her, and she was desperately afraid the wetness on her face could only come from her own tears. Impossible, when she never cried. "Get out of here," she cried. "Get out, get out, get out…!"

He silenced her, catching her in his arms and putting his hand over her mouth. "Hush, now, darling," he said, achingly gentle. "I know you're frightened. But you have to know I'd never hurt you. You can trust me, I promise. You'll believe that, sooner or later."

She looked up at him mutely over his silencing hand. She could bite him. She could seize the flesh of his palm between her strong white teeth and tear at him until she drew blood. When he finally released her, she could call for her servants and have him thrown from her house.

She stood stock still in the circle of his arms, waiting. He looked down at her, and there was tenderness in his blue, blue eyes. He bent down, and pressed his mouth against her eyelids, one at a time. And then he released her.

By the time she realized he was gone, it was too late to go after him. She sagged against the sofa, stunned, shaken. Her eyes were swollen, stinging, from the tears she wouldn't admit to. Her body was shaking, from the cold, she thought, even though her flesh felt as if it were on fire. Damn him, she thought furiously.

She'd underestimated him. She usually avoided innocent young men. They were tiresomely passionate, and far too easily entrapped. She preferred to keep her assignations with old men, roués, rakes, dissolute men who cared for nothing. Killoran was going to be her greatest conquest, a man who had absolutely no redeeming morality and was decadently handsome as well.

But Killoran had proved oddly resistant to even her

most blatant overtures. And now she had his hopeless puppy dog of a cousin declaring his ridiculous love for her.

But he wasn't the hopeless puppy she'd imagined. And the look in his eyes, the touch of his lips against her eyelids, had shaken her more than a score of encounters with more experienced men.

She would have to keep away from him. Keep his strong, gentle hands away from her. Keep his mouth away from her, keep his tender, compassionate love out of her sight.

"Damn him," she whispered out loud, rubbing the back of her hand across her tear-streaked face. "Damn him, damn him, damn him."

And in the quiet room there was no answer, but the latent, muffled sob that she couldn't quite control.

It was just past dawn. Jasper Darnley had been abed for less than an hour when the noise intruded, tearing him from a drugged sleep. He sat up, bleary-eyed, and stared around him in the murky darkness. It must have been a hell of a noise to have roused him—he'd taken more than enough laudanum to ensure that he'd sleep like the dead.

"Who's there?" he demanded sharply.

A ghostly figure began to materialize out of the shadows, and a sudden superstitious horror filled him. "Maude?" he whispered in a choked voice. "Is that you?"

The figure came into view, solidified into a sight not much more welcome than the shade of his dead sister. "Not likely," Killoran said coolly. "Don't tell me you've been plagued by ghosts, Darnley?"

"What are you doing here?" He didn't bother to disguise the panic in his slurred voice. He usually slept with a pistol, but he hadn't been in any condition to check on it when he finally collapsed onto his bed and allowed his long-suffering manservant to divest him of his clothes. It had been a hellish night, with the abortive attempt to kidnap Killoran's sister almost turning into her demise. Before he'd had her. The very notion had sent him into such a sick rage that he'd almost strangled the life out of that evil harridan who'd unhappily become his partner in crime.

It had wanted only the appearance of Killoran to make the night a total disaster.

Killoran was dressed in his usual black and white. His lace cuffs drifted down around his hands, his cravat was gone, and his jet-black hair hung loose around his face. Untidy without a wig, Darnley thought absently, fingering his own closely shaved head. But what could you expect from the Irish?

Killoran said nothing, moving closer. He didn't seem to be armed, but Darnley wasn't fool enough to discount his own danger. Perhaps Killoran was tired of the waiting game he'd been playing.

"Are you going to kill me?" Darnley demanded hoarsely.

"Oh, most definitely," Killoran responded. "That's never been in any question. But if you're asking me if I'm going to kill you now, I'm afraid not. I haven't yet derived my full pleasure from tormenting you."

"You don't torment me," Jasper said, his rasping voice making clear the lie. Killoran only smiled in response.

"If you haven't come to murder me in my bed, then go away. I'm tired."

"You do need your beauty sleep, don't you, Darnley? You haven't been feeling well lately, have you?" The concern was maliciously mocking. "Very well, I'll get to the business at hand. Someone tried to murder my sister tonight."

"Are you blaming me?" Darnley's voice rose a couple of notches in pitch. "Why in God's name would I want to kill your sister?"

"Why would you want to kill your own? You have a diseased mind, Darnley, brought about by inherent evil and aggravated by your lust for everything forbidden. You are to keep away from Emma."

"Of course." Darnley managed to summon a mocking smile.

"And you are to tell me what you know about her."

Darnley's amusement was complete. "What I know about your sister? It could hardly be more than you are already acquainted with. You must know the details of her proper upbringing, her loving family, her life of piety."

Killoran moved closer, but Darnley was too drugged to care. Even the feel of Killoran's large, strong hand around his throat, pressing against it, brought no fear to his ruined body.

"I could kill you so easily," Killoran mused. "Just a certain amount of pressure and I could crush your throat. You'd suffocate, and there'd be nothing anyone could do to save you."

Darnley stared up at him, unmoved. "That is my greatest advantage, Killoran. I truly don't care whether I live or die. And despite your efforts to prove that you are just as heartless, you still have a few sentimental longings for the auld sod and family. That's the difference between you and me, Killoran. The difference between the English aristocracy and an Irish upstart. We will always triumph."

The hand around his throat tightened for a moment, infinitesimally, and Darnley blinked. Perhaps he wasn't quite so inured to the thought of dying, after all. There were doubtless better ways to meet his Maker than suffocating in his own blood.

Killoran smiled down at him with terrifying sweetness. "It was a mistake to come after Emma, you know. I trust you won't make such an error of judgment again. Two men are dead, and I could quite easily make you the third."

"I'm not worried."

"Perhaps not. But you can answer me one question. One simple question that will keep you alive for at least another day of miserable existence. Who is helping you, Darnley? Who wants Emma dead?"

Darnley glared up at him, letting his unvarnished hatred show through. "Go to hell, Killoran. Kill me, or get out. Whichever you please."

For a moment the hand tightened further, and the breath caught in his throat. He lifted his hands, to claw at the strong, merciless arm, but his intruder seemed oblivious of his struggles. The night was growing darker around him—odd, when it should be getting lighter. The man was actually going to kill him, here and now.

There was a certain relief in that notion. What little

strength Darnley had was leaving him rapidly, and his arms fell back on the bed as the darkness began to close in on him. Death, he thought with a vague smile on his face. Maude.

Killoran released him, stepping back from the bed in disgust. Darnley still breathed. He'd be bruised around his throat, a fitting enough fate, considering he'd delivered the same to Emma's fragile flesh.

The room stank, of sweat and alcohol and drugs, and of the sickly-sweet miasma of decay. The man who lay so still in the bed was not far from death as it was—it would have taken only a moment or two to push him over the edge. "Not yet, my friend," Killoran said coolly. "You're not getting off quite so easily."

He glanced around the room for a moment, then began to search, silently and diligently, secure in the knowledge that Darnley's servant wouldn't dare approach his master until summoned. Darnley had blinded a footman, a decade ago, in one of his enormous rages, and most servants were properly frightened of him.

There was little sign of anything interesting. The servants were well paid, well trained. It was almost full light when Killoran finally had a modicum of success. A card, poorly engraved, on cheap vellum. *Miss Miriam DeWinter, Crouch End.*

Why in God's name would someone like Darnley know anyone in Crouch End? Why would he keep her card for that matter? Had this Miss DeWinter come to Darnley's house? For what possible purpose?

He could think of none, but he was assured of something more important. Miriam DeWinter was connected to his mysterious Emma Brown, or he was no Irishman.

Killoran paused over Darnley's comatose figure. The man was snoring loudly now, but his color was ghastly, pasty white and green around the edges. "You won't be needing this anymore, my boy," he said gently, tucking the card into his vest pocket. "Pleasant dreams, Darnley."

The sleeping man roused for a second, clawing toward Killoran, and a babble of curses flowed from his mouth along with a foaming spittle. He caught Killoran's arm as he turned to leave, and Killoran drove his hand into the wastrel's soft belly, as hard as he could.

Darnley's scream of pain echoed through the house. He went rigid, his eyes shot open, bulging in pain, and then he rolled over in the linen sheets and began to vomit blood. Killoran stood there for a moment, taking in the spectacle of his worst enemy, debased. And then he slipped out of the room, the same way he had entered, disappearing down the hallway before the servants could come running to see what ailed their cantankerous master.

Killoran had slept little the night before. The taste, the scent, the feel of Emma had lingered in his mind, on his mouth, on his hands. The moment he'd begun to drift off he would see her eyes again, the soft fullness of her mouth, and he would recognize the longing of an untried virgin asking for something she'd always regret.

He had heard Nathaniel return, and he'd almost risen from bed to see whether he could goad him into a fight. Verbal if need be, though fisticuffs would have been preferable. Killoran was in the mood to bash someone, to hit the person very hard, and he really didn't give a damn who it was.

But Nathaniel had been moving without his customary high spirits through the house, and Killoran had remained, still and silent in his library, listening as the lad had gone upstairs. He'd clearly had a bad night. While it was more than likely that Barbara had seduced him, he didn't seem particularly lively about it. Maybe he'd disgraced himself, as young men with no control often did. Barbara would tease him unmercifully—she often reserved her crudest moments for those young men who were most vulnerable.

And yet, when it came to that unlikely pairing, it seemed that it was Lady Barbara who was vulnerable. Lady Barbara who longed for what she could not have, longed to be what she could not be. For once Nathaniel seemed oddly mature.

So Killoran had let him go. He could find someone else to hit. And the notion of Darnley had sprung immediately to mind.

His carriage had been waiting around the corner. John Coachman was abed with a concussed head and a broken arm, and the groom who had awaited him was young and frightened of him. Which suited Killoran perfectly. He preferred people to be afraid of him. He only wished he could manage to keep Emma terrified.

But she always fought back. It was absurd—an innocent like her should have been completely helpless. Instead she managed to come back time and again after each devastating blow. She'd been attacked, almost murdered tonight, and instead of flinging herself in his arms, in his bed, or at least indulging in a strong case of hysterics, she'd simply pulled herself together.

If he didn't watch himself very carefully, he might find himself in the hideous situation of actually liking her. Caring what happened to her. When he really had no intention of caring about anyone at all, ever again.

He wasn't a man who lied to himself. And he knew the truth, whether he wanted to face it or not. It was already too late. The longer he stayed in Emma's company, the more vulnerable he became. She reminded him of a time he thought he'd dismissed long ago, she was making him human once more, and he didn't like it. He needed to finish quickly with this business and release her. Before he found himself in the unbearable position of not wanting to let her go.

He climbed into the back of the carriage before young Willie realized he was back, pulling the stairs up and the door closed behind him. "Take me to Crouch End, Willie," he called out, settling against the squabs.

He heard the shock and hesitation in the young voice. "Crouch End, my lord? Are you certain?"

"Why wouldn't I be?"

"Hardly seems like your lordship's kind of place," Willie said nervously.

"And how would you know what my kind of place is?" Killoran kept his voice low, pleasant, knowing that would terrify the boy even more.

"I grew up there, your lordship. Until I came to work for you, three years ago. My family's still there."

Killoran immediately dismissed his notion of tormenting the boy. "How fascinating. Would you say you know Crouch End well?"

"Well enough, sir."

"Then take me to the home of Miss Miriam DeWinter."

"Old Skin-and-Bones? Why would you want to go there?"

"I don't remember offering to share my plans with you," Killoran said in his most pleasant voice.

"N-no, sir," Willie stammered. "Right away, my lord."

"Does Miss Skin-and-Bones live alone?" he questioned idly, disguising his alertness.

"She used to live with her father, but he died a month or so back, or so my mother told me when I visited her last. Murdered by some aristocrat."

"Fascinating," Killoran murmured, immediately placing Uncle Horace. "Anyone else?"

"Just her cousin. No one ever saw much of her—she kept to the house. Only went out for church, and then Miss DeWinter made certain she was heavily veiled. I heard tell she was frightful ugly. Miss DeWinter wouldn't let anyone come around when her cousin was there."

"And is the cousin still there?"

"Dunno, my lord. I think she went away at the time Mr. DeWinter was killed. Why would you want to be visiting the likes of them? They're not your kind at all."

"Miss DeWinter and I share a certain acquaintance," Killoran replied. "Besides, I've never been in Crouch End, but I doubt it can be worse than the stews of Dublin. Does that satisfy your curiosity, boy, or have you more questions?"

Common sense finally seemed to penetrate Willie's thick skull. "No more questions, sir."

"Then drive on. I desire to get this settled in time to get a few hours of sleep."

"It's already daylight."

"Willie, you grow very tiresome."

"Yes, sir," Willie said hurriedly. "We'll be there in a shake." He was unfortunately far too accurate, as the horses snapped to with a jolt tossing Killoran back against the squabs.

The morning was cold, and he hadn't bothered with more than his coat. He picked up the thick fur throw and pulled it around him, ready to doze comfortably, when a teasing, alluring scent came to him.

Roses and lavender, a clever mix innocent yet absurdly provocative. The thick white throw smelled of Emma.

He clutched his hands around it, shoving it away from him. It would be far too easy to close his eyes, wrapping himself in comfort. The risk was tempting, insidious, and he had no intention of giving in to it for even a moment.

There were times when Emma Brown seemed even more of a danger to him than Jasper Darnley. And he had better do everything possible to keep from succumbing to her temptation. He couldn't afford weakness so late in his desiccated, dissolute life.

CHAPTER FOURTEEN

Miriam DeWinter was on her knees in prayer when she heard the rude pounding at her door. The house was cold, the floor hard beneath her padded knees, and she'd been intent on ordering her personal God to smite her enemies when the thunderous noise disturbed her.

There was no one else to answer the door at that early hour. She had an aversion to live-in help—women were too weak and men too lustful for Miriam's state of mind. While Emma had been there, she'd gotten by very well with a minimum of servants. Gertie saw to the sparse meals and Miriam's personal needs, and a succession of poorly fed young girls would help Emma with the household work.

It had been a convenient arrangement. Sinful natures such as Emma possessed were better off being occupied by hard work, and she had seen to it that Emma wasn't troubled by idle moments. In the past few months Miriam had been forced to hire another servant, or face the wretched necessity of joining in the endless cleaning.

But at six in the morning Gertie would be just arriving, and the man who came in to tend the fires wouldn't dare answer her door.

Miriam rose, heavily, and started the long, winding path to her front door. Down narrow, spotless hallways, unblemished by paintings or wallpaper; down uncarpeted stairs polished so brightly that they presented a danger to anyone careless enough to move with lighthearted speed through the house.

But there was no one with a light heart living in the DeWinter house in Crouch End. Miriam moved slowly, with a stately dignity, as the pounding continued, relentless.

It could be Darnley again, she supposed. He wasn't happy with her, a notion that didn't bother Miriam in the slightest. He was a fool to think he controlled her—in her entire life no man had ever controlled her. He thought he was using her to get his revenge upon Killoran, using her to get his hands on Emma.

But she was the one who was doing the using. She was the one who would extract revenge, from Killoran and most especially from Emma. Emma would die. If Darnley happened to rape her first, it mattered not in the slightest to Miriam. She would die, and her paramour as well. Miriam had failed the first time, but she wouldn't make that mistake again. She would hire her own men instead of relying on Darnley. She would make her own arrangements. And if that failed, she would do the deed herself.

She opened the door, glaring out into the early morning fog. The liveried servant who stood at her door could have been no more than twenty, and he looked frankly terrified. He glanced behind him, as if he expected to see a ghost appear over his shoulder, then turned back to Miriam.

"Beg pardon, Miss DeWinter," he mumbled. "My master was desiring of seeing you."

She peered out into the dim light. She was as nearsighted as Emma, and just as vain. The tall figure that loomed out of the fog could only be one man.

"Lord Darnley," she said in her frostiest tone. "Why are you back again?"

He stepped closer, out of the fog, and Miriam felt her first moment of real fear. "I'm afraid not, Miss DeWinter," the man said. "Though I do wonder what Jasper Darnley would find to interest himself in Crouch End."

Miriam DeWinter was a formidable woman. It took her only a moment to pull herself together, to let the icy coating of murderous rage wash over her. "I couldn't say, my lord," she said in her most waspish tone.

His smile was cool, charming, but Miriam was stonily unmoved, blocking the huge door to her house. "I wonder how you knew I was a lord," he remarked gently.

A mistake, Miriam acknowledged to herself. But not a fatal one. The man in front of her was as clever as the devil, and not far removed from him. It would take a good woman like Miriam to confront him, and best him. She had to watch every word, make certain she didn't betray herself. But it was hard, when her soul was crying out for justice and death.

"Your servant is wearing livery," she said icily. "And your carriage has a crest on it."

"I wouldn't imagine you could see my carriage through this fog."

"I have excellent eyesight."

"Indeed," he murmured. "I gather it doesn't run in your family."

She ignored that provocative statement. "How may I help you, my lord? I'm not used to entertaining gentlemen in my robe and slippers."

"I imagine not."

Miriam seethed. "State what you desire and then please leave."

"I've come to talk to you, Miss DeWinter. About your family. About your unfortunate choice of friends."

"I'm afraid I have no interest in talking with you, Lord Killoran."

"Ah," he said. "Now, surely I didn't mention my name, did I?"

"You are well-known," Miriam said firmly. "You're a rake and a scoundrel, a gamester and a murderer. I have no use for sinners like you. Get yourself gone!"

"A murderer? I'll plead guilty to the other crimes, but as far as I know, I have yet to commit murder."

Miriam's self-control vanished. "Get out!" she shrieked.

Killoran didn't move. "Of course, if you're referring to your late, lecherous father, then I must inform you that it was a case of self-defense."

He'd manage to sting her into reacting. All discretion had vanished. "He wasn't a lecher. It was her. That evil whore, luring him to his destruction. But she'll suffer for it, I warn you. And you as well. You won't benefit from his murder. I'll see to it that..." Her voice trailed off before his calm, ironical gaze.

"Yes, Miss DeWinter?" he said politely. "And how

were you going to exact revenge? Doubtless through Darnley's assistance, though I'm afraid he's not the most competent of villains. You do make an odd pair."

The last of her control had disappeared, leaving Miriam in a blind, spitting fury. "I know you have her in your house, in your bed," she shrieked, trembling with rage. "You tell her. She'll die. I'll see to it. And I'll laugh. And dance on her grave! The Lord will have justice. If thy right eye offend thee, pluck it out. Vengeance is mine..." she babbled.

"Saith the Lord," he finished for her in a calm voice.

"Insolence and blasphemy!" Miriam shouted.

Killoran nodded. "I do my best. Good day to you, Miss DeWinter. I rather think you've told me all I need to know."

"She's a whore!" Miriam called after him, ignoring the curious neighbors. "A slut, a fornicator, a creature who converses with devils!"

"I'll give her your best regards," Killoran said gently, climbing into the carriage.

"May God strike you both dead!" Miriam shrieked after him. But the Almighty failed to listen, and the sudden silence of the morning street, the icy chill all around her, brought Miriam back to her senses. She slammed the door, leaning against it, breathing heavily.

She had no doubt whatsoever that the Almighty was a man. A woman wouldn't have failed to exact instant and awful retribution.

Fortunately for Miriam's God, He had Miriam to manage things. To arrange revenge when the Almighty failed.

Miriam moved into the austere front room, sinking

down on the bare floor in an attitude of abject prayer. She would have to move fast now. Lord Killoran was obviously the devil's own henchman—with no difficulty he'd managed to goad her into revealing her hatred. Now that he'd been warned, he might do something. Take Emma away, out of harm's reach.

But he couldn't keep her safe forever. Miriam would wait years if she must.

However, patience had never been her forte. And there was a sizable sum of money—a fortune, in fact—that was out of her reach as long as Emma was alive and missing.

No, patience wasn't called for right now. Action was. And Miriam rose from her attitude of angry prayer and went in search of a hearty breakfast.

Emma was not ready to face the world. She'd slept very badly indeed. Her body ached from her tussle on the frozen cobblestones; her head ached with confusion, people going round and round in it in a circle, talking at her, warning her. Lady Seldane danced through her dreams, small, dark eyes accusing. "You love him," she said, but the voice that came from her pursed, painted mouth was Miriam's.

The dead man was there as well. Emma hadn't taken a close look at him after Killoran had shot him, but there'd been no doubt that he hadn't survived. He haunted her dreams. Blood and lust and anger, and just when she thought she might escape, he turned into Miriam, too.

Killoran stood in the shadows, watching. She couldn't see his face, only his hands, the long, slender fingers; the fall of lace from his extravagant cuffs, his long, black-clad legs. He was watching, and judging, and she knew she had to fight the three specters to get to him. He wouldn't come to her.

Someone else stood in the way. She reached out her hands, to shove, when she came face-to-face with her own pale reflection. Her double stood there, dressed in black, stopping her from going to Killoran. Stopping her from going to her doom. And all she could feel was fury and despair.

"Lord, I thought you weren't ever going to wake." Mrs. Rumson's hearty tone didn't cover her concern. "It's past noon, and his lordship will be wanting to get on the road as soon as you're ready. I've taken the liberty of ordering you a bath, and Dora's already packed your new clothes..."

"On the road?" Emma said, dazed. She sat up, staring around the room. Her door hung open, the broken latch and splintered wood painfully obvious. "Where am I going?"

"His lordship has taken it into his head to rusticate. A house party in the country, I believe, near Oxfordshire. You're to accompany him."

"You don't sound as if you approve," Emma said shrewdly.

Mrs. Rumson shrugged her massive shoulders. "It's not my place to approve or disapprove. I have no very high opinion of his lordship's acquaintances—one can scarce call them friends."

"Perhaps I should remain in London."

"You have no choice, miss," Mrs. Rumson said. "Mr. Hepburn will remain behind. You're to accompany his lordship, and to be right quick about it. He says to tell you if you're not ready within the hour, he'll have Jeffries carry you out to the carriage."

Outrage and amusement fought for control in Emma's weary brain—amusement won. "I doubt a frail creature like Jeffries would get very far," she murmured.

"Better to risk being dropped by him than carried by his lordship."

"True enough," Emma said, throwing back her covers. Arguing would be a waste of time, that much was more than clear. She was just as happy to get away from London, away from the danger of Cousin Miriam, of hired ruffians and the lecherous Lord Darnley. She would be perfectly safe at a house party. There would be chaperons, company, safety.

Her one concern was being immured in a carriage with Killoran after last night's devastating encounter. Hour upon hour, rocking back and forth in his elegant coach would be its own kind of hell, and she anticipated it with both longing and panic. He would doubtless be cool and mocking, and she would have nothing to fear. Nothing to hope for.

By the time she raced down the stairs, long hair flowing behind her, skirts trailing, she was within minutes of the hour he'd allotted her. Only to find that her alarms had been useless. Killoran was mounted on the huge black gelding he'd ridden the night before, and he barely glanced in her direction as Jeffries handed her up inside the empty coach. A moment later they were off.

Emma had spent a great deal of her life alone. Ever since the death of her father, when she'd been thrown upon the mercies of her cousin, Miriam, Emma had accustomed herself to spending by herself whatever hours weren't devoted to improving works. Reading. Playing the clavichord. Dreaming.

There'd been a certain peace in solitude. A peace that had vanished from her life completely. Not with the death of her uncle, not with her abrupt change of life. But with the simple advent of Killoran.

When he was around, she was obsessed by him. When he was distant, he haunted her. There was no reason that she should love such a man. He was malicious, immoral, unfeeling, and licentious. He was everything that could destroy her, and she needed to call upon all of Cousin Miriam's most rigid moral strictures to keep herself aloof from his decadent lure.

But even that was not enough. For whatever reason, he had become the very center of her life, and she couldn't free herself of his powerful effect no matter how much she fought it.

She must have dozed. Mrs. Rumson had packed her a lunch of cold chicken and cheese and French bread, along with a bottle of claret. Emma ate every scrap, drank most of the bottle of wine, and promptly fell into a slightly drunken stupor. She was unused to spirits, but there was little else to occupy her mind during the endless journey. Only memories of Killoran's body, pressed hard against hers. His mouth, hot and wet and demanding; his hands, deft, arousing. His touch, his kiss, his need and hers, all tied up together in a mass of aching confusion that made her want to cry out in pain and yearning.

When she awoke, the night was dark, the carriage had

come to a halt, and her head ached abominably. She heard voices. Killoran's slow, lazy drawl, mixed with other, drunken greetings.

"I thought you weren't coming, old man!" That voice was very slurred and not the slightest bit familiar. "Thought you weren't going to leave that sister of yours for a bit of hired sport."

"Don't know if that's quite the thing, Killoran," another voice chimed in. "Granted, she's only a by-blow, but there are rules. Not that I'm against having it on with your sister, but society frowns on such things. You need to keep such dealings private."

"I appreciate the advice, Sanderson." Killoran sounded cool. "But I rather think you know that I do exactly as I please in these matters."

"More power to you, I say," the first drunken voice trumpeted. "Bugger them all, that's what I say. Come on in, Killoran. There's a prime bit of muslin that might tempt even you. She has the most extraordinary pair of tits you've ever seen."

"Really?" Killoran sounded simply bored.

"Even you might get excited," Sanderson chimed in. "Why in God's name were you riding on such a cold night?"

"I brought a guest."

Emma heard him draw closer, and she shrank back into the carriage. A waste of time, of course, when the door opened.

Two men were standing on either side of Killoran. They were both shorter, younger, and drunk, and they stared in at her with almost comical expressions on their faces.

"Brought your own, did you, Killoran?" the older one said, leering at her. Sanderson, by the sound of his voice. "Can't leave the doxy be, can you? Well, they say when you develop a taste for the naughty, it's hard to go back to ordinary pudding."

"I have an idea," the other man said, shouldering his way forward. "We'll share her. Sanderson and me. We watched Barkley and Howard do it last night with one of the whores, and I've been itching to try it. You can give us advice, Killoran."

Killoran was silent, gazing at her. There was no expression on his face, his eyes were hooded; and beyond the door of the carriage, Emma could see the brightly lit mansion, hear the shrieks of laughter.

"What makes you think Killoran knows how to do it, idiot?" Sanderson demanded with drunken dignity.

"Killoran knows everything, don't you, lad? You know how horny these Irish boys are. In fact, the three of us could probably share her. After all, she has a mouth and two tits, a cunny and an arse—"

"Get away from the door, Sanderson," Killoran said in a pleasant voice.

"Come now, old chap. Don't go all possessive on us. You wouldn't have brought her to a bachelor's establishment unless you were willing to share her. Granted, she's got that innocent look to her, but I'm willing to bet she's a wild thing once you get Jack in the orchard." He reached for her, his hand grabbing hers and hauling her toward the door.

She told herself she wouldn't fight. If this was truly what Killoran had brought her for, then nothing mattered. Her innocence was something to be tossed to a pair of hungry jackals, and he would doubtless watch, as his friend had suggested, and be greatly amused.

She was almost through the door when the rough hand on her wrist suddenly loosed, and she fell back among the squabs. She heard a squeal of pain, high-pitched, almost that of a pig. She struggled to sit up, but the door was slammed behind her, and a moment later the coach took off at a punishing pace.

She held on to the door handle as she was tossed back and forth. She had no idea what had startled the horses, whether the new coachman had deemed it necessary to rescue her, whether Killoran had suddenly developed a conscience. That last possibility seemed the least likely, but she was weary, frightened, and beyond rational thought. All she could do was struggle to retain her balance on the seat as the carriage raced on into the night.

It was a losing battle. She ended on the floor, the white fur throw on top of her. She had banged her head against the seat, she had to use the necessary, and for all she knew, she was trapped in a runaway coach. So be it. She only hoped, if she was going to go over a cliff and die, that fate would be quick about it.

The wine was making its presence felt most unpleasantly. She put her face on the carpeted floor of the coach and moaned as her stomach began to perform somersaults. Maybe death wouldn't be that horrid, after all. It was survival that was getting to be a major annoyance.

The coach began to slow, imperceptibly at first. The

wicked rocking lessened, and while Emma decided not to risk climbing back up onto the seat again, it seemed likely that she wouldn't cast up her accounts. It was dark in the carriage, chilly, and between the rumbling of the wheels and the pounding of the horses hooves, she found herself drifting into a drugged stupor. If Sanderson or his disgusting friend had commandeered the carriage, at least she might manage to sleep through it. That, or throw up on them.

The coach lurched to a sudden stop. A moment later Killoran stood in the open doorway, his face hidden in shadows, his voice lifeless. "Are you all right?"

She stirred, shocked, staring at him in momentary be-musement. "Where are we?"

"At a small hunting box I won several years ago from one of my many helpless victims. Since I don't hunt I haven't much used it, but I imagine it's still basically sound. Young Willie will see to your comfort."

"And where will you be?" she asked stupidly, brazenly.

His smile was as wintry as the night air. "I'm going back to the party. I decided you would put too much of a damper on the festivities. You are, after all, merely an untried virgin, and gentlemen such as my friends ex-pect someone with a bit more talent and experience. You would be a sore disappointment to them, and they would hold me responsible. My evil reputation could never with-stand the blow."

"I imagine not." He was holding out his hand to her, impatient, waiting for her to alight. She had no choice. She stepped into the cold night air, and her legs promptly collapsed underneath her.

He was there to catch her, damn him. His body was warm beneath his winter-chilled cloak, and his leather-gloved hands were both hard and gentle on her as he held her for what surely was a minute longer than necessary while she regained her balance.

Then he released her. "Willie will see that you're well taken care of. He won't let anyone bother you."

She looked past him, to the darkened, shuttered house. The trees and shrubbery had grown close around it, she could see that much in the moonlight, but the place looked trim and snug, if not luxurious. Anything, however, was preferable to that den of iniquity they'd stopped at earlier.

"Are you really going back there?" she asked foolishly.

"Indeed. It's only a few miles, and my friends will wonder what became of me. I'm not known for passing up the occasion for sport, even if I have no taste for shooting defenseless creatures. There's a bevy of beautiful, inventive bed partners, a host of men eager to game who are no match for me, and the food and wine will doubtless be superior to whatever young Willie can scrounge up here. Is there any reason why I shouldn't go back?"

She stepped away from him, pulling her black cloak around her. Her hair was blowing in the strong breeze, obscuring her face, which in itself was a blessing.

"No reason, my lord," she said in a low voice.

He persisted. "You weren't, by any chance, thinking of offering me your own myriad charms as a distraction? Granted, the women at Sanderson's party have a great deal more experience in these matters. They know how to provide a man with exquisite pleasure. But there's something to be said for the clumsy enthusiasms of youth. Shall I stay?"

"Stay?" she repeated stupidly.

"And share your bed?" he said bluntly.

It was unlike him. He wasn't a blunt man; he seldom said what he meant. For a moment she wondered what he might do if she said yes. It would almost be worth it, to see that cool, distant expression transformed by shock.

Almost, but not quite. "No, thank you," she said with spurious calm. "I am tired from all this traveling. I'm certain Willie and I will dispose ourselves quite comfortably."

There was a flicker of something in his eyes, surprise, perhaps even a grudging respect, but it was gone as soon as she saw it. "Not too comfortably, I trust," he muttered, half to himself. "I'm not surprised you're tired. You were up late last night, fighting off ruffians, were you not? I won't offer our dubious hospitality to any of my acquaintances, then. The lodge is rather small, and I'm not convinced they'll appreciate my noble motives in keeping you away from them. They might decide to sample you themselves and see how disappointing you are. I couldn't have that."

She lifted her head, looking at him squarely. "Why not?" she asked.

His smile was icy. "Because I'm saving your maidenhead for Darnley," he said. "Pleasant dreams, my pet."

CHAPTER FIFTEEN

It was fortunate the hunting lodge was small. While apparently sound enough, it had the musty, unused air of a place long closed up. It took Willie a good deal of effort even to unlock the front door, and the dark, icy interior was far from welcoming.

But Killoran had already ridden off, without a backward glance, and there was no choice but to try to make the place comfortable. Emma did her best not to think of the bizarre household they'd stopped at earlier. If Killoran chose debauchery, she was hardly the one to argue with him. As long as he didn't drag her with him.

Her body was stiff and aching from the long carriage ride, and also from her tussle on the London streets the night before, and for a moment all she wanted to do was sink into one of the chairs and weep with hunger and weariness and something else she didn't dare to define.

She didn't. She leaned her head against the stiff chair, blinking back her tears, and by the time Willie had returned with an armload of dry wood and the food hamper, she'd managed to light several candles. She moved through the place with brisk efficiency while Willie tended to the fires.

The lodge was small and neat, a gentleman's toy house, though fallen into disuse. Mice had gotten in at some point during the past few years, making themselves a comfortable little nest out of one of the beds, but the other three rooms seemed relatively unscathed. She couldn't begin to guess which was the master bedroom—all four were small and simple, so she took the least inconspicuous of them, and the one with the sturdiest bed. The one with the unshuttered window near the peak of the roof, through which she could see the moon shining down brightly.

Within an hour the fires were laid and crackling merrily, dispelling the gloom as well as the cold. Emma made a cheerful meal of bread and cheese and hard cider, and Willie managed to pry some of the shutters off the lower windows before retiring to the small stable to sleep with the horses, after quickly refusing her suggestion that he sleep in the warm house.

"Master wouldn't like it," he muttered. "Besides, I'd rather be with the horses, if you don't mind, miss."

"I don't mind."

Willie yawned hugely. "Dunno how he can keep going on so little sleep, miss. I'm tired to the bone, I am. I'm not used to being up all night, wandering the streets of Crouch End at the crack of dawn."

"Crouch End?" She heard her voice say the words from a distance. "Whyever was his lordship in Crouch End?"

Willie shook his head. "Wanted to see old Skin-and-Bones, he did, though I have no idea why."

Emma felt the coldness descend, hardening her insides into a solid chunk of ice. She knew who old Skin-and-Bones was. She'd heard some street urchins shout it at her cousin, Miriam. "And did he see her?" Her voice was remarkably cool.

"Stood on her front step, arguing with her at the crack of dawn. I couldn't hear a word they were saying," he added, sounding mournful. "In the end she slammed the door in his face. But when he came back to the carriage, he was smiling. You know that smile he has, miss. The kind that could charm a dragon while he cut its throat."

"I know that smile," Emma said.

Her small room was toasty warm from the fire Willie had laid for her. She glanced at the bed. The hunting lodge didn't seem possessed of bed linens, and Willie had brought the white fur throw from the carriage and set it on the mattress. If she had any sense at all, she'd curl up in it and force herself to sleep.

But she was beyond forcing. She sat in the one chair the room boasted, her back to the moonlight, to the bed, and stared into the fire. She was shaking, yet she knew it wasn't from cold.

Killoran had a terrifying charm of that there was little doubt. But it was the memory of Cousin Miriam that had sent Emma into a panic. Why would Killoran even know of her existence? Had he been lying to her all this time? Was he not her rescuer at all?

Had he brought her there to die? It was always possible, and she found she no longer cared. She'd trusted him, in an odd sort of way. Knowing that he was a villain, a user, a self-confessed rake and debaucher, she'd still felt an irrational sense of safety with him. Perhaps it was simply because he'd rescued her so many times.

But the time was coming when he wouldn't rescue her. When he'd throw her to the wolves and watch. She could count on no one but herself, and if she had any sense of self-preservation, she would get away, from this place and most particularly from him.

The more she thought about it, the more determined she was. She'd been mesmerized by Killoran, by his dark green eyes and elegant hands, by his low, seductive voice and wounded heart. But he was doubtless right in saying he had no heart. And the sooner she was away from him, the sooner she could reclaim her own.

The night grew quiet and still around her. The crackle of the fire, mixed with the sound of her even breathing, her determined heartbeat, lulled her into a shallow, fitful sleep.

She dreamed of Killoran. And his deft, elegant hands.

He watched her as she slept. She looked oddly fragile for such a robust creature. Her skin was pale beneath the flame-colored hair, and the clinging black clothes only heightened the stark contrast. She looked almost ethereal, sitting there asleep in the chair.

The room was hot, the dry wood sending out waves of blessed heat. Killoran stripped off his jacket and waistcoat and tossed them across the dusty table, then turned back to her.

There were no other chairs in the room. It didn't matter. He sank down on his haunches, leaning against the wall, staring at her.

It was a bad sign, his need to get back to her. Almost as bad as his sudden decision to keep her from the debauches of Sanderson's house party. He didn't remember feeling particularly protective before in his life. It was a bad sign indeed.

A few hours, or days, on her own at that licentious party would have given her a most enlightening education. She would have learned more about men and their needs, their frailties, than most women learned in a lifetime. The knowledge would have served her well if she'd decided to be a wife or a whore, the two options open to most women.

He'd told himself he was saving her to torment Darnley, but he'd lied. He'd been saving her for his own torment.

Sanderson had brought his remarkable kitchen staff with him, but Killoran had soon discovered he wasn't interested in food. The claret and brandy had been smuggled from France, and he'd drunk too much, but even that had failed to still the nagging, unsettling feeling that had settled somewhere in the black hole where most people had a heart.

He could have found any number of games with all levels of play, from the green 'uns ready and willing to be fleeced, to the more expert players who offered him a real challenge. He'd realized he didn't care.

Even the ripest, most talented of female flesh had failed to entice him. For this particular gathering, Sanderson had imported only the highest level of tarts. Actresses; the demimonde; the occasional masked, bored, aristocratic slut seeking diversion. None of them had moved him.

"What's wrong with you, man?" Sanderson had demanded, one hand occupied with a glass of champagne, the other tucked down the front of a spectacularly well-endowed, masked female who Killoran suspected was Countess Olivier. The same woman who'd refused to dance a country dance with a lowly Irish peer, freshly arrived in London so long ago. Killoran's mouth curled in a cynical smile.

"And don't look like that!" Sanderson added, slopping champagne over the countess's creamy bosom. "You know I hate it when you smile. It's enough to give a corpse the shivers."

The countess shrieked. Killoran ignored her, glancing around the crowded, noisy room. "Is Lady Barbara Fitzhugh here tonight?" he asked, casually interested.

"Babs? No. I couldn't prevail upon her to join us. Just as well, I think. In the past few weeks she's proved tiresome. Never up for a bit of sport." Belatedly Sanderson caught himself. "Beg pardon, old man. I was forgetting that you...that she..."

He floundered, and Killoran let him. So Barbara had passed up the sort of thing she usually pretended to revel in. Interesting. And he could just imagine whose company she was preferring.

"But what about the gel?" Sanderson was unwise enough to continue. "When I got word that you had decided to join us, you said you were bringing a young woman. Not that most people bring their half sister to this kind of thing, but then, I suspect you're not like most brothers. A little overfond, don't you know?" he added with a drunken leer. "Wouldn't have minded a taste of her myself. Always was partial to tits."

"Darling!" the countess protested.

"I adore you, my sweet," Sanderson assured her. "I just want to fuck Killoran's sister as well."

"Indeed," Killoran murmured coolly, wondering why he suddenly wanted to kill a drunken fool like Sanderson. It was a great shame that one of the few rules of society decreed that you couldn't kill a man who was the worse for drink. He stared at his host. "I'm afraid my sister isn't available. I'm saving her."

"For Darnley or yourself?" Sanderson asked, showing he wasn't quite as drunk as he'd first appeared. Perhaps he was sober enough to meet him after all, Killoran thought wistfully.

"Why should you say that?" he inquired. But his host failed to recognize the imminent danger.

"Everyone knows there's bad blood between you and Darnley. Has been from time immemorial. Word has it that you despoiled his sister and she took her own life. Course, that doesn't sound much like the Maude Darnley I remember," Sanderson added fairly. "She wasn't the type to throw herself away on…well, you know what I mean, old man. She had a high opinion of herself and her value on the marriage mart. No offense, Killoran," he said uneasily.

"None taken," Killoran returned smoothly, dreaming of pistols. "And if it were true, it doesn't make Darnley much of a brother, does it? To let me go unpunished."

"Darnley's not much of a human being, if you ask me," Sanderson said with devastating frankness. "But then, you're a hard man to kill. No one even dares try anymore."

"Oh, they try," Killoran said in a deceptively tranquil voice. "They just don't get very far." Out of the corner of his eye he could see a plump, red-haired woman near the stairs, and he felt a faint flickering of interest that surprised him. He was seldom drawn to whores.

"Well, find your own pleasure," Sanderson said grandly. "There's plenty to be had. At least we won't be having the pleasure of seeing Jasper Darnley for the next few days. Apparently his stomach ailment has taken a turn for the worse once more."

"How sad," Killoran murmured in dulcet tones. "I believe I heard a rumor to that effect."

"I don't suppose you had anything to do with it?"

And that was why he put up with Sanderson, Killoran reminded himself. Because the man had just a trace more of a brain than most of his ilk.

"No more than I had to do with his recent absence from society," he answered truthfully.

Sanderson shivered with melodramatic exaggeration. "Remind me never to offend you, Killoran."

"A bit too late for that."

Sanderson seemed singularly unmoved by the notion. "Go and make yourself pleasant to Harper's latest trull. The titian-haired beauty you've been eyeing so covertly. I gather she's particularly gifted with the French talent. And you spent a great deal of time in France, did you not?"

He glanced over at the striking creature. She knew perfectly well she was being watched—it was worth her livelihood to notice such things. "I think I will," Killoran murmured. "Innocence gets to be very boring."

"I wouldn't know," Sanderson replied with a wicked leer, pouring his champagne over the countess's lush breast and proceeding to lap it up.

Killoran had no need to approach the woman. She came to him, her lush body swaying with just the right amount of seductiveness. His eyes narrowed as she glided up to him. She was beautiful. Stunningly, spectacularly beautiful, so much so that she even put Emma in the shade. But something wasn't right.

The hair, for one thing. The color was too even, too brassy, clearly not her natural shade at all. Her eyes were blue, and faintly stupid, as she looked at him assessingly. Her mouth was a rouged Cupid's bow, not Emma's generous smile, and she smelled of musk, not of lavender and roses.

And she was too damned short.

In fact, she wasn't Emma. And he looked down at her, at this luscious offering on the Altar of Venus, and felt nothing but anger and regret.

He hadn't any more time to waste on what was clearly a lost cause. Emma had bewitched him—how, he wasn't quite certain. No other woman had managed to disrupt his life, his plans, so completely. She'd sunk into his brain like a hot knife into wax, and he could think of no way of dislodging her short of burning down the night.

He had found Willie sound asleep, snoring loudly on his pallet in the stables. For some reason, Killoran hadn't wakened him, unsaddling his horse himself and brushing him down. There was something soothing about the feel of horseflesh beneath one's hands, something calming in the steady strokes of the curry brush. He'd forgotten that simple pleasure.

Once again the memory of home, lost so long ago, came crashing back over him. His love for horses, shared with his father, the long hours spent training the swift, beautiful Connemara ponies. Life had once been so very simple, so very right.

But not anymore. And not ever again.

He slapped Satanas's rump and moved away from him. Killoran could imagine Sanderson's reaction if he knew his friend had left the pleasures of a debauched party for the joy of grooming a horse. He'd think him mad. Maybe he was.

The moon had set when he went in search of Emma. He hadn't stopped to think why—he'd simply gone, with unerring instinct. The brandy still thrummed in his veins; the whore still teased at his memory. He needed to look at Emma, to find out why he'd left a talented courtesan for her. But when he'd finally come across her, sound asleep in that uncomfortable-looking chair, he'd known the answer.

Her scent filled the room—lavender and roses. He leaned against the wall, watching her, and then he knew. Whether he liked it or not, he wasn't going to let Darnley put his hands on her again. She wasn't going to be despoiled by a sick brute like Jasper Darnley, and she certainly wasn't going to have that harridan who claimed to be her cousin get near her again.

He needed to marry her off, to someone strong and decent and kind. Someone without the imagination to wound her and hurt her, someone who'd protect her and take her far away from London and the Jasper Darnleys of this world. And the Killorans of this world as well.

Nathaniel immediately sprang to mind. He was young, strong, stupidly idealistic. In fact, a noble hero, bent upon rescuing a damsel in distress. Lady Barbara was his chosen damsel, but she was already a lost cause, unwilling to be saved. She was better suited for people like Killoran, another lost soul.

Besides, Nathaniel seemed very fond of Emma. He was always warning Killoran, looking at him suspiciously, as if he suspected him of the foulest possible designs. Of course, he'd been right.

Emma would be happy in Northumberland. She'd give Nathaniel babies, and it would be a simple matter for the two of them to imagine themselves in love. If they proved recalcitrant, he could always arrange for Nathaniel to ruin her. Such things were child's play when you had a mind like his. Once Nathaniel took her maidenhead, he'd have no choice but to marry her.

It all made perfect, logical sense. Killoran would get rid of the two of them, so damnably distracting. He'd take Barbara into his bed, and perhaps even teach her to like the sport, though he doubted he'd want to exert himself that much. And then he'd find Sanderson's whore and use her as bait with Jasper.

All very sensible. Unfortunately, the plot hinged on one minor contingency. That he'd be willing to let another man take Emma.

He lifted his head to stare at her, running his hands through his thick hair. What was it about her that caught at his soul, when he no longer had one? What was it that fascinated him, weakened him, made him start believing in things that didn't exist? She was just a girl. A young woman, who'd lived a sheltered life with a religious fanatic and a lecher. A woman of courage, determination, and astonishing sangfroid, who could skewer a man without fainting, who could stand up to Killoran himself—who had terrified far braver creatures. She was just a girl. And he wanted her.

He closed his eyes for a moment. Was it the brandy that was sapping the last of his vaunted self-control? Or merely the amount of time he'd been around her? This moment had been there, just out of reach, since he'd walked into that room at the inn and found her standing, bloodstained, over the fresh corpse of her uncle. He'd fought it for as long as he could. He wasn't going to fight it any longer.

He must have intruded on her very dreams. Though he made no sound at all, eventually her eyes opened, myopic, sleepy. She didn't see him at first, crouched against the wall, and he allowed himself the furtive pleasure of watching her slow, delicious stretch.

And then she knew she wasn't alone. Her eyes flew to his, wary, squinting in the darkness.

"You're back," she said, her low voice faintly breathless with surprise. "But why? Was the orgy too tame for you?"

He rose slowly, lazily, watching the wariness in her eyes increase. "Now what, pray tell, do you know of orgies?"

"I read a lot."

"Books about orgies? You surprise me. You don't strike me as a female full of prurient interests. In fact,

there was no orgy at Sanderson's. Merely a group of un-
derdressed whores of all stations of life, some indiffer-
ent games of cards, and a fully adequate meal. Are you
hungry?" His question was almost an afterthought.

"No," she said. "But I *am* curious about something."

He glanced over at the bed. It was a large one, and
someone, presumably Emma, had brought in the fur
throw from the carriage. He wondered how she would
look, lying naked against it, her flaming hair spread out
around her. Around him.

"Ask me anything," he murmured.

"Are you going to take me back to my cousin, Miriam?"

He hesitated for only a moment. He heard the well-
disguised panic in her voice, the first real fear he'd
ever noticed in his otherwise stalwart companion.
Remembering the formidable Miss DeWinter, he wasn't
sure he blamed her.

"Willie has been indiscreet," he said in the casual voice
that was his most dangerous.

"You didn't warn him not to say anything," she protested.

"Servants in my employ shouldn't have to be warned to
keep their mouths shut. What did he tell you? That Miss
Skin-and-Bones and I were as thick as thieves? That I
tumbled her in her front hallway?"

"Don't," she said faintly.

"As a matter of fact, I learned of Miriam DeWinter
from your admirer, Lord Darnley. Apparently he and
Miss DeWinter have some sort of scheme in mind. I wondered why Jasper seemed willing to let his henchmen
murder you before he had a chance to take you. Obviously

it was your cousin who possessed the murderous tendencies. They must run in the family."

"Don't mock me."

"My dear one, I'm not," he protested lazily. "Merely
pointing out a fact."

"Did you tell her where I was?"

"I didn't need to. She was already fully apprised of
your whereabouts. Or was, up until this morning, when
I decided it might be politic for us to absent ourselves
from London for a while."

She looked at him in disbelief, clearly doubting any
noble motive on his part. She was wise to do so. "Are
you going to give me back to her?"

"I hadn't realized you were mine to give."

A faint flush mantled her pale cheeks. "You've told
me as much on any number of occasions."

"I've yet to act on it." The silence in the room was a
palpable thing. She stared up at him, and he could read
her soul in her honey-brown eyes. The fear, the wariness, the bravery. And the shy, irrational longing as well.

She longed for him. He knew it, much as it astounded
him. Not that he was unused to being sought after by
women. He'd been blessed with a certain combination
of form and face which seemed to draw both women and
men to him, even as they fought against the pull.

But Emma wasn't like other women. She was too determined, too sensible to fall for his clever ploys. But she
looked at him with her heart in her eyes, and he knew
that he'd found the one thing he couldn't resist. A taste
of innocence, after a lifetime of jaded pleasures.

He would take her. He knew it—the time had passed

for him to resist. He would debauch her. Strip off her clothes, lay her on the bed, and bring her down to his level. Make her pant and quiver and shatter in his arms. Take her, and debase her. And then let her go.

And in doing so, he'd free himself from the insidious effect she had on him. By bringing her down to his level, he'd be released from his unwelcome bondage. And there'd be no more nagging weakness, or foolish sentiment, or absurd desires.

"Do you need some help with your clothes, Emma?" he asked in a deceptively cool voice.

Her flush darkened. "No, thank you. I intend to sleep in them."

"No," he said, very gently. "You will not."

The wariness dissolved into full-fledged panic for a moment, and then she pulled herself together once more. "I will not be your whore, Killoran," she said fiercely. "If you're in need, then go back to the party and partake of the women there. I won't share your bed."

"A bed isn't necessary. If need be, I can take you on the floor. Or on the kitchen table."

Her eyes widened at the notion. "You can't make me."

He laughed then, a faint, bitter sound, full of regret. "Ah, but my precious, I can."

"By brute force, perhaps," she said, backing away from him. "And I'll fight you every inch of the way."

He advanced upon her. Slowly, silently, taking care to frighten her just so much and no more. "Not by force," he said, "and you won't fight."

He reached out for her. She slapped him, and the force of her blow whipped his head around. He paused, gazing down at her, perversely pleased to see she looked completely horrified. "I'm sorry," she stammered. "I shouldn't have… I warned you…"

"You shouldn't waste your regrets over a slap. As a means of defense, it's fairly paltry. Save your apologies for the time you skewer me." And he put his hands on her shoulders and drew her toward him fully prepared for worse than a slap.

But she was silent, mesmerized, holding utterly still as he brought her body up against his. She was shivering in the hot room, and he could feel the battle raging within her. He tucked her face against his shoulder, smiling into the darkness. A faint, bitter smile of triumph and anticipation. She would be his.

And he would be free.

CHAPTER SIXTEEN

There was no escape. In the firelit room, she knew that there was no escape at all.

In truth, if she could bring herself to fight him, she knew he would let her go. If she were steadfast and strong, she could run away from him.

Ah, but she was far from strong when it came to Killoran, and she was steadfast only in her self-destruction. Even if she ran, she'd never be free of him.

She might as well submit, since it was what her secret, shameful heart had wanted from the first moment she saw him. Cousin Miriam was right after all—she was possessed of the devil, of evil, licentious desires. And she would give herself to the devil, here and now.

She forced herself to go limp in his arms. If she couldn't bring herself to stop him, at least she could do her best not to prolong matters. If she simply lay there and let him do what he wanted to her body, it would be over soon. And then he would want her no more. Cousin Miriam and even Gertie had made that more than clear. Once a man has his way with you, your value is lost. In submitting to Killoran, she was doing the wisest possible thing, given her circumstances.

He slid his hand through her thick hair, cupping the back of her head, turning her face up to his. He looked dangerous in the firelight, brutal and satanic, and she kept very still, waiting.

"A virgin sacrifice, Emma?" he murmured. "I would have thought you'd have more pride."

"I won't fight you," she said, her voice low and faint. "I'm sorry if that's what you prefer, but I can't battle any longer. You'll win in the end, you always do, whether it's cards or dice or other people's lives."

His thumb traced the edge of her jaw. "I have the devil's own luck," he said softly. His body was very hard and fiery against hers. She was reminded again of how very powerful he was. Physically powerful. Emotionally powerful. She tried to withdraw further, into some dark, quiet place inside herself, as fear began to take over.

But he wasn't about to let her. And she knew full well that it wasn't he whom she feared. It was she herself.

The touch of his mouth against her eyelid was the first warning. His lips feathered against her skin, and her eyes fluttered closed. She could feel her heart beating, a desperate tattoo, and she tried to will herself into a calm resignation.

She had never been held so closely by a man. Never felt the strength and heat of him.

It was no wonder she was unable to dismiss him from her mind. Even as she tried to shut off her brain, her senses were playing havoc with her vain effort at self-control.

He kissed her other eyelid, and he was not a man she would have thought would be much for kissing. He kissed her temple, her cheekbone, her angular nose. And then in the shadowy night his mouth sought hers.

It was light and darkness, sin and forgiveness, hell and redemption. She put her arms around his waist, pulling him closer, closer still. She could feel the warmth of his strong back through the fine linen shirt; she could taste brandy on his mouth. His hand was between them, against her breast, and she hated the layers of cloth that separated them.

He was stealing her life, her soul, her breath. It didn't matter. She gave them willingly, courting death and despair for the heavenly torture of his mouth against hers. She clung to him, tightly, mindlessly yearning, when she realized he was trying to disentangle himself, trying to push her away.

She clung to him, her fingers digging into his flesh, desperate for him, but he was far stronger than she was and not afraid to use his strength. He thrust her away from him, and she fell back against the wall, staring at him in shock and shame.

"Tell me no, Emma," he said in a low, bitter voice. "Tell me to leave you alone."

"Touch me," she said.

"Have you no sense? No pride? I'll destroy you, as surely as if I took a knife to your throat. Tell me no, Emma."

This wasn't Killoran the cool, elegant seducer. This was a man in pain, in need. This was her man, for however brief a time it lasted.

"Yes," she said simply, waiting for him. And she held out her hands to him. They trembled slightly; she couldn't help it. He could turn his back on her, walk away, and there'd be nothing she could do. All she could do was offer herself, and wait.

The mask closed down over his face once more, and she felt despair and sorrow fill her. The pain, the need, were gone. Instead he looked at her from unreadable eyes, and his thin mouth curved in a mocking smile. "So be it," he murmured. "Far be it from me to deny a lady pleasure."

She dropped her hands, as if they burned, but it was too late. He caught them, his long, strong white fingers wrapping around them. "It will be pleasure, you know," he continued, his voice low and mesmerizing. "I have a rare gift. You yourself remarked on it. I never lose at gaming, women flock to me, and I have a magic touch with horses. I know how to take a man's fortune, gentle a stallion, and seduce a mother-abbess until she screams in pleasure."

Emma tried to pull back, but he was drawing her closer, inexorably closer, and she couldn't shake the feeling that this wasn't Killoran. This was another, darker creature who inhabited him, one she shouldn't dare trust.

But things had already gone too far. He was bringing her toward the bed, and in the wavering candlelight she could no longer see his face. "Turn around," he said, his voice faintly husky, and she did so in a fog, presenting her back to him, staring down at the bed, at the soft whiteness of the fur throw.

He pushed her hair off her back, and his mouth pressed

against the nape of her neck. His hands were deft, damnably so, as he unfastened the myriad of tiny buttons that
traveled down the length of the black silk gown. It fell
down her arms, and he kissed her shoulder blades as he
undid the whalebone corset with far more speed and dexterity than any lady's maid had ever managed.

He untied the ribbons that held her hoops, the tapes
that held her three lace petticoats. Her clothes began to
descend toward the floor in a graceful collapse, and she
stood there in her thin chemise, shivering in the heated
air.

He kissed her on the fine lawn of her chemise, his
mouth hot and damp through the almost transparent material. He sank down on his knees behind her, his hands
cupping her hips, and placed his mouth against the small
of her back.

She heard the faint, barbaric cry in wonder, knowing
yet not believing that it had come from her own throat.
His clever, clever hands were on her bare skin now, hot
against her hot flesh, running up her thighs. Her skin
was on fire, icy flames licking over the surface, and she
wanted to cover his hands with hers, pull them up, up
to her breasts that were straining against the soft cotton.
Instead she clenched her fingers, clenched her mouth, to
keep the words at bay, while his hands slid down the out-
sides of her legs, then began to move up the insides. She
panicked when he reached her thighs, clamping them together. She heard him laugh softly as he drew away from
her, and she was suddenly afraid he'd changed his mind.

But the gentle pressure on her shoulders sent her tumbling onto the cloudlike softness of the fur-covered bed.

She lay face-first across the bed, sinking into the warmth, as he climbed up behind her, straddling her prone body.

He already had the chemise up to her waist, and he pulled it over her head before she even realized what he was doing. He was sitting on her thighs, and his silk breeches were cool against her bare skin. His hands slid up her body, over her buttocks, up the line of her back, and she arched in pleasure, like a cat, unable to help herself.

"You like that, do you?" he murmured. "I thought you might. You're a sensual creature, dear heart, no matter how you try to fight it. You were made for this."

She wanted to protest. She wasn't made for this, she was made for him. But she knew he wouldn't listen. Or if he did, he might leave her, take those hard, deft hands away from her flesh, and then she thought she might die.

So she said nothing, burying her face in the soft white fur, as his hands moved up her sides, kneading, touching, stroking, dancing along the sides of her full breasts, so close and yet not close enough. His mouth followed, and he kissed her, everywhere. The base of her spine, the nape of her neck, the side of her breast, and the cleft of her buttocks, and all the while his hands were soothing, kneading, arousing.

"I could take you like this," he said in a dreamy tone. "I've done it before. I wouldn't have to see your face. I wouldn't have to look into your damned brown eyes and see that helpless look of longing. I could pretend you were as practiced a slut as Barbara Fitzhugh, and you wouldn't be able to weave your tangled web around me.

"Ah, but I mustn't forget you're a virgin. That might

frighten you for your first time. Though perhaps you could simply pretend it wasn't happening. You might think you want me to deflower you, but you don't know what you're asking. You're bartering the only valuable thing you own, and you're getting nothing in return."

The words were harsh, the voice smooth and hypnotic. She was in a dream, a trance, unable to fight him, unable to refute a word he said.

"I'm good at deflowering virgins," he said against her ear. "I've lost count of how many I've had. There's a trick to it, and it's been a while since I've wasted my time on any but the most experienced and discriminating of partners, but I'm certain it will come back to me."

No, she whispered silently, but there was no one to hear. He lifted himself off her for a moment, turning her over beneath him, and she lay spread out across the center of the bed, looking up at him as he straddled her.

He was still fully clothed, and she was naked, vulnerable. His eyes traveled slowly down the length of her, not missing a detail. He would see the abundance of her curves, the heart-shaped birthmark beneath her left breast, the scar on her hip from the time she'd fallen out of a tree. He would see what no man had ever seen before, her breasts, her belly, her...

The silence built and grew. She'd shut her eyes tightly, momentarily embarrassed out of the sensual lassitude he'd instilled in her. But finally she could stand it no longer, and she opened her eyes once more, to glance up at him, trying to gauge his reaction.

For the moment there was no telling. His eyes were hooded as he stared down at her, and she was suddenly terrified that she was being judged by a connoisseur and found wanting. No wonder he hadn't taken her to his bed. It had been no great battle to preserve her innocence. Indeed, the battle had been to lose it.

And then he leaned forward, and the mask was gone from his eyes, his face, if just for the moment, and the longing was back. "A true redhead," he murmured. "My love, you're magnificent."

Somewhere she found her voice. "I'm not your love," she said in a pained whisper.

The mask returned. "True enough," he agreed. "But for tonight, you are." His hands lifted over her breasts, paused, and the lace cuffs trailed against them. "Aren't you, my love?"

She wanted to deny it. To deny him that one piece of herself as she was giving him everything else. But she knew Killoran far too well. He'd be satisfied with nothing less than total surrender, and he would wait for her to give it.

"Yes," she said.

His hands closed over her breasts, and she bit her lips to keep back the cry of response that raced through her. His thumbs brushed against the hard, sensitized tips, and the cry escaped her anyway.

"You like that, don't you, my pet? I knew you would. Has a man ever touched your breasts before? Tell me yes and I'll cut off his hands. Has a man ever stroked you like this?" Slowly, dangerously, his fingers encircled the aching globes of her breasts, and she felt her hips arch in unbidden response.

"No," she whispered, pushing against him.

"I thought not," he said. "If you like that, you'll like this even more." And he leaned forward and put his mouth on one breast, taking it deep into his mouth, suckling her like a babe.

She gripped the bed beneath her, but the silky fur slipped through her hands. Her entire being seemed centered in her breast. His long hair fell on her, and she reached up, threading her fingers through it, pulling him closer, offering her breast to him.

There was a line of fire from the tip of her breast, where his mouth suckled and pulled at her, down to the center of her body, between her thighs, burning and hot and wet. She shifted, restless, anxious, and he lifted his head to look down at her. Her breast was hard, distended, wet from the attentions of his mouth, and she wanted to pull him back again.

"Getting impatient, Emma?" he murmured. "Good." And he covered her other breast with his mouth, using his teeth, lightly, gently.

She jerked in reaction, moaning, and he drew back. He moved off her body, stretching out beside her, running his long, hard fingers down her skin. Her flesh seemed to jump at his touch, and she realized she was covered with a thin film of sweat. The room smelled of fire and brandy and arousal, her perfume and her skin and his, and she thought she would go mad if he didn't take her. And he knew it.

He moved his hand over her stomach, down between her legs. She tightened them in instinctive panic, but he simply kissed her, hard, pushing his tongue into her mouth, tasting and draining her resistance, so that her thighs opened to his hand, and she let him touch her. His fingers threaded through her damp hair then delved deeper. She squirmed in fright, in discomfort, and then in sudden, riveting pleasure, and a bolt of reaction hit her; her entire body shook with the power of it, and by the time it was over she was exhausted, panting, staring up into Killoran's dark green eyes with dazed surprise.

He smiled for a moment, and there was something oddly vulnerable there. And then he blotted out the light as he kissed her again, and his fingers slid deeper still, two of them.

She jerked in shock, in protest, but he paid her no mind, his tongue pushing into her mouth, stroking, touching, arousing, his fingers doing the same thing. The second bolt hit her, and her body clenched, but before it left her another one came, and then another, each building in intensity, overlapping. He removed his mouth from hers, but he kept her legs trapped with his, and he wouldn't stop.

She couldn't breathe. Her body was trembling, wild, and she hit at him. He made no effort to stop her, simply absorbing the blows as he pushed on, inexorable, those deft, clever fingers touching her, taking her, driving her to a wild madness that could culminate in nothing less than life and death.

"Stop," she cried, desperate. "I can't..."

"Give it to me, Emma. Show me. Don't fight it. I've earned it. Come for me, Emma. Let me hear you scream."

She did. Her harsh, choking cry filled the room with a vast, tearing sound as her body convulsed, the last tiny bastion of control, of sovereignty, vanishing under his wicked, loving hands.

She fell back against the fur throw, dizzy. He was leaning over her now, his hands cupping her face. He whispered something against her mouth, but the words danced in and out of her mind and then drifted away. She struggled to open her eyes, but she couldn't. With her body still rippling with tiny convulsions, she sank into a powerful, healing sleep.

Killoran lay beside her, motionless for a moment. He could see the pooled tears beneath her eyelids. She probably didn't even know she'd cried. She'd hate it, he thought. She didn't like to admit weakness. Particularly weakness where he was concerned.

He looked down at her lush, ripe body. Flushed and pink from loving, and still virginal. He could probably come just from looking at her, but he wasn't going to do that. He wasn't going to touch her again.

He'd had her, more effectively than taking her maidenhead. Any man could rip past a frail barrier of flesh. He'd taken something far more important, a part of her soul that she could never reclaim. She was his now, a tiny, inviolate part of her. It would be enough.

He rose from the bed, careful not to wake her. He was so damned hard he ached, and he paused for a moment to adjust his throbbing erection, then leaned over and wrapped the white fur throw around her. She slept on, oblivious, but in the firelit darkness he could see the marks from his early morning beard against her breasts.

The fire in the front room had burned down to embers long ago. There was a faint chill in the air, one he welcomed, as he shut Emma's door behind him. It did little to subdue his fierce arousal, but it suited his bleak soul very well.

He ran a hand through his hair. Her scent clung to him, another thread of arousal, and he wanted to hit something, very hard. Instead he wrapped his icy self-control around him, sank down wearily at the rough-hewn table, and wished to God he hadn't left Sanderson's party. If only he'd decided to vent his lust on that redhead. In the dark, all women were the same. He could have closed his eyes and pretended she was Emma. He could have had her down on her knees between his legs, servicing him, and he could have kept himself separate, invincible.

But everything he did to hold Emma away from him only brought her closer and closer. He'd thought that by seducing her, showing her just how much control he really had over her, he'd be shaking off his own demons.

But it hadn't worked that way. By controlling her body, her sensuality, by taking her desire and making her explode with it, he'd simply tied the ropes tighter around himself.

He sat without moving for minutes, perhaps for hours. And then he heard the sound from the bedroom beyond, and he almost ran.

He couldn't bring himself to do so, even if it would have been the smartest choice. He simply sat there, his face composed in its usual mocking lines, and waited for her reappearance. Other women would be embarrassed, shy. Other women would hide beneath the covers, duck away from him.

But not Emma. She would confront him. He knew it as well as he knew his empty heart. He didn't turn his head when the door opened. He was sitting back in the chair, long legs propped up on the table, seemingly at ease. He waited until she came close, ready to turn and look at her when he felt something crash against the side of his face, almost knocking him off the chair. It was her fist.

"Damn you," she said furiously. She hit him again. "I hate you."

He easily caught her flailing arms, not in the mood to be pummeled by an angry woman. Not in any kind of gentle mood at all. He hauled her into his lap, trapping her there. "I suppose I should be glad you don't have a smallsword or a fire poker," he said ironically.

She paled for a moment at the reminder, and thrashed helplessly in his lap. That wasn't helping his condition in the slightest, and a distant part of him wondered how he was ever going to survive the day.

"If I did, I would kill you," she said in a small, tight voice. She was wearing her chemise again, not much protection from his curious eyes, but she didn't know that.

"I'm used to women wanting to hit me," he said. "But they usually don't do it quite so soon. You should be in greater charity with me, Emma, my heart. I just exerted myself to give you a sublimely pleasurable experience, and I left you a virgin in the bargain. Few men would have been quite so noble."

"Noble!" she shrieked in a rage. "Nobility had nothing to do with it. You never wanted me—you've made that more than clear. If you had, you would have taken me. You're not the sort of man who denies himself anything that catches his eye. I've been a game to you, a means of catching your worst enemy, and a toy to amuse yourself with. You wanted to prove to me just how powerful you were, just how helpless I was, and you did, didn't you?"

He didn't bother to deny it. "There's an element of truth in your wild accusations," he said with feigned weariness. "I'd forgotten how very tiresome virgins can be when their dignity is offended. I'm sorry. Obviously you wanted to deny me the pleasure of your quite wonderful body. I merely spared you the trouble. You should be grateful. You can still marry some decent, honorable yeoman and come to him a virgin."

She kept struggling, and he shoved her off his lap. She scrambled a few steps away and stood there glaring at him, magnificent bosom heaving, fire in her eyes. "How very kind of you," she said in an icy tone.

"I thought so. Apparently you don't agree," he replied mildly. "Would you care to explain your objections? Granted, I should have kept my hands off you entirely, but you made yourself irresistible."

"Ha!" she said, "If I was irresistible you wouldn't be sitting here fully clothed, and I wouldn't have woken up naked and alone."

He blinked for a moment. "Dear child, are you objecting because I didn't deflower you?"

"No!" she said in quiet fury.

"Then what are you making such a fuss about?"

"That you never wanted me. That you took me, used me, abased me, without having the faintest desire for me, other than a need to belittle and shame me, and—"

He moved so fast he frightened her, bolting out of the

chair and coming up to her, catching her shoulders and shoving her against the table. "I didn't belittle and shame and abase you," he said between gritted teeth.

"You didn't want me…"

"God grant me mercy!" His control finally snapped. He caught her hand and dragged it down to his crotch, pressing it against the surging heat of his erection. "Do you know what this is?"

She tried to pull away, but he wouldn't let her. He didn't know whether he was hurting her or not, and he didn't care. He pressed her hand against him, harder, rhythmically, unable to help himself.

"I can guess," she said.

Her prosaic answer stopped him only for a moment. "You bloody well can," he almost snarled. "It's a cock, my love. A painfully erect, needy prick. And I'm in that condition solely because of you, my angel. I do have my noble moments, difficult as that may be to believe. I'm saving your maidenhead for someone who deserves it. Someone who'll appreciate it."

She simply looked at him. She was breathing deeply, and he could see the darkness of her nipples against the thin white lawn. "You choose the oddest times to be noble," she said.

"Damn you." He jerked away from her, moving to stand by the table, keeping his back to her. "Go back to bed, Emma."

He could feel her eyes on his back. He could smell the lavender and roses and warm, female flesh. Go, he prayed. For God's sake, just go.

She started past him, and he kept his focus inward,

thinking of nothing at all. He would have made it if her chemise hadn't brushed against his hand. If she hadn't paused one dangerous second too long.

He caught her, no longer caring what he was doing. She cupped his face, reaching up to kiss his mouth, and it was the last straw. He ripped at her clothes, ripped at his, a maddened beast, shoving her down on the hardwood floor, covering her with his strong body.

He pulled her legs apart, roughly, and thrust into her, forgetting for a moment everything but his own wild need. She was sleek and wet, and he broke past her maidenhead before he could stop. He heard her cry, a brief, pain-filled sound, but when he tried to stop himself, tried to pull away, she simply wrapped her arms around him and held him tightly, so tightly.

He reached down and caught her thighs, lifting them up around him. It was too late now. He'd fought it, and her, and now he was the one who had lost. He'd given in to a need so powerful it overwhelmed all others, and all he could do was revel in the feel of her hot, tight body around his, the furious pounding of her heart against his bare chest, her fingers digging into his back, scratching at him, tearing at him, as he thrust into her again and again, searching for a part of him he'd lost long, long ago.

The floor was hard against his knees, harder still against her back. He rolled over, taking her with him, so that she was astride him. She looked shocked, yet triumphantly sensual, and his hands trembled as he cupped her hips, showing her the motion. Her long red hair rippled around her, rippled around him, and he could see her face knot up as she reached unknowingly for her climax.

He touched her then, reaching down between their joined bodies to stroke her, and she exploded in a wild, high-pitched little scream as her body convulsed and tightened around him, pulling and gripping him, and he had no choice. He flooded her, spewing forth, filling her.

She collapsed on top of him, as limp as a rag doll. He lay beneath her in the cold, dark room, stroking her long hair, for the moment too replete to consider the damage. She had came with the same intensity she threw into everything, and her total and complete collapse afterward left him feeling both amused and tender.

She barely moved when he sat up, carefully disentangling their bodies. He kicked himself out of his ripped breeches, scooped her up in his arms, and started toward the bedroom. He had settled her against the fur throw when her hands suddenly caught his, her eyes wide and panicked. "Don't leave me," she whispered. "Don't ever leave me."

He looked down at her, knowing he was about to send her as far away as he possibly could. "I won't," he lied. And he sank down beside her and took her shivering body into his arms.

She believed him, fool that she was. Within moments their body heat joined, and she was asleep once more, snuggled against him. Soft, warm, smelling of sex and flowers, she felt as if she belonged there. A dangerous thought.

No one belonged in his arms, in his bed. He needed to remember that. And lying beside her, his hand gently, mindlessly, stroking her hair, he stared into the fading darkness, far into the morning light.

CHAPTER SEVENTEEN

"I'm not certain this was a very good idea."

Nathaniel stopped his headlong stride down the weed-choked road to stare at Lady Barbara. "I didn't ask you to accompany me," he pointed out with a shade less than his usual deference.

"I have a stake in this matter as well," she replied frostily. "You're concerned about Emma, and I'm concerned about Killoran."

"Of course you are," he muttered under his breath.

"Besides, I don't know why you think Emma can't handle him. She's kept him in line so far, hasn't she? And he's hardly taken her all the way out here for licentiousness." Lady Barbara looked at the lodge with a faint moue. "If he'd wanted her, he could have had her in his own room, not in this seedy place. That huge bed is vastly comfortable."

She'd said it on purpose, waiting to see Nathaniel's reaction. His expression darkened for a moment, but he ignored the provocation. "I consider it any gentleman's duty to look out for the well-being of innocent young women."

"That leaves me out," she said with an extravagant drawl. "I haven't been innocent since I was in leading strings."

She tossed the statement off lightly enough, but she'd underestimated Nathaniel. He paused at the door to stare at her.

Lord, it was a sin for a man to be so handsome and so damned noble. She would have no trouble if he were simply the rotter most men were. Instead he had to look at her out those concerned blue eyes, and she started dreaming dreams that were out of the question. Why couldn't he be ugly or mean? Or both?

"Barbara—" he began, but she pushed past him.

"*Lady* Barbara," she corrected him in her frostiest voice. "I don't think Killoran is going to be any too pleased at our arriving on his doorstep in the middle of the morning. There was no need to go haring off in the dark of night."

"No need for you."

"I have my own interests to protect. I won't have that red-haired innocent replacing me in Killoran's affections," she said stiffly.

"You aren't in Killoran's affections. I sincerely doubt anyone is."

"True, but it's unkind of you to point it out," she admitted. "Then let me say I don't want her replacing me in Killoran's bed."

It was a deliberate taunt, but this time she'd gone too far. "If you share a bed with Killoran, it's not his," Nathaniel said flatly. "I've been in residence for more than a month, and I've yet to see him bring any female home."

"Except for dear saintly Emma," she said in an acid tone. "Besides, Killoran can be very discreet."

"He's hardly likely to bother." He stared at her. "What have you got against Emma?"

She gave her young hero her most brittle smile. "Jealousy. Killoran's fascinated by her, and you're ready to battle dragons for her sake."

"I'd battle dragons and worse for *your* sake."

"Too late," she said, her voice cool. "Shall we see if we can catch them in flagrante delicto?"

"He swore he wouldn't touch her. I believe him."

"Then you're a bigger fool than I thought." She pushed the door open, then paused, momentarily flummoxed.

Killoran sat alone by the fire, dressed simply in black breeches and shirtsleeves. There shouldn't have been anything terrifying about the absolute lack of expression on his face, yet Barbara felt a chill of apprehension.

"You made enough noise out there," he said coolly. "I wondered whether you were going to continue arguing for the rest of the day. To what do I owe the pleasure of this visit?"

Nathaniel pushed Barbara inside, following her and closing the door. "We were concerned."

"Indeed? About what?"

Barbara's initial nervousness began to abate. "Don't be obtuse, Killoran. Nathaniel's worrying about his little pet. Not that she's so little," she added in an acid tone. "He's afraid you debauched his innocent darling."

The temperature in the cool room seemed to drop several notches as Killoran turned his frighteningly bland expression on Nathaniel. "I hadn't realized you were en-amored of my sister."

"She's not your sister, damn it," Nathaniel said in a tight voice. "And I'm not enamored of her. I care about her well-being."

"No," Killoran agreed, some of the dangerous tension leaving him, "she's not my sister. And her well-being is none of your concern."

"Where is she?"

"Still in bed," he said lazily, his eyes alert.

"No, I'm not."

They all turned to look, Killoran more slowly than the others. She stood in the doorway, her long red hair braided loosely and tied with a strip of cloth, her black clothes neat. Barbara took one look at her and knew the truth.

"You bastard," she said to Killoran.

"Don't be tiresome, Babs. Since when have you be-come the staunch defender of womanhood?" His voice suddenly sharpened. "Don't." That was addressed to Nathaniel, who was approaching him with a furious ex-pression.

"'Bastard' is too good a word for you, you son of a bitch!" Nathaniel snarled.

"It's a waste of time to insult my parenthood," Killoran said in a voice like ice. "But I wouldn't push it if I were you. I would regret having to kill you."

"You think I'm afraid to meet you?"

"I think you're young enough and idealistic enough to think that a just cause will carry you through. You haven't lived long enough to know that only the good die young. You wouldn't stand a chance against me."

"Stop this!" Emma stepped into the room, her voice strong and angry. "You're acting like a couple of children. What makes you think you have any need to defend my honor, Nathaniel?"

"Lord, she's still innocent," Barbara said in disgust, throwing herself down in one of the rickety chairs. "In soul if not in body. Trust me, Emma, dear. One look at your face and we know just how you spent the previous night. Not to mention that bite mark on the side of your neck. Vampire tendencies, Killoran?"

In another lifetime Emma's flush of color would have amused Barbara. In another lifetime she would have watched this little melodrama with cool interest, waiting to see who would battle whom for the honor of the fair damsel. But Nathaniel's righteous indignation, and his very real danger from an experienced duelist like Killoran, made the situation deadly serious.

She was jealous, Barbara realized with sudden shock. And not of the bite mark on the side of Emma's neck, nor of the dazed look of awakened passion in her eyes. Even if Killoran was the first and only man who'd ever resisted Barbara's overtures, it wasn't Killoran she cared about.

It was Nathaniel's blind nobility that made her heart twist and ache. No one had defended her, ever, when she'd needed defending so very badly.

"Lud," she said aloud. "Aren't you making a fuss over nothing? Emma certainly doesn't look as if she's been forced to do anything she didn't want to. I think, dear

Nathaniel, we should take our leave. We're not wanted here, and—"

Something stopped her. Something in Killoran's face. No one else in the room would recognize it, but Barbara knew it. Knew the desperation and emptiness that were always hidden by the brittle smile, the cool distance, the urgent sophistication.

"Indeed," Killoran drawled. "If you're so concerned about Emma, Nathaniel, you may feel free to rescue her from my clutches. Take her back to London with you, posthaste. Take her anywhere." He leaned back, one slim, elegant hand toying with a half-drunk glass of wine. "You may leave Barbara with me."

Even a practiced manipulator like Killoran had managed to stun them into silence. All three stared at him in varying degrees of shock.

It was Emma who spoke first. Vulnerable, foolish Emma, who was clearly in love with him. Most women fell in love with the first man to bed them, Barbara thought cynically. And Killoran was very adept.

"You're sending me away?" she asked.

Killoran glanced at her lazily. "The novelty has worn off, my pet. An occasional infatuated virgin is refreshing every now and then, but in general, I prefer experience. I was thinking I might take Babs to Paris. If I put my mind to it, I think I could manage to incite even her frozen appetites."

"You keep away from her!" Nathaniel said between gritted teeth.

"Are you going to defend every female of my acquaintance against my rapacious appetites, dear boy? You'll grow very weary. If you don't force me to kill you first. Ask Babs. She's been throwing her lovely self at me these past few months. I thought it was time to take pity on her. If you like, you can take over Emma's sexual education. She's an enthusiastic student, and a fast learner. I'll wager in a few months she'll be far more adept than a dedicated whore like Barbara could ever be."

Nathaniel dove at him, his face dark with murderous fury. Barbara shrieked, leaping out of the way, certain they were going to kill each other. The two men went down with a crash, and what Nathaniel possessed in youth and fury, Killoran bettered with experience and cold-blooded intellect. Within moments Nathaniel lay, dazed and motionless, on the hardwood floor.

"You've killed him!" Barbara screamed, rushing to his side.

"Not likely." Killoran rose and took a few uncertain steps back. "I never kill by accident." He glanced around him in mild surprise. "Where did Emma go?"

Nathaniel was still breathing, and Barbara recognized with relief that he was merely dazed. She glanced up at Killoran. "Do you care? You sent her away."

"So I did," he said absently. "It seemed more than time."

"Did you have to be so cruel?"

"I doubt she would have left otherwise. Emma is a very stalwart creature, and it takes a great deal to discourage her." He moved across the room to the table. The wine had spilled, but there still remained a bit in the bottle, and he lifted it to his mouth and poured it down. "Don't you think it's about time to give Nathaniel his conge?"

"I beg your pardon?" She sat back on her heels, staring up at him.

"Take a lesson from me, my dear. Goodness and purity are not for the likes of us. You'll only break the poor boy's heart. And whatever is left of yours as well." He set the empty bottle down with a crash. "Come to Paris with me, Babs, and we'll see if I can't manage to give you a finer appreciation of sex."

"Why? You don't care about me, nor I about you," she said in a low, quiet voice. She realized she still clung to Nathaniel's hand, quite tightly.

Killoran's smile was bleak. "Precisely."

Emma climbed out the window. It wasn't that she thought Killoran or any of the others might stop her. Killoran had sent her away, in the cruelest possible terms, and Lady Barbara could only be rejoicing. If Nathaniel was tempted to help her, it would doubtless make matters worse. She already had too much blood on her hands. She couldn't risk Nathaniel's as well.

No, she climbed out the window simply because she didn't know if she could bear to look at Killoran's cool, distant, wickedly handsome face again. She didn't know whether she would try to kill him. Or burst into tears. Either reaction would get her precisely nowhere, and since her dignity seemed to have vanished with her virginity, her only recourse was to run.

Her first thought was to steal one of the carriage horses. She had no idea whether she'd still be able to ride, or exactly where she would go; she only knew a horse would take her there faster. Of course, there was always the possibility that she could take Killoran's huge black gelding, but if he didn't throw her and kill her, Killoran probably would.

In the end, she didn't have to make a choice. Willie was waiting for her. "There you are, miss," he said, moving to the carriage door and holding it open for her.

She went, for lack of anything better to do. "Where are you taking me?"

"His lordship said that was up to you. You can go back to Curzon Street if you've a mind to, or anywhere else. He's given me instructions to see you safe to whatever destination you like."

"I'd rather be roasted in hell before I go back to Curzon Street," she said in a deceptively calm voice. "Though London sounds acceptable."

"Yes, miss. London it is."

She climbed up into the coach with more speed than grace. Her body ached, and the knowledge of just what activity had caused her discomfort was like a knife to her heart. She sat back against the tufted squabs, and moments later the carriage moved forward. She didn't look out the window at the small hunting lodge. She knew that no one would be watching her leave.

She closed her eyes, letting out a shaky, shuddery breath. She could still feel his mouth against her, still feel the changes he'd wrought in her. The novelty had worn off, he'd said, and she'd had no choice but to believe him.

Why had she kept hoping that beneath his brittle, dark exterior lurked a wounded raven? Why had she thought him capable of love, or caring? He'd looked at her last night in longing, in desperation, and tried to send her away then. But she'd succumbed, like the fool she was, drawn by his wounded charm and his beauty. Foolish enough to think she could heal him.

And in the end, it was she who was shattered.

She'd recover. Of course she would. She was made of strong stock—her father had been of yeoman blood, decent, hardworking, the backbone of England. Her mother had been gentle and loving, faithful and true. Lecherous Uncle Horace had been no blood kin to her, and Cousin Miriam took after her father, not Emma's aunt.

She could weather this. It seemed unlikely that a despoiled virgin could marry decently, but that was the least of her worries. At the moment, she neither wanted to marry nor had any need to. What she did need was her money.

Not all of it. Her father's armament factories had brought in vast amounts of income—there was always a ready market for the tools of war, and Emma's inheritance was more than she could ever use in a lifetime. Cousin Miriam could keep the bulk of it. All that Emma wanted was enough to buy herself a small cottage in the countryside and keep herself safe. From the Killorans and the Darnleys of this world. From her own vulnerable heart.

Somehow she couldn't imagine walking back into that mausoleum of a house in Crouch End and simply demanding money. The very notion made her palms sweat. But she had no choice. There was no one to turn to, no one to help her. No one except someone like Jasper Darnley, who would make his own, far more dangerous claims.

She curled up in one corner of the coach, wrapping her

arms around herself. The fur throw had been left behind, and for a moment Emma remembered lying naked on it, with Killoran stretched above her, staring down into her eyes as if he cared about her. His hands had brushed her body, and in memory her stomach cramped in helpless pain and longing. God, she hated him! And God, she wanted his hands on her once more.

She slept, fitfully, off and on. When she awoke for the last time, it was pitch-dark in the carriage. She was cold, and her face was wet and salty. She backhanded her cheeks and glanced out the window.

She knew they were in the city—the change of the roadway beneath them had echoed in her ears. She couldn't recognize the area of town they were traveling through, though of one thing she was certain. It wasn't Curzon Street, and it wasn't Crouch End.

She banged on the roof of the carriage, but Willie ignored her. She considered opening the door and leaping out onto the cobbled roadway, but something kept her still. There were doubtless worse places to end up than Cousin Miriam's house, but right then she couldn't think of them. She'd been reprieved, like it or not.

The carriage came to a stop. She waited, hands clasped tightly in her lap, listening to the murmur of voices, seeing the glare of an approaching torch. By the time the door was pulled open, it was too bright for her to see, and she warded off the glare with a protesting hand, scowling at Willie's trouble face.

"Where are we?" she demanded. "This isn't Crouch End."

"His lordship told me I wasn't to take you back there. Nor to Lord Darnley's, if you was to ask."

"I thought he told you to take me where I wanted. Why should he care?" she said bitterly.

"He said if you didn't come up with a good idea, I was to bring you here."

She had no choice but to climb out of the carriage. Indeed, if it were up to her, she wouldn't get back in one for the rest of her life. She looked up at the brightly lit house, the silhouetted figure in the open doorway. "What is it?" she asked, starting slowly up the broad front steps. A liveried servant tried to take her arm, but she slapped it away. "A bawdy house?"

"Bring the gel in," a familiar voice trumpeted loudly. Emma was too nearsighted to make out details, but the immensity of the woman's shape couldn't be mistaken. She stumbled, suddenly eager.

"Lady Seldane," she said in a broken voice.

"Bring her in," her ladyship ordered again. "Can't you see the poor gel's half dead with exhaustion and hunger? Damn that Killoran, why does he have to make a botch of everything? Come here, child."

Emma tripped on the last few steps, her strength failing her. In a moment she felt herself enfolded against a massive, scented bosom, and the bellowing murmur in her ear was oddly soothing. "There, there, child. It will be all right. We'll sort things out, I promise you."

She was crying. It was absurd, Emma thought. She never cried. Particularly not in the arms of an intimidating tartar such as Lady Seldane. But weep she did, and all her ladyship did was hold her like the mother she'd never known.

Eventually the storm of tears came to a halt. Eventually she was able to disentangle herself from Lady Seldane's hearty embrace, to manage a watery smile.

"Much better, child," her ladyship said approvingly. "Everyone needs to give in to strong hysterics now and then, but afterward you must pick yourself up and get on with life. I've ordered you a bath, a light collation, and your rooms are all ready for you. For the next twenty-four hours I want you to rest. I want you pampered and cosseted and looked after."

"But what am I going to do…?"

"Don't worry about that now. We'll come up with something sooner or later. I have a few ideas of my own. Trust me, child. We'll make things right."

"I shouldn't be here," Emma protested faintly. "You don't realize what I've done."

"What have you done?"

"I… That is… Killoran…"

"He took you to his bed, didn't he? Lucky gel. If I were twenty years younger and about two stone lighter, there'd be no way he'd escape me. I gather you aren't quite so sanguine about it. No wonder. He made a botch of it, which is a good sign. A very good sign indeed."

Emma looked up at her through tear-drenched eyes. "What do you mean?"

"Killoran knows how to handle things with exquisite delicacy. It would have been a simple matter to deflower you and then dismiss you so gracefully that you barely noticed. Instead you come running to London in hysterics, and arrive on my doorstep complete with a terse note from his high-and-mighty lordship telling me to take care of you. Most promising, I call it."

"Promising of what?"

Lady Seldane's smile was mysterious. "That there's redemption in the lad, after all. Come along now, Emma. Let's get you settled. There'll be time to work this through soon enough."

She wanted to protest, but the fit of stupid, hated tears had taken the last of her reserves. She went willingly, to the bath, to the tray of dainty, invalid food in her room, to the silk-sheeted bed in the vast, elegant chamber. And then she slept.

Only to dream of Killoran.

"You're lucky he didn't kill you," Barbara said flatly.

Nathaniel stared up at her. He was lying on a bed, albeit an uncomfortable one, and the day was far advanced. The room was cold, he had the world's most vicious headache, and Barbara knelt on the mattress beside him, smelling of flowers.

"I'm surprised he didn't. Where is he?"

"Gone to some party. At Sanderson's, I believe. We weren't invited."

"I would have thought you'd be invited anywhere."

"Killoran said specifically that I wasn't to come. I gather it's rather wild."

"Aren't you used to that sort of thing?" he asked bitterly.

So it went, Barbara thought numbly. He'd finally accepted her for what she was. "Quite," she said briskly, climbing off the bed. "But since he's decided to take me to Paris, I expect he's feeling a bit territorial."

"Are you going to go with him?"

"Why shouldn't I?" She wandered over to the shuttered window, keeping her back to Nathaniel. She didn't quite trust her carefully schooled expression. "After all, Killoran is reputed to be a marvelous lover. I'd be foolish to turn down the chance to be his mistress, would I not?"

"So you admit you aren't his lover already?"

"It would be a waste of time to deny it. You're very observant, Nathaniel." She turned and gave him her most enchanting smile.

"You don't love him."

"I don't love anyone. I don't believe in it. That's for the innocents of this world. Go back to Northumberland, Nathaniel. Find another Miss Pottle. Haven't you learned by now that Killoran and I are two of a kind? We're not for the likes of you."

He was silent for a moment, and she turned away again, rather than see the contempt and disappointment on his face. It was all for the best, she reminded herself. Killoran had just given her a salutary lesson in how to be cruel in order to be kind. She could do no less.

"I suppose he would kill me," Nathaniel said after a moment, his voice surprisingly wry.

She turned. "Undoubtedly."

"Then there will have to be another way."

"Another way for what?"

"To change his mind about you. I can't count on you to have any sense of self-preservation—obviously you've been intent on going to hell since you were...what did you say? Barely out of leading strings. Someday you'll tell me why."

"Never."

He ignored her fierce protest. "So I shall simply have to rely on Killoran to give you over. I'm going to marry you, Barbara. And I've grown fond of Killoran, despite his black temper."

"You hit your head too hard," she said flatly. "You've gone raving mad."

He sat up, wincing in pain, and then smiled at her. It was a heartbreaking, beguiling smile, one that took all her effort to resist. "No, my love. I think Killoran knocked some sense into me. You'll like Northumberland. It's wild and beautiful and untamed. Like you."

"I love the city. I like shops and the theater and gay parties."

"You love me," Nathaniel said. "And sooner or later you'll realize it."

Ah, but she already realized it, she thought miserably. She just wasn't about to admit it. "You're quite young," she said. "You'll get over it."

"Over you? Never."

And she wondered whether she dared to believe him.

"Come here, love," he said softly.

She kept her distance, wary. "Why?"

"I want you to lie down beside me."

She felt her mouth twist into an ugly smile. "Of course you do," she said with false sprightliness. "I wondered how long it would take you to change your mind." She started toward him, lifting her skirts, a practiced smile on her face.

He caught her hand in his, forcing her to drop the heavy silk as he pulled her closer. "No, Barbara," he said. "I want you to lie with me. That's all."

"Don't be absurd," she mocked him. "Aren't you a man at all? I'm willing to do anything you want me to, and you—"

"I want you to lie with me. Beside me, in my arms. All night long. And nothing more."

She stared at him. At his strong hand on her slender wrist, at his fierce blue eyes. And uncertainty swept over her.

"You don't want me?" she asked in a small, frightened voice.

His smile could have broken her fragile heart. "Oh, love," he murmured, "I want you more than life itself. But not until you're sure."

He tugged, gently. She went, willingly. The bed was narrow and sagging, his body was strong and warm, and he put his arms around her, holding her close against him, tucking her face against his shoulder.

She held herself stiffly, unused to gentleness, unused to tenderness. But when he stroked her hair away from her face, dropped a kiss on her forehead, and settled back with a sigh, she knew he meant what he'd said. He was hard with wanting her, but he wasn't going to take her until she was ready.

The room was dark now, night having fallen. She felt very safe, safe enough to warn him. "It will be a long time," she whispered against the strong column of his neck.

"I'm a patient man," he said softly. "I'll wait."

CHAPTER EIGHTEEN

"I do not understand the man," Lady Seldane announced. "It really is most unlike him."

Emma glanced up at her hostess. She had been in residence for a week, a week in which Lady Seldane had fed her, cosseted her, teased her, and played cards with her, all the while refusing to discuss either Killoran or the future. Now, over an elegant dinner a deux, she'd finally brought him up, and Emma didn't know whether she was grateful or sorry.

"He's back in town, isn't he?" She kept her voice deliberately toneless as she stirred her soup.

"Who, Killoran? He's been back these past four days. Most odd—not a word from him, not even a simple inquiry as to your well-being. Most unlike the lad. He was always exact about the social details, and outrageous about larger issues."

"Perhaps he considers me beneath his notice."

"Or too much to deal with," Lady Seldane said shrewdly. "Either way, he's keeping his distance. I am not, by nature, a patient woman, and I dislike seeing you miserable."

"I'm sorry," Emma said swiftly. "I've trespassed shamefully on your hospitality. I have been thinking a great deal these past few days, and making plans—"

"You're not going back to that harridan you told me about," the old woman interrupted sharply. "Killoran says she's not to be trusted."

"His lordship has a great many opinions for someone who has taken himself out of my life. Cousin Miriam is a difficult woman, but one of the highest moral character."

Lady Seldane sniffed. "I knew she sounded dreadful. You're not to go back to her, Emma."

"I have no intention of doing so. I thought I would go away." She said it half defiantly, expecting a loud protest.

She was disappointed.

"There's merit in that notion, gel. For one thing, you'll be out of Darnley's clutches. Lord only knows where the creature is, but I don't trust him. Why in the world Killoran didn't simply call him out and finish the matter years ago is beyond me. It would have made things so very simple."

"Life is seldom simple," Emma said, giving up all pretense of eating.

"Wise for your tender years, child," Lady Seldane murmured approvingly. "If you were to disappear, it might make Killoran come to his senses a bit more quickly. He's spent the past few days doing his damnedest to go straight to hell, and as long as he thinks you're safe with me, he can carry on like that."

"I thought he was planning to take Lady Barbara to Paris."

"He said that? How absurd of him. They wouldn't suit

at all. She's back in town, as is Killoran's guest, but I've heard no word of assignations or new involvements. I gather Lady Barbara has been keeping her distance from the pair of them, and I make it my business to hear everything, even if I rarely leave my house." Her eyes narrowed. "I do know that Killoran has done everything in his power to bring himself to ruin. He has gambled, far more wildly and excessively than is his wont—"

"I thought he never lost."

"Don't interrupt me, Emma," Lady Seldane said. "Apparently Killoran has managed to rise to the challenge and lost a great deal since he's been back. He's drinking too much, he's playing too deep, and on top of that, he's made a perfectly idiotic wager that he can ride that monstrous black horse of his to Dover in five hours. Wagered that ornate mausoleum he lives in on the outcome, as well as a large amount of money. If it weren't so pigheaded stubborn of him, I'd find it most promising."

"No one could make that ride in five hours. It's not humanly possible," Emma said. "He'll break his neck."

"Oh, if anyone could do it, Killoran could. He has a rare gift with horseflesh. But I'm not certain anyone could do it, particularly someone in Killoran's current state of mind."

"Then why do you consider it promising?"

Lady Seldane just looked at her for a moment. "You're very young, aren't you, child? If the man didn't care about you, he'd hardly be so set on destroying himself, would he? Now, where would you like to go?"

"It would be better if I made my own arrangements. I've trespassed on your kindness enough as it is."

Lady Seldane's reply was suitably coarse. "Don't be absurd, child. I live a boring life, and you've brought color into it. Now, where shall we go?"

"We?" Emma echoed, astonished. "But you never go anywhere."

"It's been too damned long. I've a mind to see Ireland again. I have an estate near Sligo. What say we go there and rusticate for a bit?"

Emma looked at her for a long moment. It sounded like heaven. Without Killoran, it sounded like hell. "Yes," she said weakly, turning back to her soup.

"You'll cheer up," Lady Seldane announced confidently. "Let's forget about the past and concentrate on your future. We'll find you a husband, my dear. A tall, handsome Irishman, with poetry in his soul. How does that sound?"

Emma glanced at her across the broad expanse of table. "Killoran is Irish."

Lady Seldane smiled. "I know, dear. I know."

"They're planning to go where?" Darnley thundered.

Miriam DeWinter barely blinked. She despised Jasper Darnley to the bottom of her soul, but she was a practical woman. She needed the man. If she had any chance of succeeding without him, she would have done so. But now that Killoran knew who and what she was, it made things doubly difficult. Not, however, with this recent turn of events.

"Ireland," Miriam said again, in the patient tone of one trying to communicate with a mental incompetent. "I've had people watching her, and I just received word.

I was afraid I was going to have to handle this myself."
She glanced around Darnley's withdrawing room. It was
stuffy, airless, and far too hot. In all, not a bad sort of
room.

"And Killoran? Is he going with her?"

"I don't believe so. As far as anyone can tell, he hasn't
seen her in more than a week. He's severed all connection with her."

An unpleasant expression crossed Darnley's pasty
face, and he flicked a greasy crumb off his baby-blue
satin waistcoat. "What makes you think I'm still interested in your little plot, woman? It's Killoran I'm after. If
he has no interest in your wretched cousin, why should
I?"

Miriam considered just how far to push him. Her informants were vastly knowledgeable, but to her experienced eye, Darnley was not quite sane. Since the last
time she'd confronted him, he seemed to have deterio-
rated even more, both physically and mentally. His color
was bad, his eyes were faintly glazed, and he moved like
a man in constant, furious pain.

"I'd gathered you had a weakness for young women
with red hair," she said delicately.

"Why should I want Killoran's discards?"

"Because if you went after her, Killoran would be
forced to interfere."

"I can't imagine why. Killoran has never been the sort
for heroic gestures. When my—when a young woman
turned to him for help, he ignored her pleas, and she
ended up killing herself. It was his fault," Darnley said

fiercely. "He's hardly likely to bestir himself for a chance-met trollop."

Miriam shrugged. "Perhaps you're right. Perhaps he's content to let her go. You're a gamester, Lord Darnley, experienced in playing the odds. As for me, I'm certain Killoran will go after her. He deserves to be punished for murdering my father in cold blood, for luring my innocent niece away from the bosom of her family, for despoiling and then abandoning her. I mean to see they both pay. Killoran for his evil, Emma for her licentiousness. I can do it without your help." She rose, her stays creaking, and started toward the door.

"I haven't dismissed you yet!" Darnley snapped at her.

"I am neither your servant nor your subject." Miriam paused, glaring at him. He was petty and evil, and she knew she could make him do as she wanted, needed, him to do.

"Ireland, eh?" Darnley said, appearing to deliberate. "We can't have that, now, can we? I still have some unfinished business with the young lady. I'm not the squeamish sort, after all. Perhaps Killoran taught her a few pleasing tricks before dismissing her."

"You'll have to do something quickly," Miriam said. "They're planning to leave within a few days."

Darnley glared at her. "I never liked taking orders from women. Particularly from the bourgeoisie."

"But you want Killoran dead, do you not? And you want my cousin as your whore? I'm showing you how to get those two things. I only ask one thing in return—that when you're finished with her, you kill her. Either here or in Ireland, it does not matter to me."

"You'd hardly want to miss your chance at being in at the kill, would you?" Darnley moved closer to her. He smelled of drugs and sickness and evil, but Miriam didn't flinch. "I might even blood you," he said, touching an iron-gray curl.

She turned the full force of her baleful gaze upon him. And Darnley dropped his hand, backing away as if he'd touched an adder. "Kill her," she said again. "It's all I ask."

And Darnley nodded, a faint smile on his rouged mouth.

"This wager is madness." Killoran glanced up at Nathaniel's troubled face. He'd already drunk far too much brandy, though few people would have been able to tell. He had every intention of drinking a great deal more, and the only question in his mind was whether to wait until he arrived at his club or simply continue here alone.

He shuffled the cards lazily in his hands, staring at them without seeing. "I don't believe I asked for your opinion, dear boy. But then, that's never stopped you before. You are the most tediously judgmental soul. Perhaps it's time for you to return to the bosom of your family. Surely you've seen enough of the wickedness of the city to last a lifetime."

"You'll kill yourself," Nathaniel persevered.

"I don't really give a bloody damn." Killoran dealt swiftly, then scooped up the cards once more. "You shouldn't either. If I break my neck, then I won't be taking Lady Barbara to the Continent. Which will leave her available. I doubt she'll take you, though. She's solidly determined to go to hell, and you're just a bit too good for her."

Nathaniel took a menacing step toward him, and Killoran raised a weary hand. "Not again, dear boy. If you don't stop wanting to trounce me for insulting your lady love, you'll end up dead. I'm a forbearing man, but recently my sanguine temper has been sorely tried."

"You're not taking Barbara to Paris."

Killoran shrugged. "I offered. She agreed. There's not much I can do about it at this point. It's a matter of honor."

"Honor?" Nathaniel said. "I would say that's the one thing missing in this whole sordid mess."

"You should know. You positively reek of honor and rectitude and moral perfection," Killoran said with a faint sneer. "I'm surprised you can even bring yourself to keep company with two sinners such as Barbara and I."

"I want you to rescind your invitation, Killoran."

"Do you indeed? And why should I? Barbara is intelligent, beautiful, and experienced. A jewel for any man's bed."

"Then why didn't you take her before?"

"Perverse of me, I know. I found Emma a bit...distracting. But now that she's safely away, I can concentrate on things better suited to my nature. Such as Barbara Fitzhugh."

"How do you know Emma's safe?"

Killoran glanced at him lazily. "You *do* think badly of me, don't you? With just cause. However, on this occasion I was uncharacteristically sentimental. I made certain Willie delivered her someplace safe."

"And where is that?"

"Still pining for her? You really should make up your mind—you can't save every woman from my depredations. I thought you lusted after Lady Barbara."

"I'm in love with her," Nathaniel said in a quiet voice.

Killoran stifled his momentary irritation, though he wasn't sure why he made the effort. "I'm certain she'll find that extremely gratifying. Half the men in London have considered themselves in love with her, and she's rewarded them for their devotion. Just so long as your father doesn't hear about it..."

"You don't understand. I intend to marry her."

Killoran lay the cards facedown. "Don't be absurd. She's the daughter of an earl, and you're nothing more than a landholder. She's way above your touch—you're English enough to understand these things. You're a tediously decent, boring, honorable young man, and she's a dedicated whore. You're way above her touch. It's an impossible match."

"Nevertheless, I mean to marry her."

"Before or after I take her to Paris?" Killoran inquired lazily.

"You're not taking her to Paris."

"To be sure, I might break my neck during the run to Dover. You could always hope for that. But assuming I survive, then I have every intention of taking her with me."

"You don't want to."

"Don't be absurd. I make it a practice never to do anything I don't wish to do."

"It's not Barbara you want in your bed, and we both know it."

"You're annoying me again," Killoran said pleasantly. "I may have to kill you, after all."

"If need be. That's the only way you'll take her."

Killoran stared at him out of slitted eyes. "There's another way," he murmured, refilling his wineglass with a deceptively steady hand and pouring one for Nathaniel as well. "You can play me for her."

"What?"

"You heard me. We'll game for the fair lady's favors. Whoever wins takes her. The loser retires gracefully with no more complaint."

"You *are* a savage!"

Killoran gave him his most beguiling smile. "I'm Irish, remember? A nation of savages. Shall we say piquet? Simple enough even for an inexperienced gamester such as you to stand a fighting chance."

"I would never—"

"It's your only chance," Killoran interrupted smoothly.

He was teaching the boy to hate. Surely if he had only an ounce of decent feeling, he should regret that. But decent feeling seemed to be a conspicuous lack in his life. He sat waiting patiently for Nathaniel to take the bait.

And Nathaniel did, pulling out the chair opposite Killoran and reaching for the cards. "You're a man without decency or honor, Killoran," he said coldly.

"And you have more than your fair share. Suppose I strip just a little bit of that righteousness away from you, dear boy? All in the name of a proper education."

"You can't."

"Ah, a challenge. We shall see, dear boy." He pushed

the second glass of wine across the green baize table. "We shall see."

At first Nathaniel's skill was unexceptional. He played with the same steady intelligence and reason with which he conducted his life, and Killoran matched it, toying with him. By the time they'd opened the third bottle of claret, Nathaniel was down a bit, but not enough to signify. And that was when Killoran went on the attack.

He played with reckless abandon, with the wild instinct that always served him well. By the time Jeffries had brought and uncorked the fourth bottle, Nathaniel was more deeply in debt than his father's estate could handle, and there was a look of glazed desperation in his eyes.

Killoran watched, considered, and set the trap most carefully. He didn't stop to consider why he was doing it. As long as Nathaniel remained in London, living at Curzon Street, he would be a constant, infuriating reminder of all that Killoran could never be. The only way to be free of him, truly free, was to bring him down to his own level. He couldn't do it by taking the boy to a brothel or encouraging drunkenness; Nathaniel was too stalwart to succumb. But he could do something far worse.

He could, by simple manipulation, make Nathaniel betray the most solemn point of honor in all of England. He could make him cheat at cards.

He set it up so carefully. Despite the fact that he was one bottle ahead of his young protégé, he was far more in control of his faculties. He recognized the desperation in Nathaniel's eyes, in the faint tremble of his hands; he'd seen it often enough, in the young men who were fool enough to try to break his unnatural luck. He hadn't taken pity on them. He wouldn't take pity on Nathaniel.

"You're thirty thousand pounds down, my boy," he observed, dealing with careless dexterity. "Perhaps now might be the time to quit."

"Thirty thousand pounds," Nathaniel echoed in a hollow voice.

"Not to mention Lady Barbara's favors. I'm afraid you're not much of a challenge to a player of my skill. I'll have to see if I can find better sport at my club."

"One more hand," the young man said.

"Very well. I'm disposed to be generous. We'll play for the thirty thousand pounds. If you win this hand, your debt is canceled."

"If I lose?" he demanded hoarsely.

"Then I expect your father will be most displeased."

"We don't have that kind of money."

"That is a great deal too bad. A lesson in gaming, my boy. Never wager more than you can afford to lose."

"What about Lady Barbara?"

"We can throw her in as well. I won't lose, you know." Killoran pushed the cards across the table. "Your deal."

He rose, left the table, and applied himself to the bottle of claret. He could see Nathaniel's desperate countenance reflected in the mirror, the faint beading of sweat on his brow. He stalled as long as he could, then nearly snarled.

Nathaniel dealt clumsily, but fairly. Missing his chance.

Killoran took his seat once more, picking up the cards. Nathaniel, in all his unwitting honesty, had dealt him a winning hand.

He could see from the way Nathaniel clutched his hand

that his own was very bad indeed. And he had yet to cheat.

Obviously the boy needed stronger temptation. Killoran rose again, knocking the table with his leg, just enough to overturn the cards, exposing aces, kings, and queens. He turned his back, ostensibly missing his own clumsy move, and wandered to the window.

He was even worse a cheat than he was a card player, Killoran thought wearily when he regained his seat, a cigarillo between his teeth. It would take more than his clumsy efforts to win the game.

Killoran stared down at his hand. Even by cheating, Nathaniel could not win against the devil's own luck. There was only one thing for it, then. Killoran must cheat as well.

He didn't stop to consider the ramifications of what he was doing. "Sorry, old man. I've lost track of the cards. Could we play this hand over?"

And Nathaniel, flushed, miserable, and guilty, nodded, pushing his cheating, losing cards away from him.

It was over in a trice. Although Killoran had never cheated in his life, he knew cards far better than he knew his own soul. The proper cards were dealt, swiftly, to the proper players. The light of triumph wiped the anxiety from Nathaniel's face, at least for the moment.

"Amazing," Killoran said lazily when Nathaniel lay down his cards. "You must have the devil's own luck as well. I thought you were under the hatches for sure."

"You'll tear up my vouchers?"

Killoran smiled faintly. "Indeed. Shall I write you one

for Lady Barbara, or are you going to inform her yourself?"

Nathaniel's momentary triumph vanished in utter
panic. "What do you mean?"

"She'll need to know you've won her favors in a game
of cards. She'll hardly accept the fact that I've changed
my mind. My sins are great, but I neither lie nor cheat
at cards."

The color in Nathaniel's face deepened. "Are you sug-
gesting I won that last hand by cheating?"

"I know that you didn't," Killoran said calmly.

It was small comfort to Nathaniel. Killoran watched
him leave the room, and he told himself he could count
one more disillusioned soul to his credit.

He sat alone in the room as the candles guttered and
went out, the fire died into embers. He had no idea where
Nathaniel had disappeared to, but he doubted he'd gone in
search of his lady love. He had demons to exorcise now,
placed there by Killoran's wicked hands.

At least he could be assured that Emma was safe with
Lady Seldane.

If there was one person on this earth he trusted, it was
Letty Seldane. She was a tart-tongued old woman, his
only connection with his gentle mother, and he allowed
himself an errant fondness for her. She would keep Emma
safe enough.

Had Emma managed to forget about him? Did she hate
him? Long for him? Pity him?

She was entirely capable of that last, horrifying alternative. Emma saw things too clearly. She wouldn't waste
too much time on his worthless soul. She would know

that the blame rested nowhere but on his wicked shoulders, and she would move on. Lady Seldane would find her a good man, a decent man, make certain she was settled safely. So far from London, and from Killoran, that he might forget about her.

And if, by any perverse twist of fate, her memory intruded, he would simply consider her a momentary aberration. A fit of madness, brought about by the devil knew what.

He wouldn't think about her. He'd concentrate on Darnley. The blood of his worst enemy would go a great way toward cleansing his soul. Or muddying it sufficiently.

The night was still and dark, with scarcely a sliver of moon overhead. Nathaniel pulled his cloak tightly around him and walked blindly, neither knowing nor caring where he was going.

He'd betrayed his honor. He still couldn't believe what he had done. He'd succumbed to temptation and glanced at Killoran's hand. It went against everything he'd ever been taught. Better to have murdered, better to have stolen or committed adultery, than to cheat at cards.

And God had punished him. Even cheating, he'd still lost, and been glad of it. Until the final hand had wickedly, perversely, turned his way.

He'd almost cheated a second time. Almost told Killoran his hand was worthless and tossed it in the pile before his host could check. Not that Killoran would doubt him. He considered Nathaniel a perfect little saint, above lying, above falsehood. Above cheating at cards.

He couldn't stay in that room, in that house, a moment longer without confessing what he had done. And that was the one thing he wouldn't do.

He'd betrayed his principles for a reason. For more than just a reason. He'd betrayed them for love. Barbara would go with Killoran to Paris, Killoran would take her, and neither of them had the sense to realize they didn't want it. If the price for saving Barbara was his honor, then that price was cheap enough. He'd do it, and more, a thousand times.

And live with the consequences.

It wasn't until he was standing outside Barbara's small, elegant town house that he realized where his feet had taken him. Most of the windows were dark, and he stared up at them in blind frustration.

She hadn't allowed him anywhere near her in the past week. When he'd awakened in Killoran's hunting lodge, he'd been alone in that narrow bed, only the faint scent of her perfume reminding him that she'd slept peacefully, trustingly in his arms. He hadn't seen her since. She'd refused him when he'd called, and she'd kept her distance from Killoran, and from society as well.

Was she there now, alone? Or had she taken another of her myriad lovers and was even now disporting with him, laughing about Killoran and his lovesick cousin?

No, she wouldn't laugh at him. He knew that, deep in his heart. Killoran had said he must tell her the truth, and he knew he couldn't wait any longer. He climbed the front steps and pounded on the door, no longer caring whom he disturbed.

It took a long while for his summons to be answered.

The old woman who served as Barbara's housekeeper peered at him in the darkness. "What the hell do you think you're doing, waking a decent household at this hour—" she began. And then her gaze narrowed. "Oh," she said. "It's you."

"Is Lady Barbara at home?"

"If she weren't, it would hardly be your business, now, would it, Mr. Hepburn?" she countered crossly. "The middle of the night is no time for social calls."

He waited for her to slam the door in his face, but instead she opened it wide, ushering him in. Lady Barbara stood behind her, watching him, her eyes troubled.

"What's happened?" she asked. "Why are you here?"

"I have to talk to you."

"At this hour?"

"It couldn't wait."

The old lady snorted. "I'll take my old bones to bed, my lady. Unless you have need of me."

Barbara waved a dismissing hand in her direction. She waited until the woman had shuffled off into the shadows, then turned to look at Nathaniel.

"Why have you refused to see me?" he asked.

For a moment Barbara said not a word. Then she sighed wearily. She was holding a candelabrum in one slender hand, and he expected her to lead him into the salon. Instead she sank down on the wide, curving stairs and drew her night rail around her more securely.

For the first time he noticed how unlike her the garment was. He would have thought she'd sleep in some diaphanous creation, or in nothing at all. But she was wrapped in plain white flannel, warm and high-necked and virginal.

"It seemed the wisest course," she replied at last. "There's no future for us; you should know that as well as I do. I'm going to Paris with Killoran, you're going to find a nice, decent girl to marry—"

"You're not going to Paris with Killoran," he said abruptly.

"You can't stop me."

"I have already. I won you."

He could feel her sudden stillness. "You did what?"

"I played cards with Killoran, with you as the wager. I won."

"I see," she said after a long moment. "Killoran never loses. He must have cheated. How very lowering."

"He didn't cheat," Nathaniel said, staring down at her. "I did."

Barbara wasn't sure whether she wanted to laugh or to cry. Her stalwart hero, brought to this level. Wagering her favors on a game of cards, betraying his honor to win her. And there was no one to blame but her own worthless self, again.

"I see," she said with deceptive calm. "Then if you've gone to such lengths, I suppose I'd best make good on the wager." She reached up and began to unfasten the high-necked gown. "Would you have me here on the stairs, or would you prefer a bed? It's your choice, of course, but—"

His hand covered hers hard, stopping her. "You don't understand," he said.

"Oh, I understand very well. You wanted me. You won me. Rather silly, when you could have had me at any time, and you know it. I have no idea why you've shown such forbearance. I'm quite experienced, and adept at any number of variations, but I still think you'll find I'm hardly worth the trouble. My skills are highly over-rated. You could have received the same services from any number of society trulls."

"Don't."

"Don't?" she said brightly, her beautiful blue eyes daring his contempt. "My dear boy. And you are a boy, aren't you? I've bedded so many men I've lost count. Everything you've heard about me is true. And worse. I'm glad you've decided to stop all this tedious delay. I'm not certain you'll find I'm worth the anticipation." She waited with detached patience for his face to turn cold.

He hadn't moved. He stared at her for a long, breathless moment. And then he spoke.

"Barbara," he said very gently, his hand sliding up to touch her face, "I won't let anyone hurt you again."

She'd steeled herself for condemnation. She'd sought rage and fury. Instead, his soft words were the crudest blow of all.

She felt unbidden tears well up in her eyes as she fought the insidious effect of his words, and she flinched away from his sweet touch, unable to bear it. "I hate you," she whispered hoarsely.

He stared at her for another long moment, and his cool, strong fingers slid against her throat. "No, you don't," he said, his voice suddenly sure. And he no longer sounded like a boy at all. "You love me. And I'm going to prove it to you." And he leaned down and put his mouth against hers, featherlight. And so unbearably beautiful that she began to cry.

CHAPTER NINETEEN

Barbara closed her eyes, holding herself very still. She was accounted an expert at kissing, yet she didn't want to kiss Nathaniel. She wanted him to kiss her as he was kissing her, his lips brushing hers, back and forth, softly, then traveling across her cheekbones to press against each eyelid.

She was trembling, she who never trembled. This time he wouldn't pull back. This time she would bed the man she loved, and nothing but disaster would come of it.

A faint, whimpering sound bubbled forth from her throat, and she tried to catch it back, but he stopped. His hands were on hers, clutched tightly in her lap, and he drew back. She didn't want to open her eyes, but his hands were strong and warm on hers, and slowly she looked up at him.

Somewhere she found her faltering bravery. "Don't you want to do this, after all?" she asked him.

God, his smile! It should be a crime for a man to have a smile as lovely as his. "Not if you don't. What are you afraid of, love? I won't hurt you. You know that, don't you?"

Her mouth curved in a bitter smile, and she managed what she thought was a credible yawn. "I'm merely afraid I'll be bored," she replied. "That's always a danger if you put it off for too long. It probably would have been better if we'd given in to it days ago. Then we'd be well past it."

"Would we?" he murmured. She'd wanted him to pull away from her, hurt, with childish, outraged pride. His hands still held hers. "What are you really afraid of, love?"

"Don't call me love! I'm not your love, I'm not any-one's love—" His mouth stopped hers, gently, and she sighed, the anger evaporating.

He kissed her with slow, deliberate care, seducing her so skillfully that she found she was clutching his shoul-ders, tightly, and the quiet little sound that came from the back of her throat sounded like a mewl of pleasure. One that was real, unrehearsed, unbidden.

He drew back, and his mouth was damp from hers. Her breasts were hard, sensitive against the soft cotton of her night rail, and she felt a strange, unaccustomed ache deep inside. She wanted him to put his arms around her, but she was afraid, so afraid.

He knew it. He knew what no man had ever guessed, and her fear grew, so that she wanted to push him away, to lash and belittle him with her vicious tongue.

"Well," she said tartly, staring up at him as she crouched on the stairs. "Shall I lift my skirts?"

"You can't drive me away, Barbara. Not this time." And he scooped her effortlessly up in his arms.

She wanted to mock him for the romantic gesture, but she couldn't. She was unaccountably close to tears;

she put her head against his strong shoulder and closed her eyes.

He found her bedroom easily enough—she'd left the door open when she'd heard him in the street, and a fire was burning brightly in the hearth.

It was a whore's bedroom, and she knew it. She'd decorated it with an eye toward sin, and when he laid her down amid the red velvet hangings and the indecent carvings, she felt like weeping.

He stretched out next to her, and there was an unexpected hint of laughter in his deep voice. "I've never seen a room quite like this. I must say the night wear doesn't really match the decor."

"I can take it off," she said breathlessly. His strong hand skimmed across her stomach.

"There's no hurry, love."

His touch, firm yet gentle through the soft cotton, made her want to scream. Yes, there was a hurry. She wanted him to strip off his clothes and climb on top of her, to pound away and spend his passion in her body, then roll over and fall into a loud, snoring sleep. Only to awake and creep away in the cold light of morning, ashamed and relieved that she wasn't going to make a fuss about it.

Ah, but he was paying no attention to what she wanted. Or rather, too much attention. When his hands touched her breasts through the fabric, she moaned, not in artifice but in a shock of desire. When his hand slid beneath the full skirt of her night rail, caressing her legs, she moved restlessly. When he pulled the cloth over her head, she let it go clumsily, forgetting the coquettish tricks she had perfected.

Men liked her breasts. She was used to enduring their lavish attention. Nathaniel was no different, and yet he was. When his mouth touched her bare breast, the tip beaded up in a tight little nub of pain and pleasure, and the burning in her belly grew and centered between her legs.

She was no fool. She guessed at what she was feeling. For the first time in her life, this country boy, this man, was making her feel things she'd never thought she could.

She fought it. His mouth moved to her other breast, and she put her hands to his head, to push him away.

But she couldn't do it. She found she was cradling him against her, and when his hand moved between her legs, she first tightened against the invasion, then arched her hips.

She should have stripped his clothes from him. She should have climbed over him and used her mouth, on his flat male nipples, on his cock. She should have stopped him, turned the tables, controlled him. But she couldn't.

She could only lie there against the pristine whiteness of her sheets, surrounded by the whore's bed hangings, and watch as he tore his clothes off with awkward, passionate good humor.

He was beautiful in the firelight, his body strong and taut and finely chiseled. She wanted to tell him so, wanted to tell him she loved him, more than she deserved to love, but he kissed her again, and the time was past, the fires were burning hotter still, and when he knelt between her legs, powerful in the flickering light, she couldn't even bring herself to tell him where to find the jar of French unguent that would ease his entry. He was very large, and much smaller men had had difficulty without its aid.

But she was hot, and damp, and he braced himself above her, resting against her, and she knew she wanted him. Wanted him to complete it, finish it, now.

He pushed against her, sliding in deep, smoothly, and she let out a small cry of wonder, clutching his shoulders, waiting for the tremors to stop and the coldness to settle back down around her.

But the ice that encased her had melted. And when he moved, she moved with him, automatically at first, and then with heat, and passion, and a desperate need that she couldn't even begin to voice. It frightened her, this need. This man, who knew her better than she knew herself. He knew how to touch her, how to move within her, how to reach down and stroke her, ways other men had touched her but had never moved her.

He understood her choked, breathy little cry, so different from the studied sounds she usually made. He knew her restlessness, her heat, and her need. He knew how to love her. And when the first explosion hit her, it was so powerful, so unexpected, that she screamed, clutching at him, and his formidable control vanished, and he pushed deep, holding her, filling her, giving to her instead of taking.

He sank down over her, covering her body completely with his larger one, and through the stray tremors that still danced within her body she waited for him to sleep. But his hand threaded through her hair, his labored breathing slowed, and his teeth caught her earlobe.

It was then that she cried. Loud, noisy sobs, filling the room, which she made no attempt at quieting. He rolled off her, and she expected him to leave, and she didn't care, she hated him, and she told him, noisily, as he simply pulled her into his arms, wrapping his body around her, wrapping the red covers around them, and held her during the storm of tears. He kissed her swollen eyelids, he kissed her mouth, he held her so firmly that she couldn't run from him, couldn't escape.

"It's not fair," she wept against his strong, warm chest, the golden-brown hairs tickling her nose. "I don't want to love you."

"I know you don't, angel."

"I'm not an angel," she howled. "I'm a whore, a slut, a worthless—" He put his hand over her mouth, hard, and for the first time she saw real anger.

"No one can call my wife a whore," he said tersely. "Not even you."

"It won't work. I can't marry you, Nathaniel."

"I'm not giving you any choice in the matter. You've compromised me," he said, kissing the side of her neck. "You'll have to marry me."

"You don't understand. I've tried to tell you. I've been a whore all my life."

"All your life is a long time."

"Since I was five years old." The words were out before she could stop them, and she waited, in silence, for his disgust, his withdrawal.

His arms were still strong around her, his voice measured, calm. "A child is not a whore. A child is a victim."

"Even when she's been delivered by willing parents?

And told to please the old gentleman, and do anything he asks of her, and not to cry, no matter what?"

The arms around her were like iron. Unbreakable. "Delivered to whom?"

"The Duke of Castor."

She felt the breath leave his body, the tension dissipate. "A royal duke," he said. "It's a shame he's already dead. I would have killed him for you."

The words were so prosaic, she felt dizzy. "Nathaniel," she said weakly. "Ever since…"

"Ever since then, you've been punishing yourself for something that wasn't your fault," he said, oddly, tenderly, stern. "But you've done it for long enough, my love. You'll marry me. You'll live a faithful, devout life from now on and even manage to make me seem like a wastrel."

"I can't…"

"You have no choice in the matter," he told her once more. "You'll marry me. Because, though you've been very foolish for a great many years, you're far from stupid. And even if you wanted to keep punishing yourself, you're too softhearted to punish me as well. Marry me, love."

She stared up at him. He was mad, he was beautiful, and he was hers. As she lay there in the waning firelight, wrapped in his arms, anything seemed possible. "If you still want me in the morning," she said, suddenly shy, she who had never been shy in her life.

"I'll want you on my deathbed, when I'm an old, old man." She didn't believe him. But she loved him, so she smiled through her tears, and twined her arms around his neck, and held him close. And she was the one who fell into a deep, dreamless sleep.

Emma stepped out into the dark and empty streets of London, alone. She expected she would have more than enough time to consider the rashness and possible ingratitude of her actions. Running away from Lady Seldane, a woman who had offered her care and comfort at the worst time in her life, was hardly the wisest course of action. She had taken her hospitality and her money and crept out of the house, leaving no more than a note of thanks and apology. Her motives were noble, but as she moved quietly down the icy streets of predawn London, she had lingering doubts.

Lady Seldane was too old and too crippled by her massive weight to thrive on a journey to Ireland, one that would necessitate traveling across the country, then embarking on a boat. The old woman stayed close to home for a reason, and Emma couldn't see dragging her across the country when she hadn't chosen to go farther than her daughter's home in Essex for more than twenty years.

But there was another, more important reason to escape. Emma needed to break all ties with her past. Most particularly with anyone who knew Killoran. She needed to carve out a new life for herself, a place with no connection to Killoran or to Maude Darnley. Or to Emma Langolet. She would find a safe haven, north somewhere, as far as her limited pocket money would take her. She would find work if she could, or she would sell the broken diamond necklace she'd sewn into her petticoat. The diamonds that Killoran had insisted she keep. She would make a life for herself, far away from his memory, from the impossible yearning. She would build a happy, simple life there, and no one would ever find her.

Emma hadn't had much to pack. Her black silks had arrived from Killoran, but Lady Seldane had steadfastly refused to allow her to wear them. "You're not in mourning," she'd sniffed, and Emma had decided not to enlighten her about Uncle Horace. "No need for you to look like a crow."

Instead she'd provided a young girl's wardrobe for Emma, full of pale, flattering colors better suited to an innocent. Emma didn't feel innocent. In truth, she was glad she didn't. Never would she regret lying with Killoran, no matter what the consequences. Even if a part of her hated him, another part was still torn with love.

The streets of London were dangerous. She had learned that much, but in the past few weeks she had grown soft. Distracted by the danger to her heart, to her soul, she forgot about the danger to her life. She failed to notice the shadows behind her, the footsteps dogging her.

Until it was too late. And she was caught.

"Wake up, damn your eyes!" The stentorian bellow ripped through Killoran's skull, and he sat bolt upright, blinking, reaching automatically for his smallsword. His intruder had torn open the curtains in his bedroom, letting in the blinding winter sunlight, and through the miserable pounding in his brain he could see only the short, massive outline of his uninvited guest.

"Sleeping at this hour of the day! God knows you were never an example of rectitude, but this passes all bounds.

Did you plan to drink yourself into oblivion every day, or did you discover a faster way to kill yourself?"

His eyes focused, but his brain refused to believe what he saw. Lady Seldane never left her house. She certainly wouldn't be storming around his bedroom, at midday, haranguing him.

But then, who else would have the nerve to do so?

He shoved himself upright in bed. He slept in the nude, but Letty Seldane was a bawdy old lady, and she did nothing more than glare at him before continuing her diatribe.

"Everything has fallen to pieces, disaster is in the offing, and you sleep like an innocent, despite the fact that you must have the blackest conscience in Christendom. Have I been mistaken all these years I've known you?"

"I have no idea," Killoran murmured, stretching with just the right amount of laziness. He had no intention of letting Lady Seldane know just how alert, how wary, he was. Nor just how much his head hurt. "What *have* you thought of me all these years?"

"That you're not nearly as blackhearted a rogue as you pretend to be."

"You wound me, Letty!" he protested. "I assure you, I'm just as evil as I appear. Heartless, soulless, amoral, and wicked."

"Then it shouldn't bother you that Emma appears to have run off."

"And you let her go?"

A lesser woman would have blanched at his tone of voice. Lady Seldane was up to it. "I thought I had persuaded her to accompany me to Ireland. Some time at my house in County Sligo would have provided a nice distraction. Given her some peace, some time..."

"I don't suppose the fact that your lands are adjacent to the old farmhouse where I grew up was a factor in this decision?"

"Do you accuse me of being a matchmaker?"

"You've never stooped so low before."

"And I'm not about to now," she said with great dignity. "I happen to like that gel. I wouldn't relegate her to your tender mercies—unlike you, I'm possessed of morals. I'm certain there's someone, young and decent, who'll make a perfect husband for her. You must be twice her age."

"Are you trying to offend me, Letty? It's usually a difficult thing to do, but I will confess I drank a bit too much last night, and my temper is uncertain. I am fifteen years older than Emma, but a Methuselah in the ways of sin."

"You've been drinking too much every night, according to rumor. I'm certain your abrupt desertion of Emma had little or nothing to do with this sudden lapse into maudlin degeneracy..."

"Nothing," he snapped.

"But it's not you I'm concerned about. It's Emma."

"Then why are you here? Send someone to chase her down and bring her back. You must have some notion of where she went. Don't bother me with matters that don't concern me."

"You've been paying her bills, Killoran. That gives you some concern in the matter. You know there was no need, but you insisted. It suggests you might have a bit of human feeling left, after all."

"Simple guilt," he replied.

"That's even more difficult to believe. You're not a man to succumb to guilt. Listen to me, Killoran, and listen well. She needs help, and if you're not the man to provide it, I'll have to look elsewhere. My blasted youngest daughter chose Saturday to give birth to her first child, and the gel decided to be tiresomely sentimental and demand my presence. When I left for Essex, the plans for our discreet little journey to Ireland were in place. When I returned, I found a note from the wretched child, saying she needed time on her own, that I wasn't to worry, and that she'd be fine. She would let me know where she was in a little while."

"Then why are you worried?" A nagging, horrified thought struck him. "She isn't pregnant, is she?"

Lady Seldane picked up a delicate Chinese vase and flung it at his head. It bounced off the bed curtains and landed on the floor. "You stupid, idiotic man!" she fumed. "Doesn't a person of your experience know how to avoid such things? Of course you do—I've never heard of a trail of by-blows from you, and you've certainly bedded the majority of beautiful women here in London."

"I know how to avoid such things," he said, realizing he sounded faintly sulky. "I just…didn't."

"Carried away, were you?" Lady Seldane nodded knowingly, slightly mollified. "Most unlike you, Killoran."

"Why do you think I sent her to you?"

"Because she terrified you, didn't she? Got beneath that cold-as-ice exterior of yours. No wonder you panicked. And don't give me that look. It don't work with me, and you know it. You can't call me out, and you can't intimidate me. I've known you too long and too well. You care about the girl, you who pride yourself on not caring about a damned thing."

"Age has addled your wits."

"Yours as well," she snapped back. "Are you going to be sensible and go after her? Or are you going to leave it up to me to find a new champion? Trust me, most men wouldn't be foolish enough to let someone like her slip through their fingers."

"Send Nathaniel after her. He specializes in damsels in distress. He's more the heroic type. I have no intention of having anything to do with her. She's better off that way, and we both know it."

Lady Seldane nodded. "Nathaniel. He's a good man, from all I hear. I just wonder how he'll be able to stand up to Darnley."

There was a sudden, furious roaring in his ears. "Darnley?" he echoed hoarsely.

"You don't think a man like Darnley is going to give up, do you? He'll be after her in no time, and she has no one to watch over her. She's a brave gel, but she's unused to treachery. Other than what she's learned of yours, of course. She wouldn't stand a chance against a creature like Darnley."

"What makes you think he even remembers her existence?"

"You made certain of that, m'boy. I wouldn't be surprised if he's already gone after her. I'm afraid you set your trap too well, Killoran. He's more interested in your protégé than you at the moment. Of course, once he tires of her, he'll be back to cause you trouble, and you can dispose of him then—if you're willing to wait. However, I wouldn't think a dedicated villain such as you would be willing to leave Emma to a creature like Darnley. The things I've heard about his habits could shock even a jaded old woman like me."

Killoran had already thrown the covers back from the bed and begun to dress. Lady Seldane watched him with detached interest. "Why did you take so long to come to me?" he snarled. "You know I counted on you to watch over her, to see that she came to no harm."

"I arrived home late at night, and it wasn't until this morning that I discovered she was gone. If you hadn't been spending the last week or so intent on self-destruction, you would have remembered the danger Darnley poses."

"I didn't forget." He yanked on a cambric shirt with furious speed. "I'll find her, damn it, and bring her back to you. It shouldn't take long, and if Darnley's anywhere near her, then I'll finish with him. I should have done so years ago." He sat on the bed and began pulling on his boots. "And this time you'd better keep an eye on her. Don't let her go until you've found the right man to marry her."

She looked him up and down, approval and irritation in her small, dark eyes. "Killoran, my boy," she muttered, "I already have."

Nathaniel's mood was bordering on the celestial when he mounted the front steps to Killoran's Curzon Street house two at a time. It came as a great shock to discover Killoran was up and about at the unheard of hour of 1 P.M. He appeared at the doorway of the library, dressed in traveling clothes of unrelieved black, his dark hair tied back in a queue, his eyes clear.

"Where the hell have you been?" he demanded.

Nathaniel blinked. "I don't believe that's your particular concern."

Killoran stared at him for a long moment. "She seduced you," he said with an unpleasant twist to his mouth. "I'm surprised it took you so long to succumb. Tell me, did she put on an enjoyable performance?"

"I don't want to have to kill you," Nathaniel said carefully. "But I will."

"You can certainly try. But you'll have to forgo the pleasure for the time being. I have more important things to do at the moment."

"I forgot. Your race. It's today, isn't it?"

Killoran's laugh was devoid of humor. "Is it? I'd forgotten as well."

"Killoran…"

"Forbear to lecture me, dear boy, and I'll grant you the same courtesy." He tilted his head to one side, observing him. "Though I must confess you don't seem like such a youth today. Lady Barbara's had a salubrious effect on you. I'm surprised."

"Damn it, Killoran, keep your mouth off her!" Nathaniel said furiously. "You never wanted her."

"True enough. But I did enjoy watching your reaction to the notion," he said smoothly. "Alas, I gamed away any claim to her favors. For once, my phenomenal luck at cards has finally deserted me."

"Has it?" Nathaniel murmured. "I wonder."

"Wonder what, dear boy?"

"Wonder exactly what you were doing when you lost at cards last night."

"Nothing more than you did, Nathaniel, in the previous hand," he replied with exquisite care.

The underlying truth hit Nathaniel like a blow in the stomach. He'd been manipulated by a master, made to betray his honor. "You Irish bastard," he said bitterly.

"You're right about the Irish part. The bastard part is, in fact, not true. My parents were married in a Catholic church. Making me a worthless, disenfranchised papist. Not nearly good enough for the daughter of an earl. You two are well suited. You can save her, my little saint. Just don't make the mistake of saving me."

Nathaniel stared at him. "If you'd forgotten your race, why are you up so early?"

"It seems that Emma has departed Lady Seldane's without any warning. I must admit, I feel a certain... responsibility toward her, so I'm off to find her."

"But you can't! I'll go after her. She's more likely to accept my aid than yours," Nathaniel said.

"So she is. Nevertheless, I find I'm not willing to give up this particular task. You might inform Sanderson that I'm planning to forfeit. He'll see that word gets out." He started toward the desk, a remote expression on his face.

"My lord." Jeffries appeared at the door, his usually urbane countenance troubled. "A note arrived for you."

Killoran looked up. "I heard no one at the door, and my hearing is considered acute," he drawled.

"It arrived at the service door, my lord. A rather scruffy creature delivered it. Since it wasn't sealed, I was bold enough to read it myself."

"Bold indeed, Jeffries," Killoran conceded. "What is it, man? A dun? A death threat? Speak up."

"In a manner of speaking, my lord." He handed the filthy piece of paper to Killoran. Nathaniel watched with interest as Killoran stared down at it, his face even more expressionless than usual. And then he crumpled the paper in his strong white fingers.

"What is it, Killoran?"

Killoran paused for a moment, searching through the desk drawers with uncharacteristic haste. A moment later he pulled out a large, ivory-inlaid box. "I don't think it's your particular concern," he murmured, opening the lid to reveal a matched set of pistols.

"But you're willing to forfeit the wager. What's going on, Killoran?" Nathaniel demanded. "It can't be a duel— you'd have more warning."

"Your final lesson in social etiquette, dear boy. A wager always takes precedence over a duel," he said casually, checking the site of the pistol.

"How can you simply forfeit, then? I heard the stakes were extremely high. What did you wager?"

"Just the house. And fifty thousand pounds."

"Christ!"

"Nathaniel, you shock me!" Killoran mocked. "I didn't know you ever cursed."

"You don't have that much money."

"Unlike you, dear boy, I don't wager what I don't have. I can pay my debts. I simply won't have much left."

"Give me the note, Killoran. I'll deal with whatever it concerns, and you can win your damned race…"

"Trying to save me as well as all the other lost souls? You're a veritable saint, Nathaniel. I, however, don't wish to be saved. I sold my soul to the devil long ago, and I don't give a damn about fortunes, or horse races, or this mausoleum of a house. Sorry, but you'll have to confine your savior tactics to Barbara. I'm sure she'll be far more appreciative."

"Damn it, Killoran, what's in that note?"

Killoran's eyes narrowed. "There is a limit to my forbearance, Nathaniel. I *will* kill you as well, if you continue to irritate me."

"Of course you will," Nathaniel replied. "You don't care about Emma; you wouldn't think twice about killing me. You're evil through and through. I'll believe you. Thousands wouldn't."

"Nathaniel," Killoran said sweetly, heading for the door, "go back to Lady Barbara. Maybe if you apply yourself, you can teach her to enjoy what she pretends to crave."

Nathaniel could feel the blush rise in his face, and it was enough to stop Killoran. He stared at him for a moment, his green eyes wide with surprise. "Don't tell me you managed it?" he said.

"I have no intention of discussing my future bride with you," Nathaniel responded stiffly.

"Has she agreed to that as well?"

"She has."

For the first time since Nathaniel had known him, Killoran grinned. "I underestimated you, my boy. Take good care of her. In case I don't see you again."

"Killoran…"

But he was gone, the pistol tucked in the pocket of his black silk jacket, the door slamming shut behind him.

CHAPTER TWENTY

It was the smell that first told Emma where she was. The odor of boiled cabbage, sunk deep into the walls, that crept into her barely conscious mind with a slow, sinking terror. She opened her eyes to the darkness, not moving. She lay on her stomach on a thin pallet, and there was nothing but chilly air all around her, and thick, smothering darkness. And the sudden, sure knowledge that she was back in Crouch End.

She struggled to sit up, but every bone, every muscle in her body cried out in pain. Her head felt thick and fuzzy, her stomach lurched suddenly, and she sank back down onto the hard floor, hugging herself. She had no idea why she was here, who had brought her back. Someone had come up behind her, shoved a foul-smelling rag over her face as she struggled, and then everything had descended into darkness.

She might not have known who had brought her here in the first place, but she knew who was behind it, and all her fear and doubts about her cousin had coalesced into an unthinking terror. Miriam was going to exact her stern punishment. And if the punishment for daydreaming had been harsh, the punishment for fornication and murder would be a great deal worse.

She moved more slowly this time, trying to keep her stomach from revolting, her head from spinning off her shoulders. Carefully she rose to her knees, peering through the darkness around her. She knew where she was. It had to be one of the empty bedrooms on the third floor, made for servants, but Miriam allowed no servants to stay, not even the faithful Gertie. Emma staggered to her feet, moving toward the door. To her astonishment it opened beneath her hand, and she stepped out into the deserted hallway, her heart pounding so loudly she thought surely Miriam could hear it.

She edged toward the stairs, going by instinct rather than by sight. The darkness was eerie, threatening. There were no lights in the house at all—it was as still and quiet as death.

Emma slipped off her shoes. Over the years she had learned to move silently through this house, and she needed that silence now more than ever. She descended the narrow flights of stairs and stopped at the bottom, suddenly afraid. There was death in the air, death and disaster, and she wanted to turn and run, as far and as fast as she could. She knew this house well, better even than Cousin Miriam did. She could find a place to hide until the light that filtered into the old house grew marginally brighter. She had no idea what time of day it was—early evening, midnight, or close to dawn. She wasn't even certain which day it was, or how long she had lain in that upstairs bedroom in a drugged stupor.

She only knew that sooner or later it would have to grow lighter. If she just found a place to hide, she'd be safe. She needed time to get her bearings, to get her stomach back in reasonable shape.

The door to Miriam's sitting room was open, and the hallway was cold and dark. She could just picture her cousin sitting there, dark and malevolent, waiting for her, as she had over the years. Ready to force her to her knees, to confess sins that never existed.

Emma had lived through that too many times. She wouldn't do it again. Not when her sins were real now, and not regretted. She wasn't going anywhere near that room. She turned, ready to run, and heard a faint, piteous moan.

She wasn't a coward. She walked forward, into the darkened interior on silent, unerring feet, her eyes growing accustomed to the faint light. A fire spread a specious warmth through the room, illuminating the huddled shape of a woman lying on the floor.

"Gertie!" Emma cried, forgetting her caution and rushing to the woman's side. She lay in a pool of blood. She was alive, and conscious, but just barely, and her eyes were glazed with pain. Her clothes were torn, her skirts rucked up around her sturdy legs, and Emma stared down at her in horror, at the swollen, distorted mouth and bruised face.

Gertie whispered something, but Emma couldn't understand her. She sank to her knees beside the woman, grasping her cold hand, and leaned closer. "Who did this, Gertie? Who hurt you? Where is Cousin Miriam?"

Gertie's mouth struggled to shape a word. "Run,"

she finally managed to whisper. "Get out of here, miss. Before they hurt…"

A light blazed in the room as someone struck a tinder, and Gertie sank into silence, perhaps an eternal one. Her insides like ice, Emma looked up toward the light.

She hadn't seen her cousin, Miriam, in more than two months. In that time she'd almost forgotten the woman's power. She sat in a straight-backed chair, her stern, colorless face composed in lines of judgment and hatred, and her drab clothes covered a body that was thin and strong and hurtful. She folded her hands in her lap, and Emma could see blood on them.

"Miriam," she whispered, trying to quell the sudden onrush of fear.

"So kind of you to return to your home," Miriam said in a cool, monotonous voice. "I wondered if you would ever be willing to face your judgment."

Judgment, Emma thought with renewed horror. She knew all too well what Miriam's judgment could constitute. "What have you done to Gertie?"

"She's sinned," Miriam said calmly. "She needed to be punished. Fornication is a crime, and she is ungodly. She sought wicked congress, and has paid the price."

"What are you talking about? Gertie is as good and kind a woman as ever lived!"

"She was going to interfere. She told me I was mad. That she wouldn't stand by and let me hurt you. As if I'd hurt you," Miriam said with a faint sniff, her pale eyes alight with a fevered glint. "She confused justice with cruelty. I had no choice. She needed to be punished. As do you. We intend to see to it, you know. It's for the best—a pure death is far preferable to a life of sin. It won't be easy, though. Pain and suffering are needed to wash your soul clean."

Emma sat back on her heels, fighting down the panic. Gertie lay still, her breathing shallow and labored. "There's no need to kill me, Miriam. I left. I've given up all claim to the money. You can have it all—I don't want it. You can just forget about me."

"I can't do that," Miriam said. "Nor do I want to. *He* wants to keep you alive. He wants to make sport of you as he did with that slut there, but I shan't let him. You'd take pleasure from it, I know your wicked soul. He shan't have you. No one will."

"Who, Miriam? Who shan't have me?"

"I believe she must be referring to me."

The drawling lisp came from directly over her head, and Emma froze. She had almost forgotten the man's existence. She turned and looked up into the puce-clothed dandy's glittering eyes, and she knew who had brought her back to this place.

"Lord Darnley," she whispered.

"None other," he said, stepping over Gertie's body without a glance. "Your cousin and I have been unlikely confederates. I do believe that that connection has now served its usefulness." He glanced at Miriam's stony face. "I don't want her dead," he said pleasantly. "At least not until I've had my fill of her."

"She needs to be punished."

"Oh, I'll see to that. You may even watch if you so desire. You liked watching me with that old woman, I know you did. I could hear you panting in the background."

"No," Miriam said furiously. "I'll kill her first. After that you may take whatever pleasure is left from her."

"An interesting notion. You are a creative witch, aren't you? But I want her first. Alive and kicking. Struggling. If you like, you can hold her down for me. You can pray for her soul while I do her."

"Ungodly!" Miriam shrieked, leaping up from her chair and hurling herself upon Darnley. He struck out at her, and the two of them went down, amid a thrashing, grunting struggle, horrifying amid the dancing shadows of the darkened room.

Emma didn't hesitate. She ran from the room, from the smell of hate and violence, blindly unsure of where she was going, only knowing that she was running from certain death.

She hurtled against something large, something solid, something that hadn't stood in her way before, and she screamed, a short, shrill sound cut off abruptly by the hand clamped over her mouth. She fought the imprisoning arms, fought wildly, until a voice she thought never to hear again hissed in her ear.

"Keep still, you idiot. Do you want to bring them down on us?"

She stopped fighting. She stopped thinking, going limp in his arms in shock and relief. Killoran had come for her. Killoran would save her from those two ghouls.

"How did you find me?" she babbled. "How did you get here? They've killed Gertie, I know, and they're trying…"

He shook her, hard enough that her teeth rattled and her head snapped back, hard enough to shake the hysteria out of her. "Be quiet," he said, his hands strong on her arms.

"You aren't taking me to them, are you? You won't let them hurt me?"

"Damn it, Emma!"

"You said you were going to give me to Darnley. He'll kill me. He's already killed Gertie, and Miriam will watch and I don't—"

"For God's sake," he hissed, dragging her up against him. "I won't give you to Darnley. I'll kill him for you— would you like that?"

She thought of Gertie's body, lying in blood. She thought of those mad blue eyes and the vicious mouth. "Yes," she said, shocked at herself. And then: "No. I want to get away from here. Take me away from here, Killoran. Please."

"Sorry, darling, but I'm afraid I can't go with you. I have some unfinished business."

"Killoran, no!"

She heard him coming. The glow of candlelight, like a golden specter, signaled his approach, and she pulled at Killoran. But he was immovable, and there was a light in his eyes, a curious, deadly delight about him.

Darnley stood in the doorway. There was blood on his hands, on his clothes, and at one side of his mouth. "There you are," he said pleasantly, macabre. "It took you long enough to get here, Killoran. I was afraid you were going to ignore my summons. I should have known the combination of your red-haired doxy and me would be enough to stir you." He glanced at Emma dismissingly. "I regret to inform you, my dear young lady, that your cousin is no longer with us. She was quite mad, you know. Tiresomely so. Religious fanatics are the worst. They're so damned certain they've been anointed by God to wreak vengeance." His smile was ghastly in the wavering candlelight. "She was most unwilling to let me be the avenger." He glanced at Killoran, almost casually. "Are you going to shoot me, old boy? Not much sport in that, is there?"

"I find I'm no longer interested in sport," Killoran murmured. "However, I'm more than happy to indulge you. I'm more than a match for you no matter what the weapon. How would you like to die?"

"Bastard," Darnley snarled, suddenly dangerous. "You killed my sister. Did you know that, girl? He seduced and then abandoned my darling Maude, and she took her own life out of despair."

"You're mad," Killoran said abruptly. "I never lay with her."

"She told me," Darnley said. "I made her tell me. All the details, everything. And then I made certain that she would never let another man touch her again…"

"You raped her, got her pregnant, and then drove her to suicide," Killoran said in a deadly voice. "She haunts you, just as she does me."

"If you aren't responsible, why does she haunt you?"

"Any number of reasons. Because I didn't care enough about her to help her when she came to me. I turned her away. She wouldn't name her seducer, and I didn't believe that it hadn't been her choice."

"She wanted me," Darnley cried.

"She hated you."

"Damn you!" Darnley lifted his hand. The pistol exploded. He must have missed, for a moment later he leaped toward them. But instead of Killoran he caught Emma, falling to the floor with her and rolling, as she fought, until they ended up entwined in a ghastly embrace, Darnley's knife at her throat, his foul breath choking her.

"Let her go, Jasper." Killoran's voice was soft, beguiling, more Irish than she had ever heard it. "You don't want to hurt her. What good would she be to you if she were dead?"

"Oh, she'd be most useful." Darnley giggled. "You'd mind, you see. You'd mind more than if I killed you. I'm going to cut her throat and have her bleed to death right in front of you, and there won't be a thing you can do. I'll do it slowly so you won't be certain that it's fatal, but you won't dare move, because you know that then I will slash, so deep that I might take her head right off, and that will be a far worse pain than anything I could have…"

"Hurry up, then." There was no lilt now. Only cool, calculated boredom.

"Don't try to fool me into thinking you don't care for the wench. I know better."

"Do you, now?" Killoran's voice in the darkness held amusement. "What in God's name made you think I had a *tendre* for an overgrown bourgeoisie? Kill her, by all means, but get on with it. I want to finish this up and get home to bed. I'm going to kill you, Darnley, as I should have killed you years ago. One woman is much the same as the next. It makes little difference to me if you take Emma with you into hell."

He was lying, Emma thought. He was trying to trick Darnley into releasing her; that had to be it. But he sounded so calm, so reasonable. So very much like Killoran.

"I don't believe you," Darnley said, his voice a little less sure.

"Have you ever known me to show an ounce of sentiment? To care for any living creature other than myself? Kill her, by all means. And then I'll kill you."

Darnley staggered upright, hauling Emma with him. The knife pricked her throat, and she felt a faint trickle of blood course down her neck. In the dim light she could see Killoran, leaning casually against the wall, hands tucked in his pockets, as if he had all the time in the world.

"You won't—" Darnley said, and then jerked. A moment later an explosion rang in Emma's ears, and Darnley was flung backward. She spun around in shock, but Killoran's hard hands were on her arms, yanking her away.

"Don't," he said coolly. "The man's dead."

She struggled for a moment, dazed. "But perhaps—"

"I shot him in the face, Emma," he told her flatly. "He's dead."

She stopped struggling, staring up at him. There was no remorse, no emotion whatsoever on his dark, handsome face. "Did you mean what you said?" she asked hoarsely.

"What do you think?" His voice was savage. "Shall I stand over Darnley's corpse and give you tender declarations of love? I care for nothing and no one. I've told you that. I don't know what else I have to do to make you believe it."

She pulled away from him, and he let her go, without a moment's hesitation, leaning against the wall once more, an enigmatic expression on his face. "I believe you," she said in a dull, lifeless voice. "I'm going to check on Gertie."

She picked up the candelabrum and moved down the hall, back to the salon. Gertie lay still and silent on the floor. Miriam's body rested in the chair, the blood pooling beneath her.

Emma knelt beside her old friend. There was still a faint pulse, and she glanced around her, looking for something to cover the woman. And then she froze.

Miriam towered over her. The knife protruded from her thin chest, and she reached down and yanked it free, staring at it with a kind of numb surprise. And then she looked down at Emma, kneeling at her feet, and her smile was horrible indeed as she turned the knife blade toward her.

For a moment the world stood still. Miriam would kill her, and there was nothing she could do. Emma watched numbly, and then life surged through her, taking hold. "No!" she screamed, as loudly as she could, surging to her feet. "You won't hurt me ever again." And she lunged for the knife.

But before she reached her, Miriam's pale, mad eyes had glazed over. The knife dropped between them, skittering away. And with a final, choking sound, Miriam collapsed onto the floor, a lifeless, harmless bag of bones.

There was no sign of Killoran. Emma had thought he

would come when he heard her scream, but the room was still and silent, only Gertie's labored breathing, mixed with Emma's panic, breaking the stillness.

He'd left, she thought numbly. He'd already abandoned her, final proof that he didn't care. The grief, the pain, were so powerful they took her heart and twisted it, and she wanted scream with the agony of it. But then Gertie moaned once more, and Emma shook herself. There would be time enough for grief, for anguish. Now she had to get help for Gertie.

She heard footsteps approach the room, and joyous relief swamped her. She ran to the door, ready to fling herself in Killoran's arms, only to draw herself up short. Nathaniel stood there, his face dark with shock.

"Are you all right, Emma?"

"I'm fine. Gertie…" She gestured toward the woman lying by the fire.

"I've sent for help." He looked past her, at Miriam's corpse, and shuddered. "Let me take you out of here. There's nothing more you can do." He started to drape his cloak over her shoulders, but she tore it away, carrying it to Gertie's still figure and covering her.

"Where's Killoran?" she asked, succumbing to the weakness, knowing she wouldn't like the answer.

"Um…he's gone."

She smoothed the cloak over Gertie, then glanced up at Nathaniel's troubled face. "Gone? Where?"

"I have no idea." He caught her arm and tugged her to her feet. "Come away, Emma. You've done all you can. I just thank God I made Jeffries tell me what that note said, or God knows what would have happened."

"I would have survived. Killoran would have killed Darnley and then abandoned me, just as he did. And I would have been fine." Her voice quavered, and she tightened it, firmly. "I want to stay with Gertie."

"No!" Nathaniel's voice bordered on panic for a moment, oddly so. "Lady Seldane is outside in her carriage. Come away, and I promise I won't leave Gertie."

She looked up at him. But finally shock and exhaustion won out, and she nodded. "I'll go," she murmured. "You stay here."

"You promise me you won't run away?"

"Where would I go?" Emma whispered. And she walked from the room, from the house, from her childhood, without a backward glance. To fling herself on the warm, comforting bosom of Lady Seldane.

"She's gone."

Killoran looked up into Nathaniel's troubled face. "She is a headstrong wench, isn't she?" he said weakly. He'd slid down against the wall, unable to stand any longer, and it had been sheer luck that Emma had stormed out without peering into the shadows.

"Help is coming..." Nathaniel said.

"No. Get me out of this place."

"You shouldn't be moved. You've lost a lot of blood..."

"I've been shot before. It's not going to kill me," he said, struggling to his feet, leaning breathlessly against the wall.

"Lady Seldane has already sent for a surgeon—"

"I'm going back to Curzon Street," he said, and his voice sounded odd, far away.

"You'll kill yourself."

"Perhaps. But I'm not going to die beside Jasper Darnley." He took an unsteady step away from the wall. The bullet had lodged beneath his shoulder, but it wasn't a clean wound, and he knew it.

"Killoran, for God's sake, man!" Nathaniel cried desperately. "The bullet might have touched a vital organ. Be still. It could have nicked your heart, your lungs…"

"I don't have a heart," Killoran said wryly.

"True enough," Nathaniel agreed sternly. "Emma just ran off with it. Are you going to sit back down and wait for help, or am I going to have to force you?"

"Sentimental fool," Killoran murmured weakly. His legs wouldn't support him, and he slumped back to the floor. The hallway was already dark, but it was closing in upon him like a velvet throw, and he considered death to be an imminent possibility. "Promise me something, Nathaniel."

"Anything."

"If by any bizarre chance you're right," he whispered. "If I'm dying, you're to let me go in peace."

"Don't be absurd, man…"

"If I call out for…anyone…you're not to bring them to me. Do you understand? I don't care if I'm on my deathbed, delirious and begging. You're not to bring her."

"Killoran!" he protested.

"Promise me. On your honor." He reached out and clawed at Nathaniel's plain wool coat, exerting the last ounce of his strength.

"I promise," Nathaniel said.

Killoran released him. "You're probably right," he whispered.

"About what?"

He looked up at him and managed a brief, farewell smile. "I rather think Emma did run off with my heart," he confessed. And then, he let go, tired of fighting.

CHAPTER TWENTY-ONE

Seldane House, County Sligo, Three Weeks Later

The air was surprisingly warm in Ireland, with the tang of the sea all around. A more hospitable place than England, Emma thought wearily, staring at the burgeoning green. Spring came earlier here. When she left London and Lady Seldane, the London streets were still coated with an icy mist. But here in Ireland the sun shone. She could be happy here, surely.

If she could be happy anywhere without Killoran. Since she had no choice in the matter, she needed to behave sensibly. She had the rapidly recovering Gertie to keep her company and to chivy her into common sense. She no longer need fear Miriam's stratagems, or the deranged lusts of men. She could find peace here, she was convinced. And if she cried at night, in the large, well-appointed bedroom of Seldane House, no one, not even Gertie, knew of it.

As the days passed, a certain peace settled over Emma. A sense of waiting. Seldane House boasted only the minimal staff—an elderly couple named Murphy and a re-cuperating Gertie, but the quiet and lush beauty of the place soothed Emma's soul. By the second week the tears were gone, and she took long, solitary walks through the blossoming spring countryside, and tried not to count the days till her monthly courses were due.

By the second week she discovered the farmhouse. More of a ruin it was, set amid a valley so green and ripe it was almost magical. This was the first morning the apple trees had blossomed, and the smell in the air was heavenly, enticing her to walk farther than she usu-ally did. The sight of the old stone building stopped her.

The roof was intact, covered with a coppery-green moss. Some of the leaded windows were out, some boarded up, and the front of the house was a tangle of overgrowth. She walked up the choked drive slowly, look-ing for signs of life.

The gray stone house wasn't dead, however. Merely sleeping, like a fairy-tale creature. She could feel the heat and life in the place, the heart, waiting to be brought back to life and beauty. It came as no surprise to her that the front door opened when she tried it, no surprise that de-spite the damp and dust of the front hall, the place felt strangely like home.

She wandered through the rooms, unashamed of tres-passing. It was a large farmhouse, with room for a dozen children and more, yet there was a cozy feel to it, de-spite the decay. As she wandered through the rooms, she wanted to weep at the sheer waste of such abandoned loveliness.

She dreamed of it at night, was unable to keep away

during the day. She never asked whose house it was, but from her inexpert grasp of the Irish political situation, she assumed it belonged to some absentee Protestant landlord. One who had no love for the land.

She wanted that house, with a covetous longing that surprised her. For no reason whatsoever, the house reminded her of Killoran. Of the Killoran she thought she'd seen beneath the drawling airs and graces, beneath the mocking words and clever tricks. It reminded her of the Killoran she'd given herself to. And would again, if he only wanted her.

But he hadn't wanted her, ever. She needed to remind herself of that painful, unpalatable fact. She was simply a means to an end, and when revenge had come to fruition, he'd dismissed her, walking away without a backward glance. He'd left her to Lady Seldane's kind heart, never thinking of her again.

Well, she wouldn't think about him. She would think, instead, of this house. A woman could love a house as well as a man, couldn't she? A house wouldn't break your heart. A garden wouldn't make you weep. She would find some way to claim this house as her own, with its horse barns and lush fields and overgrown gardens, and then she would be invulnerable.

She was unable to resist the house and, once there, unable to resist touching it. The broom she found was old and shredding, but she still managed to sweep the rooms free of dust and leaves and debris. The curtains at the windows were tattered and torn, and she simply pulled them down. The Irish sun was spring-bright, even through the filthy, broken panes.

She knew how to work—Miriam had taught her that much. And she worked long hours in the abandoned house, sweeping out the fireplaces, scouring the kitchen, burning the filth and accumulated trash from wasted years.

She wanted that house. As much as Killoran had wanted revenge, as much as Nathaniel had wanted Lady Barbara. Lord, she wanted it almost as much as she wanted Killoran. And since her first choice, her heart's desire, was forever out of her reach, she intended to do anything she possibly could to attain her second.

She had money. Obscene amounts of it. With no one left alive to make any claim on it, money she'd never wanted, never used. She would use it now. She could wait to ask Lady Seldane for help, or write to Nathaniel. He and Lady Barbara would return from their wedding journey before long, and he could assist her. She would find the absentee landlord, buy this house, and make a peaceful home for herself. For the time being, she was safe, and happy. For the time being, she didn't think about Killoran above once every hour. Twice at the most.

Life was definitely looking up. Was it not, it should have been an endless trip. In truth, to Killoran, it felt far too short. He sat in the post chaise and listened to Barbara and Nathaniel make disgustingly sentimental noises at each other, and in the back of his mind was an utter dread he'd forgotten existed.

He didn't want to go back. He'd sworn to himself that he would never set foot on Irish soil again, once his parents were dead, and he'd kept that promise, one of his few points of honor. Not that honor was involved. More likely self-preservation.

He'd thought he was well past it all. Past the rage and hurt, past the desperation and resentment, until the damned boat landed, far too soon for his peace of mind.

Spring came earlier to Ireland than it did to England— one of the few benefits. The daffodils were already blooming by the side of the road, the blue sky overhead was kissed with warmth, and everywhere around him, he heard the lilting voices of his youth.

He'd always sworn nothing and no one could make him go back. That he would never care enough for anything that might make him return to this troubled land and this troubled people.

He'd broken that vow, one more among many. He'd cheated at cards, not to win but to lose, but cheating it was. He'd found mild affection in his black heart for not only a rowdy old lady but also a heroic young man, who had more decency in one finger than Killoran possessed in his entire body. He'd taken pity on a lost soul like Lady Barbara, and he'd relinquished Emma when every fiber of his being longed for her. He'd fallen in love with her when he didn't even believe in love.

He had no idea where she was, and he was grateful for that fact. During the long days and nights when he'd been feverish from the bullet wound, he'd called out for her, but Nathaniel had kept his promise. Emma was long gone, and Killoran hadn't cared whether he lived or died.

He'd lived, surprisingly enough, even though he didn't really care to. He was still weak, and pale, and the journey hadn't done much for his constitution. The two newlyweds did little for his state of mind. "I fail to see why you've brought me with you," he said testily. "You could have seen the house without me. Though why you should want to buy an abandoned farmhouse in County Sligo is beyond me. The land is good only for horses, and you've never shown much interest in them."

"It wouldn't be fair for you to sell the place to me unless you saw it one last time. What are you afraid of, Killoran? It's just your past."

"I could still kill you," he mused. "I may be weak, but I'm still treacherous. Perhaps the new widow would enjoy a jaunt to Paris, after all."

Barbara ignored him. Indeed, she seemed to have eyes for no one but her new husband, and her glowing happiness was absolutely nauseating, Killoran thought. The sooner he got away from them, the better.

Unfortunately, until he sold his last remaining possession, he had no money. He had sworn he would never return to Ireland, but also that he would never part with the last trace of his Irish heritage, the old stone farm that was all that was left of his mother's inheritance.

But he was breaking that last vow as well. He would go back to the ruined decay of the old horse farm, and he would sell it to Nathaniel for whatever pittance he offered. And then he'd be gone, to the Continent, to a short, sweet life of gaming and an early death. He found he had something to look forward to, after all.

When Emma climbed the stairs in the old house, it was already late in the afternoon. The place was growing steadily more habitable as she worked through the long days, and while she knew she should be getting back, she couldn't bring herself to leave. Gertie had settled in quite happily, content to sit by the fire and regain her strength, and as long as Emma appeared reasonably happy, she didn't bother to ask her where she spent her days. The Murphys were too well trained to question her, but if she failed to return, they would come looking for her, and she wanted no one to enter what she'd come to think of as her house.

She was growing fanciful. She would dust and clean, haul water and scrub, and in the afternoons she would stretch out on the wide, slightly mouse-chewed mattress in a big bedroom upstairs and sleep. And she would dream. Dream of a time when the house was bright and clean and sturdy, dream of a bed with linen sheets and a man beside her, and the other bedrooms filled with the noise of children. The tumbled-down farm buildings would be in repair; there'd be sheep and cattle and horses, beautiful horses. She would learn to ride, and she wouldn't be afraid.

The apple trees would grow heavy with fruit, and so would her belly. The horses would breed, the house would come alive again, and all would be well. And the man who lay in the bed beside her would hold her in his arms, tight against his body, and he would laugh.

Had she ever heard Killoran laugh? In sheer, unadulterated joy? She doubted it. He had no joy in him. The man who would share this house, share this bed with her, would be filled with love and laughter. He would be nothing like Killoran at all.

And she wouldn't want him.

She always woke up weeping. This house was not for her; this life was not for her.

She lay down on the bed, one last time. It was coming to an end, and she needed to let go. Of childish hopes, of a house that wasn't hers, of a dream that could never be. Tomorrow she would make plans to return to London. She would find a husband, someone kind, and she would have babies to fill her empty life. There was no baby from her night with Killoran, and that was one more grief.

Tomorrow she would face life once more. But for now, she would dream one last dream.

"I want to get this over with," Killoran snarled, flinging himself into a chair with only a faint grimace of pain.

"What's your rush, Killoran? This seems a decent enough inn, and it's growing dark. We'll drive out there in the morning and inspect the place; then you can be on your merry way with a bank draft in your pocket. That's what you want, isn't it?"

"That's what I want."

"Then sit back, man, and enjoy yourself," Nathaniel urged with heartless jollity. "I've ordered us a bottle of claret, and if the smells emanating from the kitchen are any indication, we'll eat well enough. The rooms looked clean, the beds well aired..."

"I doubt you and Barbara notice the condition of the beds you share," Killoran said in a sour voice. "And unless things have changed greatly in the last dozen years, the Miller's Thumb has not only a decent cellar but also an excellent cook. You'll enjoy your sojourn here."

"You know this place, then?"

"I've been here. What would you expect? It's the only inn within a dozen miles of my family home."

"Then I imagine you've sampled the beds."

"What happened to that saintly boy who arrived in London besotted with Miss Pottle?" Killoran inquired in an acid tone.

"You've managed to teach me the error of my ways. What can I say? Marriage agrees with me. I expect fatherhood will agree with me even more."

"Christ, man, how can you know?" Killoran exploded. "You've been married for only two weeks."

"It won't be for want of trying," Nathaniel said.

"I don't know if I can stand another minute in your company," Killoran growled. "You're enough to make a man spew his guts out."

"Do you find other people's happiness a little hard to take, old man? You sent her away, you know."

Killoran ignored his second comment. "I can tolerate happiness. Simpering ecstasy is another matter. I'm going for a walk." He pushed away from the table just as an old man entered the room, bearing a bottle of wine and two glasses.

"Stay and share a glass with me, Killoran," Nathaniel pleaded. "I promise not to be too happy."

The old man set the tray down on the table with a clatter, his mouth agape, his eyes filled with sudden tears. "Your lordship," he mumbled in a quavery voice. "Is it really you?"

The silence for a moment was absolute, as Killoran considered denying it. "It's me, Ryan," he said finally.

"Saints be praised," the man cried. "You're finally back home where you belong."

"This isn't my home," he said sharply. "I don't belong here anymore..."

"It weren't your fault, my lord," Ryan said earnestly. "Haven't you learned that in your years of exile? You were young and hotheaded, and a true Irishman..."

"And my parents were killed because of it."

"It weren't your fault," Ryan said again. "They caught the lads who did it, you know. Hanged them down in County Wicklow, and left their bones to rot."

"They had come for me, not my parents," Killoran said savagely. "And I was away from home, playing schoolboy pranks that got them murdered."

"Don't you go blaming yourself for the evil that infects this land. We need you here, my lord. The people need you. Ireland needs you. Don't abandon us again."

"I'm sorry, Ryan. I'm here to sell my land to my friend. And then I won't be coming back."

Ryan looked toward Nathaniel. "Another English landlord?" he said softly. "You'd do that to your own people? I don't believe you. When you walk the land, breathe the good Irish air again, you'll know you can't leave us."

Killoran stared at him, brimming with despair and frustration. Ryan was an old man, ageless even years ago when Killoran was a young lad, wild and full of ideals. He knew too much, and it took all Killoran's hard-won cynicism to fight off the effect of his words.

"I've come here for the last time, old man," he said. "I'll see the old place, I'll breathe the air, and I'll walk the land. And then I'll sell my property to an English landlord and never set foot here again." And he walked away from him, out into the early evening air.

He walked slowly, the casual, lazy pace of an English gentleman with time on his hands. Until he was out of sight of the inn. Then he began to move more swiftly, ignoring his damnable weakness and the pain in his shoulder.

He still remembered the back way, across the meadows, down through the thicket, past the stream that was swollen from spring rain. Suddenly, after waiting so long, he could wait no longer. He had to see the house, to prove to himself that it no longer mattered. The past was past; he had no ties to the land, the country, his long-dead family. He could let it all go.

He wasn't sure what he had expected. Twelve years of neglect weren't enough to send the roof tumbling in, walls collapsing. At first sight, in the twilight, it looked the same. Until he moved closer and saw the broken, boarded-up windows, the tangle of undergrowth creeping up the sides of the house. For a moment he stared as the setting sun illuminated the upstairs windows, and he felt nothing but a blessed emptiness.

And then it came back, a swamp of feeling, washing over him. His mother, laughing, beautiful; his father, in shirtsleeves, out in the paddock with the horses.

The grand manor house up North had been burned. With his parents inside, torched by Protestant bullyboys in search of a trouble-making young aristocrat who should have been grateful his rank protected his Catholic blood. His parents had burned to death and he had left, never to return. And all that remained of his inheritance was this, the farmhouse where he'd grown up, where he'd known happiness, before his father had been thrust into a title he'd never wanted, and they'd had to leave this place for death and disaster at the hands of their enemies.

He moved closer, only to realize with a start that the windows on the upper floors were open to the cool spring breeze. The heavy front door was ajar as well, and the place, for all its overgrowth, seemed oddly welcoming.

He fought it. Fought the pull. He wouldn't let it wrap around his heart again. He was growing damnably weak, to fall in love with a fierce-hearted young amazon, to start feeling sentimental about an old house. He'd dismissed Emma from his life. He could dismiss this house as well.

Someone had been there, he knew it the moment he stepped inside. He could smell soap and water, a recent fire in the grate. He could smell life in the house, and it hurt.

He moved through the place silently, half in a trance, not knowing what he expected. Whether it was the little people of his childhood fairy tales or something more dangerous, he neither knew nor cared.

He went up the broad oak staircase, listening to the familiar creak of the fifth step. There was silence all around, but he wasn't alone. He didn't know if they were ghosts or memories or travelers. He only knew where they lay.

The bedroom at the top of the stairs had once been his parents, before his father had inherited the title and the grand, cold house and the life that Killoran had hated. Here they'd been happy.

He walked into the room, moving straight toward the casement windows and pulling them closed against the cool evening air before he turned and saw her.

He'd known she would be there, irrational as the notion seemed. He felt no shock, no surprise at seeing Emma sleeping peacefully on the huge old bed in which he'd most likely been conceived. She was wearing colors, something light and green, and her hair was loose and untidy around her dirt-streaked face. And he knew immediately who had cleaned his house.

Her feet were bare. Long, narrow feet, for a large woman. Her hand was tucked under her chin, her eyes were closed, and she looked weary and immeasurably sad.

Perhaps she heard the latch of the windows, the imperceptible sound of his tread on the freshly scrubbed floorboards. Perhaps it was just that sixth sense that comes into play when one knows one is being watched. Her eyes opened, blinking, and she peered through the gathering dusk, straight at him.

"This is my house," he said slowly, so as not to frighten her.

She sat up, edging back against the carved headboard. "I didn't know," she said, breathless. "No one told me. It was abandoned, and so sad, and I..." Words failed her, and she just stared at him, with such pain and longing that something cracked inside him.

He moved to the bed. "How can a house be sad?" he asked her.

"Perhaps it missed you. Perhaps it needed you desperately, even though you'd left it, turned your back on it."

"It's better off without me," he whispered.

"It's lost without you," she said, her honey-brown eyes full of grief. "Why have you come here? You didn't know I was here, I'm certain of that."

The strands were weaving around him, gossamer-fine Irish silk. He made one last attempt to fight his way free. "It was all I have left."

"No, it isn't," she said. "You have me."

He didn't say a word. Darkness was descending around them, filling the room, and it seemed a dream. One could do what one liked in dreams, couldn't one? There was no danger in dreams.

"I have you, have I?" he murmured. "Is that a blessing or a curse?"

She didn't flinch. "It depends on how you look at it," she said. "On whether you want me or not."

"What do you think?"

"I've never been sure."

And he realized with shock that she spoke the truth. She truly didn't know how much he wanted her, needed her, longed for her.

It could be his freedom. He could turn his back on her, on the house where he'd known his happiest years, turn his back on Ireland. And she'd find a new life. She was young enough, resilient enough.

It would be his first decent act in more than a decade. An act of such nobility and selflessness that no one would even suspect he was capable of it. He could do it, and he could do it for her.

"You're mine, are you?" His voice was harsh. "Much as I appreciate the offer, I rather think I should decline."

"I'm rich, you know" she told him, nervous. "My inheritance from my father's munitions factories is quite vast…"

"I don't want your money."

"I know you don't need it, but—"

"Actually, I'm penniless," he said. "The devil's luck finally abandoned me. Too many nights of deep play, a horse race I was fated to lose. This house and some land near Wicklow are all that I have left."

She stared at him, and the faint light of hope vanished from her eyes. Perhaps for good. "Why did you leave me at Cousin Miriam's?" she asked suddenly. "Why did you just walk away once Darnley was dead?"

He managed a shrug. "I'd finished what I had to do." He picked up a lock of her long red hair and ran it through his fingers. "Lovely as you are, dear Emma, you no longer held any use for me."

"I see," she said in a muffled voice. "I should leave your property." She tried to move, but he forestalled her, putting his hands on her shoulders. She felt thinner, more fragile beneath the thin green material, and there were shadows under her eyes.

"I thought you were my property as well."

"You don't want me."

"I may be cruel, heartless, and penniless, dear Emma," he said lightly. "I never said I was a fool."

He should walk away. Now. And he knew he couldn't. One last taste. Surely he was already doomed to hell— this could give him something to think of during an eternity of damnation.

He leaned forward brushing his mouth against hers, a mere temptation. It proved his undoing.

Her breath was warm and sweet against his mouth. And hardly realizing what he did, he threaded his hands through her tangled hair, cupping her face as he deepened the kiss.

She said not a word of protest, of longing, as he stripped her clothes from her body. She lay back on the mattress, watching him as he knelt over her, and when his mouth touched her breast she arched her back. He tasted her skin, her belly, between her legs, using his tongue, and it took him only moments to shatter her deliberate control, so that she cried out in the gathering darkness.

One last time, he told himself, rising over her, unfastening his breeches. But her hands were reaching up, pulling at his clothes, and he barely noticed the pain in his shoulder as she stripped the coat off, pushed the white linen shirt away from him; didn't realize what she was doing until he felt her grow stiff beneath his hands, and heard her sharp intake of breath.

He knew what the bullet wound looked like. It was an ugly thing, red, raw, barely healing. And he didn't for a moment think he might convince her it was anything other than what it was.

"He shot you," she said. "I didn't know."

"It was merely a scratch," he lied, but she wasn't listening.

She rose up onto her knees, and she was magnificent in the shadows, her long mane of fiery hair tumbled around her lush white body. "You didn't tell me," she accused him. "That's why you left. You'd been hurt, and you didn't want me to know. That's why you didn't come to see me, why you disappeared."

"Stop thinking I have any decency!" he snapped, half mad with fighting his better instincts. "Who's to say I would have done any differently? If you had any sense at all, you would leave me. I dislike people hovering over me, I don't care about you or anyone, I don't—"

She stopped him. She kissed him. Her mouth was open and full beneath his, and he was powerless to resist, to push her away, with his hands, with his words. She kissed his mouth, his nose, his eyelids. She put her mouth tenderly beside the bullet wound, then let it trail down his chest. Her hands shoved his breeches down his hips, and her mouth followed.

She was clumsy, she was awkward, she bestowed the most erotic torture he'd ever endured. There was no way he could pretend to be unmoved by her, not when his body betrayed him. Not when his actions betrayed him, and he pulled her up, against him, and kissed her mouth.

He prided himself on being a clever lover, always in control. He had no control now, no cleverness. He pushed her back on the bed, looming over her in the darkness, kneeling between her legs. She reached for him, and he came to her, pushing in deep, trapped by her body, her arms, her love.

He thought he could prolong it, but he was helpless against the tide of need that swept over him. He needed her, needed to take her in this bed, this house, this land. He needed to thrust deep and fill her with his seed. He needed to claim her, and claim his heritage. He'd fought it for too long.

He lifted himself above her, staring down at her as the bed rocked beneath his powerful, rhythmic thrusts. Her eyes were open as well, looking up at him, and then her eyes fluttered closed as her body convulsed around him, and he came as well, rigid in her arms, no longer fighting it, and her, and his own lonely heart.

It seemed to take forever for his breathing to slow. She was curled up against him, her face wet with tears, her body warm and pliant, the smell of sex and desire mixing with the heady scent of lavender and roses, soap and water, and the fresh spring air of Ireland.

He brushed the tears from her face, gently, and she turned, a smudge of dust on one pale cheek, her hair a tangle behind her. "Do you really want me to leave you?" she asked.

For a moment he didn't move, but his hand didn't leave her face. "It would be best," he said in a measured voice.

"That's no answer. Do you want me to leave you?"

"I have no money, no house but this one. I'm a cruel, heartless bastard who cares for nothing and no one."

"Do you want me to leave you?"

"I'd make the devil's own husband. I'd never want to leave here, you'd go mad with the isolation, I'd have to spend most of my time with the horses, you'd grow weary of bearing children…"

"Do you want me to leave you?"

He stared down at her. "Never," he said. And he pulled her back into his arms.

EPILOGUE

"Da!" The demanding little voice echoed through the spotless old house. Killoran stood inside the front hallway of the farmhouse, stripping off his rough leather gloves. He was pleasantly exhausted, he smelled of horses and sweat, but he doubted his demanding eldest daughter, Letitia, would notice.

"What is it, my pet?" he replied as she flung herself at him, her flame-red hair hanging in its usual tangle down her back, her nine-year-old frame already tall and strong.

She looked like her mother. She had her father's imperious temperament. God help them all.

"Mother said to tell you she's going mad. The twins have been fighting all day, the baby's teething, and that wretched brat Colleen was playing with my very best doll. The one Lady Seldane sent me from London." Letitia's lilting voice was strong with indignation. "Why did you have to burden me with so many brothers and sisters?" she said accusingly.

"To keep life from getting boring," he said lightly, starting up the broad stairs. He could hear Emma's voice,

raised above the childish squabbles in fierce exaspera-
tion, and he found himself smiling. "We've a new colt."

All Letitia's pettish bad temper vanished. "Daylily had
her foal? Why didn't you tell me?"

"I just did, love."

Emma appeared at the top of the stairs, her hands on
her ample hips, her hair coming out of its haphazard attempt at restraint. The apron that covered her pregnancy-
filled belly was wet with soapy water; the baby on her
hip was damp from his bath and screaming in a rage.

"Why," she said in a very dangerous voice, "did I ever
marry you?"

"Because you couldn't resist my charm?" he suggested
gravely.

"Don't smile at me," she snapped back, shoving the
wet, naked baby into his arms. "I should have married
Nathaniel. In the past ten years Lady Barbara has had
two quiet, perfectly behaved children and a life of order
and calm. And what do I have?"

"Utter madness," Killoran said. "Where are the servants?"

"Nanny's got a toothache, Siobhan and Bridget have
gone to mass, and Cook is in the kitchen where she be-
longs," Emma said.

"Well, my love, if there are too many children, whom
do you suggest we dispense with?"

By that time baby Thomas, held in his father's strong
arms, had ceased his furious howling.

Colleen stood in the doorway to the room she shared
with her older sister, her elfin face doubtful, and the
twins, Mary and Ronan, appeared equally wary.

Emma glanced at them all, humor slowly filling her honey-brown eyes. "Well, therein lies the problem. I love the little beasts, even if they're driving me mad. Shall we give them another chance?"

"Perhaps that might be wise," he agreed. "Unless you'd rather send them to the workhouse."

"Sluff," Ronan said boldly with all the wisdom of his eight years. "The workhouse wouldn't take us."

"Doubtless you're right. We could sell you to the tinkers."

"You'd have to pay them," Mary piped up.

"Drown them?" Killoran suggested lazily.

"You won't even drown unwanted kittens," Letitia scoffed. "You can't fool me. Accept the fact, Da, that you've got the softest heart in all of Ireland."

Killoran grinned. "There's many who'd never believe it. If I can't put the fear of God into you, then we'll have to see if your mother can."

"It's hopeless," Emma said, tugging the twins close. "Your father's too tenderhearted for the likes of you. Let me warn you, children, that there's nothing more dangerous than a reformed blackguard. I imagine it'll be a life of disaster for all of us."

"Is that what Da is? A reformed blackguard?" Ronan asked, clearly planning on becoming a blackguard himself.

Killoran smiled at her over the children's heads, a sweet, private smile. His eyes dropped to the burgeoning proof of her latest pregnancy, and Emma's response was a helpless laugh. "Not completely reformed," he murmured.

"They're the worst kind," Emma said.

"Go on out to the barn, children, and ask Willie to show you the new foal while your mother has five minutes' peace." He placed the damp but now cheerful Thomas in Letitia's capable hands.

"Five minutes' peace? Unheard of," Emma said, but her frustration had already left her as the children clattered noisily down the stairs.

He looked at her in the sudden stillness of the upstairs hall. "Too many babies, my love?" he whispered.

She shook her head fiercely. "Not quite yet," she said.

"Too much Ireland? We haven't left in ten years."

"No."

"Too much of your dark and dangerous husband?"

Her mouth curved in a wide, delectable grin. "Never," she said.

"Then let's hope Willie manages to keep them busy for a good long time," he said, pulling her toward the bedroom.

And her only answer was a shy, seductive smile.

* * * * *

 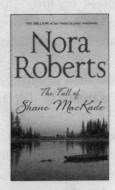 

The World of Mills & Boon®

There's a Mills & Boon® series that's perfect for you. We publish ten series and, with new titles every month, you never have to wait long for your favourite to come along.

Blaze®

Scorching hot, sexy reads
4 new stories every month

By Request

Relive the romance with the best of the best
9 new stories every month

Cherish™

Romance to melt the heart every time
12 new stories every month

Desire™

Passionate and dramatic love stories
8 new stories every month